THE MOON AND THE THORN

TERESA EDGERTON

ACE BOOKS, NEW YORK

This book is an Ace original edition,
and has never been previously published.

THE MOON AND THE THORN

An Ace Book / published by arrangement with
the author

PRINTING HISTORY
Ace edition / April 1995

ISBN: 0-441-00188-2

ACE®
Ace Books are published by The Berkley Publishing Group,
200 Madison Avenue, New York, NY 10016.
ACE and the "A" design are trademarks
belonging to Charter Communications, Inc.

PRINTED IN THE UNITED STATES OF AMERICA

10 9 8 7 6 5 4 3 2 1

Praise for Teresa Edgerton

"Edgerton writes with great sureness and sincerity."
—*Locus*

"Edgerton is a fantasy fan's utter delight!"
—*Rave Reviews*

**Don't miss out on the magical thrills
of the first two tales in this
acclaimed Teresa Edgerton trilogy . . .**

The Grail and the Ring

The rune-carved ring of an ancient mummy catapults
student-wizard Gwenlliant and her infant son into the
land of Shadows . . .

The Castle of the Silver Wheel

Gwenlliant, a very young bride, is brought to Mochdreff, a land of danger and blight in which only her
Wild Magic can save her . . .

"Edgerton's world building is original and excellent."
—*Booklist*

. . . or her other spellbinding fantasy sagas . . .

**Goblin Moon
The Gnome's Engine**
and
THE GREEN LION TRILOGY
**Child of Saturn
The Moon in Hiding
The Work of the Sun**

"One of fantasy fiction's most interesting trilogies."
—*Rave Reviews*

In those days, the wizard Glastyn went to all the christenings and all the deathbeds and all the great occasions of the greater families. If he arrived late, the baptism or the wedding was put off; if he did not arrive at all, the parents and the godparents were greatly dismayed. And when he did appear, his lightest word was received as though it were a prophecy, and sometimes the children were named accordingly. For that reason, the youngest daughter of Maelgwyn of Gwyngelli—the wealthiest lord in the realm—was named Eisiwed (penury), and there was a boy in Gorwynnion who had the misfortune to be named Gorasgwrn (big bone), which was the name of the wizard's horse.

But on the night before the christening of Cyndrywyn's daughter, Glastyn spoke words of genuine prophecy. "She will be very fair, and her hair will be like the waters of the river Arfondwy during the time of the White Flood—which will be a sign to those who see her that she has come into the world to do remarkable things."

And Gwenalarch, who was the mother of the child, replied, "Then we will name her Gwenlliant, for the White Flood, and Ellwy—which was the name I had originally intended—and also Branwen, which is the White Raven."

And so it was that the infant came to be named.

—*From* The Great Book of St. Cybi

1.

A Flurry of White Wings

The candles had all burned down to pools of wax, and the great brick philosopher's oven in the fireplace was cold for the first time in many weeks. Gwenlliant—who was fifteen years old according to the seasons, the calendars, and the clocks of the world, twelve months older in actual fact—stood in the center of the tower chamber, near the open trapdoor, surveying her domain with a puzzled air.

The guttering candles offered little in the way of light, but a few rays of pale winter sunshine filtered in through the frosty glass of the diamond-paned windows. Ordinarily, it was an interesting sort of room, largely because its collection of shelves and tables and cabinets held such a variety of arcane and unusual objects. Herbs hung drying in grey-green knots from the beamed ceiling, filling the air with their sharp, sweet, earthy perfumes. Firelight reflected from glass vessels and copper tubing, and the big brass scale with its precisely calculated lead weights.

But not today. All the interesting clutter in the room had been dusted and tidied away: the books and bottles and flasks; willow-wands, spindles, birds' nests, and besoms; amulets, talismans, and silvered mirrors; quills and inkhorns and parchment scrolls. The oak cabinets had been locked and then sealed with spells, the floor swept clean, and the ashes removed from the fireplace and the brick furnace. Yet none of this, thought Gwenlliant, quite explained the echoing sense of vacancy, the air of abandonment the place had already taken on.

As the day was bitterly cold, and it had stormed on and off ever since morning, she wore a gown of russet wool and a trailing cloak of the same thick material, trimmed with squirrel skins. Her feet were snugly encased in boots of soft grey leather, and her hair, which was the same pale color as the winter sunlight, had been braided, coiled, and pinned in a heavy knot at the back of her neck. She had come upstairs to say good-bye to the stillroom because she was about to embark on a perilous journey.

The room knows that I'm going away, and that I may not return for a long, long time. It depressed Gwenlliant to think that Tryffin, or Mahaffy, or Conn, or any of the other people who loved her, might come up to the room while she was gone and not find any promise there that she was ever coming back.

Particularly when she had spent the few brief months since her return to Caer Ysgithr trying so hard to impress her personality on the tower chamber, with just that intention. *I don't want Tryffin to be reminded of that other time . . . when I ran away. I want him to remember, instead, our wedding vows and all our plans for the future.*

A noise drew her attention toward the stairwell: a scraping of metal against stone, and then the heavy footsteps of someone climbing swiftly. A moment later, a big lean man, lightly armored, emerged through the open trapdoor and stood facing her across the gap in the floor.

"The Lady sent for me?" Meligraunce scarcely sounded winded after his rapid ascent. But those dark eyes that always saw everything registered surprise as they swept across the room, and his shaggy brows rose sharply. "You are leaving, then . . . much sooner than you had planned."

Gwenlliant could see that he had been out of doors quite recently, because his boots were spotted with damp and there were tiny crystals of ice glistening in his black hair.

"Yes, Captain, the summons arrived this morning. Sooner than I might wish, but we knew it might come at any time. That is, after all, why we planned for you to be the one to take Grifflet to his father. The only thing that has changed is that I must charge you with my son's safety a few weeks earlier."

Perhaps her voice was not so steady as she meant it to be, because the Captain's thin, mobile face expressed instant concern. "God knows, there is nothing I would not do or risk to keep the boy safe." One large hand rested briefly on the hilt of his sword.

"But I doubt our journey will be a dangerous one, since we mean to go secretly. I can't alter my form as you can, Lady, yet I can change my appearance just enough by more ordinary means. It is sometimes necessary, you know, when gathering information for Prince Tryffin, for me to assume some disguise or act some part, and I am said to be very good at it.

"As for your foster-son . . . very few people know him at all," he added. "Which is, of course, the very reason that the Governor wishes the child to travel with him as soon as the weather improves."

Gwenlliant nodded. "Though how anyone can believe the story that Tryffin has somehow quietly disposed of Grifflet to make way for Mahaffy Guillyn . . . "

"As you say, it passes belief. But there are those who might find it useful to pretend they credit the story, even though they know it to be false," said Meligraunce. "It is fortunate that the boy so nearly resembles both Rhys and Essylt; there should be no question that another child has been substituted. And those who see him with Prince Tryffin won't be likely to add up the months and discover that . . . slight discrepancy in his age."

"Yes," said Gwenlliant, around the sudden painful constriction in her throat. Grifflet was many months older than he ought to be, because she had taken him with her into the Shadow Lands, where time moved at a different pace. For part of that time in the Otherworld, bereft of her memories, she had believed that Grifflet was truly her own.

Stepping away from the trapdoor, the girl began to move restlessly around the room, her heavy cloak sweeping the floor behind her. "Will you leave immediately?" Meligraunce asked. "Or will you spend some time with the child first?"

"I have seen him . . . and attempted to explain to him, already," she said. "I doubt that he understands how long I am likely to be away. He is still a very small boy by anyone's reckoning, and he can't remember a time when I wasn't there to take care of him. I am the only mother he knows."

"Then I will try to win his trust," said the Captain. "Already, he knows me a little, and associates me with Prince Tryffin, and that is a beginning. But I will visit the nursery each day, and teach him to regard me as his dearest playfellow."

"Thank you," she said, and watched numbly as Meligraunce bowed respectfully, turned on his heel, and descended the stairs.

As soon as it stopped snowing, Gwenlliant left the stillroom and went down to the courtyard. The paving stones were slick with ice, and snow was piled up in deep drifts around the edges of the yard. A grey sky stretched overhead and a stiff wind was blowing in from the sea. But glancing up, Gwenlliant saw that the castle rooks had come out of their nests in the rookery, and had perched atop the highest tower. They would not do that if another storm were coming.

She said the word *raven*. Not as an ordinary person would say it. When Gwenlliant spoke the word in that particular way, it contained all that a raven was, it described down to the tiniest detail the nature of the bird, and just by speaking it, she made that nature her own. Before she took another breath, her bones began to shrink, her flesh and the clothing she wore to melt and take on a new form. As soon as the transformation was complete, she rose in the frosty air in a flurry of white wings, and circled the tower where the other birds were perched.

The sudden vertigo took her completely by surprise. The earth spun crazily below her, and the tower rushed forward as if determined to crush her. She landed on the roof with a thump, and sat there a moment, struggling to regain her breath and her equilibrium, before she even noticed that she had stopped being a white raven and was a girl once more.

Nothing like this had never happened before; from the very first day that she had learned the shapechanging magic, she had always been in complete control of her transformations. And while it was true that many things were different in Mochdreff—since the day that she and Mahaffy had worked the magic to heal the land—while it was also true that many spells peculiar to the Mochdreffi witches had simply ceased to work, this magic which she had inherited from her northern ancestors ought not to be affected.

However that was, her present position was disconcerting, to say the least. Not only might someone come out of the castle, glance up, and see the Governor's young wife sitting winded and dizzy on the tower roof, her perch was both slippery and precarious. The moment she shifted her weight, she began to slide, and it was only by clutching desperately at the slate-blue tiles that she was able to halt her downward progress.

She took a deep breath (but not too deep, for fear it would cause her to slip again), and wondered how she was ever going to get safely down to the courtyard again, if flying made her dizzy. *I could become a lizard and climb down the tower wall, I suppose.*

But she had never been a lizard before, and the idea of compressing herself down so small made her unaccountably queasy. A quick glance around her assured Gwenlliant that the other birds had all left the roof—startled, no doubt, by her loud and ignominious arrival—but they had only relocated on another turret not far away. She had an uncomfortable vision of herself, in lizard form, being carried off and eaten by a hungry black rook.

A raven should be easiest; she had done it so many times before. Those distant Rhianeddi ancestors of hers had made a common practice of transforming themselves into ravens, crows, magpies, and blackbirds. It ought to be second nature to her; it had been second nature, until today. So why did the idea make her feel almost as sick as the thought of becoming a lizard?

It is the only way. There is no ladder in the castle high enough to reach me, and the wind may blow me off before they can arrange anything else. I really haven't any choice.

So she said the word again, and this time, as soon as she felt the transformation take effect, she did not waste any time circling the tower, but went down as quickly and directly as she possibly could. Even so, the vertigo was just as sudden and intense as it had been before, and she landed on her feet on the flagstone pavement with another painful jolt.

Those feet, Gwenlliant gradually realized, wore soft leather boots, peeking out under the skirts of her russet wool gown. She spent a moment assessing the damage to her person and to her costume, and found that both were essentially intact, though she had ripped one corner of her cloak, probably on the tiles of the roof.

Cowardice, she thought. She did not want to leave home again; she was worried about what would happen at Caer Ysgithr during her absence, and so she had created this obstacle out of her own fears. Though her powers were prodigious, she was still a very young witch.

She glanced up at one of the buildings across the yard, at the shuttered window of the room where Grifflet was napping, under the watchful eyes of his two nursemaids. She could picture him sleeping there, with his small body curved around a pillow—as he had slept ever since she stopped sharing a bed with him—and his head tucked under one arm. He was a sturdy, confident child when awake, but there was something dark that hovered at the edge of his dreams, that made him cry out for a light and someone to sit by his bed while he slept.

Gwenlliant knew the name of that shadow. *Maelinn kills children. She sucks the life right out of them, and leaves their pale little corpses on the street or in the market square for their parents to find. And she* knows *Grifflet. The very first thing she will do if she gets past Dame Ceinwen and into our world is find Tryffin's son and murder him, in revenge for that stroke with the silver dagger.*

And that, thought Gwenlliant, *must never be allowed to happen.*

She gave a deep sigh, brushed the snow off her cloak and the skirts of her gown, and headed toward the stable.

Mahaffy Guillyn was bored and restless. He sat at the High Table in the banquet hall at Dinas Yfan, toying with the bones on his silver plate, sipping the sour wine, and listening while the other men assembled in the hall discussed his claims to be Lord of Mochdreff.

"That the Governor sincerely believes—and that all the other lords and chieftains who were gathered in Penafon that day likewise believe that they saw a wonder—I haven't the slightest doubt," Lord Gwistel was saying earnestly. "Yet the fact remains that those of us who were *not* there can scarcely credit the miraculous events that have been described. Far be it from me to question Your Grace's honor or veracity, but I ask you, Prince Tryffin . . ."

And the man went on at great and tedious length, to explain why he believed Tryffin—yet somehow did not believe him, either—while the Governor sat there and listened to it all with the same patient, attentive look that Mahaffy had seen a hundred times before in the same situation.

Stifling a yawn, Mahaffy flexed his fingers, staring at the terrible scars ridging the backs of his hands. He was used to them now, had grown to expect and accept the swift intake of breath, the suddenly averted eyes, when others saw them for the first time. His only regret was that the damage was all to his hands and not to his damnably beautiful face. *I would suffer the same and more,* he thought, *if it were all to do again*. Yet here were these men for whom he had suffered so much, and half of them pretended the thing had never happened.

"And even if a miracle did occur, if our ancient curse was lifted and some measure of fertility restored to the soil, I have never heard that an act of sorcery was any proof of special ancestry." That was Rhodri Owein, Lord Gwistel's brother, a square, heavy man with a silver cockatrice emblazoned on his black surcote. "To say nothing of the politics of the matter being so remarkably volatile. The two boys, Math and Peredur, already contending for the High Seat and so many lords and chieftains already sworn to one or the other, and now a third claimant appears, seemingly out of nowhere—"

"I beg your pardon." The Governor spoke quietly, and by doing so, commanded their attention. The others listened carefully; they had to listen or they would miss what he said. He might have dominated them by his sheer physical presence, this big golden man in scarlet and miniver, but the way he had chosen was better.

"Though evidence of his descent from the ancient princes who ruled this land in ages past is certainly new, the fact is that Mahaffy Guillyn was highly visible, even before Lord Morcant's death. I wish the same might be said of either Math or Peredur. During Lord Cado's rebellion, rather than rally their kinsmen and supporters against that murderous usurper, both boys waited out the entire conflict on the other side of the Perfuddi border, while Mahaffy remained and distinguished himself in battle, and was very nearly killed for his pains. Again, last year, when children were mysteriously dying in Anoeth, where was Math, where was Peredur then? Yet Mahaffy was at my side when I faced that menace, and again very nearly . . ."

As Tryffin continued, the hero of all these tales was sore pressed not to fidget or to squirm in his seat. Not that Mahaffy was indifferent to the important matters under discussion, not that he failed to appreciate the awesome responsibilities that would attend the high position he aspired to, but it seemed to him, at moments like this, that it was a much easier thing to lay down your life in the heat of battle, to pour out your blood on a hill in Penafon, than to sit for hours while men spoke of politics and advanced and refuted the same arguments over and over.

Mahaffy sipped his wine, glowered at his own dark-eyed image reflected at the bottom of the silver cup, and waited for his own turn to speak. That would be a little more interesting, because he never knew in advance exactly what he would say. The first part was always the same, but after that the lords and chieftains would press him harder, interrupt him more often, and ask him more difficult questions than they asked Tryffin.

The truth was—and Mahaffy had realized the fact long since—very few people actually wanted either Math or Peredur; they liked the present impasse very well, so long as it meant that Prince Tryffin would remain in Mochdreff and go on governing them as he had been doing so admirably for the last two and a half years. Mahaffy could hardly blame them for choosing a solid young man of proven worth over two beardless boys and an arrogant stripling, too handsome and spoiled for his own good.

As Tryffin neared the end of his speech, there was a restless shuffling of feet, a murmur of anticipation throughout the hall. *They are thinking it is time for the revelation of the sidhe-stone grail,* thought Mahaffy.

Unfortunately, they would have to wait a little longer. Prince Tryffin had learned to time these things carefully, in order to make the strongest impression possible: First Mahaffy would say his piece, then the miraculous other-worldly vessel would be unveiled and elevated. A hush would fall over the assembly as it always did—as it could not fail to do in the presence of such mystery and wonder— and no one would feel much like talking afterward. Not even Mahaffy, who had seen the chalice a hundred times, who had touched it, and sipped wine from it, *and watched his red blood drip into the vessel, mingling with the earth of Mochdreff*—

"For God's sake, don't turn your head in that direction," said a low, urgent voice.

Mahaffy glanced up. There was Conn mac Matholwch, Tryffin's squire and Mahaffy's best friend, resplendent in the scarlet and gold livery he always donned for these great occasions, standing on the other side of the table, offering him a dish of stewed fowl. Only, this time, he seemed to have more on his mind than Mahaffy's dinner.

"There is a man standing in the shadows up in the minstrels' gallery, who was sighting his crossbow just a few moments since, and you appear to be his target. I think he may be waiting for some signal, perhaps some distraction, before he shoots. But if you get up now, with a fine air of disinterest, and walk out of the room . . ."

With a heroic effort to go on looking as bored as he had been a moment before, Mahaffy shook his head, and pretended to wave away the proffered dish. "If I do that, he may fire anyway. And have no difficulty getting away afterward."

He moved his silver wine goblet until he was able to catch the reflection of the man with the crossbow in the polished surface of the cup. Standing in the deserted gallery, partly shadowed by a green and yellow banner hanging from the rafters, the crossbowman had his weapon cocked and loaded, though not yet aimed.

"A better plan," said Mahaffy, "would be for me to keep the fellow in sight here in this cup, while you go around behind and—"

There was a clatter of falling dishes on the other side of the hall, and everyone instinctively turned in that direction. Everyone that is, but the man with the crossbow, who aimed and released his bolt just as Mahaffy realized his mistake and turned back to look. And Conn, who had not been fooled at all, who hurled himself across the table in a frantic attempt to shield Mahaffy, and took the shaft between his shoulders. There was a sickening thud as the bolt drove home.

Mahaffy cried out in protest, too late. Conn collapsed across the board, the bowman turned to flee, and there was a sudden uproar throughout the room. Women screamed, men shouted, dogs barked, and chairs were knocked over. Half of Prince Tryffin's guardsmen ran after the escaping assassin, the rest swarmed in a protective frenzy around the

Governor or around Mahaffy. Mahaffy tried to push his would-be saviors out of the way, to get a better look at his fallen friend, meanwhile trying to be heard over the roar of the crowd as he called for a physician.

What happened, in the end, was that Tryffin made them all move aside so that he could get a better look at Conn himself. "Is . . . is he dead?" Mahaffy asked numbly.

With his fingers on the pulse point on Conn's neck, the Governor shook his head. "Unconscious but not dead, praise God."

"Is he *going* to die?" Mahaffy ran a hand through his wild dark curls.

"I don't know," Tryffin said quietly. He took out his knife and cut away some of the silken cloth around the protruding shaft. "As you can see, he was wearing his new leather armor under his tunic; the cuir bouilli and the padding beneath undoubtedly absorbed some of the impact. It looks as though the head glanced off the tip of his shoulder blade and then buried itself at an angle here in the muscle. If he was lucky, it hit a rib and was stopped before it went into his lungs."

Just then, a lean man in a black robe came through the crowd and announced that he was Brother Nefyn, Lord Gwistel's physician. While the doctor and his assistants laid Conn out flat on the table and set to work, Tryffin and Mahaffy moved away from the dais.

"If it should please Your Grace and Lord Mahaffy, it would undoubtedly be better if you were to remove yourselves to some more secure place." That was Lord Gwistel, the very picture of shock and mortification. Mahaffy almost felt sorry for the man. "How such a terrible thing came to happen under my roof, I cannot say. But I assure you, all that can be done will be done, and the rogue who has committed this outrage brought to justice."

Prince Tryffin nodded absently, and turned to speak to Mahaffy. "As he says, this room is too open and too dangerous with an assassin loose in the castle after your blood. Let Gwistel and his men escort you to some other place."

"No," said Mahaffy, as firmly as he could. "You wouldn't go, if he had taken that bolt on your behalf, so why should I?"

Tryffin sighed and made a helpless gesture. "No more I would, but I hoped you would display better sense. In God's name, at least take a seat then. In your place, I would feel weak in the knees."

As that exactly described Mahaffy's condition, he was happy to collapse in the nearest chair and cover his eyes with one hand. "Now I know how you felt when I swallowed poison meant for you, at Caer Clynnoc."

"And all the other times men have died protecting me, or because I sent them into battle," Tryffin agreed. "It's no pleasant feeling, though I am afraid that it's one you will have to grow accustomed to, if you are to be Lord of Mochdreff."

Mahaffy nodded weakly. "What are you going to do with the man who did it, after they catch him?"

"That will depend on how willing he is to tell us what we want to know."

"I mean"—Mahaffy took a deep breath—"after you have finished questioning him, how do you intend to kill him?"

There was a long pause. "As much as I might enjoy cutting the fellow's heart out with my own dagger," Prince Tryffin said at last, "I think that should be for you to decide."

Startled, Mahaffy took his hand from his eyes. All this time, Tryffin had remained so calm, had spoken so steadily, it had never occurred to Mahaffy that he was furiously angry. Now he saw that the Governor's eyes were stern, his mouth drawn in a grim line, and his hands were balled up in fists so tight that the knuckles were growing white with the strain.

"Is that supposed to make me feel better, or is it intended for—for a lesson in government?"

For such a big man, the Governor was always so light and deft in all his movements, it was easy to forget how terrifyingly destructive a man of his size and strength could be if he ever lost control. That control was evident now as he asked softly, "What do you think?"

"I think," said Mahaffy, "that you don't give a damn about my feelings just now. Considering what your own must be. Conn is your squire, your kinsman. If you are giving up your right to take personal revenge, it must be with an eye to the greater good, so that I can learn everything it means to be Lord of Mochdreff."

Tryffin shrugged a broad shoulder under the red velvet. "Say rather that I don't think there is anything that *could* be done to make you feel any better. And that if it were that easy, I would not consider you worthy to be Lord of Mochdreff or anyplace else."

While Mahaffy did feel suitably wretched, the prospect of arranging the crossbowman's death *did* soothe his wounded sensibilities just a little. He entertained himself for the next hour by staring at the row of banners up in the gallery, and devising various methods of execution.

In all these schemes he was destined to be disappointed because Lord Gwistel came back into the hall and announced that the assassin had somehow eluded the Governor's guards, escaped over the castle walls, and disappeared into the darkness and the storm raging outside. "Though my men will naturally spend the night searching for him, and spare no effort—"

"No," said Tryffin. "They can resume the search in the morning, or as soon as the weather clears. There is no sense killing a dozen men to apprehend one. What I would like to learn in the meantime is who he was and whether he left any friends behind, here in the castle. Did no one recognize him? And if he's not one of your people, if he did not come in with any of your other guests, then how, in God's name, did he get into the gallery with that damnable crossbow in the first place?"

After considerable hedging, Gwistel finally realized that nothing was going to prevent the Governor from asking a great many embarrassing questions—no matter how many men Gwistel was willing to sacrifice to the wind and the snow by way of distraction—and placed his men at Prince Tryffin's disposal, to interrogate as he saw fit. It was during the questioning of the guards from the gate that the physician came forward to report on his patient.

The bolt had been recovered, the bleeding stanched, and the wound bandaged. "A broadhead lodged against a rib," said Brother Nefyn, "not so deep as I had originally feared. The loss of blood was severe, however, and it is not always possible to tell whether the bleeding *inside* has ceased. Then, too, the wound may go bad, though naturally every effort has been made to see that this doesn't happen."

Tryffin lifted the damp blond hair from his brow. "I suppose you mean to tell me that he has survived your surgery but you have no idea if he will continue to do so."

The physician inclined his head. "We may have a better idea in the morning. Until then, we can only leave the matter in God's hands."

And Sceolan the King and all of his warriors went out hunting the white deer, one day in early spring. But the doe ran so fleetly and the King and his dogs followed so swiftly and eagerly, that he was soon separated from the other men.

Grown weary at last, he stooped to drink from a forbidden well. And the vines of the ivy and the bramble started up out of the ground, and grew so swiftly that soon there was an impenetrable barrier all around him, nor could Sceolan cut a path through with his sword, because the vines were so exceedingly tough.

Then the birds and the beasts and the hairy woodwoses came out of the bushes, to stare with their wild, dark, wondering eyes—all of them greatly amazed by the sight of the King in his leafy cage.

—From The Book of Dun Fiorenn

2.

With Holly, Ivy, and Thorn

Meligraunce slept late these dark winter mornings . . . at least since Prince Tryffin went on progress, leaving the Captain with no duties and few occupations. There was simply no purpose to rising in the dark and the cold, when the dull grey days seemed to stretch on endlessly no matter how short they actually were.

He woke one morning in late December with the distinct impression that a woman was lying in bed beside him. He could hear the rise and fall of her breathing, a sigh as she shifted position and snuggled down under the sleeping furs, trying to find a pocket of warmer air.

But when he opened his eyes and reached out to touch her

16

with his hand, he found only emptiness. It was the same hard, narrow cot that he slept on each night in the barracks: no furs, no silken pillows, and certainly no woman. And the sounds he had been hearing came from the next bed over, where another man was snoring softly.

For no reason that he could think of, Meligraunce broke out in a cold sweat, and his heart beat so hard that his chest began to ache. When he closed his eyes, tried to drift back to sleep, he realized that the dreams he had been dreaming all night long were faintly disturbing. A noisy jumble of disjointed images danced in his brain: *Mummers and dwarfish jugglers in green and gold silks . . . an army of holly and ivy growing over and around the towers of Caer Ysgithr, while the thorns that had flourished there before caught the moon in a net . . . a raven, a golden cauldron, a skull with gemstones for eyes . . .* and at the last, shortly before he woke, *a ragged scarecrow figure of a man, lost in a boxwood maze.*

There was nothing in any of this he wanted to bring back. The Captain opened his eyes, slipped out from beneath the rough wool blankets, and moving quietly, so as not to disturb the other occupants of the room — who kept the night watch and had earned their rest — washed and dressed by the thin beams of light creeping in through cracks in the shutters.

As soon as he was dressed, he went downstairs to the empty guardroom, where a fire and breakfast awaited him: ale and bread, a pot of porridge warming on the hob at the back of the fireplace, and rather surprisingly, an immense venison pie, only half eaten. Meligraunce cleared up the crusts and the wooden bowls left by the men who had eaten earlier, and took a seat at a narrow plank table.

He ate slowly, being in no hurry, his appetite uncertain. This was the third time in a week that he had imagined the woman's presence in his bed, but this was the first time the impression had been so vivid, so utterly compelling.

Meligraunce considered, briefly, the idea of moving up to

Prince Tryffin's abandoned rooms, where there would be no one to disturb his rest, no one to send his imagination reeling, merely by breathing in the dark. With the Governor and his lady both away it would surprise no one if the captain of the Governor's personal bodyguard decided to keep a closer eye on their apartments and their possessions during their absence.

The only problem was, Meligraunce had never slept entirely alone in his life. First sharing a loft with his brothers and sisters, in their father's cottage in Camboglanna, later assigned to a series of barracks and guardrooms, or bedding down in the antechamber outside Prince Tryffin's sleeping quarters when the Governor traveled, he had always enjoyed the reassuring knowledge that someone was there only a few feet off, and never divided from him by more than a single wall. Though he was ashamed to admit it even to himself, the idea of isolating himself in a vast suite of otherwise unoccupied rooms was even more daunting than the dreams and the cold sweats.

And a man half mad with boredom as it was had no need to make a hermit of himself into the bargain, the Captain decided as he left the table and began to buckle on his light everyday armor. What he really needed was something more to occupy his mind, and keep his imagination in check.

Over the years, he had performed a variety of duties on Prince Tryffin's behalf. Bodyguard, spy, personal attendant, confidante, advisor . . . What it all came down to was doing whatever was necessary to protect Prince Tryffin, and what was more, to preserve Prince Tryffin in a state of health and peace of mind that would allow him to perform the important duties which God and the High King had chosen to bestow on him. Without that guiding purpose, the Captain's own existence seemed singularly empty and unimportant.

"I am trusting you with something far more precious, far more sacred than my own life . . . which is the safety of my son." That was how the Governor had broken the news

that he would be leaving Meligraunce behind during the early stages of his journey.

Not for one moment had Meligraunce believed that. He was fond of children, and please God he was not a hard or a cruel man, but even he had to admit that this particular child was a serious political inconvenience to Prince Tryffin—more so in his way than his older half-brother, Peredur, or his cousin Math fab Mercherion—one that was likely to cause a great deal of trouble and possibly even bloodshed before another year passed. At the same time, he realized that Prince Tryffin, with that outrageous Gwyngellach sentimentality when it came to children and households and families, did believe every word of it. And if this inconvenient foster-son was precious to the Governor and to his lady, as wrong-headed as they might be in bestowing their affection, then it only made sense that protecting the child, and traveling with the child when the time came, was a logical extension of Meligraunce's ordinary duties.

Even, he thought ruefully, as he donned his cloak and left the barracks, if that meant being at loose ends for the next four or five weeks.

The snow in the courtyard was several inches deep, already crossed and recrossed with footprints, though the sun had not yet climbed as high as the walls and the yard was still in deep shadow. There was a great bustle of activity over by the stables, the smithy, and the bakehouse. As a steamy draft of air brought the scent of spices and boiling meat, the Captain was suddenly reminded of the unexpectedly bountiful breakfast: not only the venison pie, but apples and raisins in the porridge, and three loaves of bread instead of the usual two. It seemed that the cooks and everyone else in the castle, except Meligraunce himself, had shaken off their winter lethargy.

Without any conscious volition, his long strides took him in the direction of the great stone Keep, toward the rooms where three ancient noblewomen, the widows of powerful men, lived in faded splendor, occupying themselves day after day with needlework, cards, quarreling, and stale gossip.

They did not much approve of the Captain, those imperious old dames, whose tongues were so much sharper than their silver needles, deeming his dress, his speech, and his education unsuitably grand for a man of his peasant origins. But they were too feeble to make visits themselves—unable to move at all without their sticks and their sturdy little pages to support them—not agreeable enough to attract many visitors, and since their numbers had dwindled from five to three over the course of the last six months, they were so desperate for company that even *his* was welcome. Because he was well acquainted with the evils of boredom, Meligraunce had taken to visiting them every day.

They were basking in the heat of a roaring fire when the Captain found them: three crooked figures in elaborate gowns and fantastical headdresses, with coffers and work baskets lying open around them, spilling a flood of bright, tawdry materials across the floor . . . rotting silks, rubbed velvets, soiled tissue of silver and gold . . . faded ribbons, dim jewels, and dingy silk flowers.

"It is the handsome young Captain come to visit us," said Dame Maffada, glancing up from the slashed and beaded sleeve she was mending. The silk was so ancient and fragile, it had already been mended a dozen times, and the color had mellowed to a soft dusty rose, though Meligraunce suspected it had once been crimson.

The grotesque old creature leered at him so, the Captain knew better than to mistake her words for a compliment. *You may be a handsome fellow now, but you'll never live to see my age,* her eyes told him. *Your kind never do. You'll be a toothless old man while your master is still young and lusty, outlive your usefulness before you know it, live and die off the charity of your betters—and what use your long, straight limbs, your fine eyes, and the manner you've copied from Prince Tryffin, then?*

But Meligraunce, who had trained himself to be useful in

ways that had more to do with his keen mind than his strong limbs, was able to ignore the provocation. He bowed, murmured a polite greeting, and asked if there was any commission that he might perform . . . any errand into town?

"You might bring men to haul these lunatics away," said Dame Indeg, indicating the band of servants on the other side of the room, who were busily engaged with ladders and stools, hanging garlands of evergreen from the beamed ceiling, tacking wreaths made of ivy and bramble over each of the windows and doors.

Meligraunce stared at the workers, uncomprehending. "I had no idea a celebration was planned. What is the occasion?"

Dame Indeg put aside the spangled veil she had been stitching to a towering horned hennin. "Today is Christmas Eve, Captain. Did you lose count of the days?"

In truth, he *had* lost count of the days, since the holiday held little meaning, with everyone he cared about so far away. But that explained the venison pie at breakfast, and all the activity elsewhere in the castle. Or it would have done, if Prince Tryffin and his Rhianeddi bride had been in residence.

"I had no idea the Mochdreffi marked the Twelve Days of Christmas with any special observance," said Meligraunce. "That is, I knew there would be Mass in the castle chapel, and again at Epiphany, but as for feasting or anything else . . . I have lived here five years and never seen anything of the sort."

"No more have I, and I've lived my three score and ten in this land," said Dame Morag. "Heathen tricks, I call it. Trashy, foreign nonsense—"

But Meligraunce was already drifting across the room, to see what the servants had to say for themselves. He arrived just as two of the men and one of the serving maids were discussing the best way to make masks.

"Rags and flour-paste, or parchment over a wicker

frame," said the girl, who was thin and dark with a vivid color in her cheeks.

"Plaster might do, if we could get the lime; there may be some left over from when they whitewashed the stable." The younger of the two men scratched his head. "A bit brittle maybe."

"My uncle spent a year in Pennefynn, when he was a lad," offered the second man. "'*By God*,' he used to say, '*there was never anything like the Christmas Revels in Walgan.*' Everyone dressed up in feathers and furs, and the masks were terrifying: ravens and owls, foxes and great hairy devils. You will know, Captain, for you were bred in those parts."

Meligraunce cleared his throat. "In truth, I was born in southern Camboglanna, which is an immense distance and across a great river from Pennefynn in Walgan." Yet there was no use explaining this to people who had never ventured more than twenty miles from home, ignorant people to whom all foreigners were much the same.

"They never dress as foxes or devils in Treledig, or at the court of the High King. Perhaps you are thinking of the wolves and the wild men of the forest, who dance in the masque with holly in their hair." Even as Meligraunce spoke, the bright, confusing images of his dream flooded back into his memory.

The girl flashed him a dazzling smile. "Ah Captain Meligraunce, you should be our Master of the Revels, since you know all about it."

It was a tempting offer, especially with the girl tossing her head and laughing up into his face. He wanted to ask what had set off this uncharacteristic flurry of celebration, ask where they had come by the evergreens, with the nearest pine forest leagues upon leagues away. But a man who was entrusted with the Governor's secrets must not spend his time gossiping with servants. So Meligraunce politely declined, slipped quietly out of the room, and proceeded down a long flight of stone steps to the courtyard below.

No sooner had he reached the yard than someone hailed him. He turned to see one of the men from the gatehouse striding his way from the direction of the barracks.

"A lady at the gate, Captain, asking for you." The young guardsman was huffing and puffing in the sharp winter air, as though he had already been through most of the castle in search of the Captain.

Meligraunce gave him a puzzled frown from under his dark, shaggy brows, not quite certain he had heard properly. "A woman from the town, asking for me?" His family in Camboglanna was so far away, it would take weeks of travel to reach them, and he had no friends and very few acquaintances down in the town of Trewynyn.

The guard shook his head. "A great lady in a velvet gown, with jewels in her hair. She walked up the road from the town and asked for you."

Meligraunce started moving toward the outer walls. "I hope, Sergeant, that you did not leave this great lady standing there at the gate. I hope you had the courtesy to invite her in."

Hurrying to keep pace with him, the Sergeant lengthened his stride. "She said she might not enter without Prince Tryffin or his lady to speak the words." By which the Captain gathered that the visitor was a witch, a Mochdreffi wise-woman, unable to pass beyond the castle's warding spells without the ritual invitation. "When she heard you were not immediately at hand, she charged me to deliver this letter." And that, Meligraunce realized, meant that the woman actually knew him. Prince Tryffin had insisted that he learn to read, though it was not something he had practiced long enough or often enough to do very well. That he knew how to do it at all was something few people outside the Governor's household were likely to guess.

He took the letter and broke the wax seal, unfolded the piece of parchment. Though the handwriting was unfamiliar, a faint odor of oils and rare spices identified the writer even before he was able to puzzle out the words. Meligraunce felt his palms grow damp, his stomach harden into a painful knot of apprehension. Though his dreams might remain a mystery, the cause of his morning panic was now very clear.

"If you have any desire to see me again, you will find me outside the town, down by the water. If you do not wish to meet with me, be assured that I will not linger long." At the bottom of the letter was a single word: *"Luned."*

Meligraunce crushed the paper between his fingers. He was embarrassed to see, with the Sergeant still looking on, that his hand was shaking. "My thanks," he said, as steadily as it was possible for him to say anything at that moment. And the other man, correctly taking this for dismissal, turned and walked away.

As soon as the Sergeant was gone, Meligraunce smoothed out the parchment and read the first line of the letter over again, his lips silently forming the words. *"If you have any desire to see me again."*

And that, thought the Captain, standing there in the courtyard with the icy wind lifting his cloak, and every inch of his body slick with sweat under the layers of leather and armor, summed up all that he desired and all he most feared.

Yet he was forced to give Luned credit. Though the tone of her letter was curt, she had at least done him the courtesy of informing him that she would not waste the entire day waiting for him, should he wish to refuse her invitation. She was too proud and too generous to command him or to shame him into meeting her if he did not come willingly.

And a wise man, a prudent man, would take advantage of that. A man with even a shred of common sense would destroy the parchment and try to convince himself that he had never seen the letter at all.

Yet a man who had been able to resist Luned in the first place would not be holding such a message in his hand right now. Nor would he be struggling with the temptation (as Meligraunce most certainly was) to experience once more the sweetest and most dangerous moments of his entire life.

It was a tangled, rambling wood, with oak and thorn and vine, and wandering pathways leading on to yet more dark and impenetrable shade. It was so dim under the canopy of leafy boughs that even the owls nesting at the heart of the wood mistook the day for night. Gwenlliant, who had been forced to dismount and lead her dappled mare, could hear their hollow voices, the fluttering of their wings, and every now and then she caught a glimpse of round, golden eyes glowing in the dark, among the branches.

Though the forest was strange to her, the girl moved swiftly along the path, finding her way by owl-light and by that uncanny witch sense she had come to rely on more than the other five. The wood was strange to her, but she knew there was a house deeper in, a weird old shapechanging house (Dame Ceinwen's cottage that traveled between the worlds) that was entirely familiar, and it was her awareness of that house and its remarkable occupant that drew her continually on.

When she finally came out in a sunny clearing and found the house, the cottage wore a face she had never seen before: wattle and daub, with a thatched roof of dry, leafy branches.

Gwenlliant left the mare grazing in the clearing. When she went in through the low door, it was the house that she knew: the stone walls lined with shelves, the central hearth, the few rough pieces of wooden furniture, the candles and the tallow dips that made the tiny room almost too bright for Gwenlliant's eyes. She could hear the doves cooing up in the rafters, and the air seemed to be filled with floating grey and white feathers.

"Dame Ceinwen?" As soon as Gwenlliant spoke the name, a dark figure solidified in one corner of the room, a bent old woman, all sharp angles and jutting chin, in a black gown and cloak. As she moved toward Gwenlliant, a weedy, marshy odor came with her, and the girl realized that it was mist, not feathers, that made the air so bright and hazy.

"I am growing weary," said the crone, in her thin, old voice. "The time is swiftly approaching when you must either take my place here, guarding the ways between the worlds, or go out further than I dare venture, and meet your enemy on the other side of the Breathing Mist."

"I am ready," Gwenlliant said steadily, though she was by no means as confident as she sounded.

A quarter of an hour later, they were sitting by the hearth, Dame Ceinwen in her chair of woven branches, Gwenlliant on a stool at her feet.

"A dozen times, Maelinn has attempted to slip past me and enter our world," said the old woman, holding her hands out to the fire which Gwenlliant had kindled on the stones of the hearth. The wood was holly, still a little green, and the flames were a clear, hot yellow like burning wax. The Mist had dissipated, but the room was still chilly and the heat of even a small fire was welcome.

"The first nine times, she seemed daunted by my presence on the borders of reality, and turned back without a struggle. More recently, it has become a battle of wills, and she seems to grow stronger with every encounter, while I grow weaker."

The wise-woman sat back in her chair and closed her eyes. It seemed that she dozed off; her head tilted forward and she hardly appeared to be breathing. Seeing her slumped in the chair, Gwenlliant realized how frail Ceinwen was becoming. Always before, there had been a certain wiry strength in those thin limbs of hers, but now she looked as brittle as dry branches.

Gwenlliant was about to rise from her seat, when the old woman opened her eyes and spoke again. "Tell me . . . have things changed greatly in Mochdreff?"

"The false spring that followed Mahaffy's rite of atonement and the healing of the land didn't last long," said

Gwenlliant, settling back down again. "And the weather since then has been bitter—the worst winter that anyone can remember. November was nothing but storms, scouring the land with ice and snow, and some people say—"

"Scouring," said the old woman. "The land is being cleansed, in preparation for the day Mahaffy ascends the High Seat; that is as it should be. But I interrupt you. What more do you have to tell me?"

"The Wild Magic is no longer . . . accessible. Many who were great witches in the past find themselves limited to the simple spells they learned as children. And whether what they have lost has truly been returned to the land, whether the soil is really more fertile, no one will know for certain for many months. But there have been omens and portents. The day before I left Caer Ysgithr, I heard of an oracular pig in Oeth, and before that, of a griffon's egg which had been incubating on an old man's hearth for twelve long years, that had finally hatched."

Gwenlliant paused for breath and then continued. "In Cormelyn, they say a woman well past the age of child-bearing bore twin boys who walked and spoke in the hour of their birth, and then fell silent, as though waiting for someone or something to startle them into further speech. I think, with all this, the people are confused, and don't know whether to greet the next change of seasons with hope or with fear."

The old woman nodded. "Some will welcome change, some will not. That is always the way. Moreover there are families who rose to power in the Mochdreff that was, and they will be reluctant to relinquish what they hold. Nor will they be ready to accept the young man responsible for these changes as their Lord, merely on the strength of Prince Tryffin's example. If Maelinn were able to cross over from the Shadow Lands into the world we know . . ."

Ceinwen shifted in her wicker chair. "She might do much to stir up their resentment with her spells, with her illusions. May have done more harm than we know, already. But if you should enter the Shadow Lands in search of her, I think she will retreat before you, find some place to hide and remain there, hoping to escape your notice."

Gwenlliant reached up and drew the hairpins out of her hair. The winter-gold braids came tumbling down, and she began to absently separate the plaited strands and comb out her hair with her fingers. "Yes. But what am I supposed to *do* with Maelinn when I find her? Shall I try to destroy her, or merely render her harmless by taking back the memories and the power she forced me to share with her?

"And how," she added with a sigh, "am I to do either of those things?"

The old woman shrugged a bony shoulder. "That may be as the situation dictates. The first thing that you must do is gain some measure of power over her, by recognizing Maelinn in whatever shape she happens to be wearing and naming her before she names you. You will have this one advantage: She will not lead you back to her own time and place in the sacred forest of Achren, because the wound from Prince Tryffin's dagger will kill her if she ever returns."

Gwenlliant sat for a long time, rebraiding her hair, wondering if she ought to tell about the difficulty she had experienced, back at Caer Ysgithr, working the shape-change. She did not want to say anything that would dishearten the old woman. But she needed Ceinwen's advice, so at last she told it all.

"When I tried again on the journey south, it was as easy and as natural as ever. I ran with the wolves and with the deer, burrowed under the earth as a badger, yet for all that, the idea of changing myself into a bird or a fish or a lizard fills me with terror."

The crone considered for a long time before she answered. "You know the shapechanging magic is foreign to me, a gift of your people and not of mine. And that being so, I hardly know how to advise you. This much seems clear: Go as a woman when you can, wearing any face that you choose. Some disguise will be necessary. When you feel it necessary to do more than that, don't attempt to make yourself too small, since your instincts warn against it. And stay close to the earth, because air and water no longer appear to be your elements."

Ceinwen hesitated, staring into the fire, seeking some vision there that would provide further guidance. Then she shook her head. "I cannot see the end of your quest. But that in itself may be a favorable sign; if there were some compelling destiny on you, to die or to be conquered by Maelinn, I believe I would know it. Even crippled this way, you seem to have some chance of defeating her, though your victory is by no means assured."

Gwenlliant let out her breath in a long sigh. "Then I shall go and seek that chance. I would far rather take it now, by choice, than weeks or months in the future, by grim necessity."

"I believe you have made a wise decision," said the old woman, rising from her chair. "And if you go soon, I think you will find Maelinn's trail still there to be followed."

The girl stood also. "Then summon up the Breathing Mist. I see no reason to delay any longer."

And when they had ridden some distance from the lady's home, her baseborn lover took her down from the saddle, and bade her not to follow him. "For it is a great shame that a woman like you should give herself to a ragged, disreputable fellow like me, forgetting all that she owes to her clan and her people. And a woman who has been faithless once may be faithless again—which woman is not for me."

For as much as the lady wept and made moan, the rogue remained as determined as ever, and returned all that she said to him with more hard words. But as he mounted once more the bonny black steed and rode off over the lea, she kilted up her silken shirts and followed after him . . .

—*From a Camboglannach ballad, freely adapted*

3.

The Language of the Heart

Meligraunce had no difficulty finding Luned, down among the great ships and the little fishing boats. She stood at the end of a wooden pier, staring out across the choppy grey waters of the bay, a bright, arrogant figure in purple and scarlet. Her velvet cloak was lined with ermine, and the jewels in her dark hair caught the sunlight and cast it back in a shimmer of rainbow colors.

There was something in her stance, even from a distance, that told Meligraunce her letter was a lie: She meant to wait there until nightfall if necessary. And if he never came, she would return the next day, and the day after that, hoping he would change his mind.

She was also, he noticed, unattended. A Mochdreffi woman of power, even an unmarried one, had far more freedom than her ordinary sisters. She could go where she wished, meet whom she pleased, without any fear of being accosted or molested. At least, so it had been in the past. No doubt there were many Mochdreffi witches, finding their power diminished, who were becoming more timid, more circumspect in their behavior. It was a relief to Meligraunce to discover among so many changes that Luned had not changed, that she was just as beautiful, splendid, and self-assured as ever.

When she heard his footsteps on the wooden pier, when she turned and caught sight of him approaching, her eyes lost some of their coldness, and a faint smile appeared, then disappeared so quickly he almost doubted that he had seen it.

On a sudden impulse, he went down on one knee, took her hand, and kissed the tips of her fingers. It was a bold gesture—seeing that she was so far above him and that no vows of fealty or service existed between them—but she did not seem to resent the liberty, made no effort to withdraw her hand.

"I began to wonder, Captain, whether you would meet me or not."

"Lady, it would have been better for both of us, had I found the strength to stay away." He released her hand and rose to his feet. "Unless . . . you came here to tell me that you repented those words you said to me in Anoeth. That you realized how impossible—"

She stopped him with an impatient gesture. "You should know me better than that. Once I form a resolve, my mind is not easily changed. But don't let us quarrel," she added hastily, seeing him frown. "Will you walk with me and tell me . . . oh, whatever it is that friends tell each other after a long parting. What have you been doing this cruel winter, and why are you still here in Trewynyn? I've heard that the Governor is traveling north with Mahaffy Guillyn."

Though he knew her to be a friend of Prince Tryffin, it was not for him to decide whether or not to trust her with the

Governor's secrets, so he answered evasively. "I was told to stay behind with the Lady Gwenlliant. Now that she is gone, I plan to join Prince Tryffin as soon as possible. But you, Lady, surely you never came so far alone . . . I've heard that the bays and the inlets to the north are all frozen over, and the journey from Anoeth by land must have been grueling for your great-grandmother."

They left the pier and moved down the wooden walkway that circled the harbor. "Dame Brangwaine found the journey difficult—who could have expected otherwise?" said Luned. "Yet her health is much better than it was. The disease that she suffered from last year was apparently cured when the land was healed . . . though it would take a greater magic still to cure what ails her now. She has lived so long, Captain, that the very years have become a burden to her. Also, her gifts are not what they were in the past, and that seems to frustrate her. She doesn't complain, but I have heard her say that the sacrifice will be a bitter one if she doesn't live to see the results."

"And you?" said Meligraunce. "Were your gifts affected also?"

"Dame Brangwaine was very slow and careful when it came to instructing me," said Luned. "And so I was never permitted to test the limits of my power. What remains is formidable, and what I lost . . . well, I'm not likely to miss what I never knew."

Meligraunce wondered if that was true. It seemed to him that Luned, being who and what she was, must have once cherished ambitions, ambitions which she had been forced to set aside now that her powers were, however imperceptibly, diminished.

Perhaps she guessed what he was thinking, because she abruptly stopped walking and turned to face him. "My plans for the future have changed, Captain. They are very different from anything I wanted in the past," she said earnestly. "Shall I tell you what I long for now?"

He put up his hand as if to ward off a blow. "If it is the

thing that you told me in Anoeth, spare us both by not repeating it."

She moved a step closer. "And yet," she said softly, "I know that you love me."

"The more reason," he protested, "to refuse to involve you in the shame, and the scandal, and the ruin of an unequal marriage. Even supposing that such a thing were possible, that your kinsmen had no means of standing in our way. A marriage between us might not even be lawful for all that I know."

"No one *could* prevent us, if we married with the Governor's consent and with Dame Brangwaine's blessing. And why should we care for the scandal, if we were together and happy? Dame Brangwaine has seen it, and her prophecies invariably come true. She is convinced that I will bear you many fine sons and daughters, and that our descendants will wield great influence and power in the Mochdreff that is to be."

"With all respect that is due Dame Brangwaine," the Captain insisted, "I must remind you that she also pretends to believe that I am descended from kings and princes, by some back-handed connection with Prince Tryffin and his family—which I can assure you is not true."

Luned shrugged. "As you have said, it is all pretense. She hopes to convince others by pretending to believe it herself. Others *would* believe it, if you stopped denying it, and then our way would be clear."

He shook his head sadly. "And do you believe we could be happy together, if our very marriage was founded on a lie? And I don't understand why Dame Brangwaine even wants this. She seems to be the last woman who would wish to mix her bloodline with peasant stock."

They began to walk again, the Captain keeping a safe distance between them; if he came too close, he might be tempted to reach out and touch her.

"In the Mochdreff that was," said Luned, "certain qualities in a man helped him to rise to greatness, and so the principal families came to be. We were hard, ruthless, implacable. Our honor was always tempered with cruelty, our friendship with self-interest. It was the only way that we could survive and flourish. But in the new Mochdreff, a different kind of strength will be wanted: courage, integrity, intelligence, coupled with a certain adaptability that is, I fear, completely foreign to us. God knows, you are nothing if not adaptable, or you could not look and act so much the gentleman, and those other qualities are yours as well. If we married, you would pass them on to our children, and through our children to succeeding generations.

"So you see," she went on, "my great-grandmother is as proud and terrible as you think she is. She wishes to breed the pair of us like cattle, that her descendants may continue to flourish in this land. And if she wished to mate us against our will, that would be one thing—I would resist her with every bit of strength I possess . . . but since we love each other, since it is something that *we* want as well—"

"If, like Dame Brangwaine, I was willing to sacrifice your present happiness for the sake of those future generations," Meligraunce interrupted her. "If I was willing to see you pass the rest of your life in bitterness and regret, and watch whatever love you feel for me now turn to resentment and eventually to hatred.

"Besides," he added, with a hopeless gesture, "the man you have been describing is Prince Tryffin, not me. And he is the one you wanted, before you realized you couldn't have him. Do not make the mistake of believing . . . because I am permitted to walk in his shadow, because he has honored me with his friendship, because I have gained some trick of imitating his easy, gracious manner . . . that I am worthy to take his place, in your affections or anywhere else."

Luned took two steps in his direction, reached out to touch him lightly on the face. "Prince Tryffin is a great man. Who am I to deny it? Once I was drawn to that greatness, but I swear I never loved him as I love you."

He drew away from her touch. "For all that, I can't do this thing you ask me. The risk to you, to our happiness, is just too great."

She bit her lip, clenched her hands so tightly, he knew that the marks on her nails would be there in her flesh for many days to follow. "As you are such a man for caution, as you are so careful and prudent, I wonder that you were willing to share my bed that night when I sent for you . . . and all the nights that followed."

"I thought you meant to amuse yourself," he replied. "Did you imagine that you were the first great lady who was curious to try me in her bed? Ever since I was a boy and grew more quickly than all the others, women who were lonely and powerful and bored—" Meligraunce broke off abruptly. Many of the memories were unpleasant ones, and certainly none of them were anything he wished to share with her.

She opened her eyes in disbelief, gave a painful little laugh. "And that drew you to me? That was something you sought? You surprise me, Captain. Whatever I imagined, I never thought that kind of liaison would attract you."

And of course she was right. Even when the woman had been kind and the act pleasurable, the realization that he was in some sense helpless, the unspoken element of coercion, had always troubled him. Ever since he was old enough to understand what it was he disliked about those encounters, he had done all that he could to avoid them.

So why had he obeyed *her* summons, gone up to her bedchamber that first night. Because he had fallen in love with the ghost of a woman he could never have, and this one was beautiful, and alive, and willing? Or because he sensed in Luned a capacity to give him what no woman had been able to offer him before?

He remembered knocking on her door, his palms as clammy as they were now. And he remembered her look of surprise, when she answered the door, standing on the threshold in her gauzy nightdress . . . how his heart sank as he realized there must have been some mistake, even though her invitation had been so explicit.

But then she laughed tremulously and drew him into the room with her. *"Ah Meligraunce, I had made up my mind you were going to refuse me. I thought I should die of the shame . . . and the disappointment."*

What followed after that took them both by surprise, by its incredible sweetness, by its passionate intensity. It was as though they shared some language of the heart, which existed for them alone. He had lived through the next few weeks in a pleasant state of delirium, returning to her bedchamber night after night, happier than he had ever thought he could possibly be, until he woke one morning on the bed beside her, in a blind state of panic, and asked himself the question, *God in Heaven . . . what am I doing here?*

But when he tried to explain to her what he was feeling, why it would only be cruel to them both to encourage an impossible attachment, one which already promised to be stronger than either of them had ever anticipated, she only made everything that much worse by asking him to marry her. He had refused her then, as he refused her today, and they had ended the affair by quarreling.

"I went to you in a state of madness. Or else, under some damnable spell of Dame Brangwaine's. Whatever it was, I have since recovered, and I can only hope that you will do the same," he said now. She colored, then went deathly pale, but he continued doggedly on. "Because if you do not, if you can't go on to live your life as well and fully and happily as if we had never even met, then I will spend the rest of mine regretting that moment of criminal weakness."

By the look that she gave him, it was plain that he had hurt or insulted her in some way that he had never intended. But it was too late to take back anything he had said, and perhaps . . . yes, perhaps it was kinder this way in the long run. Anger would make her strong—she was that kind of woman—false hope would cripple her.

"Perhaps you were, as you say, criminally weak, and God knows that I have no use for a weak man or a timid one," she answered coldly. "Very well, Captain Meligraunce, go your way and I shall go mine. And if we are very fortunate, we will never meet again."

And because he loved her, he left it at that. As much as it hurt his heart to do so, he forced himself to make a deep silent bow, turn on his heel, and walk back to the town gate, without so much as a backward glance.

But it would be a long time before he put Luned out of his mind—if he was ever able to do it at all.

Dame Ceinwen put a big pot of herbs and water on the fire to boil, then she began to hobble around the cottage, opening up baskets and boxes and chests.

"You must not wear the clothes that you came in . . . the color is good but the cloth is much too fine," she told Gwenlliant. "There are places in the past where it might draw too much attention."

The old woman pulled out a shapeless grey garment of wool spun with flax, and a mantle of the same dull material. "But the costume of simple folk changes very little over the years, and these should serve, no matter what shadow of the past you should find yourself visiting."

Gwenlliant thanked her and slipped out of the gown she was wearing, and into the clothes the crone offered her. To complete the outfit, Ceinwen handed her a leather belt to girdle the overdress, and a copper brooch to pin the mantle in place over one shoulder.

By now, the water had come to a furious boil, and the Mist was gathering in the tiny room. The witch threw open her door, and the steam went sailing out. Soon, the walls began to creak and the air to shudder as the fabric of reality began to alter around the cottage.

It was time to leave. Gwenlliant embraced Dame Ceinwen (not failing to notice how sharply the bones stuck out under the old woman's flesh), took a deep breath of the moist air, and headed resolutely out the door.

Outside, the forest had disappeared, was no longer there, had retreated behind the shifting borders of the world she knew. Now, it was all stifling fog and quaking earth, with no trees, stones, or other landmarks that Gwenlliant could see. But after a time, her senses began to adjust to the seething chaos around her. The vapor was faintly luminous, allowing her to see a little more, and she caught a strong whiff of a familiar, unpleasant odor. It was the stench of Maelinn's abominable magic, and it was as good as a trail through the fog.

Gwenlliant walked for what felt like hours, the scent that led her growing steadily colder. If she should happen to lose the trail before she emerged from the Breathing Mist, she would not know which direction she ought to follow, and would have to wait there in the chill and the damp until the shapechanging Maelinn made her next attempt to cross the borders. It was not an appealing prospect.

Eventually, however, the Mist became thinner, and a few minutes later Gwenlliant walked right out into the brilliant sunshine of a fine spring day.

Or at least Gwenlliant thought it must be spring. She stood in the middle of a grassy plain that seemed to extend forever. Where the high green grass grew a little thinner, there were clumps of blossoming clover, and the sky overhead was a soft blue, with billowing white clouds like the sails of immense seagoing vessels. Seasons in the Shadow Lands could be deceptive, but if this wasn't spring it was the next thing to it.

In all her life, Gwenlliant had never seen land that was so flat and featureless. At first she wondered how anyone could possibly find their way in country that was so anonymous. But as she kept on walking, she realized that the grasslands were somewhat deceptive. There were hollows that were invisible until she came right up to the edge of them, and ridges that rose so gradually, the only way that Gwenlliant knew she was climbing was by the aching muscles in her legs. Once, she nearly stumbled into a deep stream bed when the ground fell away suddenly, but she recovered in time to negotiate a careful course down the steep, rocky embankment, wade across the brook, and then climb up the gentler slope on the other side.

She walked for such a long time that the sun—which had been high in the sky when she arrived—was already riding low on the horizon when she finally saw a long dark line of trees take shape ahead, and here and there, where there was a large gap between the trees, the silver gleam of a large body of water. A cloud of rising smoke just this side of the trees promised a village, a farm, or some sort of settlement.

But that was the way that Maelinn had gone, and Gwenlliant did not dare to follow too closely. If her enemy was waiting somewhere ahead, if she had somehow sensed Gwenlliant moving through the Mist, she would be certain to view with suspicion any approaching stranger, and attempt to place that person immediately under her power.

Let someone else be the first, thought Gwenlliant. *It won't harm another traveler to be greeted by my name. Let Maelinn spend a few days watching and wondering, until she decides she must have been mistaken after all, or at least grows careless.*

So Gwenlliant veered a little toward the north and began to follow the line of trees. Where there was water and a windbreak, there would probably be houses of one sort or another. She could stop at the first house she came to, ask for some work to do in exchange for her keep, and gather what information she could about the land and the people who lived there, before heading south in search of Maelinn.

She climbed another ridge, and stood looking down at a green pasture full of horses, beautiful creatures with glossy coats of white, black, grey, and chestnut. About a quarter of a mile further on, there was a long wooden hall, a pile of stones like a well, and a number of outbuildings.

At the sight of the horses, Gwenlliant thought she must

have wandered into some shadow of Draighen. That was a place she had never visited before, though she knew a number of people who had lived there. Grasslands, horses, and cattle were its principal features, also harpists, leather-workers, bookbinders, and wizards. Gwenlliant could not remember the rest, except that the Draighenach were proud, industrious people, noted for their generosity . . . except that is, when they were noisy, contentious, and covetous instead.

She grimaced suddenly, wondering what time she had wandered into. If it should happen to be the not-so-very-distant past . . . *How dreadful if that house up ahead should chance to be Dun Dessi, and I walked right in on Derry mac Forgoll and his brother Morc!*

Even knowing that was highly unlikely, she began to change her shape, before she could meet anyone who might possibly recognize her. If this was Draighen, there was no need to alter her eyes or the color of her skin, because the people who lived here would be just as fair as she was. But she did elongate her bones so that she stood taller, so that her face took on an elegant, sculptured beauty, and she darkened her hair from white-gold to an auburn so deep it was almost black. By the time she stood within twenty yards of the house, the transformation was complete.

A redheaded boy was just emerging from the hall when Gwenlliant arrived at the low flint-stone wall enclosing the yard. At the sight of an unknown woman, he angled his head back through the door and shouted to someone inside the house.

Gwenlliant felt her mouth go dry. During her previous visit to the Shadow Lands, she had fallen in with kindly, hospitable folk who had welcomed her into their home, but it occurred to her now that the people she met this time might be hostile to strangers. That certainly seemed to be the case, because a man with wiry auburn hair and a black beard came striding out of the house, and stopping halfway to the drystone wall, regarded Gwenlliant with a deep, suspicious frown.

"In the name of God: Who are you, and what do you seek at Dun Eogan?" he asked, making the sign of the cross.

Gwenlliant thought the greeting was meant as some sort of challenge or a test. If she was any sort of wicked, supernatural creature, or if she bore anyone in the house malice or carried with her any evil intention, she ought not to be able to reply in the same fashion.

"In the name of God and of St. Sianne: My name is Niamh, and I want nothing at Dun Eogan but food and shelter, for which I am willing to pay with any sort of honest work." As she spoke, Gwenlliant broadened her vowels just a little, adopting the brogue of her not-so-distant Rhianeddi childhood.

The accent was apparently close enough, because the man's face lost its dark, suspicious look and he said, a bit more cordially: "Enter then, in God's name, and we will see what work you are good for."

"I will . . . in God's name," she remembered to say, as she lifted her skirts and stepped on and then over the low stone wall. It was meant to be more of a ritual barrier than anything else, since it stood no more than two feet high.

The man led her into the hall, which was lit by torches. Only a small portion of the interior had been partitioned off at one end, presumably for sleeping quarters, making it very light and airy for a place with no windows and only two doors. A long table, beautifully carved, with benches to either side, ran most of the length of the big room, and on a raised platform at the near end a number of women sat on stools, cheerfully engaged in various useful tasks.

The two eldest were spinning flax; a brisk matronly woman was stitching what looked like a rude tapestry, in bright colors of blue, green, red, and yellow. A girl of about Gwenlliant's age was carding wool, and a young woman, who looked enough like her to be her older sister, was nursing a baby.

"This is Niamh, who asks for a place here," the man said briefly.

The woman with the tapestry put her work aside and examined Gwenlliant with a keen pair of dark blue eyes. "And what will Niamh do to earn her keep? For she appears to be able-bodied, and we have no place here for lazy or shiftless folk."

Two years ago, Gwenlliant would have been good for nothing but fine needlework—her other accomplishments had been better suited to the princess she was than to the Draighenach maidservant she now aspired to be—but thanks to the training she had received from Dame Ceinwen, and the time she had spent in a shadow of the distant past with the twelve young priestesses in the sacred forest of Achren, she could turn her hand to almost any task.

Yet she hesitated. Though Maelinn's trail had seemed to lead elsewhere, she did not know any of these people—any one of them might be a stranger only a little less recently arrived than she was. Would it be wise to seek a place under this roof, where her enemy might be lurking behind any one of those pleasant, ordinary faces?

Gwenlliant took a deep breath. "I can wash, scrub, cook, spin, sew and mend, mind children, help in the dairy if you have one, make cheeses, bake bread, dye cloth . . . and in short, do any work that is fit for a decent woman to perform."

The brisk woman up on the dais nodded. "Then be welcome, Niamh. For truth to tell, there is enough work to be done about this place that another pair of ready hands is exactly what is needed."

The Three Great Fallen Adepts:

4.

Riddles Posed,
Questions Unanswered

The next few days passed in a whirl of activity for Gwenlliant. Another pair of hands was, apparently, *exactly* what was needed at Dun Eogan. She scrubbed cups and bowls, beat laundry, scattered grain for the geese and other small fowl, milked a cow, baked bread . . . These were but a few of the tasks which occupied her, leaving little time to ask questions or even to get her bearings.

The inhabitants of Dun Eogan were plain, practical folk, who were not about to trade a roof and a place at their table for anything less than a solid day's work. Nor were they inclined to idle gossip in the presence of one who was still very much a stranger.

After "Niamh" had lived with them a week, they finally began to open up. And one evening, when Gwenlliant was sitting on the dais, watching the coarse woolen thread grow on her spindle, she heard two of the other women discussing their nearest neighbors, and took that opportunity to ask a few questions.

"The seven sons of Guaire," said Aoife, the woman who

43

employed her. "They are blacksmiths . . . and magicians. Perhaps you saw the smoke rising from their forge when you first came here."

"I did," said Gwenlliant, letting the wool slide through her fingers. "and the smoke was so great, I thought there must be a town there at least." The seven sons of Guaire sounded familiar, somehow, so she tried to get more information. "A household of magicians living so near . . . that sounds rather daunting. But perhaps you don't think so?"

"Well, and it is a little queer," said Aoife's old mother, who was sewing a linen shift for one of the children. "Though mind you, they are decent men in their way. But the wicked lord across the water changed all of their sisters into horses, and ever since that day the men have been hammering away at their forge and casting their spells along with their iron, hoping to change the young women back."

Gwenlliant drew in her breath, let the spindle fall to the floor. She remembered now, she remembered it all quite clearly. It was a story out of legend, how the evil warlock, Gandwy of Perfudd, had courted in swift succession the twelve beautiful, black-haired daughters of Guaire, who had all scorned and refused him. For that reason, he had changed them all into mares, one after the other, and then . . . Gwenlliant shuddered, remembering how the story ended. The Warlock Lord had tamed a terrible serpent that lived at the bottom of Loch del Dragon, by feeding the creature twelve beautiful, coal-black mares.

"Into horses, you say? What a wicked thing." Though it was possible, of course, the tale had been exaggerated over the years. "Have . . . have the men succeeded in changing any of the maidens back?"

"Only the one. They disenchanted the youngest with a silver bridle." Aoife glanced up from her tapestry. The hanging was almost finished; when it was completed, it would represent the deeds of Vannen, an ancient Draighenach hero, along with a wide border made up of curious knotwork beasts and flowering vines. "But there is strong magic on the older girls. They say that Gandwy put all of his spite and malice into those spells, and when it came to the last he was losing interest.

"And it is God's own truth," she added, as she selected a strand of green yarn and rethreaded her needle, "that the Warlock has left the entire clan in peace ever since, and has turned his thoughts and his wicked schemes elsewhere."

All of which explained a great deal. For one thing, Gwenlliant knew *when* she had arrived in Draighen: shortly before the downfall of King Cynwal the Fifth, and the long dark years of the Interregnum. And for another thing, she knew why the people here were so careful with their invitations and their invocations. With the most notorious sorcerer in the history of Ynys Celydonn living in his palace just across the lake, it made perfect sense.

And if the sons of Guaire are magicians as well, it's not unlikely that Maelinn has settled with them. Power always attracts her; that is why she was in Charon and in Anoeth. Besides, I know already that she went that way.

There was another possibility, but Gwenlliant did not like to think of it. If Maelinn had gone across the lake to join forces with Gandwy in Perfudd . . .

Yet Gandwy was a man who might daunt even Maelinn. And while Maelinn was invariably drawn to seats of power, she also liked to be around people who were weak in some way, the better to manipulate them. The sons of Guaire, with their single-minded efforts to rescue their sisters, would suit her much better. What would they not be willing to trade for a little of Maelinn's shapeshifting magic?

Gwenlliant picked up her spindle off the floor and went back to her spinning, her mind awhirl with possibilities. But of one thing she was absolutely certain: She had to find a way to visit the sons of Guaire.

Perhaps tomorrow. If I can slip out early in the morning, I can get there and back before anyone misses me.

But in the morning, Gwenlliant woke with a swimming head and a churning stomach. She staggered outside, knelt down in the high grass outside the house, and heaved up all that remained of her supper the night before.

Then she sat for a long time in the dewy grass, trying to gather her thoughts. Never before had she felt so thoroughly sick, so *wretchedly* weak and ill, and it was a long, long time since she had last been sick at all. Those who worked the shapechanging magic rarely contracted any disease. In fact, the thing was nearly impossible, because the body healed itself of every natural ailment with every change.

And then a terrible thought came into her already dizzy brain. Someone was evidently trying to poison her. As fantastic as that idea was, Gwenlliant could think of no other rational explanation. But if that was true . . . who was the culprit, and what did he or she hope to gain by it?

As might be expected, the blizzard covered the bowman's tracks. Though Tryffin sent out men to search every cottage, hayloft, crib, byre, woodshed, henhouse, cave, den, burrow, and hole that the countryside offered as soon as the storm abated, the results were discouraging. Even more disheartening was the fact that no one could identify the assassin or explain how he had entered the castle, though the Governor personally questioned every man, woman, and child at Dinas Yfan.

"Who can say, with so many people coming and going this last fortnight as we prepared for your arrival," Lord Gwistel explained with a nervous laugh. "And I regret to say that the defenses are not all they could be. There is, for instance, a great gaping hole where the outer curtain wall collapsed at the beginning of winter. And the stonemasons, you know, have gone south to avoid the vile weather, so that repairing the breach was clearly impossible."

Tryffin drew Mahaffy aside for some private words. "Young Math or Peredur would seem to be in this somewhere, if only as the innocent cause. Neither seems the sort to resort to murder . . . though I can't say as much for Peredur's uncles, or Math's grandfather."

"Or maybe the assassin was just a man who had no desire to see a Guillyn ascend to the High Seat," said Mahaffy grimly. "God knows, we have done little enough to endear ourselves to the other clans over the years."

Tryffin gave him a reassuring pat on the back. "Ah well. If the Mochdreffi have finally learned to stomach me—and I confess to God they've little reason to love *my* family— they ought to eventually come around to tolerating you."

After all this, the presentation and the revelation of the sidhe-stone grail fell rather flat. While the lords and chieftains gathered at Dinas Yfan were impressed by the beauty of the crystal chalice, by its otherworldly glow, though they eagerly listened to Tryffin's tale of how he had carried the vessel out of the distant past, they were now inclined to ask difficult questions. And chief among them: Why was the cup not used to heal young Conn, when he lay near death?

It was embarrassing to have to explain that the healing powers of the chalice were greatly diminished by the rite in Penafon. Any influence the miraculous vessel worked now was likely to be more subtle, more mysterious, more spiritual . . . They seemed to accept that readily enough, but no mass conversion to Mahaffy's cause followed, as it had on all previous occasions when the cup was unveiled.

Lord Gwistel and his brother Rhodri Owein *did* become ardent partisans, but that was probably just to cover their embarrassment over Mahaffy's near-assassination—and to express their gratitude that Prince Tryffin did not have the pair of them hanged for conspiracy.

The one bright spot in the days that followed was the fact that Conn did *not* die, and as soon as Lord Gwistel's physician was sure he was out of danger, he allowed Mahaffy to visit his friend.

He found Conn lying flat on his back in bed, under a pile of blankets and shaggy bearskins, grown shockingly thin and pale. At the sight of Mahaffy, the boy summoned up a weak smile. "If you have come to scold me for saving your life, spare me that much at least."

Mahaffy swallowed hard and took a seat on a chair by the bed. "Tempted as I am, I know that would be ungracious, so I'll restrain the impulse. In truth, it was nobly done, and I thank you very much. But . . ." He took a deep breath. ". . . you look like you've spent ten thousand years in Purgatory, Conn. Is the pain really terrible?"

"No," said Conn. "It hardly hurts at all anymore. But they keep dosing me with something . . . syrup of poppies, I think, and it brings on such weird fantastical dreams, I always wake up more tired than when I fell asleep." The boy yawned. "If you want to know the truth, you look ghastly yourself."

"Thank you," said Mahaffy, though he knew Conn said it just to be kind. Where other men turned haggard and hollow-eyed, he only managed to look pale and interesting, no matter how sick or depressed or worried he might be.

Mahaffy fastened his gaze on the foot of the bed. He had been told that the head of the bolt had come very near Conn's spine, and he wanted to know if the boy would be able to walk after he recovered . . . but perhaps Conn had not yet considered all the grim possibilities, and Mahaffy certainly did not want to be the first one to broach the painful subject.

But Conn gave a deep sigh. "By the way you keep staring at the covers, I suppose you are wondering if I can move my feet."

Mahaffy blushed. "My apologies. I—"

"Well, I can't," said Conn. "The truth is, I am still so weak that it is all I can do to turn my head on my pillow. But when Brother Nefyn comes in with those cold hands of his and flexes my legs to see if they still work, he seems to be encouraged by my curses and complaints. It's apparently good news that I can feel anything."

Feeling somewhat relieved himself, Mahaffy framed his next sentence carefully. "Conn, I was wondering if you would be willing to do me an immense favor."

The boy on the bed regarded him suspiciously. "That would depend on what the favor is." Someone had apparently bathed him and shaved him and trimmed his light brown hair, with the result that, even as gaunt as he was, he looked much younger than his eighteen years.

Mahaffy moved uneasily in his chair. "I know there was some plan that the Governor would knight you at Easter, but I wondered if you would allow me to do it instead. Of course, that would mean putting it off, perhaps as late as the end of the summer, and it might not be so great an honor as receiving the accolade from Prince Tryffin. But I was thinking I might want to found a new order of knighthood— the Order of the Sun in Glory—as my very first act as Lord of Mochdreff . . . and I want you to be the first one to receive it."

"It would be a very great honor, and certainly one that I would be willing to wait for," said Conn. "That is, if I am able to bear arms at all; you don't want to spoil your order by giving it to a cripple. No, I mean that, Mahaffy. It would be a poor way to begin. And if you really want to reward me, you can . . . oh, give me Castell Ochren or some such thing, instead."

The young Lord of Ochren grinned at him. "You are joking of course. But it's not so bad in Ochren, since the healing of the land. Or at least, nothing like the wasteland it was. And I have other plans for that ruin of a castle I inherited. There is someone else I would like to knight, but I know it would cause a terrible uproar, and that *would* be a bad way to begin. So I have to find some other way to reward him, something that would give him consequence, without causing a great deal of envy or fuss."

"It *is* a great pity," said Conn, knowing very well who Mahaffy meant. "But whatever happened to *'I am Guillyn and not answerable to lesser men for anything I choose to do?'*"

Mahaffy sighed and shook his head. "You know, Conn, it was just false pride when I used to act that way because pride and arrogance were practically the only inheritance that I could claim. It is different now. I have responsibilities. And everything I do will have to be answered for, one way or another."

At Caer Cadwy, the Yuletide decorations were just going up, and the wizard Glastyn and his little apprentice were walking in the snowy courtyard, discussing the season to come.

"But the days between Christmas and Twelfth Night, and between Twelfth Night and Imbolc—which is now called Candlemas—are a weird and portentous time of year," said Glastyn. "Though the light is growing, it is still a dark time, and it is said that werewolves and other skinchangers are most active during that season, that ghosts and other spirits are often met walking the roads, and that even the ancient gods stir in their barrows under the earth."

"If that is so," said Teleri, shaking the ashy blond hair out of her eyes, trying not to trip on the hem of his green wool cloak as she attempted to keep pace with him, "then why do the people celebrate?"

"They light candles to drive back the darkness," he replied ominously, "and they put out feasts . . . of dishes they prepare at that time of the year and no other . . . in order to placate the spirits of the dead.

"But they make merry," the wizard added, with a reassuring smile, "because they know there are better times coming."

5.

Of Blackbird Pies and Good Barley Ale

At Caer Ysgithr, the Twelve Days of Christmas came and went in a mad whirl of color and unaccustomed gaiety. The three old women were scandalized. "Wanton, wanton waste," said Dame Maffada, banging her stick on the chimney piece for emphasis. "They are eating every bit of food in the castle. Someone should put a stop to it!"

Just as though, thought Meligraunce, she were not living off Prince Tryffin's generosity as much as anyone. Yet, as much as he hated to agree with Dame Maffada, it did seem that the stores were being consumed at a furious rate. Not that Prince Tryffin would begrudge the expense, but he wasn't there to open his coffers or send out men to buy more food when the pantries and storerooms and granaries were empty.

And always supposing there was anything left to be bought. When Meligraunce went into town, he saw that the Christmas madness had spread there as well. It was as though the Mochdreffi—the simple folk, anyway—after all the long bleak years when there had been little to celebrate, were determined to make up for lost time. Most likely the farmers and villagers had been affected along with the townsmen and the servants, and they were feasting like gluttons, too.

"Every cow, every ewe, every brood mare in the countryside for a hundred miles around is big with young," said the Chief Cook, by way of explanation. "Even those that everyone thought were too old for breeding."

And yet, the Captain reminded himself, the livestock still had to be fed from available stores, perhaps for many weeks still ahead, before the grass began to grow again. If the hay gave out and the grain went into bread and pies for Christmas and Twelfth Night, what would the animals eat in February? To end up slaughtering them all before spring arrived would clearly be disastrous.

And while Meligraunce believed, as fervently as anyone, that the year to come would be an unusually prosperous one, the way that the apples, the pears, the nuts, and the root vegetables were coming up from the cellars to be baked and stewed, and chopped and boiled, you would think that September and the harvest were just around the corner instead of eight long months in the future.

He was not, however, in charge of running the household, and it was not his business. Garth mac Matholwch, who had managed things admirably in the past, was off in Camboglanna, seeking advancement at the court of King Cynwas, and the man who was in charge of things now was not the one to listen to advice from a mere man-at-arms, no matter how high in Prince Tryffin's confidence. So Meligraunce decided not to worry about something he could not help, to try to put the strange dreams he was dreaming every night out of his head, and make the best that he could of the holiday season.

This he accomplished in part by visiting young Grifflet in the nursery each day, and winning the boy's confidence by joining in his games and pastimes. This was perhaps a bit trying to the Captain's dignity, with the nursemaids looking on, but it made sense in the long run. When he and Grifflet left the castle together, they would have to travel swiftly and they would have to travel secretly, and Meligraunce could think of nothing more likely to draw attention along the road than a cantankerous, distrustful child.

Fortunately, though Grifflet bore a strong physical resemblance to his real parents, the Captain was delighted to discover that the little redheaded boy's personality—his sunny disposition, his sturdy, deliberate way of doing things—was pure Prince Tryffin.

The power of naming, thought Meligraunce, remembering how the Governor had renamed the boy when he adopted him. Or else some spell worked by the Lady

Gwenlliant. In any case, it was reassuring to know that Grifflet fab Tryffin, who had once been Rhys fab Rhys, was not sly like the man who had fathered him, or selfish and uncontrolled in his passions like his mother, the beautiful and treacherous Lady Essylt. It might even be that there was something in the boy that was going to make all the trouble he was causing somehow worthwhile.

Between Twelfth Night and Candlemas, the weather grew steadily warmer. Soon, it would be time to set out on their journey.

Meligraunce had already put considerable thought into his disguise. It would be impossible, of course, to do anything about his size. Being eight or ten inches taller and considerably broader than the average Mochdreffi (they were not an imposing race), he was likely to attract attention wherever he went. The trick was to change everything else, make himself so striking in every way possible, that his size was the last thing that anyone thought about.

A fastidious man—considered by some to be almost fanatically neat and methodical—what better disguise could he possibly assume than that of a battered, weather-beaten wanderer, perhaps with a touch of the rogue about him? Accordingly, the Captain began to let his hair and his beard grow out. He had one ear pierced and a gold ring inserted. As he had always been good at imitating accents and mannerisms, he spent hours in the privacy of Prince Tryffin's rooms practicing a swaggering gait and a rough way of speaking.

At Candlemas, when the decorations of ivy and evergreen came down and were burned in all the castle fireplaces, Meligraunce went up to the Governor's rooms late that night, and completed his disguise.

While most Camboglannach tended toward a ruddy complexion, Meligraunce was as fair as any whey-faced northerner; his winter pallor contrasted strongly with the warm skin tones of the common Mochdreffi. Rather than attempt to match the Mochdreffi complexion, he had decided to make himself even darker. So he dyed his face and his hands and every other bit of visible skin with the juice of walnuts, until he was as swarthy as a tinker.

Then he donned the costume he had spent the last few weeks assembling: High boots, very worn and scarred, with the tops turned down. A dark tunic and breeches that were stitched with roundels of rusty metal and other bits of harness, in a rude imitation of armor. And a long cloak that was a motley collection of rags and patches, mostly in shades of black, grey, crimson, and scarlet.

When he examined his reflection in the mirror in Prince Tryffin's bedchamber, he saw staring back at him any Celydonian's worst nightmare: a great ugly rogue of a foreigner, with more than a suggestion of the cutthroat about him. Gazing at his own image in the mirror, Meligraunce had to repress the reflex to cross himself, or to make some other sign meant to avert evil.

"And I confess to God, I hope I don't frighten the life out of young Grifflet," he said out loud.

In the dark hours when nobody else was stirring, he walked through the empty corridors of the castle, and startled the guard outside the nursery—who needed to take a second look before he recognized the staid Captain Meligraunce in his gaudy attire, and allowed him to pass through the door. Inside Grifflet's bedchamber, Meligraunce crept past the chair where one of the nursemaids was dozing, and gently lifted the small boy out of his bed.

He carried the child upstairs, where he woke him gently. Far from being frightened by his companion's appearance, the little boy was vastly amused, and made no protest when the Captain dressed him in garments as dingy and ragged as his own. He even accepted the Captain's suggestion that he might like to take a handful of soot and ashes from the fireplace and rub them into his face and his rusty red curls.

"My mother wouldn't like it," said Grifflet, as he surveyed his grimy hands afterward. "But my mother went far away. And perhaps by the time I see her, I'll have time to take a bath."

"Very true," said Meligraunce. He thought that the Lady Gwenlliant would understand, but in any event, he agreed with Grifflet: What she did not know could not possibly dismay her.

"But I wonder, now, how good you will be at playing a small game that I have devised," said the Captain, going down on one knee, the better to address his companion confidentially. "We will pretend that I am your uncle, that your mother is off somewhere in Perfudd (where she may well be for all that we know), and that the journey we are about to take is in search of your grandfather, who is a traveling tinsmith.

"It would be better and simpler if we don't use any names," he added. "For then we will both have less to remember. You call me 'Uncle,' and I will just call you 'my lad' or something of the sort, and we will see how many people we are able to fool."

Typically, Grifflet considered before he spoke. "Very well, Uncle," he said at last. And gifted the Captain with his very best innocent smile for good measure.

Meligraunce sat back on his heels with a sigh of relief. He had been watching Prince Tryffin employ that very same disarming smile with devastating effect for years now—no one knew better than the Captain what a potent weapon it could be. Armed with that and Meligraunce's own ingenuity, they ought to do very well.

They left Caer Ysgithr an hour before dawn, when no one but the guards at the gate (who were sworn to secrecy) would see them go, or be able to describe what they were wearing or how they went, afterward. In fact, they rode out on the Captain's big black gelding, but he had already made arrangements through one of the other guards to stable the beast down in Trewynyn, and exchange the black for a shaggy dun of uncertain ancestry.

"Uncle, I think I am old enough to ride by myself," said Grifflet, in his chirpy little voice. He was eyeing a particularly sturdy-looking island pony in a stall near the back of the stable in Trewynyn.

"Aye . . . well, I lack the gold to buy you a horse of your own just at the moment. But I will look out for an opportunity to steal you one, just as soon as I possibly can," said the Captain, staying in character.

He placed the little boy atop the dun, showed him the way to hang on to the saddle and to the horse's mane, then swung up behind him. "My mother says I must wait until my fifth birthday," Grifflet whispered. "It was only part of the game, when I said that."

The Captain heaved a sigh of relief. "Which is fortunate," he said under his breath, "because I am no horse thief."

They rode out of Trewynyn through the north gate, and followed the road for several days without incident.

Until one evening in Peryf, when they were traveling later than Meligraunce had planned, and two men with great knotted cudgels jumped out of the brush and attacked them, apparently after the horse.

Shielding the little boy as best he could with his own body, Meligraunce reached for the throwing knife he wore in one boot, and hurled the *sgian dubh* with deadly accuracy. The knife hit one of the brigands squarely in the throat, causing the man to stagger back and then collapse in the road. But the other man was still there, and he had one hand on the bridle.

Meligraunce caught a crushing blow on his arm before he was able to work one booted foot free from the stirrup and catch his attacker, with stunning force, under the chin. Before the man had time to recover, the Captain had the dun off at a gallop, and did not slow down for another two miles.

By then, it was not only late, but the wind was rising and

an icy rain falling. His arm did not seem to be broken, but it was aching horribly—and God help him, he could not afford to allow the bruised limb to stiffen up in the cold and become useless. He and the boy would have to take whatever lodgings were available in the village up ahead . . . which turned out to be a disreputable-looking tavern the Captain would not have considered under any other circumstances.

Not that the better sort of establishment had ever precisely *welcomed* the big, black foreigner's custom. Yet the Captain had found that a hand on each of the daggers he wore in his belt, combined with a murderous glance, was usually sufficient to convince any innkeeper that he was a dangerous man to turn away.

It said little for their present lodgings that this tavern-keeper readily agreed to provide a meal and a roof for the night, in exchange for a small copper coin. But of more immediate interest to the Captain was getting Grifflet dry and fed, before he took ill.

Soon, they were sitting by the fire, eating a late supper of boiled tripes, thin gruel, and salt herring. It was another of Grifflet's virtues that he could, and did, eat anything that was offered, and never seemed to suffer any pangs of indigestion afterward. But then, between having Dame Ceinwen for his earliest nursemaid, and trailing along with the Lady Gwenlliant through the Shadow Lands when he was a little older, the boy had never any chance to grow spoiled or pampered. *And thank God for that*, thought Meligraunce.

"Your boy looks nothing like you," said a man sitting at a nearby table. He was a rough fellow with scars and broken teeth, but his tone was amiable enough.

"He is my sister's lad," the Captain replied. "It may be that he resembles his father . . . whoever the poxy bastard was."

Meanwhile, Grifflet went on eating serenely, thoroughly accustomed by now to hearing himself discussed in such terms. As for Meligraunce, he only hoped that the Lady Gwenlliant would prove understanding, once she was restored to them, and forgive the sort of language that her son was picking up in his company.

There was a titter from another corner, and an ancient greybeard stepped out of the shadows. As dirty and as haggard as he was, the old man had clearly seen better days, for his tunic was silk and his cloak was velvet, and his hands, though gnarled with extreme age, were otherwise soft and well kept.

"A fine-looking boy," the greybeard rasped. "They do say that a child with two fathers is invariably wise beyond his years and grows at an amazing pace."

Meligraunce stared hard at him, because the old man's words were so startlingly accurate. He forced himself to answer with a smile and a wink. "Then this one should be wiser than Solomon, for he must have a dozen fathers at least."

"Aye, no doubt, no doubt," said the old man, creeping a bit closer. He bent down and said some gibberish, almost directly in Grifflet's ear, and the little boy laughed out loud and replied in the same fashion.

The incident left Meligraunce with a bad feeling that endured all through supper. When he and Grifflet bedded down in the cubbyhole the Captain's coin had purchased for the night, he asked the boy what the old man had said to make him laugh.

"He asked if I had ever tasted blackbird pie," Grifflet replied sleepily as he burrowed under the blanket they were sharing. "He said, *'ring all the bells because the cat is down the well, and if she's not rescued, there will be no sweet water to brew the barley ale.'* He said you were the Black Man who would scare off all the crows that would eat the harvest."

"Did he now?" said Meligraunce, with a puzzled frown. It had not sounded anything like that to him, and he thought that Grifflet might have put his own interpretation on the old man's nonsense.

But how, the Captain wondered as he drifted off to sleep, had this boy who had spent his entire life in Mochdreff — even allowing for a long visit to the region's shadowy past — ever picked up a bit of doggerel commonly recited by little peasant lads and lasses in far off Camboglanna?

It took three miserable mornings for Gwenlliant to realize that no one was poisoning her — though even then it required some friendly advice.

"It will pass soon. Though not, perhaps, until you have had ample time to wish yourself dead many times over," said Aoife, standing over her bed. "Do your people know that you are carrying a child? Is that the reason you left them?"

"No," whispered Gwenlliant. She covered her head with a pillow, and tried to quiet her heaving stomach.

"If the father is a decent sort of man, perhaps you should send him a message," said Aoife, lifting the pillow and continuing to speak in her relentlessly bracing way. "He may wish to marry you."

Gwenlliant felt a fool . . . several times over . . . not to have guessed. It was true that she had no younger brothers or sisters, and that she had left her own mother at an early age, to live at court — where the Queen was barren, and all her attendants were unmarried girls. She had married Tryffin at the age of twelve, and repaired to Caer Ysgithr with handmaidens as virginal as she was, the only other women of rank in the castle being the five old women who were well beyond the age of childbearing. After that, she had lived with Dame Ceinwen, who was even older, and then in the cloister with the twelve young priestesses. If there was any girl on Ynys Celydonn who knew less about the business of bearing children than Gwenlliant did, that girl had probably spent her entire life in a convent.

*But even I should have expected it. Eight weeks sharing
a bed with my husband before he left Caer Ysgithr . . .
and if ever there was a virile man, or one with more of his
will set on becoming a father, I never heard of him!*

And it explained so many things. Not only the sickness
each morning, but the dizzy spells when she tried to fly.
Also Dame Ceinwen's warning to go as a woman whenever
she could, and never to try and make herself small. Some
instinct had been trying to warn her that whatever shape she
took she must always keep a suitable place for the new life
to grow inside her.

"The man has been married two times already," she said
out loud. "I . . . I hardly think that he wishes to take
another wife."

"That is unfortunate," said Aoife. "Though you may be
surprised to learn how lonely these widowers can be."

For the rest of that day, even after she rose from her bed
and went about her various tasks, Gwenlliant existed in a
daze of delight—mingled with apprehension. She wanted
this child, there was no doubt of that. Yet she had to find and
conclude her business with Maelinn before the birth. A
newborn infant would make her vulnerable, and she had to
be strong when she and Maelinn met.

I will be strong, having that much more to fight for, she
vowed.

Later that day, she came to herself with a start, when she
heard Aoife and her daughter discussing a visit to the sons
of Guaire. "Two of the horses need to be shod, and I'm
thinking, Grania, that you are the one to take them," the
woman said.

This was the chance that Gwenlliant had been waiting
for . . . a chance to arrive at the forge, not as a stranger,
but as an acknowledged member of a neighboring household. "I would like to go along, if I may. That is," she
added meekly, "if you think I can be spared from my
work."

Aoife considered for several minutes before she answered. "It is a good plan for you to meet those fine strong men . . . now, when you need a husband," she said at last. "Yes, Niamh, I think you should go. And may the Good Lord help you to find what you seek there."

In ancient times, it is said, a smith was regarded as a kind of magician, for in his work with metals he was the master of many remarkable transformations.

And I have heard of a blacksmith in the parish of St. Gall—so recently as the time of our own fathers—who was a positive wonder-worker, besides being a man of immense strength. The people of that parish were in the habit of bringing him any horse that was ailing, or any old horse that had outlived its usefulness. The smith would take a broken-down nag, pick it up in his brawny arms, lay it down on the anvil, and beat it with his hammer until it was as good as new.

He had a son however, who was a brash youth and by no means so great a master of his craft as the father. Thinking to do as the blacksmith did, he took a fine young stallion and put it on the anvil, and beat it with considerably less happy results.

—*From* A Journey into Rhianedd and Gorwynnion, *by the monk Elidyr fab Gruffudd*

6.

Chances and Circumstances Unforeseen

The next afternoon, the two girls set off across the grasslands, leading the two chestnut colts. Even before they reached the forge, the reek of heated metal came out to meet them, and there was a great clamor as of mighty hammers beating on even mightier anvils.

This settlement was much larger than Dun Eogan, almost

the size of a village, with at least a dozen smaller buildings clustered around the great wooden hall. And surrounding them all was a low wall made of rocks fitted together without any mortar.

It was difficult for Gwenlliant to tell, with the buildings blocking much of her view, but she thought that the yard enclosed by that drystone wall was formed on the plan of a cross. She could see the broad base, and two arms running east and west of the settlement, and guessed there was another arm behind the buildings.

As Gwenlliant and her companion approached the wall, two handsome youths dressed all in red leather came out to question them. "In God's name, what brings you here?" said the taller and fairer of the two boys.

"In God's name, I have come seeking the services of a blacksmith," replied Grania. "And Niamh comes with me, because she has heard of the exploits of the sons of Guaire and wishes to see for herself if the stories are true."

After a brief exchange, the girls and the horses were allowed to enter the compound.

When one of the boys led the horses off to be shod, Grania took Gwenlliant by the hand and pulled her toward the cluster of buildings. "It is likely they will ask us to stay for dinner," she whispered in Gwenlliant's ear. "It will be a fine thing if they do, for then we'll have time to watch the craftsmen at work, and that is a thing worth seeing."

Gwenlliant followed obediently after her. In one building, men and women were tanning and gilding leather. In another, they were boiling hides in great steaming vats and cauldrons. The leather came out in bright hues of blue and scarlet. Gwenlliant would have liked to remain and see how this was accomplished—in her own time, the dyeing of leather with blue azure was a rare, secret process—but Grania drew her along to another building.

This one was more like an open stall. Inside were a dozen craftsmen making saddles and bridles, stitching the leather together with gold and silver thread.

"It is God's own truth," said Grania, "if I were a mare who had once been a maiden, I would gladly come home for the sake of a golden saddle and a bridle stitched with silver thread."

Gwenlliant thought about that. It would depend, she decided, on whether or not the maidens had wholly assumed the nature of horses—and how vain they had been while they were still young women. Before she had time to give this anymore thought, Grania was leading her on toward the smithy.

The forge was a long narrow building, three walls and a roof made of beaten copper, with one of the long sides open. Even more than the dyers and the saddlers, the smiths were hard at work.

The sons of Guaire were men of enormous stature, with bristling black hair and beards, and eyes of a brilliant blue. And though they were rough and boisterous, they seemed to be kindly disposed, for they welcomed the two young women with hearty greetings, and appointed a boy to explain to them the work being done.

These were more than blacksmiths, as Gwenlliant soon realized, for they worked with copper and precious metals as well as iron. Aided by an army of apprentices and journeymen, they were busily engaged making cups and brooches, rings and torcs, and other fine things set with sparkling gemstones, along with the stirrups and horse-shoes, and the metal parts of bridles Gwenlliant had been expecting.

There was magic at work in the forge. She could smell it, and taste it; she could feel it working in all the hollow parts of her bones. But it was White Magic, there was nothing evil about it. These men, though they hardly looked it, were wizards and philosophers working the alchemy of molten metals.

"You will honor us by eating at our table," said Finn mac Guaire, wiping the sweat and the smoke from his brow with one broad hand, and then wiping both hands on his leather apron.

The two young women gladly accepted. In truth, Gwenlliant would have been glad to stay in that place for a long time, and try to learn a little of the smiths' magic. But a slender, green-eyed girl came in through the door to say that the meal would soon be ready.

"This is my sister Nuala," said Finn. "She will take you inside and find you a place to sit in the hall."

So, while the men cleaned up, Grania and Gwenlliant followed Nuala across the yard and into the lofty, torchlit hall. There were already a number of women there, the wives and daughters of all the craftsmen, bustling about, setting the long tables with cups and trenchers, platters of steaming meat, and pitchers of mead and ale. Nuala stood a little apart from all this activity, with an expression that said, as plainly as words, that she was not the one to dirty her fine white hands with common labor.

That suited Gwenlliant very well, because she was eager to speak to the disenchanted maiden. "What was it like, being a mare?" she asked—then regretted speaking, because the girl looked even haughtier than she had before, so haughty that it seemed she had taken offense.

But then Nuala shrugged and replied in an offhand way. "It was not so bad a thing as you might suppose, running wild on the plain. And I tell you this: They will never catch my sisters half so easily as they caught me. Even if they could, there was never the wall or the fence of the paddock built that could possibly contain them."

Gwenlliant was a little surprised; it sounded like Nuala was angry with her brothers for changing her back. It sounded like she would have been glad to remain a mare for the rest of her life.

One of the men came in just then, in time to hear his sister's remark. Far from taking her seriously, he replied with a snort of laughter: "It was only the indignity of changing back . . . half woman and half horse, it was not a lovely sight. And that's not speaking of the reek of Gandwy's magic. She has a sensitive nose, our Nuala, particularly for a girl who was reared next door to a tannery."

Before Nuala could answer, they were called to the table. As Gwenlliant sat down with the others, she kept looking into the faces around her, wondering if one of them might be Maelinn. One of the boys, perhaps, a recently acquired apprentice. Though how to find out if any of the boys were new at the forge, without asking directly, was beyond Gwenlliant. Besides, they all looked perfectly ordinary, as they sat eating bread smothered with honey, feasting on mushrooms and blackberries—just like dirty, noisy, quarrelsome boys anywhere.

And why, after all, look for Maelinn here at the table, when she could as easily be a mouse nesting in the thatch overhead . . . one of the geese pecking up grain in the yard outside . . . a hawk in the sky . . . a fish in the well . . .

At least, thought Gwenlliant, she was limited to something that lived. Here in the Otherworld, Maelinn could not turn herself into stone or metal or wood, as she could across the borders in the *real* Celydonn. Still, that left a great deal of ground to be covered and Gwenlliant had only the one afternoon.

Before the others had finished eating, she excused herself from the table. Grania, assuming a return of the morning sickness, let her go out without any comment. In the yard outside, the first creature she met was a fat grey tabby. Gwenlliant knelt down and looked the cat directly in her round golden eyes. "Maelinn," she said experimentally, under her breath.

The tabby only mouthed a sharp-toothed yawn, sat down in the dirt, and began to groom herself.

So Gwenlliant went through the entire settlement, speaking to all the animals. Not one of them answered to the shapechanger's name. And by the time she had spoken to every one of them, the people were beginning to come out of the hall. As there was now very little time left, Gwenlliant perched on the low stone wall to rest and to think.

Perhaps she had guessed wrong, and Maelinn was not even there. Certainly, if Maelinn *was* there, if she had shifted her shape, worked any sort of magic at all . . .

The smith's voice spoke in her head: *"And that's not speaking of the reek of Gandwy's magic. She has a sensitive nose . . ."* And Aoife had said, back at Dun Eogan: *"There is strong magic on the older girls . . . but when it came to the youngest, he was losing interest."*

Gwenlliant drew in her breath sharply. What if the youngest sister had *not* been released from Gandwy's magic? What if the brothers had met something else out on the plain, something that had only pretended to be an enchanted mare, and was now pretending to be their sister?

Leaving her seat on the fence, Gwenlliant went to look for Nuala. She found the girl just beyond the wall, sitting on a grassy mound and deftly weaving wildflowers into her long dark hair.

"It is a warm day, too warm for housework," said Gwenlliant, sitting down in the high grass beside her, beginning to unbraid her own dark hair.

"It is always too warm for housework," Nuala replied, with a languid gesture of one hand. And that was not like Maelinn in the least; the young pagan priestess had been proud but industrious.

So, Gwenlliant thought a little longer. "Your brothers are so immensely wealthy," she ventured at last, "I wonder they have not hired a woman to wait on you. It is a shame they don't use you with more respect, expecting you to wait on yourself."

"That is the truth, and there is no denying it," said Nuala. "It was different when there were twelve of us. We helped each other to dress and to do up our hair. I wish they were with me right now."

Gwenlliant sighed, for this told her nothing. Twelve

beautiful sisters, twelve maiden priestesses—Maelinn would understand very well what life had been like for Nuala when she and her sisters lived together.

Growing a bit desperate, Gwenlliant tried again. "But the gown you are wearing . . . it is very pretty, yet I wonder, with all the fine and precious things that your brothers own, that they should dress you in anything so ordinary as wool and linen. If I were you, I would have dozens of gowns, and they would all of them be silk."

Nuala smiled dreamily. "Once, I had a beautiful gown of green silk, and a necklace of golden acorns. Another fine thing that I had—"

But then she stopped. Her eyes dilated and her face went white as she realized her mistake . . . and guessed who it was that had just been able to trick her into saying those words.

Gwenlliant named her first: *"Maelinn."* No sooner was the word out of her mouth than there was a foul, choking odor, the girl beside her disappeared, and a buzzing green insect hovered in the air, directly over the place where Nuala had been sitting.

Moving too late to hold her, Gwenlliant could only watch helplessly as the darting insect flew out of her grasp and went winging away across the plain. Because she had spoken first, Maelinn had no power to harm her nor could she assume any dangerous form, but the shapechanger was escaping simply because Gwenlliant had failed to lay hands on her when she spoke.

"Fox," the girl whispered, naming the first swift thing that came into her mind. A moment later, there was a little red vixen crouching in the grass at the top of the mound. Then with a bounding leap, she set off across the grasslands after her enemy.

Meligraunce heaved a great sigh of relief as the familiar, irregular contours of Caer Clynnoc came into view. It had been a long day's ride in uncertain weather, and the thought of the fire and the friendly faces that awaited him and the little boy, inside the castle walls, was a welcome one.

And not a day too soon, Meligraunce told himself, since Grifflet was finally beginning to show the ill effects of travel and exposure to the elements. He had developed a hoarse little cough, and when the Captain felt the boy's forehead, it was damp and hot.

As they drew nearer to the fortress, it was some disappointment to see that Prince Tryffin's dragon and sunburst banner was not among those flying above the battlements. That had been the plan, to meet the Governor in Clynnoc the third week in February—or, if Meligraunce should be delayed along the road, in Cormelyn the week after that. Since the Captain and his young charge had encountered no such delay, he had naturally expected to find the Governor waiting.

But the men of clan Glyn were utterly trustworthy. Once the Captain and Grifflet crossed that final acre of rocky ground, once they were inside those high limestone walls, the child would be safe.

"This is the place where you were born," Meligraunce told him, as they approached the gate. "This is where Prince Tryffin found you and made you his son. Tonight, you will dine with your cousins, Ogryfran and Esgeir, and with my friend Llefelys Glyn, and his brother the chieftain, who has been raising those boys since their father died and will go on doing so until Ogryfran is old enough to come into his inheritance."

It was doubtful that Grifflet understood the half of what the Captain told him, but Meligraunce thought the boy should begin to be acquainted with his own family history . . . at least the less scandalous parts. And he thought the child would find it reassuring to know that the place was inhabited by men and women who had served his own people faithfully for many years.

Grifflet nodded sleepily, gave a small raspy cough. "Will I sleep in a real bed?" he asked plaintively.

"That you will," said the Captain. "In a deep feather bed with fine linen sheets, I make no doubt. And there is a girl here named Cianwy Glyn, who will look after you as well as any nursemaid would—and better than that, because she, too, is one of your cousins."

The guards at the gate were men that Meligraunce knew, staunch fellows who could be depended on in the heat of battle. Though it took a few moments before any of them recognized their old comrade, Captain Meligraunce, in the dirty and ragged stranger, as soon as they did pierce his disguise they greeted him gladly, and passed him and the boy immediately through the gate.

They took him at once to the Keep, where a room had already been prepared against his arrival. The servants brought in buckets of steaming wash water, and poured them into a great wooden tub, and once the women had cleaned up Grifflet, dressed him in garments befitting his rank, and hustled him down to the kitchen to be fed, Meligraunce doffed his clothes and settled into that tub for a good hot soak.

Eventually, the Captain realized that he was hungry, too. Washed and shaved for the first time in a month, dressed in the rough but serviceable garments that someone had made up in anticipation of his visit—without that advance preparation, there would have been nothing in the castle nearly large enough for him to change into, once he had shed his disreputable disguise—Meligraunce found his own way down to the banquet hall, where Captain Llefelys and his brother Caradawg Glyn were waiting for him to join him.

The first thing that Meligraunce asked—even before he took a bite of the supper the servants had kept warm for him—was what had happened to Prince Tryffin, and why wasn't he here at Caer Clynnoc.

"He was delayed for more than a week at Dinas Yfan, before he went on to Ymorgan" said Caradawg. "I don't know much about it. Only, there was some sort of trouble involving young Conn. But the Governor sent word saying that he expects to remain where he is for another five or six days."

"You are to wait here with the boy if you choose," added Captain Llefelys. "Or else ride to Ymorgan and meet Prince Tryffin there, if that is what you prefer. It is not very far . . . If you left at sunrise, you would be there at noon."

And so, thought Meligraunce as he drank his ale and chewed on a haunch of greasy mutton, it had not been so easy as he had begun to hope. And of course, the best place for Grifflet was with the Governor, but with the boy possibly sickening . . . the Captain decided he could put off the decision for another day at least.

After all, what danger could possibly threaten the child *here*, where he was surrounded by the Governor's friends and his own kinsmen?

By morning, there was no fever, and Grifflet was only coughing whenever he remembered that he was supposed to be sick and when he knew that someone was watching him. He spent two hours after breakfast roughhousing with his cousins, Esgeir and Ogryfran, big boys of eight and ten respectively, until Cianwy Glyn came in and hushed them all. Then they settled down by a small smoky fire in a room adjoining the banquet chamber, where the older boys taught Grifflet how to play Mill, and Fox and Geese.

So why, the Captain asked himself, as he walked in on this scene of innocent pleasure, did he feel this sudden sharp pang of misgiving, watching Grifflet play with his cousins? There was no disputing it was a pretty picture: three young boys with hair the identical coppery shade of auburn, their heads bowed, and their bright eyes intent on the wooden game board.

And yet, Ogryfran and Esgeir were the sons of a man who had tried to kill Prince Tryffin by treachery. Was it any wonder that he suspected those boys of . . . something?

Only, then Meligraunce remembered that Grifflet was *also* the son of a man who had attempted to kill Prince Tryffin by treachery, and of a woman who was every bit as wicked as her husband.

For all that, Grifflet was a fine boy—and to be perfectly fair, there was nothing at all in his cousins' looks or actions to which the Captain could possibly take exception. Aside from the fact that they were rather spoiled and had clearly acquired an inordinate taste for luxury, like their father and their uncle, all dressed up in satins and velvets on a dirty day like this . . .

But no, Meligraunce forcibly thrust that idea out of his mind, and went in search of his friend Llefelys Glyn.

Unfortunately, the idea came back at midday, when everyone gathered in the banquet hall for dinner. The boys were well behaved, if a bit fussy over their food, and spoke charmingly to everyone during the meal. But over and over Meligraunce kept thinking: *Here are two boys with expensive tastes, and only one castle and a modest number of acres to divide between them. But if something were to happen to Grifflet—if he should not live to manhood—then there would be Eildonn for the younger of Efrei's two sons to inherit, and the older son could keep his own lands intact.*

In the hour before sunset, when Cianwy Glyn was preparing Grifflet for bed, Meligraunce met the older boys just coming in from the courtyard, looking fresh and windblown, and smelling of heather and broom. When he politely remarked that it was a boisterous sort of day for a ride over the moors, Ogryfran surprised him with a remarkably hostile glance.

"If we choose to go out riding it is no business of yours," the boy replied haughtily. And when the younger brother would have added something to that, Ogryfran silenced him with an elbow in the ribs.

It was at that point that Meligraunce stopped trying to convince himself that his suspicions were wild and unwarranted, and he went upstairs to find Caradawg Glyn, and inform the chieftain that he and Grifflet would be leaving for Ymorgan the following morning.

They left later than expected, because Grifflet disappeared from his bed before dawn, and was found a great while later, curled up in bed beside young Esgeir.

"I didn't hear any of it myself—more shame to me!—but it seems that Esgeir heard him cry out in his sleep, and carried the little lad over to his own bed to soothe away his terrors," said Cianwy Glyn, as she delivered the child to Meligraunce.

The Captain, who had spent many dark hours rocking Grifflet back to sleep after a nightmare, took the boy into his arms without any questions. He had already assumed his own disguise, minus the beard but with a fine morning stubble, and it took only a short time to dress Grifflet for the journey and hustle the little boy down to the stable.

But an hour's ride out of Caer Clynnoc, the horse began to display distressing symptoms: dropping from a brisk walk to a slow lethargic amble, then finally coming to a complete halt, despite all the Captain's efforts to urge him on.

Meligraunce dismounted and ran a hand over the horse's neck. The dun was sweating and shivering, and without the rider to impede him, reached back to nip at his own flank. And when the Captain shouldered him out of the way, and put his ear to the flank, there was a gassy, bubbling sound, which told him the gelding had come down with colic.

But how had it happened? This was not a horse with a sensitive stomach, and the clan Glyn grooms and stableboys all knew their business. They would not feed moldy hay to a horse, or straw that was fermenting, or overwater him, or neglect to do *anything* that ought to be done.

As Meligraunce lifted Grifflet down from the saddle, and began leading the shaggy dun back down the road, he suddenly remembered his encounter last evening with the sons of Efrei: how the two boys had come in from their ride smelling of heather and broom . . .

But it wasn't broom. The scent made me think of the yellow flowers, and that was where I made my mistake.

The plant he had been thinking of was called swine-weed, and it only grew in Mochdreff on particularly rocky heaths. Five years back, when he first arrived in the *degfed,* Meligraunce had once let a horse nibble on the yellow flowers, until someone warned him that the weed would soon make the animal exceedingly ill.

Now, a distant rumor of approaching riders—a pounding of hooves on the hardbeaten road and the sound of harsh voices calling out—caused the Captain to pause and to strain his ears. A large party of horsemen was apparently riding furiously toward Ymorgan from the direction of Caer Clynnoc . . . and they could not be much farther away than the other side of the next low hill.

Instinctively, Meligraunce gave the dun a slap on the rear and sent him on ahead; he would not go far, as sick as he was, but it was the best the Captain could do on such short notice. Scooping up Grifflet, he ran in the other direction, diving into the first bit of cover the countryside offered.

"Be silent and all will be well," Meligraunce hissed as he and the boy landed in a rocky ravine. Though considerably bruised and jolted, Grifflet did exactly as he was told. His face was wet with tears, his nose began to run, and his breath came and went in ragged gasps, but he did not make a single sound other than that.

Peering through a screen of desiccated heather at the top of the embankment, Meligraunce and Grifflet watched a party of a dozen horsemen go thundering past. The Captain had imagined nothing; there were dangerous plots afoot. For these were no men of clan Glyn, on the road on some innocent business—these were armed strangers, riding past with a grim intent written plain to be seen on each and every determined face.

As the troop disappeared over another rise, Grifflet wiped

his nose and turned toward the Captain with brimming eyes. "Those are bad men," he said tremulously. "We aren't playing a game anymore. We are really hiding from them."

Though he had no wish to frighten the boy, Meligraunce realized that the time for pretending was past. "I think you are right. Those are very bad men, and you and I must do everything we can to avoid meeting them."

Grifflet rose shakily to his feet, dusted himself off, and managed a valiant smile. "Don't worry, Captain. My father is the Governor of Mochdreff, and he will protect us."

He would at that, thought Meligraunce. If they could reach him safely and claim his protection, before these other men found them first.

And as Sceolan struggled in his prison of vines, a great giant of a man dressed all in skins came out of the forest and approached him.

"In the name of God," said the King, "who are you, and what do you want of me?"

"My name," said the giant, "is Hawk of the Summer Day, and what I want of you is recompense for the evil you have done here."

Sceolan found these words exceedingly strange. "May God strike me dead if I have knowingly done evil, here or elsewhere."

"You have done evil," said the giant, "and I will tell you how that is."

"Then do so," said the King.

The giant sat down on the ground among the forest beasts, and regarded Sceolan with a sorrowful gaze. "This well that you drank from has magical properties. All the creatures of the wood, when they are ill or injured, come here to be healed. But because you have approached the well without an invitation, the place is defiled and the water does no more good. And as I am the woodward and the guardian of these beasts, so I am required to make this demand: Either undo the evil that you have done here, or forfeit your life."

His words troubled the King very much, for he had certainly not intended to do any harm. "I would gladly undo what I have done here, but I do not know how that might be."

"Then I will tell you," said Hawk of the Summer Day. "There is a place a long way distant, which is called the Forest of the Daughter of the Moon, and in that forest is another well, and the water in that well is not only the *purest in the world, but no wicked or defiling thing can exist in its presence. If you were to bring back some of that water in a crystal vessel and pour it into my well, all would be here as it was before, and more than that, your trespass would be forgiven."*

"Then in God's name," said Sceolan, "tell me how I may find the Forest of the Daughter of the Moon, that I may go there and fetch that water in a crystal vessel."

But the giant shook his head sadly. "That I may not tell you. But I will give you a year and a day to send out your warriors and your emissaries to find the place and bring back some of the water. Only you must promise to return here at the end of that time, and if you have been unable to fulfill my conditions, you must be willing to die."

"That is fair enough," said Sceolan, "and I give you my word."

At that, the giant stood up and stamped his foot upon the ground three times. The thorn and the ivy that had imprisoned the King immediately released him and sank back down under the earth.

When Sceolan returned to his fortress, he called his three sons before him and told them all that had happened to him in the wood. "And I am sending the three of you out to find the well in the Forest of the Daughter of the Moon and bring back the water to ransom my life. But because the way is likely to be long and filled with perils, I will be sending warriors and servants along with each of you, and I advise the three of you to stay together."

"We will, in God's name," said the three sons of the King. And that very same day, they began to prepare for a long and dangerous journey.

But during the night, the King's sons were each taken aside by evil men who attempted to incite them to ambition and envy. "For it is plain," said these wicked men, "that whoever comes back with the water from that marvelous well, he will be King after Sceolan has died. Therefore, it would not be wise to stay with your brothers and perhaps

*allow one of them to take credit for what you have
accomplished yourself."*

*And the two older sons listened to this council, and
departed separately during the night, each taking with him
a few friends only. Which left the youngest son to follow in
the morning with the bulk of their escort.*

—*From* The Book of Dun Fiorenn

7.

*Noble Lords and
Vile Insinuations*

The banquet in Ymorgan was drawing to a close. Mahaffy had already spoken his piece—and please God, he
had been eloquent, had impressed the assembled lords and
chieftains as worthy—and he was now listening attentively,
replying as convincingly as he could, to all their questions
and expressed reservations.

The only really bad moment came when someone mentioned Grifflet. "Rhys fab Rhys fab Ogryfran . . . we
heard that he would accompany the Governor on progress,"
said Corfil Alun, one of the clan chieftains. He tugged at his
red and yellow tunic, played nervously with the ends of his
drooping moustache, and nodded in Tryffin's direction. "We
are naturally concerned for the boy's safety, so inconven-
iently placed as he is."

"Grifflet fab Tryffin fab Maelgwyn," the Governor corrected him gently, though his fingers visibly tightened on
the stem of his silver goblet. "You are forgetting that I have
adopted the boy. I hope he will join us soon . . . if not
here, then at Caer Clynnoc. Perhaps some of you noble lords
would like to ride with me when I go there, so that you can
assure your friends of the child's health and well-being.

"God knows," he added, under his breath but loud enough
for the others to hear, "I look forward to seeing that bright

little face myself. Would that he were sitting at my side right now."

It was a good answer, and the more so because it was obviously sincere. Even Corfil smiled indulgently. And as everyone else had said their say, the time had come to reveal the sidhe-stone chalice.

All this time, the cup had been sitting at the center of the High Table, directly in front of Prince Tryffin, but it was veiled in rich purple velvet worked with gold and silver threads; the form of the vessel itself remained a mystery. When Tryffin gave the signal, his two young squires, Cei and Elffin, approached the table with bowed heads and solemn gait. Suddenly, the tension in the room was almost palpable.

As the two boys—one fair and earnest, the other dark and lively—knelt on the dais before the vessel, Mahaffy felt a twinge of sympathy, for the strain on Cei's face was evident. Being Rhianeddi, and therefore deeply religious, with an inbred, almost instinctive passion for relics and ceremonies, the boy took these matters far more to heart than anyone present.

When Cei lifted the veil and Elffin elevated the glowing chalice, there was a long sigh from the assembly. The grail was large and shallow, an ancient drinking bowl carved from a single sidhe-stone that lit the air with an uncanny radiance. All around the rim was a golden band set with many lesser gemstones. And Prince Tryffin had chosen the cupbearers with an eye to the effect they would have on all viewers: Somehow, the holy vessel seemed to take on an added shade of mystery, set against the youth and innocence of the two young boys.

As the boys began to move around the chamber so that everyone would have the opportunity to see the chalice up close, there was a deep silence. Mahaffy could see the unearthly glow of the stone reflected in the faces of every man and woman the cupbearers passed. Not to be wondered at, for his own eyes were filling with tears, his heart leaping in his chest.

The sidhe-stone vessel had been a thing of beauty from the very beginning, but ever since the rite of atonement, the healing of the land, it had become something much greater. And they had been blind, back at Dinas Yfan, not to recognize that . . . Mahaffy knew that he had been blind as well. The strain and the stress, the atmosphere of suspicion, and most of all his concern for Conn, had obscured his vision. *I see more clearly now,* he told himself. They all saw more clearly.

When it was over, when the cup was covered and carried away under guard, Prince Tryffin rose from his seat and left the hall—which meant that everyone else was free to leave as well. But Mahaffy waited until the place was practically empty, then pushed back his chair and walked slowly out of the hall, heading for his own chamber in a meditative mood.

"Lord Mahaffy, a word with you." That was Gwalchmai, the oldest son of Greid of Ymorgan. His blue and green surcote, with his father's badge of a winged serpent emblazoned on the chest, was spotted with rain, and his hair and beard were damp and curling, as though he had just come in from the yard. Now that Mahaffy came to think of it, Gwalchmai had not been there during the latter part of the banquet; he had been summoned away by one of his father's servants shortly before the cup was unveiled.

"A message came . . . my father is greatly disturbed. He has asked Prince Tryffin and several of the other lords to meet with him privately in his chamber. He charged me to find you and to make certain that you came. It is vitally important; those were his words."

"Then in the name of Heaven take me to him," said Mahaffy. It was not the sort of invitation he could well refuse, even if he had been so inclined.

Lord Greid's apartments were near the top of the central tower, a long climb up a spiraling stone staircase. When

Mahaffy arrived in the candlelit bedchamber, a dozen men were there already, Prince Tryffin among them.

"Grim news," said the Governor, by way of greeting. "Word has arrived that young Math's horse apparently went mad and threw him . . . the boy escaped being trampled to death only by a miracle. Even less welcome news comes with it: There is a rumor abroad that Math's cousin Peredur is dead, and that his death was so sudden and so unforeseen, his uncles are convinced he was poisoned."

Before Mahaffy could reply, Corfil Alun was already speaking. "Unwelcome news you *say*, Lord Prince, but in truth I believe you must receive it with rejoicing. That is one less rival standing between Mahaffy Guillyn and the High Seat. And if Math had not been miraculously spared, Mahaffy's way would be entirely clear."

There was a long, uneasy silence before anyone answered. And then it was the Governor, so steadily, patiently, and gently, that had Mahaffy not seen the way every muscle in his body suddenly went tense with the effort to keep himself under control, he would have never guessed that Tryffin had just been mortally insulted. "Surely, you do not mean to imply that we are responsible. Particularly when you consider that Mahaffy himself was so recently nearly assassinated."

"And yet escaped harm," snapped Corfil. Perhaps he did not see, as everyone else in the room saw, how the Governor's breath was coming so quickly, how his broad, strong hands clenched and unclenched. "I cannot but wonder whether the whole thing might have been arranged, against this day, against any suspicion—"

Lord Greid spoke up, before the man had time to utter another reckless word. "The same might be said of young Math and the fall from his horse. If that story is even true. If I may say so, that tale arrives rather conveniently along with the other, considering these events must have occurred at a distance of several hundred miles apart. And we do not even know for certain if Peredur is really dead. Or even if that *is* true, whether he might not have died of entirely natural causes. For now, it is all rumor and conjecture."

There was a considerable lessening of the tension in the room after Greid spoke.

"There would be no need to *clear Mahaffy's way*, in any case." Tryffin's southern lilt was as soft and melodious as ever, but there was a dangerous gleam in his brown eyes. "Since his claim is more ancient and supersedes them both. If anyone would benefit by Peredur's death, it would have to be Math. Equal in rank, equal in blood, and of much the same age—it would have been difficult for the King to choose between them, even if he were willing to overlook Mahaffy or to regard his claim as spurious."

"That is true," said Gwalchmai, speaking up from his place by the door. "And what is more: The very best reason that I ever heard for choosing Mahaffy Guillyn instead is that it would be impossible to elevate either Math or Peredur without slighting the other . . . a slight which those who support the injured party might be glad to avenge by taking arms. It seems to me that Peredur's death, however it came about, alters a very delicate balance that the Governor, of all men, would wish to maintain."

Several of the other lords and chieftains, who had not taken part in the conversation up until now, began to nod and murmur their approval of what Gwalchmai had said.

And by now, Corfil was beginning to look slightly embarrassed, was fiddling with his moustache again. He blew out a long breath. "Perhaps I spoke hastily. The news was so shocking. Nevertheless, I can't help thinking—"

"Thinking," said Greid, with a quelling glance, "is the very thing that we should all be doing. It would not be wise for *any* of us to speak or to act on a hasty conclusion. Instead, let us each spend the night in silent contemplation, and meet again in the morning for further discussion."

"Well spoken," said Tryffin, his gaze softening just a little. "You are a wise man, Greid."

And as there was nothing that anyone could think of to

add to that, or at least nothing that anyone felt comfortable saying, the men began to file slowly out of the room.

It was a raw night and the shelter that Meligraunce built out of brush and dry branches did very little to keep out the wind, but at least it stopped raining before he and the boy settled down for the night. Grifflet slept curled up in a tight ball, with the Captain's cloak folded over for extra thickness and then wrapped around him, while the Captain made do with the garments he was wearing. He had slept and survived under worse conditions before this, and there was no reason to suppose that he could not do so now.

For Meligraunce, it was a long, restless night, though he thought less of his own discomfort than of the dangers facing his small companion. What should have been a few hours' journey on horseback had already stretched to two days and two nights of roundabout foot travel over rough, unforgiving country. Meligraunce had not even dared to stop and beg for shelter in any of the cottages or villages along the way, had been at some pains to avoid those cottages and villages as much as he avoided the roads, because there was no way of knowing whom he might trust, who could be depended on not to betray him and the boy to the men searching for them.

And even if Efrei's two sons had no knowledge of these present disguises, they had certainly been able to pass on a general description to any possible conspirators: a big, dark foreigner, and a little redheaded boy, and that would be more than enough.

The Captain shifted uncomfortably on his rocky bed. If he did not manage, somehow, to get that little boy safely to his father . . . by God, if he was still alive to do it, there would be a grim reckoning those other two boys had to face. He would tear those young wretches limb from limb if that was what it took to get at the truth!

By morning, the wind had died and the sky was clearing.

Grifflet woke up, demanding his breakfast, and this time would not be satisfied when Meligraunce told him there would be no breakfast this morning, not any more than there had been breakfast the morning before, or dinner, or supper either. He began to cry, sitting there in the dirt among the rocks, and it broke the Captain's heart to see him do it, considering how brave he had been up until now, how unfailingly cooperative and uncomplaining.

When it was time to break camp, and Grifflet tried to get up and begin the day's journey, he kept sitting down again, his legs were so weak—or perhaps he was just weary and disheartened. Perhaps he simply did not understand why the man who had cared for him all these weeks was torturing him now. "Cap-cap-captain, I can't-can't walk," he said, with a pitiful glance.

"Then I will carry you," said Meligraunce. He picked the little boy up and went shambling along, feeling far too lightheaded himself. At the first stream they encountered, they stopped to drink, but even though it served to quench their thirst, the water only made them both feel emptier inside.

By noon, when they spotted another village in the distance, a cluster of mean little cottages, the Captain decided the time had come for desperate measures. The boy had to be fed and so had he, because if his strength gave out, they were both lost.

He put Grifflet down in a sheltered spot and explained that he had to leave him there for a short time only. The little boy curled up on the ground and promptly fell asleep. Leaving the cloak to cover him, Meligraunce departed, hoping the boy would not wake too soon and become frightened at finding himself alone.

Running low, and keeping to whatever cover was available, which was mostly last year's dried-out heather and broom, the Captain advanced toward the village. As he drew nearer, he realized there was something afoot. The people were—amazingly—out dancing on the green, if you could call it a green, and some peddlers had stopped by and set up a number of stalls, creating a sort of fair.

Madness, thought Meligraunce, *this time of year.* What had they got to dance about, anyway, with the holidays past and spring still many weeks in the future? Or perhaps *he* was the one who was going mad, because he thought he recognized one of the dancers: an ancient greybeard in ragged silks and velvets, whirling about with a village lass.

The Captain shook his head. No doubt his eyes were playing tricks; the road between here and Peryf had been a long one.

Peering around the corner of one of the cottages, Meligraunce picked out one of the other huts, one that appeared deserted. There was no smoke rising through the hole in the thatched roof and the interior was dark and silent. Steeling his nerve, he darted across the distance between and then in past the hanging horsehide that served for a door.

As he had hoped, there was no one inside. Or at least, there was no reaction to his scuffling footsteps, or his heavy breathing as he crouched on the floor and waited for his eyes to adjust to the dark. After a few minutes, there was just enough light coming in through the smoke hole for the Captain to dimly make out his surroundings.

Dropping a few coins out of his purse to pay for what he took, he snatched up a pair of rough sacking blankets off the bed, a flat loaf of unleavened bread from the table, and by rummaging around in the single cupboard came up with some dried roots and a jug of sour-smelling ale. He wrapped up his gleanings inside one of the blankets, threw the other one over his shoulders for a cloak, and skulked out of the hut and out of the village.

When he was a safe distance away, he threw himself flat on the ground to regain his breath, then crept back to the place where he had left Grifflet.

With a meal inside of them, no matter how scanty, they both felt a great deal better, and Grifflet was ready to try his legs again. But they still had a long, weary walk ahead of them.

It was a sorry, footsore pair that finally arrived within sight of Lord Greid's fortress, a little before sunset. Prince Tryffin's flag still waved proudly above the ramparts. Yet that offered little in the way of reassurance. There was no way of knowing what sort of things were happening inside, and Meligraunce was beginning to see the shadow of treachery wherever he went.

However, unless some misfortune had overtaken the whole lot of them, Prince Tryffin and Mahaffy would be riding out of the castle along with their troops tomorrow morning. Meligraunce reckoned that the safest course was to wait until then, watch the castle gate until Prince Tryffin emerged, and then meet his party along the road.

As for tonight . . . because it was still early, the Captain had time to look about for a more suitable resting place. This he found in the ruins of a shepherd's hut. Out of some old boards and branches and some uprooted bushes, he was able to erect another makeshift shelter, much better than any that he and Grifflet had slept in in the last two nights. Crawling inside, he and the little boy shared the last of the dry, bitter-tasting roots, swallowed a last mouthful of sour ale, made up their bed using the two blankets and the Captain's tattered cloak, and immediately fell asleep.

The sun was hardly over the horizon before the castle gates opened and a large party rode out. Prince Tryffin was unmistakable—a big, broad man with the early morning sun shining on his golden hair—but there seemed to be a great crowd of men riding with him, far more than the Captain had expected.

Cutting across a rocky field in order to head the horsemen off, Meligraunce and Grifflet arrived at the road only a few moments before Prince Tryffin and Mahaffy came riding by. Catching sight of that worn and bedraggled pair standing in the dust, the Governor reined up at once.

A heartbeat later, he was kneeling by the side of the road, holding out his arms to the little boy. Grifflet flung himself into that encompassing embrace, and promptly burst into tears and great wracking sobs. Tryffin let the boy have his cry, before asking any questions, though he continued to hold him and make soothing sounds. When the sobs had died down, he wiped away the tears with his own hands; then with a piece of cloth and some water from a goatskin bag, he cleaned the dirt off his son's face.

Sitting on Prince Tryffin's knee, the little boy looked more than usually small and fragile, with his head resting on the broad front of the Governor's scarlet tunic. He gave a final tremulous gasp, turned his gaze full on the assembled company, and smiled his peculiarly winsome smile.

There was not a man in the entire party who was not visibly moved. "This is my son," said Tryffin, as though any such explanation were necessary.

"So we see," said Corfil. "Indeed we do see. He is a fine boy, and the image of . . . He is a fine boy, and it is plain that he is as fond of you as you are of him."

"And you were a fool ever to doubt it, Corfil," said a younger man with a curling black beard.

Corfil shrugged, and made an apologetic gesture with one hand. "Well, I am willing to admit that I was wrong. And having seen what I wished to see, there is no reason to continue on to Caer Clynnoc." He turned and glanced around him. "How many are willing to follow me back and tell the friends that we left behind that the matter of young . . . Grifflet . . . has been most thoroughly and gratifyingly explained?"

Apparently, all of them were, because all of the men who were not of Prince Tryffin's original party mounted up, turned back the way they had come, and disappeared down the road in a cloud of dust.

Which was all for the best, thought Meligraunce, since they left before Grifflet could say anything startlingly

precocious, or give a hint of his true age, to start them
asking questions all over again.

At Caer Clynnoc, Grifflet was immediately washed, fed,
and then bundled off to bed by Cianwy Glyn. A half-dozen
guards were stationed outside his bedchamber door and
beneath his window, and Cei and Elffin were to take turns
sitting up by his bed, because he knew them and would not
be upset by their presence. The Governor was taking no
chances.

Now there remained the unpleasant task of questioning
Grifflet's cousins. "I don't doubt for a moment they are as
guilty as you say," Tryffin told Meligraunce as they discussed the matter in the little antechamber off the banquet
hall. "But this would be an unfortunate time for me to arrest
the pair of them on such scanty evidence, with rumors
already circulating about my high-handed, not to say
murderous, methods in clearing the way for my young
wards to prosper. I can't imprison them on mere suspicion,
and as for questioning children under physical duress, that
would be unthinkable."

Meligraunce reluctantly agreed with him. Perhaps some
of the Governor's soft-heartedness was wearing off on him,
since the idea of torturing children—even these particular
children—was not an appealing one.

"If I may make a suggestion, Your Grace. Those boys are
likely to be terrified of you already. They were at hand, as
you may remember, the night you killed their father and
their uncle. With the battle madness on you, you hacked
both men to pieces, and for two little boys it must have been
a shocking experience. They were also there earlier
when . . ." Meligraunce cleared his throat ". . . when on
learning that Mahaffy had been poisoned you promised
to . . . er, cook and consume the heart of the guilty party."

Tryffin sat down in a chair, regarded him darkly from
under his sandy eyebrows. "You are saying that I should

frighten those boys into a confession. But I can't threaten them, Captain, you know that."

"I know that you are under some destiny or compulsion to always speak the exact truth as you see it," said the Captain, pacing back and forth before the fire. "Yet I've often known you to make truthful statements in such a way that those who heard you were completely misled."

Tryffin sighed and nodded his head. "I have done some sickeningly violent deeds in my time, with the battle fury on me. I suppose if I recited some of my more despicable exploits . . ." He put a hand over his eyes. "Ah God, this is not much better than beating it out of them, but we have to find a way to get at the truth. I suppose this is the best we can do. Bring them in here, Captain, as soon as we have finished eating."

With supper eaten and the pewter plates and tankards cleared away, Tryffin waited for Efrei's sons to be brought into the hall for questioning. They came in with Meligraunce, and took the seats that had been arranged for them facing the Governor across the low table. The Captain took up his position again by the fire.

"I had hoped we would meet again under more favorable circumstances," Tryffin greeted the boys, with a sinister smile that was calculated to trouble their dreams for a long time. And he went on to speak a number of other pleasantries which, somehow—later, it would be impossible for them to say exactly how—had nothing pleasant about them.

The two boys answered in monosyllables, the younger one clearly terrified, the older sullen and defiant. Tryffin took as long as possible before coming to the point, as long as he could think of these ambiguous remarks, in order to give their guilty apprehension a long time to grow. He could see it was having the desired effect, because Esgeir began to tremble, and Ogryfran was giving him murderous looks.

"I wonder now," said Tryffin, at last, "if either of you

were acquainted with young Calchas, in the days that he was Lord of Mochdreff."

Ogryfran shook his head. "We weren't, but we knew all about him. But what does that have to do with—?"

Tryffin continued to smile. "He was a terrible liar, that one. I could never tolerate anyone who lied for profit or out of cowardice; that's a black sin, where I come from. I killed Calchas, you know, when he was not so very much older than you are now. I was only a boy myself, of course. But it wasn't for his lies only—although those were quite abominable—it was because he had caused so much pain and worry to someone I loved.

"I suppose you know," he added, pulling out his dagger and placing it on the table in front of him, "that your cousin Grifflet has just spent the worst few days of his entire life." The dagger had a wicked looking blade, and there was a dragon worked into the golden hilt, a beast with malevolent ruby eyes. He had not, as a matter of fact, used it to kill Calchas or anyone else . . . it was the knife that he used to cut his meat.

There was a long silence, broken at last by Esgeir. "I don't . . . we didn't . . ."

"He doesn't understand what any of this has to do with us," Ogryfran inserted smoothly. "We've not hurt Grifflet; we've not hurt anyone."

"Not directly perhaps," said the Governor. "Yet it was certainly Esgeir who caused the initial delay that made the Captain and Grifflet leave so late in the day. And I can't think of a single reason why any of the servants or the guards would wish to poison the Captain's horse with swine-weed. The horse did come back to the stable on his own, they say, with all the symptoms, and I'm told the grooms had a difficult time saving his life, he was so far gone. Certainly, there was no one else in the castle, other than you and Esgeir, who went out riding the day before and came back wearing such guilty faces." He paused, and then continued. "I do mean to get to the bottom of this, you know."

Reaching across the table, he took one of Esgeir's hands in both of his. The boy's white hand looked small and fragile between his broad, sinewy ones. "Do either one of you know the sound of breaking fingers, the kind of a snap the bones make? Calchas did, I regret to say. He was not very forthcoming when my brother and I asked him certain questions."

There was a horrified gasp from Esgeir. He looked ready to faint, staring up into the Governor's face with wide fascinated eyes, like a rabbit or some other small, quivering thing under the spell of a serpent.

And his brother blurted out: "Take your hands off of him. If you . . . if you promise not to do him any harm, I will tell you everything you want to know."

Ogryfran swallowed hard. "It was all my fault, anyway."

"We have a bargain then," said Tryffin, immediately releasing Esgeir's hand. Watching the tension drain out of his body, Meligraunce could see what all this had cost him—and guessed how the Governor was struggling not to show his vast relief.

Tryffin nodded to the younger boy. "You can go now. I have no further use for you."

Esgeir moved uneasily in his chair, turned a painfully questioning glance in his brother's direction. "I said that you can go," the Governor repeated sharply. He had no wish to prolong the young one's discomfort any more than necessary. "Rest easy; your brother has saved you. That is, if he sticks to his word."

Esgeir slipped quickly out of his chair and out of the anteroom. "Well . . . ?" said Tryffin, eyeing Ogryfran across the table.

Ogryfran began to gnaw on his lower lip, and replied in a suffocated voice. "When we went out riding that day, we met a band of men on the road. They said we could do an ill turn to the man who had killed our father, and at the same time help our cousin Rhys to his rightful inheritance, by helping *them* to rescue him out of your hands. Esgeir didn't trust them, but I talked him into remaining silent. I was the one who put Grifflet into his bed, and then fed swine-weed to the Captain's horse early that morning. Then, right after Meligraunce and Grifflet left, I went to the place where the men were waiting, and told them which way to go."

"And who were those men?" Tryffin asked.

Ogryfran shook his head miserably. "I never saw any of them before that day. I . . . maybe it wasn't so wise to speak to strangers."

"Not wise at all," said Tryffin, sitting back in his chair. "Were there no names mentioned among them . . . nothing that gave you any idea who they might be, or who had sent them?"

Ogryfran squirmed and stared down at his hands. "Were there no names mentioned, no armorial bearings?" the Governor insisted quietly.

"There was one man . . . I saw under his cloak, and there was some sort of animal embroidered on the sleeve of his tunic. It might have been a lion, but I only caught a glimpse."

"And the hue?" said Tryffin—though if it were a badge instead of a coat of arms, the color might not matter.

"Azure, I think. That is, the light was poor so it might have been vert, but I am nearly certain the color was blue."

The Governor considered that. Lions were unfortunately common as charges and badges, but a blue lion gave him a bit more to go on. Supposing, that was, that the animal in question was not a blue tyger instead, or a panther, griffon, or wild cat . . .

"And is there nothing else you can tell me?" he asked Ogryfran. "Nothing about the way the men were dressed, or how they looked?"

"At least two of the men were wearing gold spurs. It was because they were knights that I thought I could trust them. Except for those two, the others were just ordinary men with black hair and beards. Common-looking fellows if you want to know the truth." He gave a long, shuddering sigh. "Do you believe what I have just been telling you?"

"Oh yes," said the Governor, tapping his fingers on the table. "It's a credible story, so why *shouldn't* I believe you?"

The boy continued to look apprehensive. "What are you going to do to me, now that you know?"

Tryffin and Meligraunce exchanged a glance across the room. "As to that . . . there is nothing you have done that inclines me to take any action against you at all," Tryffin said slowly. "I killed your father fairly and honorably in judicial combat—the treachery was all on his side—but it is natural enough you should feel some resentment. And I think it is commendable that you wanted to help your cousin—as you supposed. I am willing to believe that you meant that for the best, since you were so ready to defend your own little brother. Though truth to tell, it's much more likely that you almost delivered Grifflet into the hands of wicked scoundrels who meant to murder him. I hope that realization keeps you awake for many nights to come."

The Governor picked up his dragon-hilted dagger and slipped it back into his belt. "As for your less innocent transgressions—speaking to strange men, and mistreating a horse—those are for Caradawg Glyn to punish, since he has charge of your upbringing. The naughtiness of young boys scarcely falls under *my* jurisdiction. But I doubt the chieftain will let you off as lightly as I would, so you have no need to thank me for that. You can go now, if you wish."

The boy started for the door, relief warring in his face with a certain humiliating suspicion that Tryffin had fooled him. He paused on the threshold to deliver a scathing denunciation: "You never would have done anything terrible to Esgeir, even if I had never spoken, now would you?"

"I don't make war on children," said the Governor. "Or steal from them either. Having so much of my own, there is no need for me to steal from anyone. Grifflet will never be Lord of Mochdreff but he will be Lord of Eildonn, that I can promise you. Of one thing you may be certain: You will never, ever, need to protect him from me."

"Now, I suppose," said Meligraunce, as Ogryfran walked out the door, "you will spend the night feeling badly because Caradawg Glyn has them beaten."

"No," Tryffin replied, after a moment of consideration. "God knows, I would never whip a child myself, but I think I may be growing harder as the years go by. When I think what might have happened to Grifflet—and of all that he suffered as it was—I'm afraid that the thought of Ogryfran's and Esgeir's probable punishment doesn't distress me at all."

. . . *and Pefyn was horrified by the things he had seen, and with only his shirt to cover him, he ran out of the castle in a terrible frenzy. It is said he went mad at that time and lived many months in the woods and the fields.*

How he kept himself, nobody knows. Yet there was a lordly air about him even in his madness, and a strange, clear light shining in his eyes, and for that reason he was treated as a person of importance wherever he went. In truth, they say that the beggars, the pickpockets, the harlots, and the peddlers wandering the roads were all so taken with him, that they made him their Lord and did all his bidding.

—From the Oral Tradition

8.

The King of Vagabonds

It had been a long day, so the Captain went to bed unkempt and unwashed. And in the morning, he had no time to do more than splash some cold water on his face and the back of his neck, before Prince Tryffin came striding into the barracks with a letter in his hand, dismissed the other men who were just arming up, and closed the door behind the last of them.

"This message has apparently been waiting for me for two days, but I only saw it this morning. Dame Brangwaine sends the most troubling and puzzling news," said the Governor, throwing the letter down on the table by the rough crockery wash basin. "It seems that her great-granddaughter is somehow held captive by her kinsman, Lord Cernach."

Meligraunce felt the blood drain from his face, at the thought of Luned in any danger. "An abduction? How would he dare? Do you know if he has . . . harmed her in any way?"

Snatching up the letter he tried to decipher the words, but he was far too agitated to make any sense of them. "Of course you will send a troop of men to demand that he release her at once!"

Tryffin shook his head regretfully. "I am sorry, Meligraunce, but I am afraid that's impossible. Cernach is her cousin and the head of the family. And it appears—though Dame Brangwaine's message is rather obscure—that at least at the beginning Luned was willing enough to go with him. I can hardly demand that he yield her up, under the circumstances. Not without some sort of proof that he is holding the lady against her will."

The Captain was stunned. "Surely you don't mean to leave her in that bad man's power? Last year when we were in Anoeth, she and Dame Brangwaine—"

"She and Dame Brangwaine saved my life, by nursing me back to health after the shapechanger attacked me," Tryffin finished for him. "I remember it well. And certainly I have no wish to leave the lady in Lord Cernach's power. Supposing that is, that it is even possible for a man of his sort to hold a Mochdreffi wise-woman against her will."

The Governor sat down straddlewise on the only chair that the room contained. "I intend to send you to Dame Brangwaine in Anoeth to learn more about this. We both know from experience that what can't be done by force with a troop of men can sometimes be accomplished quietly by one or two daring men."

Meligraunce felt a tinge of relief. "So you are sending me off to effect a secret rescue?" he said, a flush creeping up to his cheekbones.

"Say rather that I am sending you to discover if a secret rescue is called for," Tryffin replied. "You may learn that the lady is well enough where she is. Or you may bring me information that will justify a formal demand, backed up by force, for her release."

Already, the Captain was reaching for the cleaner set of garments. "God knows, no one could be more eager than I to perform this service."

Tryffin smiled. "That I know. But I think it will be better if you maintain your present disguise a short while longer, because I would rather as few people as possible knew of your visit to Dame Brangwaine. Aside from your own feelings at the thought of that *particular* lady in distress, it seems this may be more important than we know."

Meligraunce stopped with tunic and hose in his hands as the Governor continued. "Dame Brangwaine informs me that Cernach has invited young Math and his grandfather to visit him. She does not say which of his castles they are occupying, but it may be the very same one where Luned is a less than willing guest.

"You will remember what Ogryfran told us, just last night," he added. "That he caught a glimpse of a device worn by one of the men who was hunting you: an animal like to a lion."

"And Cernach uses two wildcats combatant as a badge," said Meligraunce, his nostrils flaring and his eyes dilating. It seemed that this Cernach was a busy man. "It might well be that a second cat was covered by the cloak."

He began to don, once more, the disreputable garments he had put aside the night before. "In truth, I know little in Lord Cernach's disfavor—aside from his remarkable indifference, last year, when faced with the slaughter of more than a hundred infants and old people—yet I find it hard to believe that any form of treachery, any wicked deed, would be beyond him."

Tryffin nodded, watching Meligraunce belt his tunic, then slip a pair of long knives into their sheaths. "I hope you may be proved wrong," he said, "but I believe in my heart that your instincts are correct, and Cernach is the very worst sort of villain."

From daylight to dusk, the chase continued, across the shifting borders of the shadow realms. When the grassy plain gave way to a hard, burning wasteland with a silver sun flaming in the sky, the green fly became a sliding green serpent and went coiling and slithering across the rocky soil. But the red vixen, determined not to be left behind, became a golden lioness and continued to give chase.

Although the lioness was lithe and swift, the snake could go places where she could not: down a hole or through a narrow crevice between two rocks. Whenever Gwenlliant came near enough to get ready to pounce, Maelinn found some new way to elude her. When night came to the wasteland, Gwenlliant's cat eyes served her well, as did her ability to sense her quarry even after the moon set and the darkness became absolute. But Maelinn became first an owl and then a bat and went winging on through the night.

Before morning there was another border, with the consequent shifting of time. What was for Gwenlliant, on one side of the border, the space of a heartbeat, stretched into minutes for Maelinn, on the other side. When the lioness came bounding out of the desert and found herself crashing through thorny underbrush in a forest of dying oaks and withering elms, the only living creature she could see (and that only a glimpse through a gap in the leprous trees) was a silver elk, running so far ahead of her that it seemed she would never catch up.

Yet so long as she was able to keep Maelinn in sight, there was always hope. Gwenlliant became a white doe and continued more swiftly than before. Through the woods, across a wide river—Maelinn became a salmon and Gwenlliant an otter—then for miles upon miles of heathery moorland, they continued the chase as a dappled mare and a wolfhound bitch. Gwenlliant only dared to stop and rest when Maelinn did, and so long as she was able to keep her quarry in view.

At the next border, time shifted in her favor: When they came out on a windy mountain side, Gwenlliant was now so close she dared to change back to her own shape in order to have hands to reach and to grasp . . . but Maelinn anticipated her, went suddenly small and sleek, and as a grey mouse went skittering up the slope.

On the other side of the mountain was a town, and there Maelinn became a woman again and tried to lose herself in the crowd in the market square. Gwenlliant slid past a wagon just in time to witness the next transformation and follow the shapechanger out of the town.

Yet now the next border was just ahead, and between was a deep chasm. Maelinn flew over as a peregrine falcon, but Gwenlliant, mindful of the new life growing inside her— unable to become a bird or an insect and fly over—had to take her time, in the shape of a mountain cat, climbing down a steep, dangerous pathway and creeping along narrow stony ledges until she reached the bottom. And even then there was the long, treacherous climb up the other side still to be negotiated.

With a sinking heart, Gwenlliant realized that this delay was likely to cost her dearly, that these hours of toil crossing the chasm were likely to translate into days or even weeks on the other side of the border.

Within its bastion of crumbling granite walls, Anoeth was as hard and bitter and stony as ever. From the dirty alleys and narrow pathways where the poor lived crowded in flinty little hovels, to the wider (but somehow no less stifling) lanes where the great men of Anoeth had built their cryptlike mansions, there had never been, and probably never would be, a town so dark and oppressive.

It therefore struck Meligraunce as worthy of note—when he rode into the town on a piebald gelding he had acquired in Clynnoc—that while the flesh and the bones of the town itself had changed not at all, the people crawling about on

the skin of Anoeth like so many fleas should have altered so
amazingly.

Where they had shuffled or slunk, they now moved with
a light and agile step. Where they had arrayed themselves
solely in somber hues—muddy grey, mousy brown, and
faded black, like a city in perpetual mourning—there was
here and there a splash of some brighter color: a blue feather
in a peddler's cap, a knot of scarlet ribbons on a young
woman's bosom, a little boy wearing leaf-green hose under
his more sober tunic. And there were none of the sliding
sidelong glances or the downright hostile stares which
would have greeted a gaudy and ragged foreigner as
recently as last summer.

One buxom lass, the girl with the scarlet ribbons, even
smiled at Meligraunce as she pressed him to buy something
from her tray of bright trinkets. "A necklace of beads for
your sweetheart . . . or a golden ring for your hand, dear,
to match the ring in your ear."

He gave her a small copper coin, just for the sake of the
smile, but refused to buy any of her wares. He could see that
the color would rub off the beads in less than a fortnight,
and the ring was only made of base metal painted to
resemble gold.

At the door of Lord Cernach's brooding fortified man-
sion, it was not easy to convince the servant in purple and
gold livery that Dame Brangwaine *did* want to speak to him.
Had Cernach himself been in residence, it would have been
impossible, but with the master absent, the family retainers
were rather more concerned to curry the favor of the family
matriarch . . . who was eccentric and occasionally known
to entertain queer visitors, in her isolated set of rooms at the
back of the house.

"Tell her that a man has come to show her an item of great
value and unusual design: a silver dagger with a golden
hilt," said Meligraunce.

The dagger has been a gift from the old woman, one of a

pair she had given to him and Prince Tryffin, so he was certain Dame Brangwaine would understand.

The servant agreed to carry the message, closed the door, and opened it again just a few minutes later, to usher the Captain inside. Meligraunce followed, down a long dark corridor and up a set of stairs, taking a grim satisfaction in the knowledge that he would now appear before the old woman entirely stripped of those deceptive airs and graces which had apparently been responsible for her outrageous scheme to unite him with Luned.

Her reaction as he entered the room where she was sitting, was all that he could have wished. The old woman started violently, and her twisted hands clutched at the arms of her carven chair. However, she regained her composure and her customary ill humor quickly, and irritably waved the serving man out of the room.

Meligraunce smiled bleakly. "Now that you see me for the baseborn fellow I am, perhaps you are not so eager for your kinswoman to marry me."

But Dame Brangwaine never let anyone get the better of her in a verbal duel. "On the contrary. Even more than you did before, you look like the bastard black-sheep son of some royal house . . . the very King of Vagabonds," she replied tartly. "Do people draw in their breath and step aside when you walk by? That is not to be wondered at. You look like a man who, having everything to lose, has already lost it and consequently fears nothing. Such men are dangerous."

In spite of himself, Meligraunce laughed. And when she ordered him to take a seat, indicating a low stool to one side of her chair, he promptly obeyed her. As usual, there were too many candles burning in the room, and too many cats, lying on rugs and on pillows, or perched on the heavy oak furniture.

"We have much to discuss," said the old woman. "A great deal has happened since we did *not* meet in Trewynyn. You don't know, for instance, how my great-granddaughter came back to the place where she and I had taken lodgings, with such a wild, despairing look on her face as I had never seen before."

Meligraunce stiffened, opened his mouth to speak, but the old woman forestalled him. "What passed between the two of you is no business of mine. So Luned told me . . . and so, to some extent, I agree. I am far more concerned with the consequences, which promise to be dire. And as I have a long story to tell you, I expect you to listen patiently."

Meligraunce nodded, and prepared to listen—if not patiently, at least attentively.

"At the beginning of winter, my grandson asked Luned to marry him. This, I should tell you, startled her greatly, because far from being fond of each other, she and Cernach have always been deeply antagonistic. She refused him, of course, but he persisted in wooing her, not with words of love but with a strange, rambling discourse that troubled her greatly, and with hints of some great destiny he seemed to believe was awaiting him, a destiny she was not only to share but to play some part in the actual achievement, by opening to him *'her store of dark knowledge.'*"

A black and white kitten climbed into her lap, and the old woman reached down absently with a withered hand to stroke it. "This continued for some time, and when his attentions became too pressing, Luned begged me to go away with her to Trewynyn, that she might put herself safely out of his reach. It was madness at that time of the year, yet she was frightened and I was uneasy, and so I consented."

Meligraunce frowned. "She led me to believe that she went to Trewynyn in order to see me. And God help me, I believed her."

The old woman shrugged. "And in some sense, she told you the truth. Of all the places that were not Anoeth, of all the places that we *might* have gone to avoid Cernach, she chose Trewynyn. Which turned out to be a very poor choice indeed, since we learned only after we arrived that

Prince Tryffin and his lady were gone, and we were therefore denied entry into the castle."

"Before God! Do you tell me that Luned was abducted on the very streets of Trewynyn?" The Captain was breathing heavily. "That she was carried off right under my——"

"She was not," said Dame Brangwaine. "But she was in a reckless mood after your meeting. And in that mood, she told me that she had experienced a change of heart. She was ready to return to Anoeth and listen more favorably to my grandson's suit. I might have argued against that more forcibly, I might even have commanded her obedience . . . but I do not expect to live much longer, Captain, and it seemed to me that the time had come for Luned to learn how to curb her own impulses. Besides that, I thought she would think better of her decision on the long journey home."

One hand went up to cover her eyes, an involuntary gesture, and one that told the Captain much more than she wanted him to know, because her hand shook, if only a little, and her voice broke. "That was my mistake, for which I blame myself most bitterly."

After a moment, and as if ashamed of that momentary weakness, she dropped her hand and continued even more briskly than before. "Even before we arrived here, Luned declared that she had made up her mind entirely in Cernach's favor. On the day that we came home, he was preparing for a journey of his own. The next morning, Cernach was gone and Luned with him. I have not received a word, not so much as a hastily scribbled message, from her since."

Meligraunce abandoned the stool and began to pace the floor—much to the consternation of the cats, several of which rose, humped their backs at him, and then strolled out of the room. "This hardly seems reason enough to accuse him of holding your great-granddaughter captive. Lady, I would gladly serve you in this matter, but Prince Tryffin has charged me to exercise discretion. And that being so, if you could give me something, something more——"

"I believed that she would regret her decision eventually," said Dame Brangwaine. "And a few days after her departure, I *knew*. My powers are not what they once were, yet there were . . . signs . . . that Luned was in danger or distress. A silver mirror that belonged to her suddenly turned black. Only yesterday, a grey cat that had been a special pet of hers gave birth to a litter of deformed kittens. And the linens in her bedchamber are mysteriously stained with blood, though they were whiter than snow on the day she left. These incidents have meaning when a woman of power is involved."

This did sound sinister. "Tell me more of those hints and those promises you mentioned earlier," said Meligraunce, lengthening his restless strides. "What do you think it is that Lord Cernach really wants from her?"

"I cannot say for certain. His discourse, as I said, was inclined to be rambling and more than a little obscure," Dame Brangwaine replied. "You may put aside any thoughts of rape or seduction, however. It is clear to me that he wants Luned only for her knowledge and her power— and her vulnerability. As you may know, we sacrifice certain freedoms when we become witches. It is painful, though not impossible, for us to cross over running water, and we cannot enter a warded house or room without an invitation. These facts are well known, or I should not mention them, but there are other limitations which I may not tell you. Those who know them may be able to control us in various ways."

The old woman shook her head. "As to what he said to her: Cernach spoke of a golden cauldron . . . and of the ancient magical treasures of Ynys Celydonn, the Twelve Hallows as the bards have named them . . . and of many other strange and wonderful things that were revealed to him in dreams and visions. *'I have seen the Lady of the Ravens mow down an entire army with a single terrible glance,'* he told Luned. *'And a man without a face, who stands behind the High Seat and whispers secrets into the young Lord's ear.'"*

The Captain stopped and stared at her for a long moment; all these things sounded vaguely familiar. "I, too, have dreamed of a cauldron, and of other strange things as well, ever since Christmas. There seems to be a new influence abroad in the land and these dreams or visions may be a part of it. I am not so certain, Lady, that they may not prove to be beneficial in the end."

Dame Brangwaine nodded. "That may be so. In the case of your own dreams it may well be so. But my grandson's dreams are not of such recent date. They began last year at this time, when the children were dying, and continued through most of the summer. I believe those dreams came from the shapechanger Maelinn, and that their nature was entirely baleful.

"This would explain why he was so unwilling to see Prince Tryffin in Anoeth. Cernach was in the power of that bloodsucking succubus, and did not wish to be freed from her influence. Also, he would not wish Prince Tryffin to know that, even so early as last spring, he was writing letters to Math fab Mercherion and his grandfather, Lord Branagh."

The Captain sat down again on the stool beside her chair. "If you will pardon me for saying so, that makes little sense. What need was there for secrecy? Last spring, the Governor was still looking forward to the day that he would see either Math or Peredur on the High Seat. Even now that Prince Tryffin has his heart set on Mahaffy Guillyn instead, that is not his decision to make. His cousin, the Emperor, will make his own choice and in his own time. Of course Prince Tryffin wishes to influence that decision by rallying support for Mahaffy. But until then, it is not treason to prefer Math to Mahaffy, and the Governor would be the first man to say so."

"Yet some men in Prince Tryffin's position might make the High King's decision even easier, by eliminating Mahaffy's rivals and any man willing to speak for them," Dame Brangwaine suggested.

When the Captain sprang to his feet with words of protest on his lips, she added hastily, "You and I know Prince Tryffin better than that. My grandson can only judge by what he would do himself if their positions were reversed."

"I will take your word for that," said Meligraunce, settling back down again. "But tell me this: Do you know where Lord Cernach has taken her?"

"I cannot say for certain," the old woman replied. "But in his place, I would go to Caer Rigor, which is the best of his castles. It is located near the coast, in his domain of Cuachag, and the lands around are some of the best in Mochdreff."

"I have heard of that place," said Meligraunce.

"And so you should have done. Those lands show little sign of the blight which has afflicted so much of Mochdreff for centuries—in truth, it is from the bounty of Cuachag that much of the wealth of our clan derives, at least that part that was arrived at honestly, and not through rapine and murder."

A cat with yellow stripes and a ragged ear had joined the kitten in her lap. "And the domain has been under the able stewardship of a remarkable man for many years," Dame Brangwaine went on. "My grandson preferred, shall we say, the dissipations of life in Anoeth, and so long as there was enough wealth to satisfy his needs, he gave little thought to anything else. He knew, you see, that this steward of his, this bastard uncle, was utterly trustworthy."

The old woman shrugged. "It happens, sometimes, in our family. Most of us are proud and ruthless—though some live long enough to grow bored with our own wickedness, and so reform—but occasionally there is born one of the honorable dutiful ones, like Luned, or like the man of whom I speak. Age and senility have recently forced him to abandon his duties, yet the castle remains in good repair and the garrison in good order. It is the logical place for Cernach to go and to entertain Math as his guest."

Meligraunce rose to his feet. "Then I will go first to Caer Rigor, and see what I can learn there. As soon, that is, as you give me leave to depart."

"Go then," said the old woman, with an impatient gesture, and he moved swiftly to obey her.

But then he paused on the threshold. There was one very important question that he wanted to ask her, yet he hardly knew how to begin. "I know that the witches of Anoeth are exceedingly powerful," he said, choosing his words very carefully, "and that they are able to affect the minds of men in many subtle ways."

"That is true," Dame Brangwaine agreed. "Or at least it has been true in the past and may be in the future. It is difficult to say, among so many changes."

He took a deep breath. "Then I wish to know: That first night that Luned sent for me . . . the sweetness and the passion . . . were they real?"

The old woman curled her lip, and regarded him haughtily. "Do you think Luned would entrap you with a love spell?" she asked.

"No," he said, "but I believe that *you* would, if it suited your purposes. You have said it yourself—the men and women of your clan are ruthless and arrogant."

A faint smile appeared on the old woman's fierce countenance. "And as willing to lie to you about this as anything else. But Luned is not a fool, after all. Though I might have deceived *you,* she would have known that I was tampering with your mind and your emotions. If you believe nothing else that I tell you, believe this: What you and Luned experienced that night was real. Or at least," she added cynically, "as real as such things usually are."

Until that moment, part of him had not dared to believe it. Now that he knew the truth, instead of greeting the news with the expected joy, he felt his heart sink, because he finally understood what he had said to injure Luned in Trewynyn.

"Lady," he said softly, "I have insulted the woman I love best in the world. And I must find her again, if only to set things right between us."

. . . and now I will attempt to explain to you the Law of Opposites.

The Alchemist says, "No generation without corruption," and the Physician, "What can heal may kill." The Wizard knows that no thing can exist without its Opposite, equal in force and in substance. Male and female, bright and dark, heat and cold, weight and lightness, fixed and mutable . . . through the continuous tension and clash of these mighty Principles is the whole World created.

—From a letter written by the mage Atlendor to his pupils at Findias

9.

The Thirteenth Hallow

Math fab Mercherion was feeling rebellious. Not that rebellion had ever gained him anything . . . his grandfather, Lord Branagh, had a way of making him feel worthless and ungrateful whenever he tried to assert himself, so that Math always gave in and did what the old man wanted anyway.

Only this time, he told himself, as he climbed the stairs up to the battlements at Caer Rigor, he was going to stand firm, make his demands, and get his own way. It was only right: At fourteen, he had been of legal age for two years, and if there were any justice in the world, he would have been Lord of Mochdreff all of that time.

He stopped at the top of the stairs, shook his head, and laughed softly to himself. There he was again, thinking as his grandfather wished him to think. The fact was, he would be just as happy if the honor went to Peredur, who deserved it every bit as much as he did according to the law of Mother Right, and probably wanted it more.

As Math walked out on the allures, a chill wind was blowing and there was a sprinkling of big wet snowflakes. But the weather had been beastly ever since he and Lord Branagh had arrived at Caer Rigor at Twelfth Night, two weeks since, and this was the best day so far for getting out of the rooms he shared with his grandfather and making a thorough exploration of the outer regions of the castle.

Caer Rigor, the royal castle . . . it was called that because of the enormous wealth of the men who had lived there, wealth rivaling that of kings and princes. And it really was a magnificent place, in a gloomy sort of way, with all those statues and tapestries and purple velvet hangings, the room where the Lords of Cuachag kept the bones of their enemies, gilded and set with gemstones, and that vast and intriguing boxwood maze down in one of the many gardens. Probably there were a great many other interesting things as well, though Math had yet to see them. As Lord Cernach was not yet in residence, many of the rooms were locked.

But what interested Math most of all was the clandestine midnight activity he had been observing over the course of the last two weeks, activity centered around one of the towers, an ancient structure set off at a distance from all the other buildings and surrounded by a private garden of its own. That was the real reason he had come up to the battlements today, to get a better look at that tower. And he was pleased to discover that he could see quite well from this lofty vantage point.

Down in the enclosed garden, through a net of leafless black branches dusted with snow, it was possible to see someone moving about: a short, squat person in gaudy orange and scarlet, a little old woman with red hair, a hump on her back, and a hooked nose.

Math had tried to warn his grandfather. *"There are dwarfs in the castle . . . one of them is a hunchback! And they are up to all sorts of nasty tricks, coming and going through secret doors and passageways in the middle of the night."* Lord Branagh had only responded with a quelling glance and the cold response that Lord Cernach must certainly know his own business best, and if he chose to keep dwarfs or other oddities at Caer Rigor, that was certainly nothing that Math need question.

Math did not see it that way at all. Most everyone said that dwarfs were the worst sort of ill luck, it was common knowledge, and he could tell that Lord Branagh thought so, too, by the look of pained distaste on his face.

Now Math crouched behind the parapet, trying to see without being seen himself. Pulling up the hood of his deep blue cloak to cover his straw-colored hair, he peered around one of the limestone merlons. He had to admit that the dwarf was not doing anything particularly sinister at the moment, just pacing back and forth as though she were taking the air, but—there!—she was stooping now, and drawing some sort of pattern in the snow. It looked like a circle with a cross at the bottom . . . and then a star . . . and then a wiggling line that might be a snake.

He drew in his breath sharply. So the old woman was a witch, as well as a hunchbacked dwarf. Math felt a chill slide down his spine. He had the utmost respect for the wise-women of Mochdreff, but dwarf *and* witch seemed an unfortunate combination.

"Lord Math." The name shattered his reverie, and brought Math out of his crouch, feeling distinctly embarrassed at being caught spying. Even on such a disreputable old creature as the dwarf. A man in armor was striding toward him. Iolo, his name was, the Caer Rigor guard captain, and Math rather liked him.

For which reason he felt suddenly impelled to confide in the man. "I was watching the dwarf down in the garden."

The guard nodded. "Best not to inquire too closely," he replied. It was strange the way two different men could say the exact same words and they would come out sounding entirely different each time. If Lord Branagh had said that,

Math would feel as though he were being reproved and put in his place. When Iolo said it, they were suddenly on the footing of friendly conspirators.

"And as long as Isaf Danan calls this place home, the luck should hold," the guard continued enigmatically.

Math, of course, had no least idea who Isaf Danan was, or what he had to do with dwarfs, or good and bad luck. And he was about to ask, when Iolo went on speaking.

"Lord Math . . ." until King Cynwas acknowledged that he had the better claim and made him Lord of Mochdreff, it was not really proper to address Math as "Lord" anything, but Branagh made all the guards and servants use the title anyway ". . . your grandfather has received word that Lord Cernach will be arriving sometime in the early afternoon. He asks you to go back to your rooms and dress yourself in a more suitable fashion."

Math felt his pulse begin to race. He had never met Lord Cernach and was exceedingly eager to do so. The man who owned this remarkable castle, who was so free with his hospitality, must certainly be worth meeting. So without asking any further questions, Math followed Captain Iolo across the allures and down the stairs to the garden below. At the foot of the steps, they parted company, the guard heading toward the gate, and Math toward the rooms that he shared with his grandfather.

Unfortunately, Lord Cernach did not appear to be either pleasant or fascinating, when he first came into the Solar where Math and his grandfather awaited him. Not only was Cernach cold and abrupt, Math thought he could hear the man distinctly grinding his teeth as they exchanged greetings.

But perhaps that was just because the Lord of Cuachag was tired after his journey, his fine clothes and his soft leather boots were splashed with mud, and because he and the lady he brought with him were already quarreling when they came into the room.

The woman, on the other hand, was utterly magnificent. Math was only just beginning to be interested in females at all—except for the tawdry ones that his grandfather told him were only good for a moment's pleasure—but this woman looked like a princess: dark and graceful, and as richly dressed as Cernach was himself, all in purple and claret, with a great deal of fur trimmings, though she had somehow avoided most of the mud.

She, too, was speaking between her teeth and under her breath. "The woman has been dead for an entire year and you did not tell me! She was good to me when I was a girl, and I think you might have considered that I would want to know."

Cernach made a dismissive gesture as he stripped off his doeskin gloves. "Her death slipped my mind. In the name of God, Luned, she was only a servant. And after all, you can choose a girl from the village to take her place."

Luned sniffed loudly—it would be outrageous, Math thought, to characterize anything that came out through that perfect, imperious little nose by an undignified term like "snort." "If I had known she was not here, I would have brought my own woman with me." As she spoke, her bosom heaved and her eyes flashed in a way that Math found very interesting. "Do you really suppose that a girl from the village will know how to look after my gowns, my jewels, and my hair?"

She was gracious, however, to Math and his grandfather, when Lord Cernach introduced her as his cousin and his betrothed.

"I hope you will enjoy your visit to Caer Rigor. It was one of my favorite places to live when I was a girl. Though perhaps you are already a bit too old to enjoy the maze or the secret passages and staircases as much as I did."

Then she said something that was really confusing. "I was sorry to hear of your accident, your brush with death. And your horse going mad and having to be destroyed . . . I hope, at least, he was not a particular pet."

Now it happened that Math had suffered no such accident, and more than that, his horse—which he had been riding practically since he was old enough to ride, and which he considered a babyish sort of mount for someone his age—was a docile little mare, no more in danger of going mad and being destroyed than he was. She was probably eating hay in the stable right now. Math was opening his mouth to say so, when his grandfather silenced him with a ferocious glance.

"It was a recent gift," said Lord Branagh. "I thought such a high-spirited stallion was an inappropriate mount for a young boy, but Teign and his sons insisted, and we did not like to insult them by refusing."

The name meant nothing to Math, but it apparently meant something to Luned, because she drew her delicate dark eyebrows together in a frown. "I had no idea," she said, "that Teign and his sons had come over to your side. They have always been so closely allied with Prince Tryffin."

Lord Branagh smiled grimly. "I begin to wonder, myself, whose side they are really on. The gift may not have been so well meant as I originally thought."

Math was astonished. He had never before heard his grandfather speak anything less than the absolute truth—at least the truth as Lord Branagh saw it, which was not necessarily the same thing—but now the old man had just uttered a whole series of lies in swift succession. It was more than puzzling, it was disconcerting.

An obsequious-looking servant crept into the room just then and spoke in Lord Cernach's ear. As soon as the fellow oozed out again, Cernach turned toward his cousin. "Since the woman you asked for is not here, these fools neglected to prepare your bedchamber. Your things have been taken upstairs to my apartments for the time being. There is a small room there, set aside for my squires and pages, where you can wash, change your clothes, and rest until we meet for dinner. The boys can make do in the antechamber."

"Very well," said Luned, though she did not sound

enthusiastic. In fact, some of the fire was beginning to die from her eyes, and she looked nothing so much as apprehensive.

Math was disappointed, too. In Lord Cernach's apartments, he would have no chance to speak with her privately, or ask any of the questions that he was hoping she could answer.

But several hours later, when they all sat down in Lord Cernach's magnificent dining hall, and prepared to eat from Cernach's golden dishes and drink from Cernach's jeweled goblets, the lady appeared to be in better spirits. She also, unfortunately, seemed to be on better terms with her betrothed, which fact Math found oddly disturbing.

Jealousy might have something to do with it. As one dish after another was presented to him, as he methodically chewed and swallowed, all the time keeping his eyes on the engaged pair, Math was willing to admit to himself that envy *might* be a factor. Though he rather thought that Luned was one of those exciting things that you might like to admire from a distance—like a thunderstorm, or a raging flood—without actually wanting to acquire the thing for yourself. As for Lord Cernach, despite his elegant airs and graces, the arrogant way that he spoke and held himself, he was really just a fussy little middle-aged man, old enough to be her father probably. And when Luned spoke of their approaching nuptials, when she smiled at him, showing all those pretty white teeth, or fastened that burning gaze on his pasty face, her bridegroom-to-be seemed singularly unmoved.

As Math lifted his goblet and sipped the flowery spiced wine, it was clear to him that the man was not worthy of her—if indeed anyone ever could be.

When the meal was finally over, when Cernach's squires and pages were clearing the dishes away, Luned turned to address her cousin once more. "I would like to know more of these plans of yours. If we are to be married, surely there should be no secrets between us."

Math's heart sank. Now they would go off someplace together, to speak in private, and again he would have no opportunity to talk to her himself.

But Cernach surprised him. "I have waited until tonight to explain more clearly, because I can show you these things better than tell them . . . and enlighten young Math and Lord Branagh at the same time."

Rising from his seat and taking a torch from the wall to light their way across the dark courtyards, Cernach led his guests to the walled garden where Math had watched the dwarf woman moving about earlier. The door to the tower was locked, but Cernach wore the key on a chain around his neck. When he removed the chain, he surprised everyone by handing the key to Math.

"This may well prove to be the key to your kingdom," he said with a flourish.

The boy thought that was silly and affected. Even so, he did feel a flutter of excitement as he fitted the heavy iron key in the lock and the stout oak door creaked open, revealing a long flight of stairs on the other side.

As Cernach had the torch, he naturally led the way— though not before taking back the key. They climbed the broad stone staircase and came to a landing and a half-open door. There was a glow of firelight on the other side, and a blast of heat came out to meet them when Cernach pushed the door the rest of the way open.

Inside the room, Math glanced curiously around him, growing more and more interested and puzzled as he did so. This chamber was evidently some kind of goldsmith's or jeweler's workshop. There was a furnace and a cooling vat, scales, tongs, a great many tools that Math did not know how to name, a long workbench, ingots of gold and silver, books, scrolls, parchments, and papers . . . and last, but by far the most significant, the two dwarfs male and female whose recent activities had caused Math so much concern.

Seen up close, there was something disquietingly familiar about the little old woman, with her hooked nose, improbable red hair, and her gown so extravagantly slashed and daggered, patched and beribboned, in shades of scarlet, black, and orange.

"This is Brangwengwen," said Cernach, with a wave of his hand in the female's direction. The dwarf left her seat on a stool by the furnace, spread her full skirts, and made a bobbing curtsy.

Math stopped turning in place, stopped trying to see everything at once, and stared at Cernach instead. *"Brangwengwen?* Not the same Brangwengwen who waited for so many years on the—"

The boy stopped just in time. His grandfather always referred to the Princess Diaspad as *"the sorceress harlot"* and to the odd collection of servants she had gathered around her as *"those malignant abortions of nature."* But whatever aversion Math might feel toward the dwarf herself, he knew what was good manners and what was not, and he did not think the old woman would like to hear her former mistress described in such terms as that.

"It is the same," Cernach replied with a chilly smile as he put the torch in a ring by the door. "There is only one Brangwengwen, and she is a woman of vast occult knowledge."

"So I have heard," said Luned, so low that only Math could hear what she said. When he turned to look at her, he could see that her eyes were sparkling with contempt.

So it was not just Lord Branagh's grudge against the Princess Diaspad, Math told himself. There was something really sinister about the dwarf. And it was something more than the woman's diminutive stature and the hump on her back, because Math did *not* think that Luned was the kind of person who worried about that kind of bad luck.

"And this is Brangwengwen's godson and fosterling, Bagdamagus, who is a skilled goldsmith," Cernach continued.

As the little man rose from his seat and made a deep, graceful bow, Math was surprised to discover that he rather liked the looks of him. The dwarf had a pleasant face, honest and cheerful, and he was very neat as to his immaculately trimmed short beard and his leather garments. And after all, Math reminded himself, the fellow could not really help it, being born deformed and unlucky. At least he practiced a respectable trade and did not consort with harlots and evil sorceresses, as his notorious little god-mother did.

The boy was suddenly disposed to look on the goldsmith favorably. It was one of his worst failings, Math's grandfather always told him, this tendency to form attachments or aversions practically on sight, although Math thought it was better than being like Lord Branagh, who bestowed his affections so very sparingly.

"But since you already have a . . . witch . . . at your disposal," said Luned, with another audible sniff, "I wonder why you have been at such pains to bring me here as well."

For the first time, Lord Cernach showed some visible emotion, aside from contempt or irritation. He was actually quivering with excitement as he took Luned by the hand and pulled her over toward the dwarf's workbench. Following after them, Math saw that what he had originally taken for a crude clay boiling pot was in fact a model for something considerably more elaborate, presumably to be later cast in metal.

"I spoke to you of dreams and visions," said Cernach, in a low, thrilling voice. "How a woman came to me as I slept, a lady simply clad in scarlet linen, yet she wore such jewels as the queens and princesses of Ynys Celydonn wore in days long past. At her bidding, I seemed to rise from my bed and I followed her out of the city and into the countryside. She took me into a barrow, into the tomb of an ancient king beneath the earth, and there many secrets were revealed to me, many mysteries unlocked . . . it seemed to me that we spoke of many deep things."

"Yes, yes," said Luned impatiently. "So you told me. But when am I to learn the real matter of these . . . ancient secrets."

"Much of what she told me has faded from my memory. Yet I do recall that she took me into a cavelike chamber within the tomb, and I saw there the legendary magical treasures, the Twelve Hallows of Ynys Celydonn," Cernach continued. "The Sword of Cleddyf Difwlch, which once drawn could never be sheathed again until it had tasted blood. The Golden Comb and Silver-handled Scissors of Nerth Digon, which would not groom the beard of a coward. The Spear of Madog that was so fiery . . . but I needn't repeat them all to you, for you know their number and attributes as well as I do. But of the Thirteenth Hallow—of which the bards speak only in guarded whispers—she told me more than any of the rest. How it was destroyed but is destined to be remade, what its powers were, what its cost, how it was far more powerful and precious than any of the other treasures."

"And this treasure, I suppose," said Luned slowly, "is the golden cauldron you mentioned when we were in Anoeth. The Cauldron of Cerridwen, you named it then."

"Yes," he replied raptly. "The Cauldron of Cerridwen. To be cast in twelve different sections, then fastened together by silver rivets. What you see here on the bench is only an idea of how it will finally be made. No doubt the design strikes you as primitive."

Luned bent down to examine it more closely. "The design is certainly very ancient. I have seen something like it only once before. That was in the cottage of a village witch . . . the sister of the serving woman we were discussing earlier. She used it to brew up her simples and potions, and she told me that she found the cauldron buried in the earth—I suppose she must have been out robbing graves at the time, but being a young girl, I did not inquire too closely."

She straightened up and faced Cernach across the work-bench. "You told me the cauldron would be a thing of surpassing beauty, with twelve—or is it to be thirteen?—rare gemstones set into the gold."

Cernach nodded. "Twelve gemstones, chosen for their symbolism as well as their beauty. And other potent symbols worked into the design, because it is not to be like an ordinary cooking pot, but rather more in the nature of a chalice or—"

"Or a vessel to counter the powers of the sidhe-stone cup that Prince Tryffin is carrying on progress with him from one part of Mochdreff to another," Luned finished for him with a challenging glance, as she moved around the bench to view the cauldron from the opposite side.

"Yes," said Cernach. "To counter the devastating powers of the sidhe-stone vessel, should Prince Tryffin and Mahaffy Guillyn attempt to turn those powers against us, once Math raises his banner, and I openly declare my support."

At this, Math was startled and could not help blurting out: "*Does* the cup that Prince Tryffin brought out of the past have devastating powers? Everyone says—"

"You must not believe everything that you hear," said Cernach, with a stern look. "That vessel is very dangerous indeed, if Prince Tryffin should choose to make it so. What can heal can also kill, what can mend may also harm. Properly . . . or perhaps I should say *improperly* used, the cup could stop an army in its tracks, and strip the very flesh off of the soldiers' bones."

Luned's eyes were beginning to smolder again. "And we are to believe that Prince Tryffin would turn these destructive powers on us all, without provocation?"

"Certainly not," said Cernach. "That is . . . if you, who have known him so well, say otherwise, then I am willing to amend my own thinking. Yet we may still push him to that point of desperation in the coming conflict of arms."

Math swallowed hard. "Nobody told me there was going to be a conflict of—nobody said anything to me about making war against Prince Tryffin," he said, with a reproachful glance in his grandfather's direction.

"It is Prince Tryffin who makes war against you. With subtlety and with guile, rather than with any honest weapon," Lord Branagh replied sharply. "Were you willing to wait forever to claim what is yours?"

"It is not our intention to strike the first blow," Cernach inserted smoothly. "Only to make it very clear that you refuse to be denied your rights any longer. Then it will be for the Governor to respond as he sees fit. Naturally, we must prepare ourselves, arm ourselves in every way possible, in case Prince Tryffin sends his troops to arrest you."

This sounded rather better. Mostly because Math didn't really believe that Tryffin would attack him. Everyone knew that Prince Tryffin preferred negotiation and discussion to force of arms. The Gwyngellach, Math had always been told, would talk you to death if you gave them half a chance.

"These pictures and symbols I see worked into the clay appear to be incomplete," said Luned, beginning to circle the cauldron again. "By my count, seven of the sections are blank, and the others have an awkward and unfinished look to them."

"Naturally," said Cernach. "As I said before, much of what my ancient princess told me has faded from my memory. That is why I am relying on you to assist Brangwengwen in completing the design. I know it is not the work of a day or even a few weeks. You will need to examine many scrolls and magical texts, recall to mind all that you know of history, legend, and song, gleaning a bit of information here . . . a scrap there. And then it will be necessary for the two of you to discuss what you have learned, in order to place the correct interpretation."

"It will require all of these things," said Luned, turning toward the door. "And even then, I am not certain that we can accomplish it."

As the men followed her through the door and out to the narrow landing, Math remembered to stop and take down the torch, to light their way down the broad staircase. For this, he was amply rewarded by a smile from Luned. It reassured him, too. He did not think that anything bad would be allowed to happen if Luned was a part of this conspiracy.

But in the courtyard outside, Cernach drew his cousin away from the others.

"Though you attempt to conceal it, I can see that what I have proposed troubles you," he said, so low that Math could barely hear him. "If you will come with me, I will show you something that should help you to understand what you see only dimly now."

Luned nodded, and Math saw that she *was* looking pale and distraught . . . though perhaps that was only the effect of the moonlight. She allowed Cernach to take her by the hand and draw her across the yard, away from that part of the castle where Math and his grandfather had their rooms.

Math made to follow them, but Lord Branagh called out to detain him. "What passes between them is no business of ours, boy. They are united by blood and soon will be even more to each other. Also, it is time that you were in bed."

Reluctantly, Math followed his grandfather across the yard. So now it was "boy" and not "Lord Math."

And how—he asked himself—was he ever going to stand up to Prince Tryffin and assert his rights, if he could not even convince his own grandfather that he was no longer a child?

The boy rode down into the Valley of Lamentation. He was seven days crossing the plain. On the seventh day, he came to a mean dwelling. He entered the hovel with great misgivings and sat down by a fire that was burning on the hearth.

There were some large bones lying about on the floor, and a great black pot was cooking on the fire. When the cauldron began to boil, the lad lifted the lid to see what was inside. Then a great fear came over him, for the pot was filled with the blood of men.

Just then a woman came into the house. She was very beautiful, but there was something odd about the way that she walked. The boy realized that her hips and her legs and everything below the waist were put on backwards, so that her toes were pointing behind her.

"What is that you are cooking in this pot?" he asked her.

"I am boiling a hero," the woman replied. "His heart, his blood, his brains, and his liver. And when I have cooked it all down so that it is no more than you or I might hold in the palms of our two hands, then I will cool it and keep it in a green glass bottle. And I will take a sip of that brew, whenever I feel that I am in need of courage."

—*From* The Black Book of Tregalen

10.

The Stones of Caer Rigor

Behind the stables and beyond the mews there was a frozen carp pond, shining in the moonlight, and beyond the pond was the shell of a building with two high towers. Most of the structure lay in ruins, the result of a careless ancestor's alchemical experiment gone wrong, but one of the towers had escaped serious damage during that explosion and was still maintained as a luxurious residence. In that tower, Luned had lived for much of her childhood, sometimes with Dame Brangwaine, sometimes with only servants to look after her when the old woman traveled.

It was to a familiar door at the base of the tower that Cernach brought her now, and Luned could not help wondering whether he was planning to appeal to some sentiment of family loyalty by arousing childhood memories.

Certainly this was a portion of the castle steeped in family history. The long spiral staircase leading up to the roof had been the scene of many duels and slaughters over the centuries, and Luned (she blushed to think of it now) had spent hours as a child searching for bloodstains.

And on the lower floors, you were still supposed to be able to detect the reek of that ancient explosion on certain days of the year, when the wind was blowing from a certain quarter. Though Luned was thoroughly convinced this was only the result of vapors rising off a narrow tract of marshland lying between the castle and the sea.

Tonight there was no time for searching out bloodstains or sniffing out explosions. She followed Cernach up several flights of stairs and down a long corridor to an airy suite of rooms. Cernach went into the antechamber first, then extended a hand to assist her in crossing the threshold. "Enter, Luned, and be welcome."

The room was warded; Luned remembered that even before she entered. There was a stone set into the floor just outside that was carved with an ancient pattern, and this created the warding spell that would have prevented her from entering without Cernach's invitation. As she crossed the threshold, her trailing velvet skirts brushed across the symbols cut into the stone, and she felt a brief, warm tingle coming up through her feet.

Once inside the inner chamber, Luned glanced around

her. Though the room had stood empty as long as she could remember, it was now a sleeping room, boasting an enormous bed with crimson hangings. Fine wax candles were burning in all of the sconces, a fire was blazing on the hearth, and on an oak table flanked by two chairs someone had arranged a flagon of wine and two jeweled goblets.

It looked to Luned as if her cousin was planning a seduction. She turned toward Cernach with her eyebrows raised. "In God's name, why did you bring me here?"

There was also, strangely, a fresh scent of mortar, and the stones in the walls were all jangling with . . . something, some sense of upheaval or violation. But Luned's attention was all on the bed.

Cernach began to laugh, which was disconcerting because it was something he rarely did. This time it was high-pitched, almost hysterical, and he was laughing so hard that he had to sit down on one of the chairs by the table. "Ah, sweet lady, I have no designs on your fair white body," he wheezed.

She continued to stare at him disapprovingly, finding the racket he was making extremely distasteful. "Sometimes, Cousin, I think you are not quite right in your mind."

He laughed for so long that she began to feel impatient. She was just turning to leave the room when, with a final gasp and a tremor that shook his whole body, Cernach contrived to master himself, and urged her to stay.

"I am not mad. Call me, instead, a man inspired by his miraculous visions," he said, rising from his seat and picking up the flagon of wine. "Let me pour for you, Luned. Talking is thirsty work."

With a shrug, Luned accepted the goblet he offered her, wrapping her fingers around the stem. She hardly thought he would be foolish enough to drug or to poison her, but she gave the wine a surreptitious sniff anyway.

"Perhaps you would like a piece of unicorn's horn to dip in the cup," Cernach suggested dryly.

"Perhaps I would like you to begin to answer some of my

questions," she replied. With a sweep of her skirts, she sat down in one of the chairs. "When we were in Anoeth, you promised me many things. And chief among them, that you would one day be a ruling power in this land and that I would share that power with you. Just how do you intend to achieve these things by helping young Math to claim his inheritance?"

Cernach sat down in the other chair, facing her across the table. "When Math is the Lord of Mochdreff, I will be his closest, his only real, advisor. The boy is malleable, he can be easily molded and influenced. In time, he will be nothing more than a figurehead and I will be the real power in Mochdreff."

Luned took a sip of wine. "You . . . and not Lord Branagh?" she asked, frowning at him over the rim of the jeweled goblet.

"Lord Branagh is an old man," Cernach replied coolly. "He will not live much longer. In fact, I believe I can guarantee that, once he has served his purpose. Do I shock you?" he asked, as her frown deepened. "But the man is a palpable villain. He is the one behind the attack on Mahaffy Guillyn's life. I don't doubt that he had something to do with the tragedy that overcame Craddoc and his entire clan, shortly after Lord Morcant died. And I shudder to think what he has in store for young Peredur. We can't have so cruel and ruthless a man influencing our new young Lord."

Luned could not help smiling at the irony. Then she grew serious again. "I implore you, Cousin, to be more open with me. Can you really be so ignorant as you pretend? Or do you imagine that I am? I have seen and handled the sidhe-stone cup in Prince Tryffin's possession, and there can be no doubt that the power it holds is only healing and protective. Even before the curse was lifted and the chalice reconsecrated, the cup could not do what you say—stop an army, or strip the flesh from men's bones."

Cernach shrugged. "Then it appears I was misinformed. Thank you, Cousin, for enlightening me."

There was a long pause, during which Luned continued to eye him narrowly. "This cauldron of yours is a pagan thing; I suppose you know this?" she said at last.

He poured himself a cup of wine. "And is that what troubles you?"

"No . . . at least not entirely," she answered, shaking her head. "I consider myself to be reasonably devout, but I have spent enough of my time delving into ancient mysteries to understand that our pagan ancestors were not necessarily wicked, as the Church would have us believe. And there are even objects, relics of the Old Religion, as well as places and traditions, that seem to contain in them some power for good."

"And so?" said Cernach, yawning behind his hand.

"But there is also something, some force of evil— whether it was in the world before men were, or whether they created it, I don't pretend to know—that has existed in this land for at least a thousand years. When its reputation becomes too ugly, it takes on a new form and a new name, and the men and women who worship that power pretend to be followers of the established Church in order to cloak themselves in respectability. In our own time, they call themselves the Black Canons and they are evil incarnate. Prince Tryffin met with them in Ochren, two hundred years in the past, and they called themselves the Knights of Jerusalem and the Order of St. Pellam. But in pagan times, they put on the trappings of the Old Religion."

Cernach took a sip of wine. "This is all most interesting, though not entirely unknown to me. But you wax eloquent, Cousin, and you are slow in coming to the point."

She moved restlessly in her chair. "In the ancient sacred forest of Achren, Prince Tryffin met with a priest who worshipped a goddess by the name of Cerridwen. Not the Cerridwen of the Old Religion, for whom young women are still named today—not the White Cailleach, the Lady of the Ravens. This was an aspect of that cult of evil, and they worshipped a genderless thing with a voracious appetite for bloodshed and suffering. And so I cannot help wondering: May not the vessel that appeared in your dreams be an object associated with that religion, with *that* Cerridwen?"

"But why should the idea even occur to you?" asked Cernach. "Why should this object of such exceeding beauty call to your mind a religion associated with dust and bone and blood?"

"The vessel of destruction you described to young Math and his grandfather," said Luned. "That is what put the idea into my mind. Can you tell me, in truth, that is not the cauldron you intend to create?"

"I am willing to swear that on my life," her kinsman replied, with such a straightforward glance that she could not doubt him. "But let us suppose just for an instant that I am lying to you, and that the powers of the cauldron are just what you fear. Do you think it would be necessary to make use of them . . . or that the threat alone will be sufficient to gain us all that we desire?"

Luned considered for a moment, one daintily shod foot tapping the floor. "You may be right. Prince Tryffin hates wasting lives, even the lives of the common folk, and if you could make him understand the cauldron's destructive potential, the incredible carnage that would result, he may be willing to accept any conditions we might choose to impose."

"Why, then," said Cernach, "you can easily see, there is nothing here that need trouble your conscience."

She took another sip of the wine, made an impatient gesture. "You said that you wanted to show me something. Something that would ease my mind. I suppose it must be of great value, since you keep it here in one of these warded rooms."

Luned did not understand what she had said to amuse him. "Have you not guessed, Cousin?" he said with a smirk. "The warding stone in the corridor outside . . . By my orders, the dwarfs chipped away all the mortar surrounding it, lifted the stone, replaced it with the pattern reversed, and then mortared it back into place. I had the wards at all the windows reversed in much the same fashion. And I blush to disclose that when I asked you in, there was a certain amount of deception involved, for you might have entered easily without an invitation. For you to cross back over that threshold is another matter, however." His smile grew broader and he lowered his voice for effect. "*You* are the valuable thing that I will keep in these rooms, Luned. You alone."

She gave a tiny gasp as she realized how he had tricked her, but then she struggled to regain her composure. She was angry, but it would not do to let him know how angry until after he had answered all her questions. "But why, Cernach? Why have you done this? Are we not allies, are we not soon to be married?"

Cernach shrugged. "Merely as a precaution to assure that we *remain* allies. In case you should be tempted to change your mind, or to betray to Math or his grandfather anything I have said to you in confidence. This way, you will be constantly reminded that your own best interest depends on me. As the master of Caer Rigor, I am the only one who can free you."

Luned sat fuming in her chair. "I could kill you for this insult. Do you think I could not?" she inquired in awful tones. "I could stop your heart, make the blood boil in your veins, strike you dead by uttering a single word—"

"But you will not," said Cernach with another smirk. "Because if you do, you will remain in these rooms for a long, long time. The servants have been ordered not to enter this building at all; they were told you require privacy for your meditations, and that any who disturb those meditations will suffer the harshest discipline. No one will realize that you are a prisoner. Probably you would die of hunger and thirst before anyone came looking for either of us."

Luned ground her teeth. "I could make you suffer such torments, you would scream for mercy. I could twist your very vitals until you *begged* to be allowed to release me from this room."

"And yet, I would have to be on the other side of the door to extend that invitation," he replied. "Once out and safe, secure in the knowledge that the warding stone would repel your spells, I would be likely to forget all my promises. And you would still be trapped."

He picked up the flagon and poured himself another cup of wine. "You had better make up your mind to it, Luned. You are going to remain here and do whatever I ask of you, until such time as I am ready to let you go."

In the frustrating days that followed, Luned had ample time to explore the boundaries of her prison. It consisted of three connected rooms and a private stair leading up to a fourth chamber at the top of the tower. All of these rooms had windows, but in the lower chambers they were filled with leaded glass, and while the upper windows were tall and arched and open to the breezes, they were located so high above the ground that it would be difficult to communicate with anyone below.

That was supposing, of course, that anyone came even so close as the carp pond, anyone other than the two dwarfs, Cernach himself, and the mute serving woman that Cernach sent up to wait on her.

"You have arranged it all most cleverly," Luned admitted grudgingly, when Cernach came to visit. "Here am I, surrounded by people I have known all life, yet I can't speak to any of them. No one suspects that I am held prisoner here in my childhood home."

Cernach bowed, accepting that as a compliment, which she supposed it was. She could admire his low cunning, even while she deplored his morals. From what anyone could see through the windows, she moved freely from room to room, there were certainly no visible locks or bars confining her, and the sluttish serving wench—who could not hear or speak, but was insolently expressive with her kohl-rimmed eyes—could be seen entering or leaving the tower two or three times a day.

Luned thought about using the woman to carry a written message: to one of the guards perhaps, or her uncle Isaf, but she could hardly trust the woman to deliver her message where it was meant to go. The creature's name was Gleis, and Luned remembered her well; she was one of Cernach's discarded playthings and had always been devoted to him.

For a time, Luned also contemplated scratching a message on some heavy object, a plate or a cup for instance, then tossing it out through one of the upper windows. Then she remembered that most of the castle folk were illiterate, and that being so, they were likely to carry the message to Cernach himself for translation.

It was all very frustrating. Angrily pacing the floor, moving with a restless energy from one room to the next, Luned scolded herself for the reckless resolution which had finally brought her to this miserable pass.

She had not been thinking clearly at the time she first conceived it; she could see that plainly now. Wounded, angry, insulted . . . she had certainly been all of those. *"I will spend the rest of my life regretting that moment of criminal weakness,"* Meligraunce had said. But Luned had believed that when he spoke of weakness, the Captain was really thinking of her: a woman so spoiled and pampered she had never known pain or fear or want.

Trembling with shame and indignation, she had spent a sleepless night pacing the floor in her lodgings at Trewynyn, just as she paced in her prison now. At the time, it had struck her as particularly shameful her very reasons for being in Trewynyn. If Meligraunce knew that she lacked the courage to face Cernach's determined wooing, if he knew that she had simply turned and fled . . .

But that was when Luned began to plan. She would return to Anoeth, but not to confront Cernach. What had seemed in Anoeth to be little more than the ramblings of a madman began to appear as possibly significant, the seeds of some plot with far-reaching implications. So, she would go to Cernach and pretend to be intrigued by his promises. Then she would insinuate herself into his confidence, learn exactly what he was plotting, and as soon as she knew . . . find some way to thwart him.

It had seemed such a brilliant scheme at the time. She would prove her courage, prove her determination, and Meligraunce *must* be so favorably impressed, he would understand that she was the woman he was destined to marry.

Unfortunately, it began to look now as though she had accomplished just the opposite. Eventually, Meligraunce would hear that she was here with Cernach, and he would naturally believe that she had gone over to Prince Tryffin's enemies out of mere spite, that she had joined Cernach and Lord Branagh in their treasonous plot, only to assuage her wounded feelings.

I am well served for my pride and my folly, she scolded herself as she paced the floor. *But—God in Heaven!—help me to find a way to see that others may not suffer as well.*

Every day or two, the dwarfs came up to see Luned— sometimes Brangwengwen only, though often Bagdamagus came along just to carry papers and parchments, books and scrolls across the warded threshold. Sitting on a little stool that she carried up the stairs with her, Brangwengwen would remain outside the door while Luned drew up a chair just inside. Then, each with a great musty book lying open in her lap, they would discuss what they had read, and what it all meant.

The books and scrolls in question included a number of ancient texts belonging to Luned's great-grandmother, seven books of the blackest magic imaginable—relics of Dame Brangwaine's wicked youth and even more appalling middle age—long since abandoned. She had left them behind at Caer Rigor, instead of destroying them, because the books were all magically sealed . . . though Luned, unfortunately, as Dame Brangwaine's apprentice, knew how to open them all.

They were fierce, horrible books written by reckless women and men, often in their own blood. Just reading a few of the spells they contained made a cold grue come over her, and after she was done reading them, Luned always felt dirty and weary and degraded.

"Take the fat of an Unbaptized Infant," one spell began. And another: *"For the Boiling of the Heart of a Hero."* And besides the spells, there was much dark lore which seemed to point to the origins and the uses of a vessel much like the golden cauldron.

". . . the hag had a great boiling pot, which stood on four feet like a beast, and when she put a dead man in, a live one came out, though now he was a creature entirely devoted to her will." This was written in a book bound in crimson leather and edged with gold. And a book inscribed on a fine-grained vellum—which Luned feared was human skin—recounted the tale of a witch who had prolonged her youth and beauty by distilling and drinking the souls of young boys.

These weighty volumes she was at great pains to keep out of the dwarf's hands. Luned lied to Brangwengwen, saying that she had not yet discovered the names and the spells to unseal those books, and she only examined them by the light of a single candle when she was alone in her rooms at night.

There were other books, however, that passed freely between them, volumes bound in velvet or leather with great iron bands, which had belonged to the Princess Diaspad and now belonged to the dwarf. These books were terrible enough in their way, but they were the work of lesser magicians, and could only hint darkly at things that Dame Brangwaine's books revealed more clearly.

Luned's plan, in the absence of anything better, was to hamper the dwarf as much as possible by offering the worst sort of council. Sometimes Brangwengwen would catch her out, and then Luned would be forced to admit her mistake, excusing herself by saying that she was preoccupied, or that it had been a slip of her tongue, sometimes even by pretending ignorance. All this was humiliating, for Luned hated to look a fool, but she knew that she deserved whatever pain or indignity this masquerade was likely to cost her.

"We should have lodestone," Luned would say, "which is very powerful, besides being sacred to the ancient god of war and therefore harmonious with our purpose."

The dwarf woman would pinch up her face disapprovingly. "But lodestone is a foul, ugly, base sort of stone, and what is more, antithetical to rubies. And we have already determined there must be rubies in the eyes of the sacred swine. Lord Cernach said that he dreamed of rubies."

Luned would pretend to consider. "Well, perhaps you are right. I was thinking we might wish to devise a kind of dynamic opposition. The tension between those stones—"

Or when they were discussing the decorations, she might suggest a scene out of popular legend. "Madog with his spear, and the bodies of his enemies on the ground in a circle around him—the effect should be terrifying."

"I don't understand your thinking," Brangwengwen would say with a lowering glance. "Madog is just another name for Mabon, a hero of the Gwyngellach . . . and perhaps a distant ancestor of Prince Tryffin. We don't want *him*."

And so it would continue for an hour or so, until Brangwengwen grew weary and gave up the discussion, picked up her little stool, and went waddling off.

Unfortunately, in order to keep up the pretense of cooperation, Luned was forced to share some part of her knowledge, along with the bits of misinformation that she was offering the dwarf. And she sometimes wondered if Brangwengwen was growing suspicious. In which case, she might be learning quite as much from Luned's evasions as from anything Luned actually told her.

One day, about three weeks after she first arrived at Caer

Rigor, Luned made a mistake and spoke without thinking, when the old woman let slip the news that young Math would be asked to take part in the final rituals.

"But Math was born of the line of the Lords of Mochdreff. That line is not so ancient as Mahaffy's or bound to the soil in the same way, but even so . . . don't you realize what might happen if Morcant's heir were to take an active part in—in setting up the one vessel in opposition to the other?"

"I can guess," said Brangwengwen, with a sharp, arrested look on her face. "Oh yes, I can guess quite easily." That she remained so calm, considering the subject under discussion, made Luned's blood run cold.

"But . . . is this something we really want?" Luned persisted. "Will the boy benefit by being handed the lordship of a dying wasteland, a land cursed and then cursed again?"

Brangwengwen merely shrugged. "As his ancestors were before him," she said. "What greater honor could the boy aspire to?"

Luned sat staring down at her hands, tangling her fingers together. Math had impressed her favorably; so had the little goldsmith. It was hard to believe that either one was as ruthless as the other conspirators. Yet so often had she been mistaken, Luned was beginning to doubt her own judgment.

She gave a deep inward sigh. As it was, she had probably said too much already, asked too many questions. Too late (as usual) she was beginning to wish that she had held her tongue. From now on, she must try even harder to keep her thoughts and her reactions to herself.

But one morning, in the first week of March, Luned had an unexpected visitor. As she turned away from her vantage point at one of the arched upper windows, she realized, with a start, that there was a little old man watching her from the other side of the room.

"Uncle . . . what are you doing here?" she asked, with her hand on her heart. "What a turn you gave me."

Isaf Danan laughed softly as he crossed the floor to give her a friendly kiss on the cheek. "Your nerves are not what they once were, Luned. And you never would have admitted that anything frightened you, when you were a little girl."

Luned smiled a twisted smile, felt unexpected tears filling her eyes. It was so good to see a friendly face—and more than that, a face that was not disfigured by envy, greed, and a lust for power. "Perhaps some of my pride is deteriorating along with my nerves," she whispered.

Then her heart sank, when she remembered that he was a warlock of sorts, and realized what it had cost him to visit her here. "Uncle, you should never have crossed the threshold in the room below, because now you are a prisoner, too."

The old man laughed again. "Do not trouble yourself on my account. I was master of Caer Rigor for half a century, and I come and go here exactly as I please."

As the full meaning of his words sank in, she felt a sudden stab of hope. "Then help me to escape, if you can. Invite me to cross that threshold, and set me free."

Uncle Isaf smiled sadly. "Three years ago, when I was Cernach's steward, I might have helped you. But now it is all very different, and what Cernach has taken from me I can't regain. It is true that the castle knows me, every stone in the place vibrates with my name, and there is not a warding spell at Caer Rigor that can hold me, but any more than that . . ."

He shrugged, turned away from her, and began to hobble around the room, peering through one arched window and then another. "It is a pretty aviary he keeps you in. A gilded cage for a very fine bird."

She swallowed hard. "Uncle Isaf, do you know what Cernach is planning to do here?"

Luned knew that some people, Cernach especially, were inclined to believe that Isaf Danan had grown simple in his old age. They were therefore accustomed to speak freely in his presence, as though he were a small child or an idiot. She also suspected that the old man had other ways to learn things, ways that he did not openly discuss.

Now he nodded his head. "Young Cernach was always the one for great ambitions. So were you, my dear. Has that really changed?"

"Yes," she said. As there was never any telling how much the old man knew, she had decided to be honest with him. "Or at least the substance of my ambitions has changed. I have fallen in love with a man with remarkable qualities and I . . . I aspire to be worthy of him. That is a greater ambition than you can know."

But this was not the time to discuss her hopes or her heartaches. "Uncle," she said, bending her head close to his, speaking low and urgently, "you must do something for me. As you are a good man and an honorable one, you must send a message to Prince Tryffin, or to Captain Meligraunce at Caer Ysgithr. Tell them of Cernach's conspiracy. And in the meantime, we must . . . we *must* do all in our power to hinder him."

Her great-uncle smiled sweetly. "Help is coming, Luned. Do not fear." And he beamed at her so seraphically that she really wanted to believe what he said.

Yet she knew him better than to accept anything he told her, without making certain first that she understood him completely. "Are you trying to tell me, Uncle Isaf, that a message has already been sent?"

He did not answer her question, only repeated the same words as before. "Help is coming."

And that was far more frustrating than it was reassuring. Unlike Cernach, she knew that Isaf was neither mad nor simple. But she also knew that the old man sometimes became confused, and that his sense of the passage of time had never been good. He would disappear for weeks and weeks and then act surprised that anyone had missed him. Or he would speak of events that were fresh in everyone else's memory, not as though he had exactly forgotten them, but as though they had happened decades before.

So when he told her that help was coming, that could mean almost anything. It could mean that help would arrive tomorrow . . . or years and years in the future.

I am as ancient as the sphere of the moon
And the stars in the firmament.

I know the names of the grains of sand on the beach
And the language of the four winds.

I was originally made of earth and stone
Water, metal, and flame.

I have been in many shapes
For I am endlessly malleable.

I have been a string on a harp and a note of music.
I have been a tear, a prayer, and a curse.

I have been fish and flesh, bird and serpent.
It is a question for bards and for scholars
how I was created.
—A poem written on the margins of a manuscript
found at Caer Lludd, in Rhianedd

11.

Bones and Eggshells

The mountain cat that was Gwenlliant gathered herself
for a final leap over a fall of rocks, and at last reached the
top of the path leading up out of the chasm. As she crossed
the border and felt the faint sensation that invariably
signaled a slippage in time, it was to arrive amidst a flurry
of snowflakes, in a flat, unfamiliar winter landscape.

The level country that stretched before her now was

lightly wooded; the trees were pines, powdered with ice, and the occasional skeletal leafless oak. Her quarry was nowhere to be seen—nor was any other creature that could conceivably be Maelinn, except for a flock of birds, flying high and dark against the grey winter sky.

But Gwenlliant had expected this. Maelinn had probably arrived days ahead of her . . . even weeks or months. It was going to be difficult to find her. The trail had gone completely cold. As much as the cat wrinkled her nose and expanded her nostrils, she could not catch even a whiff of her enemy's magic. Probably Maelinn had traveled a considerable distance before changing shape again.

A jingling of harness, a murmur of conversation, warned the cat that a party of horsemen was somewhere near. Crouching low so as not to be seen, she watched them approach downwind: ten or twelve riders, boys and young men, on a narrow road winding through the trees. Even from a distance she could see they were dressed for a long journey, in high boots, woolen scarves, warm cloaks, and tunics of sheepskin, leather, or fur.

Changing to a white wolf, the better to disappear against the ice and snow, Gwenlliant followed after them, loping along at an easy pace, making use of what cover the trees provided, and keeping to the east as much as she could, because the wind was blowing that way and she did not want the horses to scent her. The wolf followed the riders as closely as she dared, hoping to pick up some snatches of conversation, to learn who these men and boys were, where they were headed . . . and most of all, the when and where of this new country.

They were a noisy, cheerful lot, especially the slight young man with the curly hair who appeared to be their leader. He rode at the head of the party, continually scanning the country on both sides of the road. More than once, the wolf stopped and crouched low to the ground, certain that he must have spotted her, but then continued on when he gave no reaction.

Surely, if he had known there was a wolf keeping pace with them, apparently stalking them, he would have warned his companions. He would often shout something back to the others, but it was always some joke or comment on the conversation, which the other youths seemed to appreciate.

By the time they stopped by the side of the road, to make a fire and eat a meal out of their saddlebags, Gwenlliant knew some of their names and had a fair idea of their personalities. The leader was Rhufawn. He had a goatskin bag filled with spiced wine that he passed around to the others. A tow-headed boy who rode on a shaggy pony and appeared to be considerably younger than any of the others had a number of nicknames—mostly in reference to his size—but his real name appeared to be Caílte. Tegid and Cet were twins, dark and intense, and Findabhair turned out to be a girl, dressed as a youth for traveling.

While the others continued to eat and talk, Rhufawn stood up, stretched, and left the camp, calling something back over his shoulder that Gwenlliant did not catch. Out of curiosity, she went slinking after him, to see where the young man might be going. He plowed through the snow in his rabbitskin boots, went between the pines and over a rise, out of sight of the others. Not until he paused in a clearing, did it finally occur to Gwenlliant that he probably wanted privacy for a very natural reason.

She was turning around to trot back toward the camp, when he spoke out loud. "I can see you there, behind the trees. I am very fond of wolves, myself, but I wish you would come out and speak with me. It is always polite, when meeting new people, to appear in your own true shape."

Gwenlliant hesitated. But she was in trouble, anyway, if Maelinn was anywhere near and had heard what he said. So the wolf finally crept out into the open, and obligingly shifted her shape. Or at least . . . she became a human female, a thin girl with a plain face and mouse-colored hair and as little resemblance to Gwenlliant as possible.

"That is close enough, I suppose," said Rhufawn with a smile.

Gwenlliant felt herself blushing, sitting there in the snow. "How did you know?" she asked.

He laughed, and offered a hand to help her up. "Let us just say that there are wolves, and things that are almost wolves but aren't . . . and that I know better than most people how to tell the difference. You look rather chilly," he added, stripping off his leather gloves. "May I loan you these and my cloak?"

As garments suitable for a warm spring day near Loch bel Dragon were clearly inadequate in this harsher climate, Gwenlliant accepted his offer. The cloak was of green wool lined with with scarlet, and delightfully warm coming off his body. And truth to tell, he did not look as though he really needed it; he was still wearing a number of tunics in various shades of green and gold, and wool leggings above his boots. But the gloves she refused, because he needed them as much as she did, for riding on a day like this.

"Would you like to come back to our camp and share our meal? And you can ride along with me afterward, if you are tired of running on four feet. You needn't worry," he added, with another reassuring smile, "because I have no intention of telling your secret to any of the others."

Strangely enough—because she really knew very little about him—Gwenlliant realized that she trusted him to keep his word, trusted him to take her safely along, wherever he was going. It was hard not to, gazing into that lively, humorous face.

And now that she saw with a woman's eyes instead of a wolf's, she thought he reminded her of someone, with his curly brown hair, hazel eyes, and fair northern complexion, though she was not certain whom. *Maybe one of my Gorwynnach cousins . . . probably all of them. They all have that hair and those eyes.*

Also, she could not even remember the last time she had eaten, and her stomach was beginning to grind uncomfortably. She supposed that a woman in her delicate condition should be eating more regularly, and that was as good a reason as any for accepting his hospitality.

"My thanks," she said. "My name is Etain. And . . . I would like to ride with your company."

Back at the camp, no one acted particularly surprised to see Rhufawn return with a young woman on his arm. It appeared that he was always doing unexpected things, one way and another, and conjuring up a girl in the wilderness was the least of his accomplishments.

"Next time, please, find some lovely damsels for the rest of us," said Cet. And Findabhair, who was sitting beside him, reached over and playfully shoved his face into a snowbank.

After that, they all made room for Gwenlliant on the ground around their campfire, offering her oatcakes, cheese, boiled eggs, and dried apples, and a warm drink of something that tasted of bitter herbs. Now that she could see with her own eyes again, their cloaks, tunics, and scarves made a brave display against the drifts of snow: gold, green, red, blue, purple, and tawny. Their horses were glossy and of good quality, and everyone looked prosperous and well bred rather than grand or imposing.

They were, she soon learned, all of them students of the wizard Atlendor at his school in Findias. That is, Tegid amended, some were returning students and the rest were new students they were escorting to Findias from Murias in Cuan. So Gwenlliant knew that her pursuit of Maelinn had brought her back into Draighen—but this time more to the north, between Cuan and Findias, and in the shadow of a time closer to her own, though still almost a century in her past.

Rhufawn fab Rheged was the full name of her newfound friend, which meant that he was not Gorwynnach as she had first supposed, though he answered her query by saying that his mother was Gorwynnach, more or less, and one or two of his paternal ancestors . . . "And my stepfather, which, of course, doesn't count." He was the senior pupil among the returning students, and apparently a favorite of the wizard.

"Though he does seem to deserve it," said a boy named Cei, with a deep sigh. He looked nothing at all like Gwenlliant's own Cei, the boy who had been her page and was now Tryffin's squire. This one was short and solidly built, with lank brown hair and light grey eyes, and had just enough of a southern lilt to probably come from Walgan. "Rhufawn was apparently born knowing everything, which is why we all defer to him."

Findabhair laughed, throwing back her head. She was tall and slender, with a roses-and-cream complexion, and hair that was only a shade or two darker than Gwenlliant's customary winter-gold. Besides that, she was strikingly, even startlingly, beautiful and seemed to know it, but was pleasant in spite of that. "Rhufawn was raised in the woods with the outlaws, the pagans, and the wild animals. It is no wonder that he has picked up some odd bits of knowledge along the way."

So, mounted on the back of a chestnut gelding, riding pillion with her arms around Rhufawn's waist, Gwenlliant made the long journey to Findias . . . certain that Maelinn, too, would be inexorably drawn to that seat of power, and toward Atlendor himself. How could she possibly resist an opportunity to meet a whole school of wizards, to say nothing of their mentor, the greatest of the wizard-adepts before Glastyn?

And as they all cantered over the snowy countryside, as Gwenlliant listened to the young men (and the one young woman) discuss their aspirations, their wonderful, terrifying, fascinating studies with the famous wizard, she became more and more interested herself.

On the second day, Rhufawn glanced back over his shoulder and said: "You should ask Atlendor if he will take you on as a pupil, Etain. There aren't many girls at the school, and I am sure that Findabhair would welcome another."

But the other youths laughed good-naturedly at the

suggestion, and Findabhair said, with a shake of her head, "Rhufawn, you don't even know if she *wants* to study wizardry. Or has any talents in that direction."

"Yes, I do," said Rhufawn. "From the questions she asks and the things she says, it is easy to see that she knows a great deal about it already."

"I think that I *would* like to join you all at the school," said Gwenlliant thoughtfully. She was remembering her brief time of study with her cousin Teleri, who was the High King's wizard—and how Teleri had said that she would have a far better chance of learning wizardry after she had first mastered her natural gift for witchcraft. Gwenlliant had more or less accomplished *that* when she learned the shapechanging magic.

It was also amusing to think that she might, if she was lucky enough to be accepted at the school, be receiving instruction from the ancient wizard who had taught Glastyn, who had taught Teleri. *I might even meet Glastyn himself, there at Findias,* Gwenlliant reflected, and wondered if she would recognize him.

Glastyn was not even his real name, it was just something that people called him, and he had been close to a hundred years old when Gwenlliant first met him. If you did not count meeting him the day she was christened, that was, and Gwenlliant did not.

So how, she asked herself silently, could she possibly be expected to recognize that fierce old man who had seen and experienced so much, looking out through the eyes of an untried youth?

Though February had been a wet month, March promised to be a dry one. There was even something alluringly springlike in the air as Meligraunce rode north from Anoeth. The branches of the birches were heavy with catkins, the buds on the maples were beginning to open. A faint blue haze of heather appeared on the hillsides, and there was a green mist on the fields where optimistic farmers had planted their winter wheat. *It is starting to happen,* thought the Captain. *Soon we will know for certain if the curse was lifted and the land truly healed.*

Those random outbreaks of high-spirited celebration which had been occurring ever since midwinter now seemed to have reached epidemic proportions. In practically every village he visited, it seemed that people were either preparing for a fair or a festival, or discussing festivities just past. Most of these celebrations were poor things, the resources of the people being so meager, but . . . a garland of fresh green leaves on a maiden's brow . . . a thornbush decorated with colorful rags and then paraded through village streets . . . a figure made of rushes and set up in the market square for the swineherds and the goosegirls to dance around . . . there was something remarkable, fantastical, even intoxicating about all of these things, in a land where nothing of the sort had appeared during the last millenium.

Sometimes, Meligraunce half-suspected that he brought the infection with him, because it frequently happened that when he entered a village or even a tiny settlement of three or four houses, the children ran out to meet him, chanting rhymes and singing fragments of old songs, about the Black Man and the Green Man, the holly and the ivy, the snails and the tailors, the Lady of the Ravens, poor pussy in the well, waiting for the butcher's little boy to rescue her . . . and other bits of nonsense. What astounded the Captain most was the dawning realization that he had never heard Mochdreffi children *sing,* much less dance in the streets, or beg strangers to take them up into the saddle so they could impress their friends and relations by riding into town on a big piebald horse. Yet they were certainly doing all of these things now.

But in Cuachag, where the signs of spring were unmistakable, it was much quieter. Here where the land was more fertile, the promise of a good year to come more evident, the villagers and the herdsmen more prosperous and comfortable-looking to begin with, there were no celebrations, just people going quietly about their farming, their herding, and their other occupations, with a light step and a bright eye, certainly, but their sense of anticipation seemed to be mixed with a dose of apprehension.

The children here did not recite Camboglannach, or Perfuddi, or Rhianeddi nursery rhymes, though they followed the big, black stranger with their eyes when he rode into a village. They seemed to know something but were not quite sure of it yet—or perhaps they knew more than their neighbors to the south, and that knowledge tempered their hopes with a little fear.

Effron was the name of the village near Caer Rigor, just a stone's throw from the castle gates, located between Cernach's fortress and the marshy country lying to the east. It was a settlement of about fifty cottages and shops, with a church and an inn, almost large enough to be called a town rather than a village.

The guady sign over the door of the single inn was not encouraging, since it depicted a grinning golden skull with jewels of cheap red glass glued over the painted eye sockets. But once inside, Meligraunce saw that the inn was clean and respectable. Besides, there was no place else for him to stay.

When told that the big black foreigner would be visiting Effron for several days, the innkeeper nodded his head, accepted the coin the Captain offered him, and led him upstairs to a long room with several cots. "You may choose whichever bed you like, for you're not likely to have much company this time of year. Of course, if you would prefer one of the private rooms, it will cost you twice as much."

Meligraunce told him that he would not mind sharing, and then followed the man downstairs to stable his horse.

In the days that followed, Meligraunce sometimes walked out on the streets of the village, in order to maintain the pretense that he actually had business there. He would have liked to visit the little lime-washed church, but that hardly seemed an appropriate action for the sort of rascally man he was pretending to be. Besides, there was no telling with Mochdreffi churches and their schisms and heresies, and perhaps he was better outside.

He was able to observe, from a vantage point on the village green, that the only castle folk who visited the church were a shock-headed youth in fine clothes, presumably Math (Meligraunce had not seen the boy in four years, so he could not be certain), a stiff old man, and the guards who escorted them. Which either meant that Lord Cernach had his own chapel inside the castle, or had no relationship with God at all. The Captain, naturally, was prepared to believe the latter, though he did wonder uneasily why Luned never appeared at the church. In Anoeth, she said prayers every night in a little room set aside for that purpose, and she always heard Mass on Sundays.

But most of his time, Meligraunce spent in the public room at the inn, listening to the conversations of the men of Effron who came in occasionally for a tankard or two of barley ale. They were angry and agitated about something; Meligraunce had learned that much by the second day.

Some of the bits and pieces he picked up seemed to be no more than a natural suspicion of Cernach. ". . . foreigners swarming about at Castell Emreis, and his fine lordship in residence *here*, who never cared a straw or a rush for the place before . . ."

Other fragments were enough to make his hair stand on end: ". . . perhaps even dead and her bones already added to his collection, our poor pretty lady . . ." And then the only slightly more reassuring reply: "She's been seen at the windows in the South Tower, you know that. More likely, she's taken ill and no one but that wench, Gleis, to mind her . . ."

It did not take a blackened silver mirror or a litter of two-headed kittens to conclude that Luned *was* in some kind of danger or difficulty, just as Dame Brangwaine had feared all along.

But, God help him, what was Meligraunce to *do* about it? Climb over the high stone walls of the castle some fine night, slink through the shadows to the South Tower, scale another wall, and carry the wounded or ailing Luned off, slung over his back? There was a certain appeal to the image, but Meligraunce preferred to wait and watch a little longer, in case something more practical in the way of a plan should happen to present itself. It was not that he thought he could *not* accomplish such a daring rescue, it was simply that he was not entirely convinced that he could, and a failed attempt might do more harm than good.

It also occurred to him that any chains or prison bars that could contain a witch of Luned's formidable talents might present something of a challenge to a man like himself.

The best thing that he could do, in the absence of any plan, was to stroll out beyond the village and around to the south, to get a glimpse of the tower where Luned was either ailing or imprisoned. This scouting expedition was entirely unsatisfactory. At least from a distance, the walls of the South Tower looked smooth and sheer, and even the lowest windows seemed much too high to be attempted. Nor could he see any way up to the roof except by means of some interior staircase—or unless one should chance to take wing like the ravens, the rooks, and the seagulls that he observed circling the tower and perched on the parapet at the top. It was at times like this that Meligraunce wished for a little of the Lady Gwenlliant's Rhianeddi witchcraft for himself. Would that Luned had a touch of that gift, too, but her ancestors had lost that talent, along with their covenant with the land, a thousand years ago.

He returned to the inn in a bitter mood, glaring up at the grinning death's-head sign as he passed. He sat in the common room sipping his ale and racking his brain for something . . . anything . . . in the way of a reasonable plan.

"It is very good ale," said a creaking voice in his ear. "I've heard that they brew it in eggshells."

Meligraunce glanced up to see a familiar figure in dirty silks and velvets standing next to him: the greybeard from the tavern in Peryf, who had amused Grifflet with his gibberish. He was not speaking gibberish now, but it was still nonsense.

"No doubt," said Meligraunce with a grim smile, "they also serve blackbird pie."

The old man nodded and laughed. "On occasion . . . on occasion." He made a little skipping dance, circling the Captain, then took a seat on the other side of him. "You've been out searching for your sweetheart. I like a man who knows the value of true love, indeed I do—none of these courtly posturings all for show. But you were searching for someone the last time I met you. Let me see if I can remember . . ." He pulled at his long grey beard. "I have it. The little lad with the red curls and the two fathers: You were taking him to his grandsire. Did you ever find him?"

Meligraunce took a sip of ale and cleared his throat. "It happened that we found his father instead. One of them, anyway."

The Captain felt a dim stirring of excitement. The old man was probably addled, but Meligraunce could not accept that these continued meetings were a coincidence. He thought there must be some meaning behind it all, if he could only fathom it. Whenever he was with the old fellow, every dream he had dreamed for the last several months came back into his mind and suddenly seemed to be invested with hidden portents.

"I believe that I saw you at a village fair between Clynnoc and Ymorgan," said the Captain. "Though a festival without any feast seems pointless enough to me."

"Ah well," said the greybeard. "Where there is little to eat, you can always *throw a few more stones into the stewpot, and all the guests will be fed.*"

And that was another fragment of nonsense rhyme out of the south and west. Meligraunce's head was beginning to buzz, but not with the ale. He had the incredible sensation that he was about to experience some revelation.

"You have a rare memory for children's songs, to say nothing of a gift for turning up where you are least expected. Have you ever traveled to Camboglanna? Perhaps you are the one teaching these songs and rhymes to the children of Mochdreff."

As the Captain spoke, his companion was fidgeting about in his chair, playing with his whiskers or just making restless motions with his fingers in the air. Now he leaned forward, as if to communicate some secret. "I can move like the wind sometimes. But I can't take all of the credit, oh no. They feel these things instinctively, the common folk do, but especially the children."

He leaned back, put a finger beside his nose, and nodded wisely. "They live closer to the land, the farmers and the herdsmen, they watch the seasons turn. With the healing of the land, the old knowledge, all the things *your* countrymen have known all along, is beginning to return to them."

The buzzing in the Captain's head stopped, the mist in his mind lifted, and for the first time in a long time, things began to make sense.

It was the curse that had set the Mochdreffi apart, he realized. Now that had been lifted, they were becoming more like other people . . . the Camboglannach, Rhianeddi, Gwyngellach . . . all the men and women of Ynys Celydonn, who were really more alike than they were different, though they liked to pretend that their differences were vast.

And while it was incredible to Meligraunce that this understanding should come to him through the ravings of a mad man, they did say that lunatics and simpletons sometimes had inspirations that were denied to other men.

"Then the rite of atonement, Mahaffy Guillyn's act of contrition for the sins of his ancestors, it *did* heal the land," he said wonderingly. "Even as we sit here, the common Mochdreffi are celebrating the millenium. But the lords in their grand castles are too busy squabbling over precedence and who will rule them, to see what is perfectly obvious . . . not only to the folk who live off the land but the craftsmen in the towns, even the castle servants."

"Mind you," said the old man, "the danger is not past. Those great lords can still spoil it all, with their quarreling, their penchant for bloodshed."

Meligraunce nodded. "The Governor and Mahaffy Guillyn must prevent them from ruining everything. I suppose that is in the songs, too: *the birds that would eat the harvest.*"

He turned suddenly, to stare directly into his companion's eyes. "Before God! The cat in the well . . . what can you tell me about her?" The cat and the Black Man were always linked together in the children's songs.

The old man smiled sadly, shaking his head. "I can't help her, neither can you. Unless, that is, you should happen to be *the butcher's apprentice.*"

"I may be too old for the butcher's little boy." The Captain's hands strayed, instinctively, toward the knives he wore in his belt. "But I am a hired sword, a captain of mercenaries."

"Well, well, that's as may be," the greybeard replied. He moved closer again, and said in a loud whisper: "What you need is a way inside the castle."

Meligraunce frowned. With a sudden sinking sensation he realized that he had spoken far too freely. "And what if I do? There is no way in; any reasonable man can see that. Lord Cernach has nothing to fear from me."

The old man began to giggle quietly. "Ah . . . but Cernach is frightened anyway. He sees enemies lurking everywhere. Being treacherous himself, he cannot trust anyone else. He has asked Captain Iolo to recruit more guards. Do you see the irony? Because there is your chance, my friend . . . being that you are, as you say, a hired sword."

Meligraunce let out a long breath, considering that idea.

But then he shook his head. He simply could not believe that things would arrange themselves so conveniently. "Not likely, I fear. I am a stranger here," he said, "and as you can plainly see, my appearance is against me."

When the Captain came downstairs in the morning, the common room seemed to be full of armed men wearing Cernach's livery. A bad sign, but as he had already been seen coming down the stairs, he would only rouse suspicion by turning right around and climbing back up them. Meligraunce realized that he had no choice but to hope for the best, walk boldly in, take a seat by the fire, and demand his breakfast.

No sooner had he taken a seat on a bench, than one of the men approached him. There was something familiar about the man; after a moment, Meligraunce recognized the man who was always in command of the guards escorting young Math to church. He was also wearing a better quality of armor than the rest, so Meligraunce had no difficulty identifying his counterpart: This would be the Caer Rigor guard captain, the one the greybeard had mentioned.

"I have been told that you are a hired sword," said Captain Iolo.

Meligraunce shrugged, trying to look amiable and harmless, though he realized the difficulty. "I have been, in the past, but times are hard and, as you can see, I was forced to sell my sword in order to eat."

"Another one can be provided, if you are willing to serve Lord Cernach."

It was a long moment before Meligraunce was able to convince himself that—as fantastic as it sounded—he had just been offered a position in the castle guard, had been all but hired on sight. And even though the old man had in some sense prepared him for such an offer, the circumstances struck Meligraunce as highly suspicious. Even somewhat sinister. And yet . . . if Cernach knew he was there, why not send men to overpower him, to carry him inside by force? Why should there be this, or any other, pretense?

"You hesitate," said the Caer Rigor captain. "Perhaps I was misinformed, and you are not for hire after all."

Meligraunce shook his head. Thinking quickly, he had reached the conclusion that this might just as easily be Luned's way of sending him some message, of getting him inside the castle where she could speak to him. The guards would be local men, mostly from Effron, the rest from other villages in the surrounding countryside, and from what he had heard here in the tavern, they felt more loyalty toward Luned than they did toward Cernach.

"My skill if not my bartered sword is certainly for hire," said Meligraunce. "Though I doubt you will find any armor to fit me."

In truth, he hoped they would not. Lord Cernach knew him very well; they had met and spoken together on many separate occasions. However, Meligraunce believed there were certain people—like Dame Maffada, like Cernach himself—who did not actually *see* him when they met. What they saw, instead, was a frightening anomaly, a man who challenged all of their preconceptions about men of his class, by dressing, speaking, and holding himself as though he belonged to theirs.

As he was right now, dirty and battered and gaudy, he would be just as invisible as any other peasant, but in a decent suit of armor, there might be just enough of the old Captain Meligraunce to spark recognition.

Much to his relief, the man from Caer Rigor waved the idea aside. "We will take you as you are. You are a formidable sight, God knows. But what is your name, friend? How are we to call you?"

"My name is Avallach," said Meligraunce, saying the first thing that came into his mind. "Avallach fab Annwn."

. . . and as night came on, the King's eldest son realized that he was lost in the rambling wood. After he had wandered for a great while longer, he came to a clearing where there was a pool of bright water shining in the moonlight, and a hideous old woman sitting on a fallen tree by the water.

"In the name of God," said he. "I am looking for the well in the Forest of the Daughter of the Moon. Can you tell me the way to that place?"

"God knows," said the hag, "nothing would be easier for me than to tell you that."

"Then do so," said the oldest son of Sceolan.

She was the ugliest woman that the prince had ever seen. Her nose was long and red and dripping. Her teeth were yellow and snaggled, and she had two long tusks like a boar. Like a boar's, also, were the bristling hairs on her chin, but at the top of her head she had three hairs only: one red, one white, and one black. More than that, she was bent and wrinkled and crabbed, and her breath was hot and stinking.

"I am the Daughter of the Moon," she replied, "and this is my forest and my well."

The King's son told her why he had come and what he wanted there in the forest. "And if you will not grant what I ask, then the life of Sceolan will be forfeit."

"There is no reason for you to fear that," said the hag. "You may leave this place happy and successful, if you choose. But I must tell you, the water in this pool is not given freely. There is a price you must pay in order to get it."

"Then in the name of God, who knows everything," said the prince, "tell me the price."

*"A kiss on the mouth," said the Daughter of the Moon.
"And your promise to marry me afterward."*
——*From* The Book of Dun Fiorenn

12.

*The Dictates of Duty,
the Promptings of Love*

A great, colorful assembly had gathered at Castell Gauvain in Cormelyn, the largest company that Tryffin and Mahaffy had addressed so far. There seemed to be banners everywhere: in the hall, suspended from the rafters; in the stony corridors; and hanging from the battlements in every courtyard.

The castle was a regular menagerie of heraldic beasts: blue boars, scarlet tygers, silver harpies, black swans. There was also a great assembly of celestial bodies: comets, moons, and stars, worked in gold and silver thread. And, of course, there were the usual swords, flaming spears, disembodied arms, and axes, caltrops, pheons, and galleys, dear to the hearts of the quarrelsome Mochdreffi.

Lord Balin had called together all of his kinsmen, all of his dependents, all of his friends . . . in short, anyone over whom he exercised any degree of influence at all. It promised to be a grand, a momentous, occasion, because many there had already been converted to Mahaffy's cause, and Prince Tryffin had said that the potent influence of their excitement, their enthusiasm, would likely carry the others as well.

Not only Lord Balin, who had called so many forth to meet him out of sheer good will: Lord Gilfaethwy was there, that gruff old man, and Morgan Killian and Nefn Chenoweth, who had been his enemies but were no more, largely because Mahaffy had somehow blundered, last spring, into a kind of solution for resolving their feud.

Young Cadllyn Lochein, Gilfaethwy's squire, a scant year older but considerably wiser, showed promise of turning out far better than expected. He went about the place very quiet and discreet, in Gilfaethwy's blue and tawny. But the best thing of all was that Conn had recovered enough to travel to Cormelyn, and came riding through the gates of Castell Gauvain, bravely decked out in the scarlet cuir bouilli, the day before the feasting and the discourse began.

Of course, there were the others, still to be won over. The Lords of Scoithan, Barra, and Corroc had arrived several days early, bringing along with them their oldest sons. Two chieftains—of clans Brennan and Eifion—arrived with their wives, *all* their children, and also the family matriarchs, two ancient, venerable wise-women in terrifying horned headdresses. Most impressive of all, the great Lord Macsen of Dwrnach and Duleiven, Lord Balin's powerful kinsman, arrived with two dozen retainers, all of them dressed in green and gold. Soon, a banner with his arms, a moon and a thornbush on a green field, was hanging among the lions and swords and comets in the hall, and his badge, the staff with ivy, seemed to be everywhere.

With all these lords and chieftains, their families, servants, and general hangers-on, Castell Gauvain was so full that all the beds and cots and blankets and straw-filled mattresses were not sufficient, and the less important folk were sleeping rolled up in their cloaks on the floor. That nobody seemed to mind the crowding boded well.

At the feasting the first night, Mahaffy thought that he made a good impression. Though many had seen it already—at the assembly in Penafon the previous autumn—the sidhe-stone grail was greeted with awe and delight. As the chalice passed through the hall, glowing softly in young Elffin's hands, not a man, woman, or child remained unmoved.

The second night was even more encouraging. The Lords of Scoithan and Corroc went so far as to pledge their support, and Brennan and Eifion were clearly on the verge—thanks, in part, to the influence of the two matri-archs, who had apparently arrived with their minds made up.

But the next morning, a private interview with Lord Macsen in the garden was so thought-provoking that Mahaffy went immediately looking for Prince Tryffin afterward. He found the Governor in the Solar with Grifflet, sitting on the flagstone floor by the fire, intent on a game of jackstraws.

Mahaffy smiled, a smile tinged with envy.

"I don't wish to intrude, as I can see that you are so pleasantly engaged," he said. "But if you can spare a moment . . . ?"

"I can," said Tryffin, looking up with an entirely unself-conscious grin. "Truth to tell, he was beating me anyway. Small fingers have the advantage." He gave the little boy a pat on the head, rose quickly and lightly to his feet, and dusted off his hands. "What did you want to ask me?"

Mahaffy made a vague gesture in Grifflet's direction. "It's not anything I would care to have repeated elsewhere. Not that I question your son's discretion, but . . ."

"But three-year-olds have a tendency to babble," the Governor finished cheerfully. "Grifflet, my lad, tell one of the guards outside the door to take you to Cei or Elffin."

The little boy gathered up his jackstraws, shoved them into a pocket, and obediently headed for the door. "No doubt you think I spoil him," said Tryffin, as soon as Grifflet was out of the door.

Mahaffy shook his head. "How could I possibly judge you? I don't know anything about fathers and sons. My own father died when I was younger than Grifflet and my mother soon after, and as for my Uncle Cado . . . you know what a cold man he was."

Prince Tryffin took a chair, and indicated that Mahaffy should do so as well. "I have an excellent father myself, and I try to be like him. I wish you could meet him, because he is the best man in the world, for wisdom and for kindness."

But then, seeing the skepticism so clearly written on Mahaffy's face, he laughed and added: "The man that you met in Annwn, the King of the Fairies, was a poor copy, you know. Just as Prince Gruffydd was not so much like me as he first appeared to be."

Mahaffy smiled faintly in return. "I do know that. And as I said, I am in no position to judge. Lord Cado was more nearly related to me than Grifflet is to you, and yet I think there was never so much as an affectionate word or glance between us in all the years I spent with him."

"Then I pity him even more than I pity you," said Tryffin, "for the pleasure he denied himself. You must know it is a grief to me that the Lady Gwenlliant has given me no children as yet, though God knows I can hardly blame her, as young as she is. Grifflet makes the waiting easier, by filling an empty place in my heart.

"But it was not, I think, to discuss my family life that you wanted to speak with me."

"No," said Mahaffy, taking a deep breath. "It was to discuss my own. That is . . . what I want to ask first is: How important is Lord Macsen? How much difference would it make if we won his support?"

A tiny frown creased Tryffin's brow. He leaned forward in his chair. "You haven't quarreled with the man or any of his people, have you?"

Mahaffy shook his head emphatically. "Nothing like that. I have a particular reason for asking, but I would rather not go into that immediately."

So the Governor thought carefully before he spoke. "You know that before we came here we had Peryf and Oeth with us, Ymorgan, Cormelyn . . ." He recited a long, long list, all of them names with which Mahaffy was familiar. "And as for Lord Macsen, besides Dwrnach and Duleiven which he holds in his own name, he is regent for the young lords of Mwrhaeth, Gobrwy, and Rhichdwr. Besides that, his sons have married heiresses in Penllyn, Richta, and Llech Obwry—he is a very canny man—and there is some sort of kinship with Barra, which I think is the reason that Cynddyllig is holding back. He wants to see how Macsen goes first.

"With Macsen lending his support . . . well, it wouldn't be sufficient for us to carry the day," Tryffin concluded, "but we would be close, we would be very close."

"That's what I thought," said Mahaffy. "The reason I ask is because Lord Macsen told me this morning that he would pledge himself at once, if I agreed to marry his youngest daughter."

For several moments, there was no sound in the Solar but the crackling of the fire. "And what have you decided?" Tryffin said at last.

"I was—I was hoping that you would be able to advise me," Mahaffy replied.

The Governor frowned at him. "How can I advise you, when I don't know the lady any more than you do? Except to say that you should ask to make her acquaintance first, to discover whether you actually like her." And when the younger man looked disappointed: "I am not being sentimental, Mahaffy. Though I *am* Gwyngellach, my mind doesn't run on love matches only. I realize that a political marriage may be the best thing in your circumstances. But I tell you this: If you and the girl are disposed to loathe each other on sight, any alliance sealed by your marriage would have a poor chance of lasting long enough to do you much good."

Mahaffy mulled that over, tapping his fist on his chin. "That is sensible, I suppose. But the truth is, I am ready to like her, sight unseen."

"Because of all that her father can offer you?"

A log on the fire fell with a crash, and the flames flared up, making the room a little brighter for a moment.

"I would be lying if I said that wasn't part of it. But it is more than that," said Mahaffy. "We were talking just a few minutes since of the way I was raised. You know, I never felt that I really belonged to any place or to any family. I did have Dame Ceinwen, and, of course, she was an admirable nursemaid, but Lord Cado would decide that he wanted me with him at court for some reason, and off I would go to Caer Ysgithr, where she couldn't follow. Or he would drag me along somewhere else, according to his changing fortunes. Or it would be dame Ceinwen herself who wandered off on her own, playing all three Fates and the twelve Good Fairies all rolled into one, in her own little fairy story."

He gnawed on his thumb. "I knew that what she was doing was important, but I missed her anyway. And when you asked me to be your squire, and took me into your household . . . you know that Garth and Conn were the first real friends that I ever had. The Lady Gwenlliant has been like a charming little sister to me, and you . . . ah, well, I won't say that you have been like a father, because you are rather too young for that," said Mahaffy, not very neatly evading what he knew was a sore subject.

Tryffin folded his arms across his broad chest, shifted position in his chair. "For all I may seem so stricken with years, I am barely older than you are, Mahaffy. I was younger than you are now when the High King first made me Governor of Mochdreff."

Mahaffy decided that it would probably be tactless to express astonishment. He had known this, actually, but he was inclined to regard Prince Tryffin as . . . well, certainly not stricken with years, but immeasurably older and wiser than *he* was.

In any case, the Governor graciously allowed the subject to pass. "I suppose that what you are trying to tell me is that since the rest of us will be leaving Mochdreff some day soon—going back to Camboglanna or Tir Gwyngelli, while you remain here to govern Mochdreff—you think it would be a fine thing to take a wife and start a family in the meantime. And if the lady's father should happen to be in a position to help you to your rightful inheritance, then so much the better."

"Yes," said Mahaffy, with a sigh of relief. "That is it exactly. That may sound ingenuous, I know. But truly, no one knows better than I do the misery that unhappy families can make for themselves. Yet I will try very hard to be a kind and patient husband, and if Lord Macsen's daughter is willing to make a similar effort, I don't see why we shouldn't be reasonably happy together."

There was another long pause, while Tryffin rose and paced in front of the fire, a pause that stretched so long that Mahaffy began to fidget in his chair.

"I suppose you must be aware of the young lady's . . . hardship," the Governor finally said.

"I know that her face was scarred when she was still very small," Mahaffy replied. "And that the scars are evidently bad enough that she always wears a veil at any large gathering. I know, too, she has been here at Castell Gauvain for five days, but has remained closeted with the other women all of that time. Yet if the lady is virtuous, intelligent, and well bred, as I have heard that she is . . . then I don't think that I should let anything else affect my decision. I know that *you* would not, if you were in my place."

"God in Heaven! That seems to be your excuse for everything these days," said Tryffin. "How do you know what I might have done in your place? I married a girl whose very presence in a room makes my heart beat faster, whose beauty is so great that merely thinking about it I sometimes forget to breathe! What makes you think that I could possibly be wise enough, if there were no Gwenlliant, to choose a wife for any better reason than her pretty face?"

"Well, for one thing"—Mahaffy hesitated, and then plunged on ahead—"the Lady Gwenlliant is certainly pretty and she does have a winning way about her that makes people love her almost immediately on making her acquaintance. But she is not, by any standards that I ever heard, a great beauty. She may even be a little pale for some men's taste. That you regard her as irresistibly beautiful is utterly charming."

The Governor actually looked surprised, standing there by the fire. "It never occurred to me that other people might not see her the way that I do. But we at least agree that she is pleasant to look at. Are you certain that you would like to marry a woman of whom . . . perhaps . . . that might not be said?"

Mahaffy felt himself blushing indignantly. "You think because I have this face that makes everyone either love me or hate me on sight, that I am vain and place a higher importance on outward appearances than I should."

"I think," said Tryffin, "that since you are so remarkably good-looking yourself, you must be accustomed to receiving the favors of beautiful women. That your tastes, when it comes to lovemaking, may be more refined than you know. And that it would be a very cruel thing for Lord Macsen's daughter if you found this out *after* you had married her."

The young knight frowned darkly. "I admit I have never made love to a woman with scars on her face, but the truth is, I prefer to sleep with girls who are ordinary and amiable. You are forgetting that I had ample opportunity, when I was still very young, to observe the activities of my beautiful cousin Dahaut. And of the Princess Diaspad. I try not to judge beautiful women unfairly," he added, "but when one of them gets too close to me, I just can't help it, my skin crawls."

The Governor sat down again in the chair across from him. "Ah God. I am sorry to hear that, Mahaffy. The more so, because I played some part in Dahaut's . . . activities. But if this is really true, then perhaps Macsen's daughter is the perfect wife for you, after all. And in truth," he added thoughtfully, "it seems to me that while you asked for my advice, you had already made up your mind to marry her."

Mahaffy considered that. "I think that perhaps I did, though I didn't realize until just now. There is another reason, too. If I can gain Lord Macsen's allegiance by marrying his daughter . . . well, it is something that I can do for myself, finally. Something you have had no hand in at all. It is not that I don't appreciate what you have done, or that I could possibly have accomplished so much without you. But if I am to be Lord of Mochdreff, I shouldn't owe it all to you."

Much to his relief, the Governor did not seem inclined to argue with any of this. "Then you will tell her father immediately that you are willing to marry her in return for his support?"

"No," said Mahaffy, slowly. "No, I don't think I will. For her sake, I am going to take your advice. I will tell Macsen that his daughter and I need to meet at least a few times, have a chance to become acquainted, before I ask for her hand.

"And if she doesn't like me, or if the idea of marrying anyone at all makes her unhappy," he added fiercely, "I won't allow her to be bullied into accepting me, no matter what her refusal may cost me!"

Mahaffy was waiting with Conn in the dark little chapel beyond the orchard when Lord Macsen's daughter arrived for their arranged first meeting. Though he had been talking and enjoying himself just a moment before, Mahaffy felt his stomach plunge at the sight of the slender veiled figure in green and grey, who came in through the chapel door with two serving women following after her. So much depended on this first meeting.

She came in with a silent, gliding step. It was hard to tell under the silvery spangled veil, under so many heavy garments, but she appeared to be thin—almost like a boy in her proportions. Yet he liked the way that she moved. In that stony chapel, dimly lit by flickering candles she seemed light and graceful, almost ethereal.

Mahaffy cleared his throat, and Conn tactfully slipped away, followed by the lady's two attendants. And suddenly,

Mahaffy realized that he had nothing to say to her, though he had planned it all out in advance.

"Tifanwy . . ." he said, trying to buy time while he thought of something better, but nothing better came to mind. "It is a pretty name. I do not recall that I ever heard it before."

And that, he told himself, *sounded so stiff and so stupid, I am sure that she loathes me already.*

She made no response, did not even move, standing there by one of the pillars, scarcely breathing. It came to him then that perhaps she had never been alone with a strange man before. At the very least, her circumstances were such . . . her dealings with the opposite sex must have been such . . . that she was probably shy and reclusive. In which case, her present situation must be extremely daunting.

He smiled as pleasantly as he knew how. "I—perhaps someone should have presented us formally. I am Mahaffy Guillyn." He waited a moment for her to reply, and when she did not: "If you would like to call one of your women back, I won't be insulted."

Tifanwy shook her head, just the slightest movement under the veil. "No," she said tentatively. "I suppose—I suppose we ought to begin to get used to each other."

At least she had a pretty, melodious voice. But it made her seem younger, more like a child. Mahaffy knew that she was almost nineteen, a long time for a girl to remain a spinster, and between that and the misfortune that caused her to wear the veil, she had probably given up on the idea of marrying a long time ago. If her father had not prepared her well in advance (and Macsen did not seem like the sort of man who would consult his daughter before arranging a marriage for her), this whole thing must have come as a distinct shock.

"I hope," he said, "that we will do very much better than grow accustomed to each other. I am looking not only for a wife but a friend as well."

Through the sheer silken veil, he could see that her hair was a rich chestnut color, and while he had only a general impression of her features, they appeared to be good. As for the scars: they were completely invisible, at least at this distance.

"I didn't know that you were looking for a wife at all," Tifanwy said skeptically, moving toward the altar. "I was told that a marriage between us was my father's idea."

Mahaffy laughed nervously. "As to that . . . I have been thinking about marriage for a long time, but I hadn't yet made up my mind if there was anyone I wanted to ask."

Someone had told him that her eyesight was weak. Between that and the veil, and the fact that he was standing some distance from the candles on the altar, it occurred to him that he was probably nothing more in her sight than a sinister shadow.

He took a hesitant two steps in her direction. But the moment the light fell on him, Tiffany recoiled with a gasp. Retreating to her former place beside the pillar, she stood there trembling, as though she would have liked to retreat further, if she only dared.

It's my damnable face! thought Mahaffy. Apparently no one had been kind enough to prepare her, no one had thought to tell her that her intended bridegroom had been as cursed with beauty as she had been cursed with its lack.

He wanted to cry out in protest. He wanted to say to her: *Don't let this spoil everything! Don't think, Tifanwy, just because this is the way that I look, that I haven't a heart to give you—a heart that has never been given before. You, of all women, ought to know how little physical beauty really matters.* And he wanted to show her the marks on his hands, so she could see that he was as brutally scarred as she was, just in a different place.

But he could not do or say any of those things. They were much too personal, and besides, even to hear him speak of her scars might cause her pain.

So Mahaffy tried, instead, to think of something he could

say that would show her what sort of person he was—or no, the sort of man that he wanted to be, that he could be, maybe, with the right sort of woman at his side to help him. Only, what could he possibly say to favorably impress her?

"I would like you to know me better," he began. And then he remembered something. He remembered why it was that people generally liked Prince Tryffin, what it was about the Governor that made even people who were prepared to hate him eventually warm to him. It was because he was always interested in *them;* no matter how mighty, no matter how humble, Tryffin was genuinely fascinated by what they had to bring to any discussion. He always listened patiently even when they were horribly talkative, and if they were shy, then he found some way of drawing them out.

"But first," Mahaffy said, taking a deep breath. "I would like to learn something about you. What are your interests, and how do you occupy yourself when you are in your own home?"

And he prepared himself to be fascinated by whatever it was, even if it should be something boring and ordinary.

"I play on the harp," she said faintly. "I have a white bitch named Findulias, who is going to have puppies. And I have a garden where I grow herbs. You can hardly be interested in that."

Mahaffy blew out the air he had just swallowed. This was more promising than he had dared hope. "But I am interested. You can't be raised—as I was—by a witch, and not take a certain interest in growing herbs. Do you prefer . . . cooking herbs or medicinal ones?"

She had stopped trembling by now, and though it was difficult to tell, he thought she might even be smiling under the veil. "I like whatever I can coax into growing."

"Mother of God! I forgot you lived near here, right on the edge of the barrens," he said. And he thought that a girl who had the patience and the determination to make a garden grow under such lamentable conditions must be rather extraordinary. "Have you ever . . . propagated roses? I hear that is difficult under the best of conditions."

Taking her by the hand, Mahaffy led her over to one of the stone benches, and now she came willingly enough. He went on determinedly asking her questions, hoping none of them sounded too forced, too stupid, until she surprised him by laughing out loud.

"Are you always so eager to please . . . are you always so very kind?"

Mahaffy stopped and stared at her, until he realized that his jaw had dropped and that he must look like a fool. With an effort, he recovered himself. "I can see they haven't prepared you properly, that no one told you a thing about me. I am a Guillyn, and everyone knows that we are abominably selfish."

Tifanwy laughed again, and it was a light, pleasing ripple, like water in a stream. "So you are modest as well as beautiful," she said. "And this time, she did *not* flinch away from the word as she had flinched at the sight of his face. In fact, the way that she said it, he was fairly certain that he was making a very good impression.

Mahaffy certainly hoped so. Sitting there on the bench with her little white hand clasped in his, he realized that he had never before wanted anything as much as he wanted her.

As soon as he heard the familiar rattle of metal outside his door, Math crept out of bed and began to dress himself. The sound he had just heard, as he knew by now, had come from the two guards who watched each night at his bedchamber door; it came when they both settled down on the floor of the antechamber and took out a pair of dice and a leather cup. It was the same thing that they did every evening at about the same time, and they would continue to play and to make their wagers for an hour or so, until Math's grandfather interrupted them by coming upstairs and passing through the room on the way to his own bedchamber.

As the guards had learned to listen for the sound of Lord Branagh's approach—so as not to be caught dicing by that stern old man—Math had learned to listen for this other signal, telling him that the men would now be too busy over their game to remember to look in on him. At least not until his grandfather appeared, to remind them of Math's existence.

Once he was dressed, he slid a hand under the feather mattress, searching for the coil of rope he knew was hidden there. It was not difficult to find: more than twenty feet of good braided hemp. He pulled it out from under the mattress, and headed for the nearest window.

Fortunately, the leaded glass casements in this part of the castle could all be unlatched and opened. It was the work of only a few minutes for Math to push open the window, knot the rope around a steel spike he had driven into the stone wall three weeks earlier, scramble over the chest, and toss the rest of the rope over the sill and down the outside wall. It took rather longer to lower himself to the ground—especially tonight, when his tunic caught on a sharp stone projection, and he dangled for what seemed an eternity, ten feet above the ground, before he was finally able to free himself.

He landed softly in the courtyard below, and paused to say a quick prayer of thanks that at this time of year the moon did not shine on this part of the castle so early in the evening. Otherwise, the rope left dangling from the window would be certain to draw attention sooner or later.

Moving lightly and swiftly, and a little breathlessly, Math headed across the yard and around a corner of the Keep. Keeping to the shadows as much as possible, he at last arrived directly under Lord Cernach's apartments.

There was a tree in that part of the garden that Math knew well, a birch that he often climbed. Sitting in the lower branches, about six feet from Cernach's bedchamber window, it was possible to catch parts of conversations . . .

usually between Cernach's squires and pages as they waited to help him prepare for bed, but sometimes between Cernach and Math's grandfather: private discussions of men and weapons, letters of defiance, and many other things that were never mentioned when Math was observably present.

Math had only the vaguest idea what they were planning, and that, of course, was precisely the reason he was so eager to learn more. Once, ominously, he had thought that he caught the word "poison" followed by something that sounded like "brooch" and then the name of his cousin Peredur. Much to his frustration, there had been no way of determining, then or afterward, whether the two men had been actually discussing something they *planned*, or something—some rumor, perhaps not even accurate—they had merely heard about.

But if the conversation was perfectly innocent, if it was only a story that Lord Cernach was repeating, then why had no one said anything about it to Math in the two weeks since?

Unless, of course, they were afraid of frightening me. If somebody else had Peredur poisoned, I might be next. Math found that thought peculiarly reassuring, though he knew it ought to send shivers down his spine. That was because the alternative was, in its way, so very much worse, because it was horrifying to think that Peredur might be dead right now, might have been poisoned to make way for *him.*

Math was about to swarm up the trunk, when a noise on the other side of the yard caught his attention—just a soft scuffling of feet as though someone had slipped and nearly lost his footing. Instead of climbing, the boy dodged behind the birch, then peered cautiously around the trunk.

Someone was moving silently and furtively across the yard, flitting from shadow to shadow. Math drew in his breath, felt his heart begin to pound. So he was not the only one making surreptitious nighttime expeditions through Caer Rigor.

Although, of course, the fellow might be on some comparatively innocent mission . . . maybe one of the guards, on his way to an assignation with one of the serving wenches.

Reaching the relative darkness of the garden, the man straightened up, and stood not a dozen yards from Math's hiding place. As Math's eyes had already adjusted to the shadows, he could see the fellow quite clearly.

The man was much, much too tall to be any of the guards that Math knew. He was practically taller than anyone the boy had ever met. He must, therefore, be one of the new recruits, perhaps the terrifying, fascinating foreigner he had heard some of the serving girls discussing earlier. But even though the girls had sounded interested, it seemed rather soon for the man to have found himself a sweetheart inside the castle.

He might be a spy . . . he could even be an assassin, thought Math, his pulse racing.

When the man began to move again, Math followed him. Except that now there was nothing furtive about the big man's movements. Far from skulking in the shadows, he walked quite openly out into the moonlight and began to stroll in the direction of the barracks.

Was I wrong? Math wondered. *Or did I reveal myself in some way that I don't even know about? Did he see me or hear me behind the tree, and suddenly start sauntering along that way to lull my suspicions?*

Standing there in the darkness of the shadow of the Keep, the boy felt torn in two directions. Duty told him that he ought to report this fellow, in case he really was dangerous. But what if the foreigner's movements were in fact quite innocent—or even supposing they were not, and he was off on some sinister errand for Cernach or the dwarfs? In that case, common sense told Math that reporting what he had seen would only get himself into trouble. Because then he would have to explain what *he* had been doing, lurking in the courtyard when he ought to be in bed.

Looking at it from every possible angle, it was hard to know which was the wisest course to take. Of one thing only could the boy be certain: the stranger bore watching. And Math himself was the one who was going to have to do it.

Magic makes women wise and men into lunatics. Which is to say . . . in neither case does it change them very much.
— *A Mochdreffi proverb*

13.

The Luck of Cuachag

At Caer Rigor, Meligraunce was feeling uneasy and frustrated. He was feeling that way because the cold sweats had returned that morning. When he first opened his eyes, he had been absolutely convinced that Luned was pressed up against him in bed. And this time, the disappointment when he discovered that she was *not* there had been just as keen as the sickening wave of panic that followed.

To make matters worse, he had been inside the castle for two days and two nights, and still he was no nearer to rescuing Luned, to even finding her or speaking to her. His one secretive nighttime expedition to the South Tower had ended suddenly in the courtyard, when an uncanny sensation, a prickling between his shoulder blades, had warned him that someone was watching.

He knew very well that he had no special perceptions, no second sight or sixth sense, like some of the people he knew, but the Captain had learned to trust his own instincts. Sometimes, he had learned, there were things that you heard without realizing you heard them, things that you saw through the corner of your eye which did not quite register, yet you knew they were there. So he had obeyed his instincts and returned to the barracks — and was asking himself this morning, as he ate his bowl of barley porridge and washed it down with hard cider, whether he might not have made a serious mistake. Perhaps it had been Luned herself watching from a tower window, willing him to come and rescue her. Perhaps she had waited for him all night long . . . and he had failed her.

Walking from the barracks to the armory, where he was to meet Captain Iolo, Meligraunce reflected that he had been better off at the inn, where at least he was able to listen to gossip. Inside the castle walls no one mentioned Luned, even obliquely. Or if they did, only in whispers among trusted friends.

He found Captain Iolo straddling a rough plank bench, and polishing a piece of armor. Iolo was very careful and precise in the matter of his harness, which Meligraunce thought admirable. A man of his own stamp, though you would never think it to see them together now: the neat little man in black leather, diligently polishing his plate armor until it shone, and the tall man standing over him, in gaudy rags and rusty scraps of metal.

"You appear to be settling in," said Iolo, by way of greeting. "And the serving maids are all aflutter. They are hoping that you will ask them all to dance at the revels tonight."

Meligraunce frowned—not for the serving girls but for the unexpected celebration. "Is there some holiday . . . some local festival that I don't know about?"

The other man shrugged. "Is a reason necessary?" He picked up a second piece of armor, one of the cuisses, and set to work with his scrap of cloth, but now there was a crease between *his* eyes, as though he were trying to analyze something, some impulse, that remained somewhere just beyond his comprehension. "We are hungry for pleasure, and the world is greening," he said at last. "Reason enough, I should think."

"Reason enough," Meligraunce agreed. But there was an uneasy question he had been wanting to ask since he first arrived, and as he and Iolo were finally alone together, he thought he would venture it now.

"In the matter of my settling in," he said, sitting down on the plank across from Iolo. "I don't precisely understand what it is that I am doing here. That is, I understand my duties well enough, but I don't understand why you were willing to hire a man you knew nothing about. A man of foreign ways and habit."

Iolo smiled and shrugged again. "You are a friend of Isaf Danan, and that was recommendation enough."

Meligraunce cleared his throat, wondering whether or not it would be wise to inform his Caer Rigor counterpart that he knew no such person. But before he could say that he did not, it suddenly occurred to him that he did.

"In the matter of Isaf Danan . . . we met some while back, but I had no idea he had any connection with the people here."

"Aye, he seems to be restless, now he is no longer the Steward here," said Iolo. "Wandering about the country-side like a moonstruck old beggar. No doubt there are people who take him for just that."

It gradually dawned on the Captain exactly who they were discussing. This Isaf Danan, this crazy old man, was actually Luned's bastard great-uncle, the man that Dame Brangwaine had described in such detail—neglecting only to mention his name and his somewhat startling appearance. *"One of the honorable dutiful ones . . . it happens some-times in our family"* was what she had said.

Now it happened that Meligraunce knew many stories about wizards, warlocks, and wise-women wandering the roads in disguise—a form of amusement peculiar to their mystic tribe, which also provided them with ample oppor-tunities to test the character of everyone they met. However, it seemed to Meligraunce that not only had the testing part been conspicuously absent in all of his meetings with Isaf Danan, but that Isaf himself made a more than usually convincing madman.

When he tried to delicately intimate as much to Iolo, the Caer Rigor captain only answered with a smile: "If by wandering in his wits you mean that he has difficulty distinguishing his dreams and visions from reality, that was always the case. He was ill for a long time as a boy, and after he recovered, they say he had *ambitions.*"

Which, as Meligraunce knew, was the Mochdreffi way of saying that the old man had suffered from brain fever in his youth and that he became a warlock as a result. With the women, they were either born with the gift or they were not. If gifted, they developed their talents through instruction from an early age. But in men, the gift was usually latent and only appeared later in life, after some accident or illness or trauma led to a bout of delirium or mental collapse from which the victim emerged as a warlock, more or less in full possession of his powers.

"Though nothing much ever did come of it . . . beyond the visions and a certain odd talent for prophecy," Iolo continued. "For all that, I have never known Isaf to make a poor decision or to misjudge the character of any man. He is still highly regarded, and most of the folk in these parts, you will find, call him the luck of Cuachag."

In her tower prison, Luned was curled up in a chair, reading one of Dame Brangwaine's books. She had not really meant to open it, but the books were beginning to exert a terrible fascination—she was always wanting to touch and to handle them, to stop whatever else she was doing to run and make certain that she had not . . . somehow . . . managed to lose or misplace them. And today, just walking past the table where they rested, a compelling urge had suddenly come over her, to pick up this book, settle in a chair, and spend the next few hours deciphering the small, crabbed hand in which it was written.

"For the working of the Spell, which is known as a Tagharim: Take two hundred black cats, and roast them on spits . . ." Luned was not so absorbed in the text that she failed to hear the footsteps approaching. She slammed the

book shut, jumped to her feet, and whirled around to face the door.

"You are as nervous as a cat," said Cernach. He was standing just her side of the threshold, in his fussy silks and velvets, grinning at her in a way that Luned considered little short of demented. More and more as the weeks passed by, he seemed to be less and less himself. *And I, poor fool, always assumed that any change must be an improvement.*

"Is that one of my grandmother's books?" he asked, coming all the way into the room. "I was under the impression—as I can see, a false one—that you were unable to unseal them. Now, how do you suppose I came to be so woefully mistaken?"

Luned felt the blood drain from her face. "I can't even say how I managed to open it . . . what I said or did to make it fall open. And now you have spoiled everything by startling me so."

He sauntered around the table and chair to the place where she was standing, and took the volume out of her hand. But after a careful examination, he gave it back. "You are haggard, Cousin. Why not ask Gleis to bring up some of her face paint? It looks ghastly enough on her, but you seem to be in need of it."

Glaring at him resentfully, Luned flung herself into the chair. "You keep me caged here like a wild beast; it's no wonder that I am restless and out of sorts. Nor do I appreciate the fact that you send your trollop to wait on me. If you think that I am still going to marry you, after all the insults you have heaped on me," she added with a hiss, "I fear you are sadly mistaken."

"Don't give it another thought," Cernach replied, with an airy gesture. "Fortunately, a woman of power need not be careful of her reputation, and I'm not obliged to do the honorable thing, or attempt to make you an honest woman. So long as you do all that you have promised, so long as you continue to direct your efforts toward the creation of the cauldron, I don't much care what you choose to do afterward."

Luned smoothed out the skirts of her sapphire velvet gown. "Be certain that I mean to keep my promises. Why else but to aid you did I come to this place . . . and walk into this wretched trap of yours?"

"I sometimes wonder about that myself," said Cernach. "Brangwengwen says that you sometimes come up with the most surprising suggestions. And she and I both wonder why Bagdamagus is suddenly apprehensive, why he asks so many questions about the origins of the cauldron and its intended uses."

As well he might, thought Luned. She was beginning to believe that the younger dwarf was in serious danger. Yet angry as she was, apprehensive as she was, there was only so far that Luned dared go. Cernach would expect cross words, a disagreeable manner—what else could he expect, considering the way that he kept her confined?—but he must never guess the depths of her anger, her determination to thwart him, if she possibly could.

"I never see the little man but when he is with Brangwengwen," she said with a shrug. "If he is having pangs of conscience, that is his affair entirely." In truth, she would have dearly liked to warn the goldsmith . . . to be careful what he said, to put himself out of harm's way as soon as the cauldron was cast and completed. She spent hours trying to think up ways to secretly convey the message right under Brangwengwen's nose, but had never been able to come up with a single reasonable plan.

Cernach crossed the room, and stood gazing out one of the diamond-paned windows, down at the orchard below. "You are going to be of service to me one way or another, Luned, be very certain of that. Though I sometimes find myself wondering whether you might not still feel some loyalty to Prince Tryffin . . . and that peasant lover of yours."

Luned drew in her breath sharply. "I don't know what you are talking about."

"Of course you do," said Cernach. "Do you really suppose that I didn't know you were degrading yourself with Prince Tryffin's guard captain most of last summer? Maelgwyn's bastard, as Dame Brangwaine chooses to think of him, but even if that should happen to be true, he is no fit paramour for you, Cousin. I sent men to kill him again and again in taverns and alleys, you might be interested to know, yet he was always too quick and too clever to fall into my traps."

Luned bit her lip. "If you know so much, then perhaps you know also that when I abandoned my pride and went begging to him in Trewynyn, it was only to learn that he had already replaced me with—with the wife of a wealthy merchant," she lied.

"Ah." Cernach raised his eyebrows in mock indignation. "And thus we discover the true reason behind your willingness to make common cause with me. The bastard half-brother has the poor taste to prefer another woman to you, and, of course, Prince Tryffin must pay the price. But really, Luned, we can't let Captain Meligraunce off so easily. He has insulted a woman of my house; I must redouble my efforts to have the saucy rascal killed."

Luned ground her teeth. She knew very well that any plea for mercy coming from her would fall on deaf ears. And anyway, she suspected that her cousin wanted Meligraunce dead on general principles, which had little or nothing to do with her. So she only smiled and replied sweetly: "When you finally do it, I wish I might be there to see it."

Cernach appeared to consider. "Do you know, that is an excellent notion. Brangwengwen tells me that the cauldron must be washed in blood before it becomes anything more than a pretty ornament. We were thinking of slaughtering one or two goats, but a man would be even better. A big man with a great deal of blood in him . . ."

Luned laughed unsteadily. "Let us hope we are ready to

consecrate the vessel before the Captain could possibly be brought all the way from Trewynyn. It is a long journey, as I know so well."

Cernach continued to smile at her. "As you say, Cousin, it is a long journey. Would that he were here, conveniently to hand . . . but as he is not, I suppose we must do without him."

As soon as Cernach left her (which was not soon enough), Luned sprang up from her chair and began to pace the floor. Time was growing short. One day very soon they would start casting the cauldron—and on that day she would have to stop hoping for some miraculous rescue and openly defy him.

Not that this would prevent the dwarfs from completing the cauldron, they were so close already, or that Luned could stop Brangwengwen from boiling up horrors once the cauldron was cast. It was simply a matter of pride and of conscience to let Cernach know at the end that she wanted no part of him or his despicable plots.

Suddenly, Luned stopped pacing, assailed by a terrible doubt. *Even in that I may aid him instead.*

She knew very well that Cernach had only put forth the notion of killing Meligraunce and using his blood to consecrate the cauldron to see how she would react.

But he had also said, *"You are going to be of service to me one way or another."* Up until now, Luned had been horribly afraid that Bagdamagus was the chosen victim— unknown to Brangwengwen, of course. Now she was not so certain.

Because, while the blood of a man, even a very small one, would serve better than a goat, how much better the blood of a witch, of a Mochdreffi wise-woman with formidable powers, instead?

At sunset, Luned climbed the stairs to the upper chamber and stood by the open windows, inhaling the damp evening air. It made her feel stronger, somehow, and more determined than ever to find some way out of her difficulties. *What a coward I have become,* she scolded herself, *What a weak, pitiful thing to give up so easily!*

At the very least, she could always kill Cernach—stop his heart, stifle his breath. Though she had threatened to do so that first night, it had all been a bluff. Dame Brangwaine had carefully shielded her young apprentices from knowledge of the death spells, which were strictly forbidden . . . and something a woman might burn for, even in Mochdreff. But Luned knew how to do it now. There were a hundred ways in the books he had given her, and not a single one of them beyond her abilities.

It will just be a simple matter, she thought, *of twisting and perverting every skill that I own, that I ever employed as a healer.* Yet what was that, compared to what Cernach was undoubtedly planning? And no more than he deserved, for putting the spells into her hands. *If I don't burn in Mochdreff, I shall certainly burn in Hell.* But to kill Cernach, to cleanse Mochdreff of his plots and his schemes and his beastly small-mindedness would certainly be worth it, whatever the consequences.

Which might, she realized, be dying of thirst and starvation in these very rooms. Would Gleis and the dwarfs really allow that to happen to her—could they possibly be so cold and so cruel? Gazing out at the gaudy sunset, Luned decided that they probably would, if only out of fear. They wouldn't dare to approach her after what she had done to Cernach.

Well, what if she did die? Did she want to live . . . with the shame of whatever assistance she had rendered Cernach still clinging to her, when the man that she loved must forever regard her as an evil, treacherous woman? *Yes, I do,* thought Luned. *I do want to live.*

The more that she tried to put the thought aside, the more she realized that it was true. She wanted to go on living, even if it was only to continue as she was. She was not ready to pass on to whatever shadowy existence was waiting for her on the other side of death. Her hands gripped the stone windowsill, in the sudden intensity of her desire to live.

But that is even better, she told herself grimly. *What glory would there be in giving myself up, if I* wanted *to die?*

Looking out across the courtyard, beyond the carp pond and beyond the orchard, her gaze chanced to fall on the boxwood maze, where she had spent so many pleasant hours as a child. In those winding alleys, in those green, woody recesses, she had played by herself or with the servants' children, and it had seemed like a spot set entirely aside from time and circumstances, a place with a magic that was all its own.

Allowing her gaze to travel even farther, she realized with a jolt of surprise that there was some sort of celebration going on in the far courtyard. What Luned had at first mistaken for the usual evening activity now appeared to be something very different. Someone had kindled a bonfire, and there were couples and threesomes dancing around it, an intricate country dance. And when she listened carefully, Luned could just pick up the sound of someone blowing softly on a wooden flute, someone else beating time on a bodhran.

It was hard to make out the faces of the dancers at this distance. Even if she could, she would be hard pressed to recognize any of her childhood playmates, now they were grown. Yet her gaze was caught and held by a certain pair of dancers: a buxom, flirtatious girl and a striking big man in rags and tatters—

A lean, muscular fellow with dark skin, who moved with a peculiar grace. A man with a dangerous smile—even from this distance, she thought she caught the glitter of strong white teeth as he curled back his lips—who undoubtedly considered himself irresistible to women. And a man whose large, work-coarsened hands were nevertheless gentle and knowledgeable at caressing . . .

Luned felt her knees turn to water and the soles of her feet begin to tingle. With a gasp, she leaned against the cold stone wall, put her hands to her burning cheeks. She had been imprisoned too long, had gone too long without any real company, if she reacted this way to the sight of a stranger, and a dirty vagabond at that.

Lifting the hair from her suddenly damp forehead, she struggled to regain her composure. What she must do now was walk sedately downstairs to her bedchamber, kneel by her bed, and make her evening devotions. Yes, that would really be best. It would calm her mind and cool her blood. And in just another moment now . . . when she did not feel so weak in the knees . . . she was going to do it.

But instead, she turned around and stole another look out the window.

Down in the courtyard, the dance was ending, the couples and threesomes drifting away. In spite of herself, Luned found herself searching for the flirtatious girl and the man who had partnered her. The girl was nowhere to be seen . . . but there was the man, unmistakable because of his size and his gaudy scarlet patches, just slipping in through an entrance to the maze.

An assignation, thought Luned. *What else did you expect? He is going to lay that slut right down on the ground and they are going to rut like animals.*

It was after all, what common people did, and it was certainly nothing to Luned if they did it, nothing to her if they kept on doing it from now until dawn.

So why did she suddenly burst into tears . . . and why was she pounding her fists against the rough stone wall, until the skin broke and her hands began to bleed?

. . . A lusty man in his youth (it is said that he fathered more than two dozen children), at last Atlendor became entirely devoted to the life of the mind and the spirit. At the age of one hundred and fifty, he gave up eating and drinking, in the hope that the body would wither but the mind remain.

This the Church considered blasphemous, and so he came to be known as one of the Fallen Adepts.

—From Glastyn's Chronicles of the Isle of Celydonn

14.

A Fair White City

Findias was remarkable, like nothing Gwenlliant had seen before, a real city rather than just a large town, vast and crowded and bustling with activity. It was also a city built partly by wizardry, as could be seen by the fantastic architecture: soaring towers of pearl and ivory, gates of intricate iron traceries, marble statues and columns and portals of colossal proportions. This was Findias at the height of its splendor, before Atlendor died, his spells unraveled, and the structures created by wizardry started to decay. The Findias of her own time was an ordinary medieval town, though it certainly possessed some fascinating rubble.

But this was only the shadow of the city that was, Gwenlliant reminded herself—clinging more tightly than ever to Rhufawn as he maneuvered his horse through the crowds. It was possible that the real Findias had never been quite so gorgeous, quite so breathtaking. She thought of Annwn, the shadow Gwyngelli, where Tryffin had been

185

forced to ransom poor Conn from seven years' servitude by playing at Chess with the King of the Fairies . . . Like Annwn, this might be the legend and not the reality, a city of dreams, hopes, fears, and aspirations, bearing only a distant, confusing resemblance to the real Findias. But who could possibly have dreamed anything half so splendid as this?

"Are we near the school of wizardry?" she said in Rhufawn's ear. They had somehow gotten separated from their friends as they moved through the crowded streets. Gwenlliant kept looking for them, but there were so many people and horses and wagons on the street already, that she had practically given up hope.

"The school is not actually *in* Findias," Rhufawn answered. "That is, there is a house not far from here, where we can rest after our journey, where Atlendor will come to speak to you and the other students in another day or two, and decide whether you are suited to study with him. But the school itself is a kind of . . . fortress . . . on an island in the bay.

"It would be difficult for me to do it justice, so I won't try to describe it," he added. "Especially as you will be seeing it for yourself very soon."

"If I am allowed to go there," said Gwenlliant, feeling suddenly doubtful. "If Atlendor decides, as you said, that I am suited to study with him."

"He will," Rhufawn replied confidently. "When he sees what you are already capable of doing, Etain, he will *want* you to come to the island." He lowered his voice. "And we don't talk about these things except in private, but no one at the school will mind that you are a witch. After all, Atlendor is an Adept—that means that he is a warlock as well as a wizard and a priest. Though, of course, he studied wizardry first."

Gwenlliant nodded. The accepted wisdom outside Mochdreff was that wizards alone had the necessary discipline and control to use all but the blackest magics without being corrupted. Witches, however, who came by their talents naturally and often without any reliable instruction, were generally shunned as tools of the Devil . . . if not subjected to worse things.

It was a situation that continued to perpetuate itself: Witches were dangerous because they acted in ignorance, but since they were unable to study or to practice openly, how else could they learn to master the gifts that they could *not* ignore, except by practicing their art furtively, by picking up knowledge in bits and pieces, and often from unreliable sources?

Now they were riding through a kind of open market, vaster than any market that Gwenlliant had ever seen. And the goods displayed in the stalls and the tents came from every corner of Ynys Celydonn: furs and amber from Gorwynnion, and every sort of object you could possibly imagine carved out of bone, wood, and ivory; hawks, hounds, and bolts of rich fabrics from Camboglanna; bearskins and barrels of ale from Walgan; rings, bracelets, and torcs of Gwyngelli gold; dried herbs from Perfudd, and shaggy grey ponies from Aderyn; and from Findias itself, leather and illuminated prayer books.

"As it happens," Rhufawn continued, "Atlendor likes to take Wild Talents and train them. Not only does that make them less of a threat to themselves and everyone else, but they often show the greatest promise of someday becoming Adepts."

Gwenlliant thought about that as they came out of the market and turned down another street. "Rhufawn," she whispered in his ear, "are you talking about me . . . or are you describing yourself?"

Her companion laughed. "What do *you* think?" he said.

She shook her head; though he could not see it, Gwenlliant knew that he could feel the motion, they were sitting so close. What she *thought* was that a young man who could tell the difference between a shapechanger and a real wolf must know considerably more about wolves than she did—or else more about shifting shape than either Gwenlliant or Maelinn.

But all that she said was: "I think that when you want me to know the answer to that, you will tell me yourself."

Rhufawn brought her to a large white house with many fair chambers. Findabhair, Cet, and their other companions of the road had already arrived, and greeted them, the moment they came inside, with the only slightly surprising news that Atlendor was already there.

"Of course, we *knew* he would be able to predict the exact day we would all arrive," said Findabhair, "but he *might* have been too busy to come at once. You are fortunate, Etain, because if he accepts you now, you can continue on to the school with the rest of us tomorrow."

Caílte, Morfan, and Gildas were already consulting with the wizard in some inner chamber. Gwenlliant was to meet with him after supper. The three boys came down after only the briefest visit, looking pleased, relieved, and excited, though, unlike Etain, they had already been accepted by letter and the wizard's final approval was little more than a formality. "You will like him," said Caílte, in Gwenlliant's ear, when the students all sat down at the supper table. But that was beside the point—the question was whether or not the great Adept would take to *her*.

After a meal which Gwenlliant neither tasted nor remembered afterward, Rhufawn took her upstairs and as far as the door, then gave her a friendly push into Atlendor's sanctum. It was a large room, with tall windows overlooking a snowy garden with statues and frozen fountains. The wizard was standing by one of those windows.

He was not in the least what Gwenlliant had been expecting. He was old; there was not the least question of that . . . but he was not old and earthy, like Dame Ceinwen . . . or a fierce old man with a beard, like Glastyn, who wore all his experience in his face. In Atlendor's case, it seemed that age had refined him to a kind of sculptured, crystalline purity; his hair was so white and so fine, it appeared to be made of spun glass, and his skin was so thin and translucent, you could see the shape of his bones and the pattern of pale blue veins on his hands. His dress was clerical: a long white robe with a cowl, sandals on his feet, and a silver cross on his breast, suspended from a heavy chain. He greeted Gwenlliant with a gentle smile that was almost tentative.

"Take a seat, my child, and tell me about yourself. You come highly recommended. Cet and Tegid and Findabhair all have good things to say about you, and Rhufawn is convinced you will make an Adept before we have finished with you."

Gwenlliant slipped nervously into the chair he offered her. She already felt guilty, and she had not even begun to lie to him yet. However, she managed to spin him a long rambling tale: about her aunt who was a witch, a friendly alchemist who had briefly befriended her, and all the adventures which had brought her alone and on foot into Draighen in the middle of winter.

He listened attentively, without a single interruption, but when she had finally finished he smiled sadly. "It is a hard and frightening world for those who are born to the Wild Magic . . . It can be especially terrifying for children. Perhaps when you have been with us a little longer, you will feel safe enough to tell me the truth."

It took several moments for that to sink in: The wizard had not believed a single word that Gwenlliant told him . . . but he had accepted her into his school in spite of it.

And then she was so ashamed for the lie that the truth came pouring out before she could stop it. Or as much of the truth as she dared to tell him: her early experiences with witchcraft and wizardry, her marriage to Tryffin and the expected baby, and finally, how she had come to the north chasing a dangerous shapechanger.

"Perhaps Maelinn is already there at your school . . .

perhaps she lied to you as I just did, and you treated her just as kindly," Gwenlliant concluded.

"That is entirely possible," said Atlendor. "It is even possible that I already have an idea who she may be. But it is also possible that she came to me hoping to make a new beginning, planning to do better things with her life in the future."

Gwenlliant bit her lip. She had not been able to tell Atlendor where she really came from, or the whole truth about Maelinn, because these were things that she was forbidden to speak of here in the Shadow Lands. It was precisely because the Shadow Maelinn had learned what she never should have that the trouble began in the first place. Unfortunately, some of these omissions also served to cover the worst of Maelinn's crimes. "Then what . . . what do you mean to do, now that I have told you these things?" Gwenlliant asked uneasily.

The wizard shook his head. "My child, I have studied during my lifetime a great many arts, but before all else and above all else, I am a wizard. I value harmony, order, and proportion, and have found that the best way to maintain all of these things is by meddling as little as possible in the lives and the fates of others. I will not betray you to this . . . Maelinn . . . nor will I betray her to you. Yet it's clear that some compelling destiny binds the two of you irrevocably together. Therefore, I leave it up to you and to her to find each other, and to do what has to be done."

Gwenlliant furrowed her brow, not entirely sure what he meant. "Then I am still accepted as a student at your school . . . you are not going to turn me away?"

"I believe I have already said that you are welcome to join us," he replied with that gentle smile. "One thing only do I ask—and that is a request, not a command. Can you trust me enough to give me your name? For it is easy to see that the one you gave Rhufawn is not your own."

Though it was not a command, Gwenlliant could tell that it *was* a test of sorts. And sometimes, as she knew very well, it was necessary to take certain risks . . . sometimes, you just had to decide who you could trust and who you could not.

So taking her courage in both hands, she whispered the word: "Gwenlliant."

The old man nodded and patted her hand. "Then be welcome, Gwenlliant, and also be assured that you will never hear me speak that name again, until you give me permission to do so."

In the dark of the maze, Meligraunce paused, listening. He was beginning to think he had been made a fool, lured in with implied promises, and then left to lose his way. There was a movement, a soft intake of breath off to his left, but as he slid a few steps in that direction he came up against a boxwood barrier.

"I can hear you breathing. Before God, come out and face me, and tell me what this is all about," he whispered.

There was a breathy giggling, almost in his ear. Meligraunce whirled, but his reaching hands caught only empty air. "Come a little closer. I will make it worth your while," came the maddening reply.

Grinding his teeth with frustration, the Captain followed the sound of that voice, twisting and winding through the dark patterns of the maze, until he suddenly came out in moonlight in an open area at the heart of the labyrinth. Cernach's uncle, Isaf Danan, was crouched on a little turf-covered mound at the center. "It was no easy thing, drawing you away from your female admirers. Have you forgotten, already, who holds your heart?"

"Neither waking nor sleeping," said Meligraunce. "But the women are less guarded than the men. And I thought one of them might be the wench who is waiting on . . . I thought one of them might be carrying cream to the cat in the well. If so, I thought the woman might help me find her."

Isaf Danan nodded wisely. "Oh yes . . . our pretty black

cat with the sharp, sharp claws. But if it's that wench Gleis you are looking for, you'll not find her dancing with the others."

"Where will I find her?" asked Meligraunce, coming out of the shadow of the boxwood and moving in his direction.

"Of little use, even if you did find her. She's not quite right in her mind, poor Gleis, since Cernach grew tired of her," the old man said with a pitying smile. "What you need, my friend, now you have found a way into the castle, is a quick secret way back out again."

Meligraunce frowned. "I have just arrived and I tell you this: I have no intention of leaving, until and unless I have Luned with me."

"No, no," replied the old man, beginning to look agitated. "Of course you must not go without pretty Luned. But you may have a bit of difficulty getting her out through the gate or over the walls. There is a better way." He made a fist of one hand and thumped it on the ground. "There is a better way, right here."

The Captain went down on one knee in the grass beside him. "Do you mean to tell me . . . are you trying to say there is a secret passage or tunnel leading out of the castle?"

"Better than that," said the old man. "Something much, much better. Right here, my friend, here on this spot. For what—I ask you—is a maze but a kind of a pattern?"

Meligraunce felt his heart sink. "You are trying to say that there was once a pattern spell here. But those spells have all faded; no one can work them since the healing of the land. The greatest witches in Mochdreff have all tried and failed."

"Ah . . . but have *you* tried?" said Isaf, from his crouch. "The power of the pattern spells is fading, but certain people can still make use of them. In truth, many powers remain to men such as you and I . . . men who have traveled between the worlds." He lowered his voice to a whisper. "A man who has walked the night under a dozen spinning moons, or watched his own reflection step out of the mirror . . . he can't help being changed by something like that."

"How do you know I *am* such a man?" Meligraunce asked sharply. "Did we meet before that night in Peryf? Do you have some idea that I'm not who I say I am?"

The old man let his feet slip out from under him, and sat right down on the turf. "You told everyone back at the inn, when you named yourself for the King of the Sidhe: Avallach, son of Fairyland. But I was the only man there who understood."

Meligraunce nodded slowly. While he was in the Otherworld he had been led to believe that he had gained special powers—though none of those powers had actually revealed themselves since his return. But it was said that a visit to the Shadow Lands gave power to a man in proportion to the stature and the power that he possessed already. For someone like Meligraunce, that might mean very little; for someone like Isaf Danan, born into a family of powerful witches, it might be enough to make a boy who had been perfectly ordinary up to that point into a mad warlock with a muddled gift for prophecy.

A man who has seen his own reflection step out of a mirror. It was said that a man who met his own ghost in the Shadow Lands courted madness. Meligraunce well remembered how disconcerting Prince Tryffin had found it to meet even an imperfect likeness of himself in Annwn: Prince Gruffydd, who was and was not his counterpart. But what if Isaf had actually met *himself* at an earlier age . . .

That set off an ominous train of thought: Perhaps this man before him was not the real Isaf at all. Perhaps this was Isaf's shadow, or perhaps it was somebody else's ghost who had stolen Isaf's memories and identity, as Maelinn took Gwenlliant's, and then went mad. That would explain a great deal.

But then the Captain shrugged. Even if that was true, it did not follow that Isaf's madness would be as murderous as Maelinn's. After all, if there *had* been a substitution, it had happened a long time ago, when Isaf Danan was just a boy. And this man before him . . . whoever he was, whatever he was . . . was known to be kindly and wise.

The Captain decided to trust him.

"If I can escape through the maze but Luned cannot, what use would your pattern spell be to me?"

"If you hold her by the hand, she can pass through with you. Though you must not loose your grip even a little, because if you happen to do so during the moment of transition, she will be cast back here abruptly and may take some harm."

Meligraunce nodded. It suddenly occurred to him that they had finally abandoned this business of the cat in the well, and were discussing Luned openly. "If I can bring your great-niece this far," he said, "I won't be inclined to let go of her. Not until I have her safe, and maybe not even then."

The old man laughed. "And that is a promise I shall expect you to keep. Come then . . . what are you waiting for? I will show you the pattern, so that you may work the spell for yourself."

Jumping to his feet, the old man led him down one alley, around a corner, and then through a long and complex pattern. But Meligraunce had a good memory, and he counted his steps. The fifty-first step brought them back to the mound.

There was a sudden disruption in the air around Isaf, just before the old man winked out of existence . . . then it was the moonlight and the maze and the turf-covered mound that went out like a candle as Meligraunce felt himself hurled into darkness.

"What *is* this place?" said the Captain. There was water soaking into his boots and the footing was uncertain. Moreover, a weedy, marshy odor was penetrating his nostrils, and everywhere he looked there was water, mud, and rank upon rank of bulrushes shining like silver swords in the moonlight.

"We are out in the fenlands between the castle and the sea. That should be evident," Isaf replied. "But if you mean how far *out* into the marsh: If you walk to the east about twenty yards and peek through the rushes, you will see Caer Rigor in the distance."

Meligraunce followed his instructions and discovered that the old man was telling the truth. "But where is the way to take us inside again?" Now that he knew the way out, the Captain wanted nothing so much as to go right back and resume his search for Luned.

He frowned at his companion. "You can return through the gate and no questions asked, but I doubt they will let me pass so easily. And . . . I don't see any portal here."

The way back for any pattern spell was an integral part of the whole pattern; it only worked if you had gotten so far by means of the spell in the first place. And when the final part of the pattern was not some piece of architecture like a door or gate, it was still some more-or-less permanent landmark, like the path between two venerable trees, or a fissure in the rock. There was nothing of that sort here.

Isaf led him through the mud and the weeds and the rushes, to a higher and drier piece of ground to the north. There, someone had arranged three immense boulders in a primitive trilithon. But Meligraunce was not entirely reassured. These arrangements of standing stones were invariably quite ancient.

"This spell is an old one, then. How many at Caer Rigor know that it exists?"

The old man shrugged. "About that, I can only guess. Perhaps no one knows but you and I . . . perhaps half the garrison and all of the servants. What does it matter? Even if Cernach knows, his men can't follow you through."

"No," said the Captain, after a moment of consideration, "but they can come out to this part of the marsh by ordinary means and pick up our trail almost immediately. Nor would Lord Cernach have to *know* that we had the power to use the spell. If I were in his place, I would send my men to the marsh just on the chance, and he may do the same. In which case, his men may be close on our trail before Luned and I are more than a few miles from the castle."

The greybeard paused, just the Captain's side of the stone portal. "Well then," he said before he disappeared, "once you leave Caer Rigor, you must just keep on running until you are safe."

The hour was late, too late for visitors. And because Luned had finally convinced Gleis that she did *not* want assistance with her gowns or her hair, even Gleis could not be expected before morning. Another long, restless night stretched before her, but Luned knew that whether she spent the night pacing or trying to sleep, the result would be much the same. With a sigh, she went into her bedchamber and began to slowly undress.

There was a soft padding of footsteps out in the antechamber, and the door flew open before Luned could protest. So she was standing there with her velvet gown unlaced and sliding off her shoulders, when the man came striding into her bedchamber.

Luned felt the blood drain from her face, then rush back in again. It was the man from the courtyard, the one who had danced with the serving maid and followed her into the maze. *He saw me watching him; he thought I wanted him.* Remembering what she *had* been thinking, Luned was ready to die of shame.

For all that, she was not going to allow herself to be mauled by this big shabby fellow. She pulled up her gown to cover her shoulders, lifted her chin in the haughtiest manner possible, and the words that would send him away were already hovering on her lips . . . when the man spoke. "Can it be, Lady, that you don't know me? Or is it just that the sight of me fills you with disgust?"

She did know him then, and the knowledge went through her like a knife. Luned gasped, took several stumbling steps, and threw herself into his arms. "I thought . . . I thought I would never see you again. God help me, I thought you would despise me. I was afraid that you would never, never know . . ."

"What would I never know?" he asked, with his face in her hair. "That you love me as truly and deeply as I love you? If I ever doubted your love, if I ever gave you reason to doubt mine, then I was a fool."

She laughed weakly. "You had reason enough to doubt me. I was so proud, so selfish. And afterward—" Remembering the circumstances, remembering why she was here, Luned suddenly drew away from him.

"You should never have followed me, Captain. This is a wicked coil you find me in, and if you should be harmed in any way, I will never forgive myself."

"Where else should I be but here, if you are in danger?" he replied calmly, taking her once more into his arms, his big warm hands finding the place where the dress fell open and there was only the thin linen shift covering her back.

And that was so like Meligraunce that she wanted to laugh again. One moment the ardent lover, the next so cool and practical, you would hardly guess he was capable of any emotion. "But how did you know to find me here? How *could* you know?"

"Dame Brangwaine said that she thought you were coming here. She sent Prince Tryffin a letter, because she was concerned for your safety. She was convinced you were in deadly peril, after your silver mirror turned black, after your cat gave birth to a litter of deformed kittens."

She took a deep breath, wondering how she was ever going to tell him. Nevertheless, he deserved to know the truth. "Meligraunce . . . I brought my silver mirror with me. And all the cats at our house in Anoeth belong to my great-grandmother."

There was a moment of silence while that sank in. "I see," said Meligraunce. "Dame Brangwaine lied to me. I said that I needed some proof that you were actually in danger, and she obliged me by providing some." He shook that off with a bitter laugh. "Yet she warned me that her methods were ruthless."

His warm, caressing hands on her back were making her shiver, making her want to forget everything else but the hardness of his body, the gentleness of his hands, and the burning sweet longing that was building inside of her. She swallowed hard, and struggled to remember what they were talking about. "Dame Brangwaine's methods are ruthless, but her intentions are good. I beg you to believe that much at least."

"I believe I have known that for the last year," he replied. "And it seems that she did not lead me so far astray, after all. What, in God's name, is your kinsman scheming to do here, and why did he bring you to Caer Rigor to help him?"

Glancing around her, Luned suddenly realized that the door was still open and they had both been speaking naturally, without bothering to lower their voices. Reluctantly, she slid out of his arms again.

"As soon as we are finished speaking you must go as quickly as you can to warn Prince Tryffin," she said as she closed the door, took Meligraunce by the hand, and led him over to the bed, where they could sit and talk quietly together. "You must tell him everything that I am about to tell you."

"Most certainly I shall, and take you with me," he replied. "I had thought to find you behind prison bars, but since that is not the case—"

"Yet I am a prisoner here, for all that," Luned interrupted him.

And she proceeded to tell him everything that had happened to her and everything that she knew. "And for whatever other purpose they mean to use the cauldron, they also intend to wound the land all over again," she concluded.

Meligraunce stared at her, his eyes deeply troubled. "But

what can they hope to gain from that? It is too cruel and too senseless."

"They want things to be as they have been all along. You should remember what I told you, about the men who came to power in the Mochdreff that was. Cernach senses, I think, that there will be no place for him in the new order. And, of course, we know the shapechanger's motives in sending those dreams.

"As for Math and Lord Branagh," she continued, "I am not certain they understand exactly what is at stake. It is convenient for Lord Branagh to believe that the ritual that you and I witnessed in Penafon was only a sham. If the land was truly healed, that gives Mahaffy Guillyn too much legitimacy. If the curse was not lifted, then Branagh's conscience remains clear on that point at least . . . and I think it would be difficult, if not impossible, to convince him just how dangerous the cauldron is."

She frowned thoughtfully. "Brangwengwen insists that Math knows everything, but I can't help wondering if she is lying. They never allow me to speak with him, not since that first night, and that in itself makes me wonder. Also, though we had little opportunity to become acquainted—"

"I had ample opportunity to observe Math when he was Lord Morcant's page, when Prince Tryffin's duties as deputy to the Lord Constable took us to Caer Ysgithr," said Meligraunce. "He may have changed, but I hardly think he could change that much. I think we may be reasonably certain that they are lying to him . . . deceiving him about the true nature of the cauldron. Unfortunately, he is greatly attached to his grandfather, and is likely to go on believing his lies, whatever anyone might have to say against him.'"

Meligraunce's lean muscular hand tightened around hers. "How close are they to casting the cauldron?"

Luned closed her eyes, leaned her head against his shoulder. "It can't be much longer before they are ready to begin. Another few days, a week at the most." Her eyes flew open as she remembered what it was that she hoped to do before that day came. "There is one thing that I can find the courage to do, now that you are here. I can kill Cernach. I think I will enjoy blasting his filthy little soul to perdition."

To his credit, Meligraunce did not even flinch—not from the idea that she *could* kill her cousin, not from the idea that she would. Instead, he weighed the suggestion carefully in his mind before he spoke, and went on caressing her hand as he did so.

"If it should come to that, I can do the job myself with a knife . . . and no question afterward that witchcraft was involved. But what would be the good of that?" he asked, a note of discouragement creeping into his voice. "I doubt I would have the opportunity to kill Lord Branagh as well, and then there would still be the dwarfs, even young Math—if he should turn out to be more guiltily involved than we think. The boy and his grandfather are always surrounded by guards. And there may be other conspirators that we don't know about. There is no use killing any of them if we can't kill all of them."

Luned had to admit that this was sensible. Even so, she was not certain that she could resist the opportunity to kill Cernach the next time she saw him. Which might not be for a long time, his visits were growing so infrequent. It could be that they would never meet again, until he came with his minions to cut her throat and collect her blood. The question then would be: Which of them could work faster—she with her magic or Cernach with his knife?

"Besides," said Meligraunce. "I would like to keep him alive. Perhaps I can surprise him outside your rooms one of these days, and force him to say the words that will release you. You said that he usually comes alone."

"No," said Luned. "You can't linger here. You have to warn Prince Tryffin first, and then come back for me later if you can.

"Do not think," she added, with a proud lift of her chin, "that I will thank you if you allow me to be the cause of so much harm, so much suffering, if you deliver the warning too late because you are trying to rescue *me*."

He carried her hand to his lips and dropped a kiss on the palm. "In my heart, God knows, I tremble at the thought of leaving you behind. Yet I know you too well and respect you too highly to doubt your resolve or to stand against it. But let me stay a few days more, to see what chances develop. We can spare that much time, at least."

And Luned agreed, not because she believed in those chances, but because she realized that she could not bear to sacrifice those last few days together. "But listen carefully to what I have to tell you: The cauldron is to be cast in seven parts, and those seven parts joined together with silver rivets. This will take several days, and besides that there will be the polishing and the finishing, the setting of the gems. We will know when they have begun casting, because a great smoke will begin to rise from the tower where Bagdamagus has his workshop, and no doubt there will be much coming and going between that place and Cernach's rooms.

"On that day," she said, "you must make up your mind to go. If I am free to go with you . . . well and good. If I am not, you must not hesitate, you must be willing to leave me behind and go to the Governor as quickly as you can. Will you promise to do that? Will you give me your word?"

His grip tightened and his eyes went bleak, but he nodded his head. "Lady, I give you my word. I will carry the warning to Prince Tryffin, whether I am able to take you with me or not."

Now that was settled, Luned rose from the bed, shrugged the dress off her shoulders, allowing the sapphire velvet to slide to the floor, until she was standing there with nothing on but her shift. "Then let me make use of the time remaining to us," she suggested, in a low, husky whisper. "Let us make good use of the time."

He closed his eyes and replied with a shudder,

"Ah . . . if we only could. But as you can plainly see, I am much too dirty to even touch you."

Luned laughed softly under her breath. "There are some rags and a basin of water. Take off these remarkable garments you are wearing and I will help you to bathe yourself."

And when he opened his eyes, she offered him both her hands. "Did no one ever tell you, Captain, it is highly discourteous to keep a lady waiting?"

. . . but honor—personal honor, which is a fine, careful, scrupulous intention to do what is right, no matter what costs or consequences should happen to attend, no matter if others should agree that he has acted correctly, no matter if he should be vilified, condemned, scoffed at, repudiated, and denounced on every side—is among the Knight's most valuable possessions.

Yet for all that, he should not ignore the even greater value of a good reputation . . .

—From the diary of one Anguish of Eyrie,
Knight of the Order of St. Sianne and St. Gall

15.

A Nice Set of Scruples

When Math came down to join his grandfather and Cernach for breakfast, Lord Branagh favored him with a disapproving glare. "What sort of costume is this for a long ride? Go upstairs, boy, and change into something more suitable."

In the act of taking his place at the table, Math hesitated, one hand on the back of his chair and his knee on the seat. "*Are* we going riding? No one said so before. Where are we going?"

There was a silent exchange of glances between the two men; then Cernach cleared his throat. "Our apologies. It seems we have discussed the matter so often between ourselves, it never occurred to either of us that you hadn't been told."

Lord Branagh waved Math into his seat. "As it appears that we were at fault, you may break your fast . . . and then go up and don your riding gear. But do not dawdle. We wish to reach Castell Emreis before noon."

Math obediently slid into his chair, nodding to the servant who was offering him a slice of veal pie. "I have never heard of Castell Emreis," he told Cernach. "Why are we going there?"

Cernach made a disparaging gesture. "It is the least of my castles. But we thought it might make a pleasant morning's ride. Also, it is very ancient, and we thought you might find the place of . . . historical interest."

And that, thought Math as he helped himself to a dish of greens boiled with bacon, was the first lie of the morning. He was getting quite good at detecting them. Even the stupid lies like this one, which was clearly unnecessary, since he would find out all about it as soon as he arrived at Castell Emreis, anyway. It was as though evasions and outright untruths had become such a habit at Caer Rigor, that his grandfather and Cernach had begun to lie as a matter of course.

Math ate his breakfast without much interest, then went upstairs to his room to change into his riding leathers. He arrived in the courtyard by the stable, three-quarters of an hour later, expecting to be scolded for the delay, only to discover his grandfather and Cernach, not even mounted, in the midst of a discussion about how many guards to take with them.

"We had decided on two dozen," Lord Branagh was saying huffily. "Now you announce that you are bringing half that number."

"You are mistaken," said Cernach, pulling on his riding gloves. "We had *decided* that so large a troop would be highly conspicuous. Twelve is more than sufficient. In truth, it is almost too many."

Taking matters into his own hands, with typical arrogance, Lord Branagh turned his back on his host, and gestured toward a pair of men who were lounging on the other side of the courtyard. "I will not have my grandson imperiled. You, fellow . . . come over here and bring your friend with you. And the insolent-looking rascal by the well. He will make up in size what we lack in numbers."

Math opened his mouth to speak. The "insolent-looking rascal" was the man he had watched go creeping around the castle two nights before; the man he suspected was a spy or an assassin. But remembering why he had kept silent this long, the boy decided to hold his peace a little longer.

Of course, there was now a delay while horses were saddled for three more men, but that was accomplished with reasonable dispatch, and soon everyone was mounted and riding out past the gate.

What Lord Cernach had described as a pleasant morning's ride was a brief journey past well-kept fields and neat little villages, followed by a much longer ride through country that became increasingly wild and broken. It was a land of rugged ridges and deep ravines, and the only things that grew there were heather, whin, and broom. They had ridden right out of Cuachag, Math guessed, and into some other holding of Cernach's, and they were crossing land so poor that no one considered it worth cultivation. Someone must have lived there sometime—why else would there be a castle?—but it must have been a long time ago.

By the time that Castell Emreis came into view, Math was prepared for a ruin, and that was exactly what it was: an ancient fortress with crumbling walls and shattered towers perched on a rocky rise. He had *not* expected to see so many men camped in the ruins, or so much activity once he rode inside.

There were parties of horsemen tilting at rings, and foot soldiers practicing with sword and shield, bowmen shooting at targets . . . and a ragtag army of less disciplined men who were doing none of these things, and were engaged instead in drinking, wrestling, lounging, or whoring with camp followers.

There were also two parties of stonemasons repairing the outer walls, as though preparing for an imminent siege.

"Who are these men?" said Math, glancing around him, when he and his companions dismounted. "What are they *doing* here?" Though he had an unpleasant feeling that he already knew.

"This is your army," said Lord Branagh. "These are the men who will set you in your rightful place. It is only right that you should inspect them, because soon you will be leading them into battle."

Math frowned. "You told me there might not *be* a battle. You told me—" But his grandfather was shaking his head, and the boy realized that these were not matters to be discussed openly.

And as it turned out, inspecting his troops consisted of trailing behind his grandfather and Cernach, while they strutted about looking important and asked a great many questions. On the rare occasions that Lord Branagh paused and remembered to ask Math if there was anything he wanted to know, the boy just shook his head. It was obvious enough what was going on here.

Only a few of these men were really his. That is, most of the troops that were actually drilling were Lord Branagh's men, and here and there among the tilters or the bowmen Math recognized the badge of some petty lord pledged to his cause, someone who sent a scant handful of men to support him. But the loungers and the dicers and the whore-mongers—which was to say, the majority—were plainly mercenaries and not even hired swords of the better sort.

Judging by the evidence, it was not difficult for Math to conclude that no one really wanted him to be Lord of Mochdreff. No one but his grandfather and some of his kinsmen, no one but Lord Cernach, who was supporting Math for some devious reason of his own. Oh, there might be those among the petty lords and the clan chieftains who were willing to speak up for him, because they truly believed that he had the better right . . . or because they didn't want Peredur or Mahaffy Guillyn . . . or because they perceived some political advantage in playing the various sides each against the other . . . but none of those lords and chieftains cared enough to actually *fight* for him, not even enough to send a respectable number of their own men to fight in his cause. It was utterly demoralizing.

Not, Math told himself, that he had his heart set on being chosen anyway. Yet the not being wanted, the being rejected practically sight unseen, that was what hurt. *But why should anyone want me? I allowed myself to be carried off into Perfudd like a baby, during Lord Cado's rebellion. And ever since Mahaffy Guillyn declared himself, Grandfather and I have been skulking about from place to place like we were fugitives . . . though nobody ever threatened us that I know about. The truth is, if I had any choice in the matter, I wouldn't want me, either.*

In a daze of misery, Math went wandering off by himself out of the camp and past the archery range. *And to make matters worse, I have been too much a coward to tell my grandfather I would much rather not—and now we are probably in so deep there is no getting out.*

He stopped at the foot of the high stone wall which had been occupying the stonemasons earlier. There were beams shoring up a portion of the wall, and the masons had erected a scaffold. It seemed as good a metaphor as any Math could think of for his so-called cause. That wall and Math's makeshift army: They were both equally unsound.

Overhead, there was a scraping of stone and the sound of something slipping. As Math looked up to see what was happening, he heard his grandfather sharply calling his name. ". . . come away from there, boy. Can't you see it is dan—"

That was all he heard, because then there was a creaking of beams and the sound of stones shifting—and before Math could think or react, something heavy hit him with such force that he went tumbling across the yard, and everything went abruptly black.

Math came slowly back to consciousness, lying on his back on the ground. As he tried to focus his eyes, a lean brown face slowly took form hovering somewhere over him, and a dirty hand with broken nails was extended to help him up.

"My apologies," said a gruff voice. "I never meant to hit you so hard. A fine thing to shove you out of the way of those stones and then practically break your neck myself."

Math nodded vaguely, accepted the hand, and rose unsteadily to his feet. Somehow—he was not sure when it had happened—a great many people had suddenly arrived, and they were all milling around trying to get his attention.

"Ah God, were you hurt, my boy? Can you hear what I say to you?" That was his grandfather, with a white face and a shaking voice. Math had never seen the old man look so terrified in all his life. But when he replied that he thought he was well enough, his grandfather recovered very quickly. Going all stiff and haughty again, Lord Branagh turned to address the tall figure standing at Math's side.

"That was well done. If you had not moved so quickly, it is likely Lord Math would have been buried beneath those stones."

The boy's eyes went misty and he might have fallen again, but someone—it might have been Captain Iolo— reached out to prop him up. And as the babble of voices around him subsided, as his mind gradually cleared, he came to realize that the man he had thought was a spy or an assassin had just saved his life . . . at considerable risk to his own. There was a pile of rocks and splintered beams in the very place where Math had been standing when the big man knocked him out of the way.

"My thanks," the boy whispered as he shook off the hands supporting him. It was the most that he could manage.

"In truth, that was very well done," said Cernach grandly. "Captain Iolo, this man deserves to be rewarded. A barrel of ale and double rations in the barracks tonight."

Hearing him speak, Math was ready to die of humiliation. Rather than honoring the man who had just saved his life, Cernach acted like someone who was tossing a bone to a dog. Math saw the big man's eyes flash, his lips curl back in a dangerous smile; it was clear that he felt the insult as deeply as he ought. If there was anything needed to complete Math's utter demoralization, this was it.

But then the man did something that made the boy think again. Rather than spit in Cernach's eye and take the consequences, he bowed his head, shuffled his feet, and actually mumbled a few words of thanks.

Math felt ready to weep with rage and disappointment. So he *was* a spy after all, God rot him. There could be no other explanation. Because a man who was capable of such a look as Math had just seen would *never* stand there and accept such an insult, would never degrade himself before a swine like Cernach—unless there was something truly important at stake, something important enough to make him swallow his pride.

And it was bad enough to go blundering about like a blind idiot and have to be rescued, but to be rescued by a man who was probably your sworn enemy was infinitely worse.

Math felt his grandfather poke him in the side. "Paltry," the old man was murmuring. Or that was how it sounded to Math. Apparently, Lord Branagh was also offended by Cernach's manner—or perhaps he just thought that his grandson's life was worth more than a pot of gruel and a few pints of ale. "In the name of all that is good, boy, remember your position. Give him the ring from your hand."

Math shook his head. It was the proper gesture, he knew, in the absence of something more useful like a sword or a horse. And if Math were really the Lord of Mochdreff, he would wear several rings for just this purpose, to bestow on the spur of the moment for services rendered. Unfortunately, he had only one ring, a narrow silver band with a very small stone, and it seemed a tawdry sort of recompense . . . not just for Math's life but for Cernach's beastly manner.

But it was then that Math remembered his dagger: The hilt was gold and the blade was the very finest steel. He slipped the dagger out of its sheath, and held it out. It was possible, of course, that he was handing over the very blade that would cut his own throat—since there was no way now that he could report what he had seen the other night—but fair was fair, and honor had to be served. "Please take this. It's not nearly enough, but it is all that I have to give you."

The others were already drifting away when the foreigner shook his head, and replied in a low voice. "As to that, I thank you, but I can't take your dagger, Lord Math. No, nor the ring from your hand."

Well, of course he can't, Math realized. The dagger was far too meaningful a gift, and so was the ring. To accept either one was to imply some relationship between them: an oath of fealty and service, a reciprocal vow of patronage and protection. A man who had been sent to cut Math's throat or to learn his secrets could not—in honor—accept either one.

Although, now that he came to think of it, it seemed to Math that the fellow was displaying a nice set of scruples for a spy or murderer. Perhaps the foreigner thought so too, or perhaps it occurred to him that he was betraying too much. In any case, the man abruptly changed his mind.

"There is no need for you to offer your pretty dagger to reward a fellow for doing no more than his duty. But if you will have it so, I will accept the ring after all. It comes to me now that while it may be too small for this great rough hand of mine, I can have it melted down and remade to wear in my ear."

"Yes," said Math, with a weak smile as he slipped off the ring. "You can wear it to . . . to remember me by, I suppose."

At Lord Balin's castle in Cormelyn, the feasting had come to an end. The petty lords and the clan chieftains, Lord Balin's guests, had all packed up and left, along with their families and their retainers, and only the governor and his household lingered on, planning what was to be done next.

"Lord Macsen made it clear that he expects to see us in

Dwrnach within the week," said Prince Tryffin as he walked in the garden with Mahaffy and Conn, and Lord Balin and his sons. "I admit that I hoped for some such invitation, if things went well here, though I never thought he would want us for more than a few days. But if you go as his daughter's suitor, Mahaffy, I suppose we must stay for a fortnight at least, and that means drastically changing all of our plans."

For just a moment, Mahaffy felt as though the world were falling away beneath his feet. "But we *do* have to go. You said yourself, he is the single most important man we can win to our cause. God knows, we can't afford to insult him now, when we are so close to an agreement."

"No more we can," said the Governor, laying a broad hand on Mahaffy's shoulder. "We will just have to send word to our friends in the north not to expect us before the middle of April."

And he went off with Lord Balin and the rest to arrange for a messenger, leaving Mahaffy and Conn alone in the garden.

"I hope you know," said Conn, "that if we go to Dwrnach, you will never be allowed to escape without first betrothing yourself to Lord Macsen's daughter. People are saying that she is already madly in love with you, and that if you encourage the girl by going to visit her, her father will hang your head on his bedpost if you disappoint her."

Mahaffy winced. "More likely it is Macsen who is in love—and not with me so much, as with the match itself. I wish I *could* believe that she was so deeply attached. Because truly, I have no desire to get out of marrying her. On the contrary: It is something I want so much, I can't help fearing that it will all go wrong somehow before I can ever get the lady to the altar."

Conn stood playing with the hilt of his dirk. "Why should anything go wrong? As you say, Lord Macsen favors the match, and so does Prince Tryffin. What else is needed? You

can't believe that Macsen is the sort of man who would
allow his daughter to choose her own husband."

"Not choose for herself, no, even though he seems to be
really devoted to her," said Mahaffy. "It is true that Macsen
wants to see Tifanwy at Caer Ysgithr, and he wants his
grandchildren and great-grandchildren to rule Mochdreff.
But for all that . . . I don't think Macsen will give her to
me unless he is convinced that I will treat her with all the
kindness and respect she deserves.

"God knows," he added feelingly, "if I had anything half
so precious, I would be very careful whose hands I left it
in."

Conn stopped playing with his dagger and began to look
interested. "You sound like you are the one who is already
in love. But how can you be attracted to a young woman you
have never really seen—much less feel anything more?'

"Perhaps I can't," said Mahaffy as they began to walk
down one of the garden paths. "It may be the very fact that
I have never seen her face that makes her so intriguing.
Conn, I could hardly sleep last night, for thinking of ways to
get her alone the next time that we meet. Really alone, so I
could talk her into removing that damnable veil and . . .
well . . . since I am planning to marry the lady, I suppose
that I shouldn't say what *else* I was thinking. But I tell you,
I was willing to go to far more trouble to remove that veil
than I ever put into getting any other girl to strip naked. And
it was the first time, the very first time, that I remember
losing sleep over a woman."

A faint heat crept into his face, and Mahaffy lowered his
voice. "I don't mean that I lack the same appetites and urges
that other men have. Just that if a woman says 'no,' I have
always been perfectly happy to look for the same thing
elsewhere."

Now Conn looked surprised as well as interested. "*Do*
they say 'no'? If anyone had asked me, I would have sworn
that you had never been refused in your life."

"Mother of God," said Mahaffy, with a snort, "you have

a poor opinion of women if you really mean that. I would never have thought that of *you*, Conn. Do you honestly believe that every woman I meet is so overwhelmed that she is ready to fall into bed with me?"

"Well . . . since you put it that way . . . no," Conn replied. "Of course, there are virtuous women, and girls who are already in love with somebody else, and all the rest of it. I just thought, with all your advantages, that you must show amazingly poor judgment in the women you· choose to approach, if you find yourself being refused very often."

Mahaffy frowned, trying to remember. "Ah well, if it comes to that, I don't think that I ever have been refused, exactly. I mean, there are some women that you *know* will go to bed with you, and some where you know there is simply no hope, and others that probably would with a little coaxing . . . and with the girls that require coaxing, I just never bother."

They climbed a rocky embankment above the garden and reached the orchard, where the apple trees were already covered with white blossoms. "But you do feel that you would like to 'bother' with this one?" asked Conn. "If she required coaxing, I mean."

"Yes," said Mahaffy vehemently. "Or else why would I spend half the night spinning schemes that I know in my heart I can never put into effect until after we are married?

"I know that I want her. But as for anything deeper, more lasting," he continued, "I really can't say. I know her to be intelligent, virtuous, and gentle. I admire her for all these reasons. And when I think of her voice, her laugh, the way that she moves, there is no doubt in my mind that I like her far better than any other woman I have ever met. But when it comes to love, when it comes to passion, I'm not even certain that is something I can feel for anyone."

The path under the apple trees was mossy and damp, a little slick. "Feel love or *fall* in love, do you mean?" Conn asked, paying as much attention to the placement of his feet as he was to the conversation. "They are not exactly the same thing."

Mahaffy shook his head wearily. "They might as well be, so far as I am concerned, since they both appear to be equally out of my reach. I grow fond of people sometimes, I can feel friendship and loyalty . . . to you, to Prince Tryffin. That seems to be the most that I can summon up."

He made a deprecating gesture. "The less agreeable emotions, I do very well. Pride, resentment, guilt, shame . . . I have mastered them all. I think it may be something in the blood. The Guillyns have always been a selfish lot, you know, and it seems to me that we are incapable of forming really strong attachments. Even worse, we never seem to show any natural sense of kindness or kinship even within the family. You have only to consider the history of my clan."

Conn thought a moment before he answered. "Your uncle Cado and your cousin Dahaut . . . they certainly never displayed any kindness that I ever saw. Dame Ceinwen is capable of disinterested actions, though I would hardly call her warm-hearted." Then he brightened. "The Princess Tinne was a great and tragic lover. You can't deny that she was desperately in love with Prince Mabonograin."

Mahaffy shook his head. "But the Governor had to go all the way back ten centuries to find her. She was probably the only one. A Guillyn finally fell in love and it turned out so badly, not one of us has been willing to try it again for a thousand years."

His friend was beginning to look confused. "Then why," Conn asked, "if you are so sure that you can't love her, do you have your heart set on marrying Lord Macsen's daughter?"

"Because," Mahaffy replied, "I think that what I do feel for her is as much as I *can* feel. And that, if I can't have her, I may never be able to feel this much again."

They left for Caer Wsyg in Dwrnach, two days later. They arrived just at sunset, and Lord Macsen came out into the courtyard to greet them personally, carrying a torch in his hand. "Come in, come in . . . I am pleased to see that you keep your promises so promptly."

He ushered them inside, where a fine suite of rooms had already been prepared for them, and supper was not long in coming, carried up to Prince Tryffin's chamber on silver platters by a regular army of servants in Macsen's green and gold. There was only one thing lacking, so far as Mahaffy was concerned, and that was the presence of Lord Macsen's daughter, who had retired early.

As for Macsen himself, he seemed less inclined to discuss the alliance or the betrothal than to pose a number of questions concerning the sidhe-stone chalice. Mahaffy was puzzled, and so was Tryffin, until their host finally enlightened them with a single question.

"Can the cup from the Otherworld heal my daughter's scars?"

Mahaffy and the Governor exchanged an uncomfortable glance over the supper table. "No, Lord Macsen," said Tryffin regretfully. "I wish that it could. It had healing powers once, but those have faded."

"Then what," said Macsen, pounding a fist on the table so that the plates and the goblets and the silver serving dishes danced and clattered, "is the good of the thing? It seemed when I beheld it that I was in the presence of a mystery, but all that I can remember now is a light and a sweet odor. All very well, but how do you intend to use it to make Mahaffy Guillyn the Lord of Mochdreff? It is not a weapon, it is not a medicine for healing. What good will it be to any of us if it comes to a battle?"

It was a startling question. Up until now, the miraculous vessel had seemed to be self-explanatory. Most who had seen it had been impressed, some few had not, but no one before had ever thought to ask its purpose. Prince Tryffin sat rubbing his chin, as though at a loss for an answer. *Either that,* thought Mahaffy, *or he expects me to say something. I did say that I wanted to do this myself.*

And certainly, if anyone could explain the chalice, it ought to be him. While Tryffin had brought the vessel out of the Otherworld, Mahaffy had been the one most intimately connected with the cup since then. But how to explain the ineffable?

Mahaffy cleared his throat. "Lord Macsen, the purpose of the cup is to bring men of good will together in fellowship. You saw how we were all affected, when the chalice was revealed at Castell Gauvain."

Thinking quickly, he went on. "Most who are exposed to the radiance of the cup are uplifted by the experience. Yet for those who come to the feast with an intent to deceive, or carrying malice in their hearts, the light is almost too bright for them to bear. It causes such discomfort, they become gruff and irritable, and leave the hall afterward loudly proclaiming that the whole thing was a sham, that they saw nothing, felt nothing. Not all who can bear the light will necessarily become our friends; not all who can't will necessarily stand against us. But the difference is . . . that we know which of our foes will fight us honorably, and which of our so-called friends are likely to betray us. I think you can recognize the value of that."

Lord Macsen nodded slowly. It seemed that Mahaffy had struck the right note. "And yet," said Macsen, with a sigh, "I wish that it might have helped my Tifanwy. God knows, she deserves well."

"In the light of the sidhe-stone grail many things are revealed," the Governor said gently. "Perhaps the beauty of your daughter's soul with all the rest. But it would be cruel to make the experiment . . . to appear to give her healing and then take it back again."

There were tears in Macsen's eyes as he clasped Tryffin's hand. It was a strange moment, this bald display of sentiment from a powerful Mochdreffi nobleman. Of course, Prince Tryffin had a positive genius for drawing out the best and the truest emotions in other people, but Mahaffy chose to regard this particular instance as a sign of

things to come. The rite of atonement had healed more than
the land; it had healed some deep wound in the spirit of the
Mochdreffi people. Though perhaps not everyone who was
affected wanted to be healed—and even when they did, it
was going to be a long, slow process.

After that, Lord Macsen grew more cheerful; he even
became expansive over the wine and sweet wafers that
were served at the end of the meal. "You have only to say
the word, Lord Mahaffy, and my daughter will be yours. We
could arrange for the exchange of rings, a formal betrothal,
tomorrow if you wish."

"God knows," said Mahaffy, "there is nothing I would
like better. But the lady herself . . . is she ready to have
me so soon as that?"

Lord Macsen made an airy gesture. "She is a little uneasy,
a little agitated. What would you expect from an inexperienced girl?"

Since inexperienced girls generally fell under the heading
of "women who had to be coaxed," Mahaffy could not
really say that he knew *what* to expect. That being so, he
was willing to take Lord Macsen's word that a few
reservations were perfectly normal.

"In that case, Lord Macsen, make whatever arrangements
are necessary," he said. "Appoint the hour, and I will be
there to claim your daughter."

The hour was noon, and they met in Lord Macsen's
private chapel. The arch above the altar had been decorated
with boughs of flowering apple, and burning wax candles
had been placed on every available surface: the altar, at the
foot of the statues in all the niches, even on some of the
unoccupied benches.

When Tifanwy came in with that silent step of hers,
looking small and fragile in a trailing gown of heavy white
brocade, a circlet of ivy leaves worked in gold, and a green
silk veil, Mahaffy felt his throat tighten, his palms go damp.

They knelt together before the altar, while Lord Macsen's

confessor said a blessing over them. Her hand, when Mahaffy took it and slipped on the ring, was as soft and pretty as he remembered. In a voice that was even sweeter than he remembered, she plighted her troth, and then slid a ring from her own hand onto his finger.

Now there was nothing left to do but to wait for her to lift the veil and receive his kiss for the very first time. With the blood pounding in his ears, Mahaffy watched the silken veil flutter as Tifanwy hesitated . . . then, with a gesture more suggestive of desperation than anticipation, she flung the veil back over her head and shoulders, so that her face was finally revealed.

Mahaffy let out his breath in a great sigh of relief. Her face was a perfect oval within its frame of chestnut hair, and her skin gleamed with a pale ivory radiance in the light of so many candles. She had a soft, vulnerable-looking mouth, and large dark eyes, and she was . . . not beautiful, thank God, but certainly appealing.

As for the scars, they were barely visible: one small one above her right eyebrow, a long one on her right cheek; and the other tracing the line of her jaw. A glance was enough to assure Mahaffy they were hardly worth thinking about.

He was bending to kiss her on the mouth, when it suddenly occurred to him that a girl so shy and reserved might not enjoy such intimate contact with a man she hardly knew. There would be plenty of time for that between the betrothal and the wedding, when they were better acquainted. So at the last moment, he swerved and brushed his lips across her left cheek instead.

It was a mistake. He knew by her sharp intake of breath—even before he drew away and saw the look of pain and betrayal in those wide brown eyes. *She thought that I flinched. Oh God, she thought that I flinched.*

And he could not even make it better by kissing her on the other cheek, the one with the scars, because the veil went down again like a barrier between them.

There was nothing he could say . . . nothing that

she would believe if he *could* say it with so many other people there to hear it . . . certainly nothing that would take the memory of the hurt away, even if she did believe him.

The only thing left for Mahaffy to do was to get to his feet, take her damp little hand in his, and lead her out of the chapel, past a long line of her family and well-wishers.

And all the while, he was silently berating himself for his fatal clumsiness, his brutal, bungling, misplaced instincts. *She may not have loved you, but she was ready to like you, and now she probably never will. You have spoiled it all yourself, you criminal fool!*

But at least, he thought numbly, he had finally solved the riddle of his cold-hearted ancestors. It was not that the Guillyns were unable to *feel* love—it was simply that they were incapable of inspiring it.

"In ages past," said the wizard Glastyn, *"a maze was regarded as a sacred enclosure. A place for meditation, a place for revelation . . . and no one who entered ever emerged unscathed or unchanged by the experience."*

"But why was that?" asked his young apprentice. They were sitting in the wizard's laboratory by a roaring fire, and Teleri had spent most of the evening watching the pictures in the flames and describing what she saw—an exercise, said Glastyn, in divination. His statement seemed to come out of nowhere.

"Why was that?" the old man repeated. *"Because like a crossroads or boundary, a maze is a place neither here nor there, and so represents every place and no place . . . all at the same time."*

16.

In Exchange for a Life

It was almost midnight when Meligraunce was finally able to sneak out of the barracks and glide across the courtyard toward Luned's tower. It was a dark night, the moon no more than a milky glow behind a thin screen of clouds and all but a few of the stars obscured, yet the Captain moved warily.

He had almost reached the door at the foot of the tower, when he realized that he was not alone. Someone small and light-footed was following him across the yard. Drawing one of the knives out of his belt, he whirled around, ready for a fight, but the footsteps came to a sudden halt—and the shadows were so deep, it was impossible to make out the form of whoever was pursuing him.

"You have nothing to fear from me, Captain Meligraunce," said a breathless voice out of the darkness, a voice which the Captain immediately recognized as belonging to young Math. "I owe you far more than a silver ring, and I always pay my debts. Besides, it would be a pity to kill me, so soon after you saved my life."

The boy moved a little closer, so that Meligraunce could just see his outline. "Will you come with me into the maze, where we can talk undisturbed?"

Meligraunce slipped the knife back into his belt, and followed Math into a boxwood alley. There was the sound of steel striking flint, a spark of fire, and the smell of burning wax. Then the boy seemed to materialize out of nowhere, holding the stump of a candle in one hand, shielding it with the other.

"I had hoped you would not recognize me, it has been such a long time," said Meligraunce. "Lord Cernach sees me every day and never guesses, though he and I were actually acquainted as recently as last summer. But I suppose I gave myself away when I refused to accept your gift of a dagger."

Math smiled faintly. "I already knew that you were a spy, though I didn't know whose . . . I was the one watching you, a few nights past. And today, when I finally decided that you must have come from Prince Tryffin . . . well, it was not so difficult to go from there.

"I do remember you a little, you and Prince Tryffin both," he added. "And I've heard of your exploits since Lord Morcant died. The wonder is that you remember knowing *me*."

Meligraunce shook his head. "I remember you well enough. I remember a boy who played fairly and honorably at games with the other lads, who defended rather than bullied those who were smaller than he. I remember a boy who was easy and friendly with the servants, without pride or contempt. If I did not remember all of those things—if I had any reason to doubt that you were speaking the truth when you said I had nothing to fear—my knife would be at your throat right now . . . unless I had already killed you. It is fortunate for you, Lord Math, that I have such a very good memory."

"Please," said the boy, "it is not 'Lord Math' as yet, and you know that as well as I do. Yet it puzzles me why you saved my life in the first place, even if you do carry some agreeable memories from when I was younger. Considering all that you have seen today, you can hardly regard me as anything but a—a dangerous enemy of Prince Tryffin."

"And if you had just let me die," Math continued, "you could have spared yourself the dangerous business of spying on me."

The Captain folded his arms across his chest. "Now, there is a fine excuse for cowardice. I will have to remember it, the next time I find myself in a similar position. In truth, I acted on impulse, saving your life, yet I believe I would have done exactly the same even if there had been time to think. What I saw at Castell Emreis was a young man just as surprised as I was to see troops gathering there."

There were things that Meligraunce wanted to know from this boy—things that he thought Math might be inclined to tell him, if he read the boy's character accurately—and he decided that the best way to inspire confidence would be to offer a few pieces of information of his own. "Besides that, no one sent me here for the purpose of spying on you . . . that was only incidental. Dame Brangwaine asked me to come here to rescue her great-granddaughter."

Math drew in his breath sharply. "So she *is* a prisoner here. I was beginning to suspect that, because no one has let me in to see her since the first night she arrived. I kept thinking I might like to pay her a visit, but they said it would only make her angry to be disturbed, that she didn't want visitors, and . . . and I rather liked her, you see, so it seemed important to make a good impression."

By the pink tinge stealing across Math's face, the Captain was able to recognize a budding infatuation. "As to that, she always speaks well of you," he said kindly. "I believe she would welcome a visit, because she has many things to ask you, many things to tell you."

With a gesture to follow him, Math led the way through the maze toward one of the nooks with a bench and a fountain.

"You said you were in Anoeth with Dame Brangwaine recently?" he asked. "Then you must know better than I do what is happening out in the world. Have you . . . do you know if my cousin Peredur is well?"

"I am sorry," said the Captain, feeling a strong resentment that this task had been left to him. "Peredur is dead, and there is talk of poison."

Math sat down on the bench with a thump, and the light of his candle wavered. "And his little half-brother? I am afraid I don't remember what they are calling him now."

"Grifflet fab Tryffin," said Meligraunce. "Now that I think of it, he looks something like you, except for your yellow hair. More than his brother did, anyway. When I last saw him, Grifflet was safe in the Governor's care. But before that there was an attempt to abduct or murder him, and one of the men involved wore a device similar to Lord Cernach's badge."

The memory made all the anger he had felt before come surging back. "If I knew for certain that Cernach was to blame, I tell you I would gladly take his throat between my two hands and shake him until his neck snapped."

"I don't know if he was to blame or not," said Math. His face had gone white and there was something about his breathing that made the Captain guess that he was very close to tears. "I *suspect* there are wicked things being planned here, but I just don't know. And my grandfather . . ."

He glanced up at Meligraunce with a pleading look, as though he were seeking his approval somehow—or perhaps only absolution. "Lord Branagh is a tyrannical old man. I have seen him be very cruel. But he has always, always been good to me. Even when Lord Morcant was still alive . . . even when Calchas was alive, and there was no idea in anyone's mind that I would ever be important to anyone. I am the only one of Lord Branagh's grandchildren to whom he has ever shown a hint of tenderness. And . . . and I know that he is not Peredur's grandfather, or Grifflet's, but still I find it hard to believe he would wish either one of them harm, seeing that there is *something* of me in both of them."

Remembering how Lord Branagh had looked and acted after Math's narrow escape, the Captain was willing to give him the benefit of any doubt. "It may be that Lord Cernach plans these things, and your grandfather only learns of them afterward. Though Luned has said that her kinsman lays the blame for Peredur's death on Lord Branagh, we can hardly consider Lord Cernach a reliable source."

Math swallowed hard. "They both tell lies, you know. That beast Cernach and my grandfather both. I hardly know who to believe anymore."

The candle in his hand had nearly burned away, but the moon had come out from behind the clouds, and when Math blew out the candle, there was still enough light to see by.

"Will you tell me this," said Meligraunce, studying the boy's face carefully as he spoke, "do you really wish to be Lord of Mochdreff?"

"No," said Math, "but it doesn't matter whether I do or not. It is my duty, you see—now more than ever, with Peredur gone and because Grifflet is too young for anyone to want him. I owe it to my clan and to my bloodlines. My grandfather said so, and it is not one of his lies. He has been saying the same thing ever since Morcant died, and . . . and he used to be a very truthful man."

Meligraunce shrugged. "It is a fine thing to pay respectful heed to the words of your elders. Especially for a young boy. But if you will pardon my asking, how old are you now?"

"Fourteen," said Math. "I was born in the summer, so I am almost fifteen."

"Then by the laws of Mochdreff you are a man—and have been so for almost three years," the Captain reminded him. "And maybe it is time that you decided for yourself just where your duty lies."

Math gave a deep sigh. "Yes, I begin to think so, too. Though I still may decide that Lord Branagh is right."

He glanced up at the sky, then shook his head, as though something about the phase or the position of the moon troubled him. "I am out much later than I usually am, and perhaps it is not so wise to risk it, but . . . will you take me with you to visit Luned? You can trust me, you know. I'll guard your secrets as though they were my own. It's the least I can do under the circumstances. Also, you said that she had things to tell me, and I would very much like to hear them."

"Yes," said the Captain. "I think that would be an excellent plan."

In Luned's bedchamber, the boy sat on a stool and listened quietly to all that she told him. Yet by the expression on his face Math was only growing more and more confused. Apparently, nothing he had learned so far had served to enlighten him.

"I am sorry to tell you these things," said Luned. She was sitting in a chair, much higher than his stool, and she bent down to speak in his ear. "If it gives you any comfort, I would not tell you any of this if I did not believe you were strong enough to bear it."

Math sat up a little straighter, taking heart from her words. "My grandfather says that nothing really happened that day in Penafon, though I have always wondered how he could be so certain, since neither of us was there. Here in Cuachag, things are so pleasant it is easy to believe that things are changing, but when we went to Castell Emreis, it was so barren and grim, I knew that Lord Branagh must be right after all. For all that, I will not risk harming my land or my people. Cernach can do whatever he wants with his golden cauldron, but I will not come near it, I won't have any part of it. Just in case it should happen that I *could* curse the land, by doing what Cernach wants me to do."

"They might force you to do it," said Luned, a frown beginning to form between her dark eyebrows. "They might hurt you in ways you can scarcely imagine."

Math shook his head. "No, my grandfather would never allow that to happen. He will shout in my ear, he may even strike me, when he discovers that I am not ready to obey him, and it is likely I will subsist on bread and water for the rest of my life," he said with a twisted grin. "But nothing terrible will happen to me. Besides, you said yourself that the cauldron can probably still be used to their advantage, even if I refuse to do what they want."

"He is speaking the truth, I think," said the Captain, from his place by the door. "For one thing, Lord Branagh seems to have an eye toward his grandson's dignity. That alone should be enough to keep him from beating or abusing the lad for Cernach's satisfaction."

Luned sat back in her chair, looking ever so slightly relieved. "Well then, that is one evil thing that we need not fear. Yet there is still so much . . . !"

"No one is going to hurt you, either," said the boy. "I am going to help you to escape, Lady. You may think that I am hardly the person to do so, but the truth is, I may be the only person who can."

Luned continued to gaze at him with a skeptical smile. "I can see that your intentions are good, anyway. Yet I saw Cernach's men bring in great armfuls of wood, earlier today, and leave them by the door of the dwarfs' tower. If you are going to rescue me, it will have to be very soon. In another day or two, Bagdamagus will begin to cast the cauldron."

She did not say that Meligraunce would be leaving as soon as that happened, because with Math still apparently determined to stick by his grandfather, the less he knew about that the better.

Yet she had apparently said enough, because the boy nodded in a grim sort of way as he rose from his seat. "A few days at most . . . I will keep that in mind."

⚜

She was a golden ship with scarlet sails and she plowed a furrow through the dark waters of the Bay of Findias, leaving a glittering silver wake behind. She was a small ship, a crew of six was enough to man her, so the old wizard sat on the forecastle, leaving all the work to the sailors . . . Had there been a squall or a deadly calm he might have bestirred himself, but there was just enough wind to fill the sails, and the ship sped on through the night.

The island where they were heading, so Gwenlliant had been informed, was fourteen miles from shore. Down in the tiny dark cabin, sitting on the floor because she had been too ill to make it so far as the bunk, it seemed to her a very great distance, those fourteen miles, a voyage of epic proportions. And why on earth had Atlendor chosen to put his school on an island when Findias, glorious Findias, the city that was practically the wizard's own creation, would have welcomed him and his students with open arms?

The door of the cabin opened and Findabhair crept in, still in tunic and hose like a boy, carrying a lighted lantern. She sat down beside Gwenlliant and put a comforting arm around her. "Poor Etain, are you always so seasick? Or have you never been on a ship before?"

Gwenlliant managed to shake her head. "I am never seasick . . . or at least I have never been seasick before. The motion of the waves is so dreadful . . . Are you sure we aren't riding through a storm?"

"It is a beautiful night," said Findabhair. "I wish that you could come out and see it, because the air might do you good. Still, I can understand your wanting to be private when you are feeling so ill. Would you like me to help you over to the bunk?"

"No," gasped Gwenlliant. "I am afraid of falling. If I fall, I might injure the ba—"

But she had stopped too late. Findabhair was now regarding her with a pitying glance. "So that's how it is. No wonder you are having a difficult passage." She hesitated. "I don't wish to pry, but . . . Etain, are you married?"

Gwenlliant nodded her head. She was much too miserable to think up a lie. "Yes. But my husband is a long way away. And—and this is a secret that only Atlendor knows, so please don't tell anyone, not even our friends."

"I will not say a *word* to anyone. But if any brute of a husband comes looking for you," said Findabhair fiercely, "you can be very certain that none of us will allow him to harm you."

Gwenlliant saw that she had given the wrong impression, but did nothing to correct it. While she would have liked to trust the beautiful Draighenach girl, she thought she had taken enough risks already.

"You had better not let Rhufawn see you this way—he can't endure pregnant women, especially the young ones, and especially when they are ill," Findabhair went on. And when Gwenlliant turned an astonished face toward her, the young woman laughed.

"I didn't mean that the way that it sounded. Only that he gets sad and terribly, terribly worried. I think that someone he loved very much died in childbirth, when she was really too young to be having a baby." Then, realizing what she had just said: "Findabhair, where is your tact?" she scolded herself. "I have an idea that the girl was much younger than you, Etain, so you needn't worry about *that*. Rhufawn always says that if he ever had a daughter, or a niece, or any sort of female apprentice in his care, he would take great pains to make certain she didn't marry too early. He would lock her away in a tower somewhere and keep her at her studies, so she wouldn't have time to look at a man until she was eighteen or nineteen at least."

To Gwenlliant, this all sounded faintly familiar, like a story she had heard about someone she knew, but with her head spinning and her stomach in knots, it required too much effort to try and remember. She wondered if seasickness was ever fatal. "How . . . how old, do you think, was the girl who died?"

"Oh, not very old at all," said Findabhair cheerfully. "Perhaps fifteen or sixteen. Of course, I have known girls who were married that young and younger, but I think it is simply a scandal."

And Gwenlliant—who might have said a great deal on the subject under ordinary circumstances—felt much too ill to do anything more than nod her head, close her eyes, and lean against the older girl's shoulder.

The sailors dropped anchor at midnight, about a hundred yards from the island. Because there were jagged rocks thrusting up out of the ocean on every side, they did not dare to bring the ship any closer. They lowered two long rowboats down on ropes and then threw a ladder, also made of ropes, over the side for the wizard and his students to descend.

Gwenlliant climbed down queasily, and experienced some trouble with her tangled skirts. When she finally landed in the bottom of one of the boats, she sat there breathing hard, gulping down as much of the salt air as she could. It helped some but not enough, with the boat pitching and tossing on the little wavelets.

Caílte and the other youngsters were wildly excited. The moon was full and so bright it was more like noon than midnight, and the fortress on the island was revealed with a kind of dreamlike clarity. "It is not a castle at all . . . it is more like a lighthouse!" said Caílte.

"Then it must be the most immense lighthouse in the world," murmured Gwenlliant, interested in spite of her sickness. The island was roughly circular and perhaps a hundred feet across; the towering structure was built all the way out to the water. When it was high tide, as it was now, the waves actually slapped against the lower walls. And the tower went up and up to such a dizzying height that Gwenlliant was certain it could only have been built by sorcery.

There were no windows or entrances down by the water—else the place would have been flooded in every storm—but there was a set of narrow, shallow steps built out from the wall, made of the same flinty stone. Climbing those steps, as Gwenlliant soon discovered, was like traversing a treacherous mountain ledge; the way was so narrow and the steps so slippery, she had to inch up sideways, clinging to the wall as much as possible. And even before she reached the gates, she was looking straight down a sheer forty-foot drop to the sea.

Once through the intricate triple gates, however, it was all light and warmth, a vast entry hall blazing with torches and *four* vast fireplaces built into the walls, as well as a broad central hearth. The flames burned blue and looked cold, but they gave off a steady comforting heat. *Wizard Fire,* thought Gwenlliant. *And no wonder* . . . With dozens of young magicians on hand, it was a small thing to maintain the pale flames which required so little fuel.

Gwenlliant knelt down on a sheepskin rug by one of the fires. As she held out her chilly hands toward the blaze and felt the heat soaking into her bones, she gave a deep sigh of pleasure.

"Well, Etain." That was Rhufawn, dropping down on one knee beside her. His layers of tunics were wet with sea spray, his chestnut hair damp and curling. He did not look as though he minded either of those things. In fact, there was a gleam in his hazel eyes, an intensity bordering on hunger in his pale face, that she had never seen before.

For the first time, she understood why he had become a wizard, and why he was so good that the others all envied his talents. Magic excited him, it elated and thrilled him, it filled him with the same kind of pleasure that other men found only in bed or in battle. "How do you think you will like it here?" he asked.

Gwenlliant glanced around her. Except for the fires, there were no visible signs of magic, but she could *feel* it, oh yes, she could detect it unmistakably with every one of her other senses. It whispered in the air, it vibrated in the stones, she could taste it and smell it, but it went deeper than that. It was part of the balance and proportion of everything she saw here, it was the equilibrium that taught her the difference between up and down, it was light and shadow, distance and depth. Just to enter this place, just to sit and gaze, to feel and to know, was to understand more of the Science of Wizardry than Gwenlliant had ever thought possible.

She took a deep breath, and gave Rhufawn such a smile as (had she only known it) transformed the plain face she was wearing with its beauty and warmth. What she *thought* was that she was going to like this place better than any other place she had ever been before.

> . . . at last, Pefyn came to a place, a deep cut between two
> hills, a valley of broken stones. Near the center of that
> valley was a circle of mighty megaliths, many of them still
> standing. And because he was weary and full of sorrow, he
> sat down on the ground and began to lament his ill fortune.
>
> Pefyn spoke to the stones, and the stones spoke back to
> him.
>
> —From the Oral Tradition

17.

Speaking with Stones

Evening meals in the gloomy Caer Rigor banquet hall
with Lords Cernach and Branagh always seemed interminable . . . sufficient purgation (Math liked to think) for any
sins that he had managed to commit during his brief
lifetime.

Tonight, however, the boy was brimming with excitement. He dominated the conversation, plying Lord Cernach
with enthusiastic questions about armies and battle plans,
who would be sending troops in the future, ways and means
of enlisting greater support.

"Lord Caradoc and Lord Dyfan, they were always fond of
me—treated me with every kindness when I was a boy at Caer
Ysgithr," Math heard himself babbling. "Clans Machain and
Owein, Gilcoch and Kilorran . . ."

He brought in every name he could think of that was not
absolutely committed elsewhere, while his grandfather and
Cernach sat there and smiled, sipped their wine, and nodded
insincerely. They were humoring him, as the boy knew
perfectly well. It was not his place to make plans or to woo

followers—all this was for "wiser" heads—but they could hardly come out and say so directly, since the ostensible goal of all this planning, the premise from which everything began, was to prove to the world that Math was ready to take up the reins of government in his own right.

"But then . . . ah God, I was forgetting—" Math's face fell and he brought the recitation to a grinding halt. He sighed deeply, and began to toy with the stewed mussels on his plate, shaking his head and muttering under his breath.

"Yes?" said Lord Branagh. "Speak up, boy, and spare us these vapors. What is troubling you now?"

Math hesitated, fidgeting in his chair. "Grandfather, where can I meet with those lords and chieftains? I can hardly entertain them at Castell Emreis. You always say I should be careful of my dignity, but who will respect me if I am forced to receive envoys and embassies at that crumbling ruin?"

Though Math spoke directly to his grandfather, it was Cernach who answered, with a casual wave of one hand. "You need not trouble yourself over that, Lord Math. You can meet with them here, of course." And since he was lying anyway, Cernach apparently decided to become creative. "We will invite them all to a great feasting at Caer Rigor, and reveal the cauldron before a multitude. The Governor and Mahaffy Guillyn with their tawdry sidhe-stone goblet will be nothing beside it. It will be a truly splendid occasion."

Math brightened. "It does sound splendid. In fact, it sounds perfectly wonderful. And I think . . . but no . . ." Again, his eyes lost their sparkle and the bright smile turned wistful. "My grandfather and I have imposed too long on your hospitality. We really ought to go home to Caer Cachamwri. While it is hardly so grand as Caer Rigor, we could certainly hold the feasting there. It would be more appropriate, you know, to receive the lords and the chieftains in my own home, the place I was born and reared." Assuming once more that bright, hopeful look, he turned toward Lord Branagh. "Grandfather, I am sure you must agree with me. We ought to start making plans to go home at once."

Lord Branagh, who had just started on a bowl of milk soup flavored with herbs, stopped with the golden spoon halfway to his lips. "It is certainly worth considering, yet there is so little time——"

"Nonsense," broke in Cernach, a little snappishly. "You must regard *this* as your home. You are welcome to stay here as long as you wish, Math, and you mustn't even think about leaving."

Having disposed of that topic, and eager to take up matters closer to his heart, Cernach turned to Lord Branagh. "The letter of defiance that we send to Prince Tryffin . . . If you will meet me in my bedchamber this evening——"

But Math was not to be fobbed off so easily. He had made certain plans of his own—though the exact nature of his plans Lords Branagh and Cernach were very far from guessing—and he was not ready to give them up. "I am sorry to interrupt you, Lord Cernach. But this is very, very important to me. A point of honor, you might call it. The lords and the chieftains who we hope to impress will respect me more if they meet me on my own ground. If we hold the feasting at Caer Rigor, they'll know very well that you are the lord here and I am only your guest. In truth, so long as my grandfather and I remain here, we are nothing but . . . but pensioners, living on your charity. It is really rather shocking, now that I come to think of it, how badly we have imposed on you."

Apparently, Math was more persuasive than he had dared hope he could be; Lord Branagh was looking troubled, as though what he had just heard struck some chord. "I had not thought . . . There is some truth in what you say. Perhaps it would be best if we——"

"Utter nonsense." Cernach was breathing rather loudly through his nose. "I don't know what you are talking about.

I have already put my home and everything in it at your disposal—what more could you ask?"

Now Lord Branagh was glaring at him for the interruption, and it actually looked like there might be a quarrel brewing. So Cernach mastered his irritation and changed his tactics.

"In truth, young Math," he said with a false, condescending smile, "you are the lord here . . . I am only your obedient servant." As he spoke, a deep shiver passed through the stones of the castle, but he continued on, completely oblivious. "And any guests that you choose to invite here will be made aware of that important fact. Let there be no question. What I promise, I will perform."

Liar, thought Math. *There will be no feasting, there will be no guests here, and your promises are not worth anything.*

But for all the insincerity of that offer, the words alone had been sufficient for Math's purpose. It was time to yield gracefully, and the boy did just that. "Well, of course, if you put it that way, I can see that your plan is best. And I thank you very much, Lord Cernach."

And if I am very lucky, thought Math, *Cernach will never guess how* truly *grateful I am.*

Meligraunce and Math met down in the courtyard, just outside the tower where Luned was imprisoned. "By God," said the Captain, "you appear to be in a mood of wild excitement. Did you have much difficulty slipping past your guards and out of your rooms tonight?"

Math shook his head. "No more than usual. I am becoming quite expert at this sneaking and skulking, you know. If you are ever looking for a bright young lad to take on as your apprentice spy and assassin, you could hardly do better than to consider me." His eyes were dancing in a way that Meligraunce had never seen before—in the past, there had been a certain wariness, the look of a boy who was always expecting some reprimand or other slight unpleasantness, but that was gone now—and he seemed to stand a little taller.

"You have asked Lord Cernach and your grandfather to explain their plans more fully, and they have dazzled you with their predictions of a brilliant future for you," Meligraunce guessed, with a sinking heart.

The boy laughed softly, under his breath. "I know their schemes, Captain, but they don't know mine. Neither do you, but I think you will like them a great deal better than Cernach is likely to. Please, please, let us visit Luned at once. I have something particularly delightful to tell her."

The Captain studied him a little longer, then shrugged. Meligraunce led the way into the tower and up the winding stairs to the corridor outside Luned's rooms. He knocked on the antechamber door before pushing it open.

Luned came running to meet him, with her hands outstretched. "I am glad that you came. Can you smell the fires burning? They are heating the furnace tonight. This may be our last meeting."

She was lifting her face to kiss Meligraunce, when she caught sight of Math, lingering in the passage outside. The light in her face died—she had hoped for a last few intimate moments before she and the Captain parted—but she was swift to conceal her disappointment.

"Come inside, Math, and be welcome," she said graciously. "You have been a good friend to both of us, keeping our secrets. It is a pity our fellowship lasted so briefly." She held out her hand invitingly.

"No, Luned, you must come out and join *me*," said the boy, grasping the hand that she offered him, and pulling her past the threshold and out into the corridor.

It was a moment before Luned and Meligraunce were able to grasp what had just happened, that she had actually stepped out beyond the wards. Then she gave a little cry of delight which she smothered with one hand, and stood staring at Math with wide, dark eyes. "I am free. Math, you have *freed* me. But . . . but how, my friend?"

Math laughed. "I can't tell you the whole thing, because there isn't time. You have an escape to make, as I remember. It's enough to tell you that Cernach was so immoderate in his professions of hospitality, this evening, that he actually told me that Caer Rigor was mine to use as I saw fit.

"I daresay that I will have a difficult time holding him to that," Math added with a grin as he put Luned's hand into the Captain's, "because I don't suppose he really meant a word of it, but . . ." He shrugged.

"Yet the stones of Caer Rigor heard him speak, and that was enough to give you the true lordship," Luned finished for him. "Well, you are a clever boy to realize the meaning of his words so quickly, and to act on his mistake."

"I think there was more here than a slip of the tongue," said Meligraunce, with a dawning smile. "You tricked him into saying it, did you not? You already had some such plan in mind when you said that you would rescue the lady and that you were probably the only one who could."

"Some such idea, yes," said Math. "But I didn't want to tell you exactly what I had in mind, in case it didn't work out."

He turned toward Luned. "I suppose you have spent these last weeks thinking what you would do, if only you could pass the threshold first. What now . . . Will you cast some spell over the guards at the gate?"

Luned and the Captain exchanged a glance; Meligraunce nodded, almost imperceptibly.

"There is a pattern spell down in the maze," she said. "That way is open only to a few, but the Captain, as it turns out, is one of those few. With him, I may pass through to safety, though not on my own. But Math . . . will you not consider coming with us?"

"No," said the boy. "I am tempted, but my duty really does lie here. Also, once Cernach realizes that you are gone, I don't doubt that he will have all of his men out combing the countryside, but if *I* disappeared, too, they would be half killing themselves with searching. You have a better chance of escaping without me."

"He may realize what you have done, how you have tricked him," Luned insisted. "He is a wicked, vindictive man, my cousin Cernach, and I do not like to think what might happen to you."

Math, however, had made up his mind. And the Captain thought that this new air of purpose and determination became the boy very well. "He will certainly guess if I go with you. Or if he catches us all here talking."

Luned went pale. "You are right, Math. We are not wise to linger here. I never know when Cernach or Brangweng-wen may decide to pay me a visit. The best we can hope for is that no one will notice that I am gone until that wench Gleis brings my breakfast in the morning. We'll not get far during that time, traveling on foot."

Hand in hand, she and Meligraunce started down the stairs, Math trailing behind them. At the foot of the steps, however, the Captain stopped.

"If you will not come with us now, Math, the next time that we meet . . ."

"We may be fighting for opposite sides on the field of battle. I thought about that already," said Math, with a grimace. "Or I will be standing trial with the other traitors. I—I considered that, too. But Captain, you owe me nothing. You saved my life, and what I did tonight is only fair payment."

Meligraunce shook his head. "There are some things that are beyond calculation. You can't reckon them out and say, I did this and you did that, and now we are even. Wherever we meet, and under whatever conditions, we will still be friends." He gave the boy a swift clasp of the hand, and then followed Luned out into the yard.

"Meligraunce!" He could hear her whisper, but it was almost impossible to make her out in the shadows at the base of the tower. "I am going to put on a spell of invisibility. As you may know, that is difficult to do when one is moving, but I believe I can maintain it until I reach the heart of the maze. Also, a word will shatter it. So you must just take it on faith that I am following you and not try to speak to me."

Meligraunce nodded, and struck out across the courtyard. They were both moving so lightly, he could not even hear her footsteps following. But once he reached the maze, he thought he felt something touch him and again a little later, moving down a boxwood alley, just the lightest contact, as of her skirts brushing against his leg.

When he arrived at the turf-covered mound, she was there waiting for him. "You are certain you can remember the pattern?"

Meligraunce thought that he did, yet he experienced a moment of doubt. There was but one way to find out. Hand in hand, he led her through the sequence of movements as he remembered them. At the last second, his fingers tightened their grip, and he pulled her into his arms and hard against his body.

The spell took them both in the same instant, and whisked them through the night.

The next thing Meligraunce knew, he was standing up to his ankles in mud, staring down at the reflection of a round yellow moon in the water. Luned moved against him, raising her head from his chest. "You need not tell me where we are, because the air is unmistakable."

There was a soft whickering sound behind him, a faint splashing. Meligraunce released Luned, whirled in place, and drew out his sword in one smooth motion. A large shape loomed before him, a dappling of dark and light among the rushes.

"I'd have a care with that sword," said a voice. "You have very nearly eviscerated your poor horse, and I must tell you that I was at great pains to bring him out here for you."

Luned began to laugh. "Great-uncle! In God's name, what are you doing here?"

The old man came out from behind the piebald gelding. "Assisting you in your escape, my dear. Now that the butcher's boy has brought you out of the well, and the Captain so far as this, it came to me that you might need a horse." He seemed inordinately pleased with himself.

"But how did you know that it would be tonight?" asked Meligraunce. Then he answered his own question: "Why do I ask? You predicted this all from the very beginning. You knew exactly how it would all turn out and tried to tell me; I simply failed to understand."

Isaf Danan nodded. "Yet we have reached the end of my foreknowledge. Only a madman could predict any of the things that have happened already—not even a madman can say what comes next. But see . . . I have made this one last provision for you." He reached into the gelding's saddlebags and brought out a bundle of fabric which he then shook out. "A gown and a cloak, Luned. Not so fine as what you are accustomed to, but more practical where you are going."

Luned took the rough garments of wool and held them to her breast. "And gratefully accepted. I hope you will see that whichever of the serving girls you took these from is amply repaid."

"For you, Captain, a cloak also, less gaudy than the one you are wearing," said Isaf, producing something dark out of the second saddlebag. "I would sink that one in quick-sand, were I in your place, along with Luned's velvet gown. It would be just as well if Cernach and his men give out the wrong description when they begin searching for you."

Luned was already thinking along the same lines. She was stripping the jeweled pins out of her hair, the rings from her fingers, the bracelets from her wrists, and casting them into a deep puddle. The Captain frowned at the waste.

"There is no need to toss all your jewels away, when you are likely to miss them later. Though it would certainly be foolish to wear anything so eye-catching while we travel, we can carry them secretly with us. Besides that, we may need to sell them, in order to speed our journey."

Luned flushed. "You think me arrogant and thoughtless, I suppose. And perhaps not without cause. But I tell you, after so many months in Cernach's luxurious prison, I feel as though I am shedding my chains."

Seeing that Meligraunce continued to frown, she tugged off the last of her rings, an ornate golden band set with opals, and held it out on her palm. "Take this one, then. The sooner you sell it, so much the better, because the sight of it offends me."

Meligraunce hesitated before accepting the ring. And then, on an impulse he did not entirely understand, threw it out across the marsh with a sweeping gesture. "It is gone, then. We will have to make do with the coins I carry in my purse."

"And I am gone as well," said Isaf Danan. "May we meet again under more favorable circumstances." He waded off through the mud and the rushes, leaving the Captain and Luned, flushed and indignant, to work out the rest between them. They were both of them too involved in their argument to pay him more than a passing glance.

"That was unnecessary," said Luned. "I said that you might sell the ring if you choose. Now you will blame me if we starve along the road."

"Blame you, Lady?" Meligraunce's eyebrows rose sharply. "I wouldn't presume. You must just tell me what you think ought to be done, and I will do the best that I can to satisfy you."

She was breathing heavily and her eyes were flashing. "Do not patronize me, Captain. I know that I have little hope of escaping, even yet, without your help and guidance. Tell me what I must do, correct my mistakes if you must, but do not insult me."

"Mother of God," he said. "Is that all you can think about at a moment like this? But believe me, a woman who throws diamonds and gold into the mud needn't concern herself with what a common fellow like me thinks of her."

Luned's hand flew up as though she would slap him, but then she let it drop again. "Why are we quarreling?" she asked softly. "There was none of that when I was Cernach's prisoner. Now that I am free, does it necessarily follow that we must resume the . . . the unpleasantness there was between us in Trewynyn."

"No," he answered with a sigh. "No, it does not. My apologies. And I was in the wrong, anyway. It seemed to me, when you dropped your jewels in the water, that you were casting away the price of a poor family's existence for many years." He passed a hand over his eyes. "That was foolish . . . No one can eat diamonds, gold, or opals. Your jewels have value only as they are beautiful and give you pleasure. If they remind you of things you would rather forget, they are worthless. You were wise to throw them away."

She opened her mouth as if to reply, then apparently thought better of it. She handed him the clothes that Isaf had given to her, and began unlacing her velvet gown. Meligraunce took the clothes, but after a moment of hesitation, he turned himself halfway around so that he was facing away from her.

"Gallant, Captain, yet hardly necessary," said Luned. "You have seen me without my clothes before this."

"I have," he replied, without looking back over his shoulder. "But then I had no need to think of anything beyond your pleasure and mine. We cannot afford the sort of . . . distraction . . . the sight of you now might provoke."

Luned laughed softly. "Perhaps you are right. But we can't run forever—eventually, we must stop and rest." She moved so close that Meligraunce could feel her breath like a kiss on the back of his neck.

"Then we shall see," she whispered in his ear, "what may be accomplished in the way of distraction."

Names, Numbers, Figures, Signs, Symbols, Rhythms, Rhymes,
Configurations, and Applied Will are the basis of all Magic.
Add to these the four elements . . .

—*From* The Geometry of Magic
and the Harmony of Numbers

18.

At the Heart of the Storm

The days were long but full of interesting things to do and to learn in Atlendor's island fortress. Because Gwenlliant was new, she was assigned to study with the younger students. "But if you progress as quickly as the Master thinks that you will, you may move on to one of the other classes in another few months," she was told.

Besides herself, Caîlte, Morfan, and Gildas in the class, there was a quiet boy named Gwefl, a boisterous one named Ifor, and a highly precocious pair of twins (cousins of Tegid and Cet) who were only seven years old. When Gwenlliant first learned that one of the older students would be guiding their studies, she had hoped for Rhufawn. But Rhufawn spent most of his time with Atlendor, his studies were so advanced, and instead, there was Maeve, a girl of about her own age, who was brilliant and intense . . . so brilliant, in fact, that she had started where Gwenlliant was starting *now* less than six months ago, had advanced at a breathtaking pace through that class and the one above it, and so had earned her place as tutor to the apprentice students. Unfortunately, she wanted for patience—which was a great lack in a wizard *or* a teacher—and it was whispered among the

243

other journeymen students that she would not hold her position long.

Or so Gwenlliant learned from Findabhair. "No one likes Maeve, no one but Rhufawn and Atlendor. The Master is such an idealist, he gives everyone the benefit of the doubt. Eventually, of course, he will realize that it would be a kindness to everyone, even Maeve, to have her removed."

Could Maeve be Maelinn? Gwenlliant was nearly certain that she was. Or, at least, the logical part of her mind said so. What else at the school was so much like Maelinn? Still a doubt persisted, because she had no *sense* of the thing being true, no intuition. And Gwenlliant was always lingering somewhere near when Maeve was doing her own lessons with the journeyman students, hoping to catch her actually working magic, because then she would know. But Maeve—as everyone told her and Gwenlliant soon learned for herself—was devoted to theory rather than practice.

The pride of the school was a vast library devoted to magic, herb lore, medicine, alchemy, and natural philosophy, more than five hundred volumes in all. The possession of so many books was a wonder; Gwenlliant could remember a time when Tryffin had men out searching for weeks to provide her with just three great volumes bound in calfskin. Merely to contemplate Atlendor's wealth of books was dizzying . . . even, or perhaps especially, after Gwenlliant learned that the wizard had penned a great many of them himself.

The library was one of the central chambers, a circular room lined with shelves, tier upon tier, reaching up to the ceiling twenty feet above, each shelf literally crammed with the weighty, ponderous tomes. To claim one of the books on the upper shelves was an immense undertaking, involving a swift climb up a ladder, then a slow, precarious climb back down again, trying to balance yourself and the great awkward thing all at the same time. For Gwenlliant, with her bouts of vertigo, it was a distinct challenge.

And then, if you had selected the wrong book, it would

not even open—or if it did, you could not read it. The books were wonderful, for besides containing a lifetime's worth of knowledge, they were beautifully made: bound in leather, brass, or iron, the parchment pages inside illuminated with pictures or diagrams in brilliant colors, and the whole embellished with much gold leaf. Many were sealed by spells, and could be unsealed only by invoking the proper names, and the rest were written in cipher. This was the way that the wizard directed the studies of his various students, without actually supervising them.

"If Atlendor meant you to read that book," Maeve would wearily explain, every time that one of the apprentice students chose the wrong volume, "he would have taught you the names and the cipher."

Panting and sweaty after one such effort, Gwenlliant wondered resentfully why Maeve never warned anyone *before* they made the climb back down, since she must know very well which books were allowed to them. As she leaned against the ladder, with a volume bound in blue leather clutched against her chest, Gwenlliant glared at Maeve, and would have responded tartly, had not Rhufawn come into the library just at that moment.

"Why thank you, Etain, I wanted that particular book," he said cheerfully, smoothly slipping the book out from under her arm. "It was kind of you to fetch it down for me."

He wandered over to one of the long oak tables in the center of the room, put down the heavy book with an audible thump, and opened the cover. So it must be one of the books in cipher, thought Gwenlliant—had it been sealed, he would have carried it away to some private place before opening it.

On an impulse of curiosity, she moved closer and peeked over his shoulder. It *was* one of the books that she could read, after all. Not only did she know the cipher, but the diagram on the open page, in red and brown ink on creamy vellum, was entirely familiar. She was just opening her mouth to say so . . . when she remembered when and where she had last seen that particular volume.

It was not the same book, of course. This book was only a shadow, and Gwenlliant had once held the reality in her hands, back at Caer Cadwy when she was a child. It had been one of Teleri's books, old and faded and battered by time, because it had passed through a great many hands before the young sorceress found it at the Princess Diaspad's fortress in the north of Mochdreff, and brought it back home with her to Camboglanna. And during the brief time that Teleri had labored in vain to make a precocious witch-child into a wizard, Gwenlliant had studied from that book.

Rhufawn glanced up and caught Gwenlliant looking over his shoulder. "It is not one of the difficult volumes; you'll all be reading it very soon . . . at least the early pages," he said, smiling at Caílte and Ifor across the table.

Absent-mindedly, he reached out to Gwefl, who was standing on his right, and ruffled the boy's fair curls. "But there is a passage on sidhe-stones that Atlendor and I were discussing . . . neither one of us thinks that it's entirely accurate."

When Rhufawn was finished with the book, he asked Gwenlliant if she would like to walk up to the roof with him, for a breath of fresh air.

"You mustn't disrupt my class," said Maeve. "I am sure that you would never allow any of the rest of us to wander in and carry off *your* students, if you were tutoring."

"You are entirely right. My apologies," said Rhufawn, his smile undimmed, his good humor unimpaired. But in spite of his apology, Maeve continued to look displeased, and she followed his progress out of the room with a stony, unblinking stare that told Gwenlliant perhaps rather more than she wanted her to know.

Maeve wants Rhufawn. And the reason she is so disagreeable to the rest of us is because she not only can't have him, she can't even provoke him into a quarrel, is unable to rouse him even to anger, much less anything better.

Gwenlliant could hardly blame her. Rhufawn was attractive, not only because he was lean and graceful, with a fresh complexion and all that curly hair, but because there was a kind of tension about him at times, a passionate intensity that was very exciting. *If I were not already a married lady . . .*

But even that thought was traitorous; Gwenlliant was shocked at herself for thinking it. She was married to the best and the handsomest man in the world. How could she even think what she would do or feel without Tryffin? How could she consider what it might be like to be in love with a man who understood magic . . . and by extension, must understand *her*, in a way that even the most extraordinary ordinary man like Tryffin could never hope to match?

When a storm swept into the Bay of Findias, life at the fortress became positively thrilling. Waves crashed against the tower walls, waves that were sometimes so tremendous they almost reached the lower windows, forty or fifty feet above the rocks. As the winds and rain continually lashed the tower, the school of wizards was engulfed by the elements in dynamic collision.

"Shocks and harmonies of shocks, that is how Atlendor describes it, and why we are here, why the school is on an island," Cet explained to Gwenlliant and some of the other apprentices, one stormy day. "At the heart of any tempest there is a balance point, a place of perfect equilibrium, and once we can find it, we will know as much of wizardry as any man or woman needs to know."

"You have simplified it, Cet, until it means practically nothing," said Maeve, in her disagreeable way. A number of students had gathered in one of the large chambers connected to the hall, and were watching the storm through an open window. "What you ought to tell them—"

"No," said Findabhair. "He has distilled it down to its

very essence." Since arriving at the school, Findabhair had abandoned her boyish garb. Today, she wore a gown of scarlet wool trimmed with miniver, and the pale waves of her hair fell in a shimmering cascade almost to her knees. "These things *are* simple, or ought to be. It is your understanding that's at fault, Maeve . . . the thing is too light and airy for you to grasp, so you want to weigh it down with an excess of words and ideas."

"You are both right," said Rhufawn, ever the peacemaker. "Findabhair, because she understands the beautiful simplicity of the principle . . . and Maeve, because the apprentices are not yet ready to reach out and grasp that airy principle *without* some weight of excess words to slow it down for them."

Findabhair laughed. "I stand corrected. How wise you are, Rhufawn—it is a wonder your beard is not longer than Atlendor's. How do you combine so much knowledge with your tender years?"

Not expecting an answer to her playful question, she strolled over to the window where Gwenlliant was standing, and put a hand on her shoulder. "Come away from there— your hair is wet and your gown nearly soaked with the spray. You must be chilled right down to the bone."

Gwenlliant shook her head. "I like it," she said. "I like to feel the wind whipping around me, and the rain in my face. There is something out there, some . . . force of nature. I can't even name it, yet even so, I feel that I could reach out and touch it, learn to control it."

"And so you will, some day soon," the older girl replied soothingly. "But for now come away. Sit by the fire and warm yourself, and I will comb out your hair. Then you can return the favor by braiding mine."

Gwenlliant followed her into the hall and over to one of the rugs by the central hearth. As they sat down on the sheepskin together and Findabhair drew an ivory comb out of a pocket in her skirt, Gwenlliant felt her throat tighten. She had never had a friend so close to her own age, no sister or cousin to share confidences with, or to exchange any of the other fond, intimate little services that young women in most households performed for each other. At Caer Cadwy, she had been a sort of a pet for the older girls, and it had been much the same at the cloister in Achren. At Caer Ysgithr, as a new bride she had been alternately spoiled and bullied by her own attendants. But never a friend and equal, until now.

What a fool I am, to form attachments in this place, Gwenlliant told herself as Findabhair gently teased the tangles out of her windblown hair. *Even though wizards live a long, long time, the real Findabhair, the real Rhufawn, almost certainly died before I was even born. Even if they were still alive, even if I met them again in the Outer Celydonn, they wouldn't know me, because I was never really there in the true past.*

Gwenlliant stole a glance through the arched doorway. Rhufawn was talking to Cet, probably about some alchemical principle or some other aspect of magic; his face was animated and his eyes were flashing with excitement.

Even if I were foolish enough to try and stay here, I could never mean anything to him. No one even knows to what extent these ghosts, these shadows, are self-aware, but we do know that they are constrained to repeat all the important events of their earthly existence; there can be no significant alterations. And because of that, because there was no Etain for the real Rhufawn . . .

She gave a deep sigh. *Even if I were wicked enough to try and lure him into bed with me . . . even if I were lucky or unlucky enough to succeed . . . he would probably kiss me on the forehead in the morning, thank me most kindly and sweetly for a pleasant evening—and promptly forget that anything had ever happened between us.*

That night, Gwenlliant tossed and turned on her narrow bed, in the room that she shared with Findabhair, Maeve, and two other girls. Perhaps it was just the storm that made her so restless, but Gwenlliant was afraid it was something more than that. She had been too long in this place, had fallen victim to its various allurements, was far too tempted to stay forever, and was suffering the twinges of a guilty conscience.

But I have a husband and a little boy that I love with all my heart. The pang that accompanied that thought was more than just guilt, it contained real longing. She moaned and turned over on her side—and felt something fluttering inside her, a stirring, a stretching, a warmth flooding her.

She was out of bed in an instant, shivering with excitement. The child had moved, the new life . . . no, her *son* . . . had actually moved.

For the first time, he became real to her, a real person not just a potential. In a flash of prescience, she could see him quite clearly: a sturdy little boy with hair as winter-pale as her own. He would have Tryffin's brown eyes, his patient, practical way of approaching things, yet there would be something of her brother—long-lost Garanwyn—in him as well. His name would be Tristan.

"Tristan fab Tryffin." She whispered the name, and it had a good sound to it.

But now, more than ever, she was far too excited to sleep. She pulled on the garments that Rhufawn had bought for her in Findias: green gown, soft black boots, and a tartan mantle which she pinned in place with a silver brooch. Then, walking softly so as not to awaken the others, she slipped out of the bedchamber and moved down the long corridor toward the library.

Even through the thick stone walls, she could hear the booming of the waves, the savage howling of the wind. It was no night for sleeping, and perhaps it was no night for study. Still, she had to find some way to pass the time until dawn. Gwenlliant pushed open the door to the library, and was surprised to see that someone had set a lighted branch of candles in the middle of one of the tables.

As her eyes gradually adjusted to the dazzle of candlelight, she saw that this someone was one of the younger boys, sitting on a high stool and studiously addressing an open volume bound in blue leather.

"It is late, Gwefl, you should be in bed," Gwenlliant said as the boy looked up at her, his eyes heavy and his face flushed like Grifflet's when he was half-asleep.

She closed the door behind her as she spoke, not really expecting him to follow her advice. Gwefl was quiet and gentle, but he could be stubborn. Moving in his direction, she dropped a motherly hand on his disheveled curls. "Now see . . . you have grown so sleepy and stupid, you can't read the book and you are probably wondering why. And look here, it is the wrong one, the one that Rhufawn was read—"

She withdrew her hand, took a step backward as a light flared in her mind. Besides Atlendor and the journeyman wizards, there were only two people at the school who ought to be able to read this book: Gwenlliant herself, and the person who carried so many of Gwenlliant's memories.

But . . . Gwefl? He was gazing up at her, obviously puzzled by her sudden recoil, looking at her with such limpid innocence in his eyes, she was reminded all over again of Grifflet. *But it won't hurt him if I am wrong, if I make a mistake.*

So this time, Gwenlliant did *not* make the same mistake she had made by Loch bel Dragon. She took a firm grip on one of the boy's slender shoulders just as she said the name.

"Maelinn."

There was a grinding of bones, a shifting of flesh under her hands. A cloying, sickening stench filled the air. And a moment later, Gwenlliant was no longer looking down at the quiet young student of wizardry; she was staring directly into the eyes of her worst enemy.

For two days and the night between, it was nothing but riding and walking for Meligraunce and Luned, or else hiding in ditches, copses, hedges, and caves . . . never for very long. As soon as their pursuers were far down the road, it was up into the saddle again, Luned riding pillion with her arms around the Captain's waist, and another long wearisome ride.

As for food and drink, there was little of that: a handful of water when they passed a stream, oakcakes and cheese bought from an inn and quickly consumed. Once they put enough distance between themselves and Cuachag, Meligraunce had promised, they could relax the pace a little, stop and eat a heartier meal, perhaps even sleep in a bed. But the distance never seemed to be enough; there were always Cernach's men on the road—if not where the Captain could see them, at least so near that Luned could sense them.

By the time that a storm swept in from the south on the morning of the third day, it was almost welcome, they were both so weary. If the men searching for them stopped, then so might they. Except now came the search for shelter. They were crossing a bleak stretch of moorland through the pounding rain, and the only village they passed, they did not dare enter, because Cernach's men might have also been driven there by the raging elements. A solitary cottage or hut was what they needed.

At last Meligraunce spotted something. It appeared to be little more than an irregular heap of planks and thatch from a distance, but proved to be an abandoned drover's hut when they finally arrived. Luned ducked inside through the low doorway, while the Captain took the piebald around to a kind of lean-to stable at the back. He unsaddled the gelding, rubbed him down the best that he could with some old straw, and spread a blanket over his broad back.

"By God, I wish I had oats and hay to give you now," Meligraunce told the horse, "but I swear there will be hot bran mash in great steaming buckets as soon as we safely arrive . . . somewhere."

Having done all that he could for the animal, he joined Luned in the musty interior of the hut. She had contrived to make a fire from some sticks she had found outside and piled in the middle of the floor. She had done so without benefit of the flint and steel that the Captain carried with him. "It's a fine thing to have a woman of power on hand to make a fire by magic," he commented, as he stripped off his wet outer garments, the cloak and the tunic, and crouched by the fire in his shirt and his breeches.

"Even a witch has difficulty making a fire when the wood is so wet," said Luned. She had removed her own cloak and spread it out on the floor by the fire to dry. "I wish I could conjure us a table and some chairs to sit on . . . a bed with a feather mattress . . . but I am afraid that our cloaks will have to do for all, once we can get them dry."

"I wish I could offer you better surroundings, and all the luxuries to which you are accustomed," he replied wearily. "Unfortunately, Lady, this is the best that I can do."

Her eyes flashed in the firelight. "I had all the amenities at Caer Rigor, all but the most important, which was my freedom to come and go. I don't regret my present circumstances. For your sake, I wish this place were more comfortable . . . you have done so much on my behalf, and it is plain to see that you are ready to drop from exhaustion and lack of sleep. For my own sake, I welcome this opportunity to—to live as you have lived in the past, to share the same hardships, and prove to you that I am strong enough to endure them."

Meligraunce smiled faintly, looking up from his place by the fire. "My family was never so poor as this. I have, on occasion, been forced to live hard, but the cottage where I was born and lived as a child was twice the size of this one and very well made. My brothers and sisters and I always had food on our plates, clothes on our backs . . . my father was accounted quite prosperous by the other farmers and herdsmen in the countryside around."

Luned bit her lip. "I suppose that I have insulted you now. You must forgive my ignorance," she said, in tones of the deepest mortification.

But the Captain only laughed. "I am not in the least offended. In truth, I am deeply touched by your willingness to sleep in the dirt and eat cold porridge three times a day, all for my sake, if you think that's how you would live as my wife."

"I would walk barefoot through Hell," she said fiercely. "I would sleep naked in the snow. I would—"

He rose from his crouch, came around to her side of the fire, and pulled her into his arms. "I would never allow you to do any of those things. Luned, if you lived like the kind of peasant you are thinking of, you would be a toothless old hag in another ten years; you would be weak, dirty, emaciated, humble . . . yes, you *would* be humble, at least outwardly, and grateful for whatever scraps more prosperous folk were willing to toss you. Do you think I could bear to see you that way?"

"No," she said, leaning her head on his shoulder. "Of course you couldn't . . . no more than I could bear to see you in that condition. But you are strong, intelligent, you have Prince Tryffin's favor. Meligraunce, I can live the sort of life that you *are* going to make for yourself, if you will let me. Have I not proved to you these last two days that I am not so . . . so spoiled and fond of luxury as you thought me?"

He drew her closer, tipped back her head, and lowered his own so that he could kiss her throat. "What you seem to be proving," he said against her skin, "is that I am going to be incapable, after this, of living without you."

Her gown came off easily, and along with the two cloaks made a damp but soft pile for them to lie on. Their thin linen undergarments were little impediment, and though tired and dirty, they were both eager. The roughness of his beard, his hard, hungry kisses against her soft flesh, drew a new wildness from Luned. It was not at all like the first time, or any time since, but it was equally satisfying in its own way.

And when it was over, when they still lay tangled in each

other's arms, still breathless from the dizzying sweetness of their joining, there was no doubt in his mind or in hers that they were both going to fight to spend the rest of their lives together.

The price of blood is always blood, the price of a life is blood, bone, and flesh. If you wish to meddle in matters of death and life, it is better to do so with clean hands . . . but if you cannot, it is always advisable to have a suitable sacrifice ready to hand.

—*From* Moren Clydno's Book of Secrets

19.

The Price of Treason

The letter of defiance was written and sealed, then sent on by messenger to Prince Tryffin in Cormelyn—all without Math's consent. But when the boy heard that the deed was already accomplished, he insisted on knowing the contents of the letter. Reluctantly, Lord Branagh provided his grandson with a fair copy, written out by Cernach.

Math sat in a high-back chair with the parchment in his hand, reading the document carefully. And when he came to the end, he threw it on the floor with a contemptuous gesture. "This is . . . is outrageous. It is so provocative, that when he receives it, the Governor will have no *choice* but to gather an army and wage battle against us."

"And if he does?" said Cernach coldly. "We are prepared for him. Indeed, we have only to receive word that he is gathering his troops, and we can strike first. No one will blame us, once it is known that he is mustering his forces."

"If you do strike, it will be without me leading your troops," said Math, equally chilly. In a way, he was relieved now that he had finally made up his mind. He only wondered why it had taken him so long. "And everyone *will* blame us, who sees this letter, because it brands us all as traitors to the King, to the Governor, to every principle of law and—"

"Math," said his grandfather, in thunderous tones, "what do you mean when you say you will not be leading your own troops? I hope to God you have not turned coward. Of course you must ride with the rest of us, when the time comes. Anything else would be unthinkable. The morale of the men, the impression your absence would make on the petty lords and the clan chieftains who have already pledged themselves to support—"

"I don't see that," said Math, gripping the arms of his chair. "You have done everything else without me already. Why in the name of all that is holy should you require me to do anything now? And God knows, I have no desire to wed myself to a losing cause—and one I consider highly immoral into the bargain—because Prince Tryffin obviously has the superior forces."

"Why?" said Cernach, reaching out and taking the boy's chin roughly into one hand, tilting it back so that he spoke directly into Math's face. "Why should you wed yourself to our losing cause? Because it is your cause, boy, and as you can plainly see, if anyone pays the price for its failure, it will have to be you."

Math slapped Cernach's hand away. "I would advise you, Lord Cernach, not to maul me in the future. I simply won't have it." And there was something in the way that he said it that made the older man back down immediately.

"Besides," Math continued, "I don't think that I *will* have to pay for your failure. Prince Tryffin is a reasonable man, and God knows that Mel—that the men around him are reasonable as well. When he sees that your letter was sent without my signature, he will realize that you acted without my consent. In fact, he is such a reasonable man, that he might even spare *you*, if you come to your senses immediately and sue for forgiveness."

There was a shuffling of feet and a clearing of throats.

"Math," said Lord Branagh finally, "the letter of defiance is signed with your name and sealed with your seal."

Math sprang up from his chair. "Who *dared* to forge my signature? If it was you, Cernach, I swear, I'll—"

"Do not make threats that you can't carry out," Lord Cernach hissed. "You are under my roof and in my power; think again before you make any heedless promises."

Then (perhaps deciding that it did not become him to lose his composure, all for the sake of a beardless boy), he became very cold and haughty again. "It seems to me that you have lost your senses, young Math. You have been most reasonable and biddable up until now. Why this sudden defiance?"

But Math shook his head stubbornly. "I asked first and I want to know: Who signed my name to that letter?"

"I did," said Lord Branagh. "As your grandfather—and in some sense your guardian—it seemed only appropriate that I sign in your name. Which hardly makes it a forgery at all."

Then Math surprised both his grandfather and Cernach by laughing out loud. "Not only a forgery, but a clumsy one at that. I don't suppose you realize it, Grandfather, since you never *do* ask me to sign things, and I never send you letters because we are almost always together, but I don't even use that black letter script that you do." Reaching for pen, ink, and paper, he wrote out his name in a round uncial script: ᶜᴰᴀᴛᶣ. Then he passed the paper over to his grandfather. "It will be easy enough to prove that I never signed your wretched letter, particularly since I intend to be very forceful in all my denials."

There was a long frozen silence, broken at last by Cernach. "Think again, Math. You are behaving as though Prince Tryffin's victory were assured. But with you or without you, we are going to win. Are you forgetting the golden cauldron? Bagdamagus has completed the work; all that remains is the consecration, and this miraculous vessel will be ours to use as we see fit. Against the powers of the cauldron, the Governor and Mahaffy with all of their troops will be nearly helpless. And once we have triumphed, it is for *my* pardon and your grandfather's pardon, not for Prince Tryffin's, that you are going to be begging."

"That may be," said Math. "Though if you are so certain of that, why are you wasting your time arguing with me? You have no idea if your damnable cauldron spells are going to work—with Luned doing everything that she dared to befuddle Brangwengwen, and without the blood of a wise-woman to consecrate the thing as you had hoped—"

"And how do you know these things?" By now, Cernach was livid. "Did you visit Luned behind my back, in spite of my orders to stay away from her? What lies did she tell you, before she ran off with that gypsy mercenary? And just how long and to what extent have you been betraying us?"

"Betraying you?" said Math. "I betraying *you?* You seem to be forgetting that you are both of you pledged to me, not the other way around. You, Grandfather, have said from the beginning that you had no other goal than to win me my rights. And you, Cernach, sat in your own hall and declared that you were my most devoted servant. But what have you done, what have the pair of you done? You imprisoned Luned, you plotted to murder her, you conspired with dwarfs to curse the land, you spread stories about my horse going mad and nearly killing me, you poisoned my cousin Peredur, sent men to abduct his baby brother . . . and all this in *my* name, without ever once asking for my opinion or even telling me what you planned to do. And after all this, you dare, you actually have the nerve to accuse *me* of treachery?"

Math turned on his heel and walked toward the door, but he paused on the threshold for a final word. "That is," he said, "the greatest piece of damned *impudence* that I ever heard in my life!"

After the boy was gone, Lord Branagh sat down in the chair his grandson had just vacated. He passed a hand over his brow. "I have never seen him so. I hardly know what to make of it."

Cernach ground his teeth. "That boy of yours is well nigh incorrigible. I hope you will be able to handle him better in the future."

The old man sighed. "And yet, he was in the right . . . on some points he was in the right. We acted badly in sending out the letter with his name on it. That was dishonorable; I can't think how I came to consent to it."

"What does any of that matter now?" said Cernach. He began pacing the floor, one hand fidgeting with the hilt of his sword. "You must bring him to a more reasonable frame of mind. You must exert your authority . . . use force if necessary. We must not be tender with him, Lord Branagh. He is pleased to think that the Governor will show him mercy, but that will not happen. So do not think to spare the boy pain now, when it may cost him his life later."

Lord Branagh frowned. "I am not quite certain what you are suggesting. Though he is, in many ways, no more than a boy, he is much too old for me to chastise like a child."

Cernach laughed nastily. "I don't mean that you should switch him like a naughty little boy. This is no time for such weak measures. There are horsewhips down in the stables. Have Math stripped and beaten in the courtyard for all to see . . . the humiliation alone should be enough to break his will. If that doesn't suffice, there are instruments of torture down in—"

"Before God," roared Lord Branagh, springing to his feet. "Do you actually suggest that I have my grandson, the rightful Lord of Mochdreff, publicly abused like a common churl?"

"He may or may not be the rightful Lord of Mochdreff— but whatever he is, he is weak and he is spoiled," sneered Cernach. "By God, if he was mine, you can be certain that I would not spare the whip."

Lord Branagh had gone as white as death, and his hand rested on the hilt of his own sword. "This goes far beyond a mere disagreement over methods and policy. I see that you have been lying to us all along, with all your protestations of respect and loyalty. And Math was correct, Lord Cernach, you are damned impudent. You have insulted my grandson beyond forgiveness, and in doing so, you have insulted me. I demand satisfaction; indeed, I will have satisfaction, unless it should happen that you are as cowardly as you are false and impertinent. Come out with me to the courtyard and—"

"No need for that," said Cernach, reaching for his sword. "We can settle it here." Both men drew at once—Branagh, perhaps a little sooner, because his hand was closer—but Cernach was younger, faster, and more agile.

The old man barely had his blade out of the scabbard before Cernach lunged, thrust, and impaled him through the vitals. Lord Branagh fell to his knees on the floor, in a great gush of blood, taking the sword with him. Cernach calmly pulled out his dagger, reached over the old man's head, and thrust the blade between his shoulders, again and again.

Eventually, Branagh obliged him by dying.

Math woke in darkness. Someone was sitting on the edge of his bed, shaking him insistently by the shoulder. "Grandfather . . . ?" he asked.

"It is I, Captain Iolo," said a familiar voice. "Lord Math, I fear that you are in grave danger. You must leave Caer Rigor as soon as possible."

The boy sat up, rubbing the sleep from his eyes. "I don't understand. Or perhaps you don't. Whatever you may have overheard, my grandfather would never—"

"I am sorry to tell you," said the guardsman, "that Lord Branagh is dead. Lord Cernach has murdered him. I believe that he has lost his mind, and that you may be his next victim. That is why you must leave at once."

Math was dazed. It was too much for him to absorb all at once. Lord Branagh dead? That just could not be; if Branagh was gone, then Math was entirely alone in the world.

"I . . . are you sure that he is dead? Could it—could it be that you are mistaken, that he was only injured or . . ."

"I am sorry," Captain Iolo repeated. "I helped to carry the body out of the room. There is no doubt at all. I would spare you the details, but there is no possibility that a man could sustain such injuries and still live."

As the guardsman spoke, Math became aware of somebody moving in the darkness, somebody edging around the perimeter of the room. "Who else is there?" he asked sharply.

"A friend," said Iolo. "Someone who can lead you to safety." A light flared, and a bent figure in ragged velvet appeared out of the darkness, carrying a candle in his hand. "Do you know who this is?" the guardsman asked.

"Yes," Math answered. "It is the old madman. I have heard the servants refer to him as the luck of Cuachag. How can *he* help me?"

The old man tittered softly, but the Captain looked at Math reprovingly. "He is Isaf Danan, Lord Cernach's uncle. A man of great wisdom and inspiration." Seeing that this information had failed to make the proper impression, Iolo added: "He is the kinsman, also, of our Lady Luned. She trusted him, and so should you."

This sounded a little better, enough that Math climbed out of bed and started searching for his clothes.

The old man bent his head and whispered something in Iolo's ear. "He wishes me to tell you," said the Captain, "that he is a friend of Avallach."

Math paused, in the act of pulling on his hose. "I don't know anyone by that name. Or, at least, not that I can remember."

"The man who saved your life at Castell Emreis," the guardsman explained patiently. "The big dark foreigner, who carried our lady away."

"Oh," said Math, fastening his points. "*That* Avallach. I don't believe that anyone told me his name, now that I think of it."

Iolo rose from his seat on the bed. "Lord Math, I dare not pass you through the gate. Not just for my own sake," he added shamefacedly, "but because the other men would suffer as well if Lord Cernach had reason even to suspect. Yet there is another way, a secret way, and Isaf Danan is the only man in the castle who can show you that way. Will you not trust him, and allow him to help you?"

Math paused, and looked at the old man directly. "Are you the one who showed Cap—are you the one who taught Avallach the pattern spell?"

Old Isaf nodded his head.

"In that case—" said Math, taking a deep breath, then reaching for his tunic and slipping it over his head—"In that case, I believe that I will trust you, and go wherever you lead me."

Lord Cernach sat alone in his room for a long time after the body was carried out. It was an interesting sensation, actually killing a man. He had almost forgotten what it felt like to do it personally, after all these years of ordering it done but never actually soiling his own hands with the deed itself. It was much easier than he remembered. He thought that he recalled a kind of shock, a horror afterward, but there was nothing of that now. This time, he just felt numb, more detached than anything else.

I ought to feel angry. By God, I should. The thought brought a little rising resentment. Luned on her way to warn Prince Tryffin, Lord Branagh dead, and it hardly seemed likely now that young Math would cooperate in the tiniest detail—no matter *what* was done to him—once he learned his grandfather's fate. *And here I sit, branded a traitor by my own hand, and all for nothing, nothing . . .*

The lady of his dreams had led him astray. But how could that be possible? The dreams had been so bright, so clear, so utterly alluring. At least in part. There had also been times when the whole thing was frightening, when his pagan princess crouched over him, drawing the breath right out of his lungs, grunting and moaning in a kind of ecstasy. *"By this you shall know what a terrifying enemy I can be."*

"But where are you now, my Lady of the Ravens? Where are you now that I could use your basilisk eyes to slay Prince Tryffin's approaching army?" he asked out loud. "And where is my pretty little puppet prince to do and speak, to come and go, according to my whim? These things you promised me."

A tiny voice spoke in his head—whether it was the lady of his dreams, or some cool, logical part of his own mind, he did not know. It said: *Win your battle now. Use the golden cauldron. When you are victorious, you can find another figurehead and rule through him. In defeat, Mahaffy Guillyn might be willing to make terms with you. And if not, there is always the other boy, the little one . . .*

"As God is my witness, I will do it!" he said, leaping to his feet. He stepped over the bloodstains on the floor, snatched up his cloak—for the night was a cool one, and only a fool or a madman would go out uncovered—and headed for the tower where he kept the dwarfs and the cauldron.

In Bagdamagus's tower workshop, the two dwarfs were hovering over the cauldron, engaged in the task of final polishing. The furnace was cooling, but there was a fire on the hearth and the flames reflected off the surface of the golden vessel: its rich ornamentation of birds and beasts and men, and the sparkling gemstones that served as their eyes.

Brangwengwen glanced up as Lord Cernach entered the room. "It is done," she said with a smirk. "The Thirteenth Hallow is now created, and long before needed. Did I not promise you, Lord, that all would be done to your complete satisfaction? Old Brangwengwen knows how to reward those who are willing to befriend a poor old dwarf."

"It is done," Lord Cernach said, regarding the grotesque little creature coldly, "but not before time. We must work the final rituals tonight, because I intend to make use of the hallow immediately."

Bagdamagus frowned. "You said the cauldron would only be used at your hour of greatest need . . . that you intended it only as a final defense," he said, pausing in his work, with the polishing rag in his hand. "Lord, it is not possible that Prince Tryffin and his men could arrive so quickly."

"There is no better defense than a sudden, unexpected offense," said Cernach. "Why wait until the Governor and his men are at the gate? Come, it is for me to decide the politics and the strategy of our cause . . . you and your godmother are only here to obey me. And I will be obeyed," he added, drawing out his sword. "Make no mistake about that."

Despite the implied threat, there was a stubborn look on the sturdy little goldsmith's face. Brangwengwen, however, was inclined to be conciliating. "Lord, Lord, he meant no impertinence. Naturally, all will be done according to your desires. But you see, we can serve you best if we understand the situation completely. Why such precipitous action? Is there some danger that we don't know about?"

"And if there is, what then?" said Cernach, between his teeth.

"Why, then," said Brangwengwen, hopping about on one foot, in one of her odd small dances, "we will proceed with great dispatch. But if there is not, then perhaps we should take another day or two, to consider what ought to be done for the blood. A goat will do at need, as we discussed, but how much better if we can find a suitable replacement for . . ." She paused and gave a sideways glance in the goldsmith's direction. No one had told Bagdamagus that Luned had been the intended victim; no one had told him that a human victim had even been contemplated.

But Cernach was not interested in sparing the feelings of either dwarf. "A replacement for Luned?" he said, and laughed cruelly at the expression on the goldsmith's face.

"Another wise-woman to give up her blood? And where on a moment's notice can we find another witch, let alone one nearly so gifted?"

The answer to that question came into all three minds at once. The old woman gave a wailing cry and fell to her knees in supplication, and Bagdamagus reached for one of his hammers, just as Cernach was drawing his sword.

The hammer sailed through the air, missing its target by a bare inch as Cernach ducked his head. The dwarf went scrambling for another weapon, but it was too late—the larger man was already on top of him.

The sword did very well for dispatching the goldsmith; a single hacking blow between the shoulders and the dwarf crumbled to the floor in a pitiful little heap. But when it came time to kill Brangwengwen, Cernach lifted her bodily off the floor, and dashed her head against the stones of the furnace.

It was a long, nasty, drawn-out process, hanging up each of the dwarfs, one after the other, from a hook in the ceiling, opening the proper veins, and collecting the blood in a shallow silver vessel. It was, if possible, an even nastier job using the blood to wash the cauldron. By the time he had accomplished so much—chanting the proper chants, making the gestures that Luned and Brangwengwen had devised between them—Lord Cernach felt more like a butcher than anything else. Still, he had not dared to trust anyone else to perform the task, after so much treachery already.

Dirty and exhausted, he went down to the well in the courtyard, carrying a wooden bucket in one blood-stained hand. Back and forth, back and forth, it took more than a dozen trips to fill the golden cauldron. Then Cernach arranged the sticks that would make the fire: nine special kinds of wood, carefully chosen for their magical qualities by Brangwengwen. *The creature has actually been quite helpful*, thought Cernach. *I really must see about rewarding her. After I have punished her and her godson for sneaking off, just when the most difficult work had to be done.*

The water in the cauldron began to boil, a faint cloud of steam appeared; a cloying stench, like something many days dead, began to fill the chamber. Cernach sang the final chant. Slowly, something formed inside the cauldron, just above the surface of the water: an emaciated head with dark, burning eyes, followed by a long neck and a skeletal body, queerly jointed. As Cernach watched in growing excitement, the thing solidified.

Placing both hands on the rim, it stepped over the side of the cauldron with an awkward long-legged grace, and a second figure began to form above the water. Soon, there was a crowd of hollow-eyed phantoms standing in a silent circle around Cernach, awaiting his orders.

"Go south toward Cormelyn," he commanded them. "And once you have passed out of Caer Rigor, kill every living person in your path. Do not cease the slaughter until I command you to do so. And look, especially, for Prince Tryffin and Mahaffy Guillyn: a big golden man with a dragon and a sunburst emblazoned on his shield, and a beautiful dark-haired boy with scars on his hands. Spare the youth if you can, but above all do not allow him to escape."

With a shambling gait, the cauldron creatures moved toward the window. One at a time, they climbed over the sill and disappeared from sight. When Cernach went over to another window and looked out, he could see them climbing down the tower wall, their long bony fingers finding crevices and projections amidst the stones that he could not even make out. And still, more and more of the creatures continued to appear in the room and followed the others . . . out through the arched window, down the side of the tower. Walking disjointedly across the courtyard, they heaved themselves over the outer curtain wall and shambled across the fields—an army of horrors marching toward Cormelyn. Somewhere, far in the distance, Cernach heard a long, terrible cry, as something died. By the time that all the water had boiled away, dawn was staining the eastern sky a bloody crimson.

Cernach stifled a yawn. The sun was rising, and still there was so much to be done. He must wash, discard his soiled silks, put on fresh clothes, perhaps have a bite to eat. Then he would set about the tedious business of killing young Math.

*. . . when the youngest son of the King arrived at the pool
in the middle of the forest, the Daughter of the Moon was
waiting for him, as hideous and as fearsome as ever, just
as she had awaited his brothers. But this time, she was
exceedingly cross, having been disappointed twice before.*

*When he asked her, politely, for a little of the water, she
replied sharply, nor could she be coaxed into naming her
conditions, until the youth had been standing there talking
for half the night.*

*"Very well then," said the hag. "The first condition is a
kiss from your lips and the friendship of your body."*

*"Done," said the Prince, without hesitation, though he
shuddered inside at the sight of her great red eyes and those
frightful teeth. "In God's name, it shall be as you say."*

*"My second condition is your ring on my hand, and all
the courtesy that is due to your wife."*

*"That you shall also have," said the Prince, a little less
quickly, because the sight of her wrinkled body and her bald
head dearly oppressed him. "I swear it on my soul."*

*"And finally," said the hag, "my third condition, which
you will find much harder to perform than any of the rest:
You must do all these things with a willing spirit and a light
heart, else no good will come of any of them."*

—*From* The Book of Dun Fiorenn

20.

A Cold Supper

They were just beginning to prepare for the wedding
when the letter arrived at Caer Wsyg. It had gone to Castell
Gauvain in Cormelyn first, and so it was ten days old when
it finally came into the Governor's hands. Prince Tryffin

called Mahaffy, Lord Macsen, Lord Balin, and various others together in his rooms, and they passed the letter from one to the other, shaking their heads over the contents.

"I would never have thought such a thing of Math," said Mahaffy. "Of course, he is years younger than I am, and we were never really friends, but I thought I knew him better than this would seem to indicate."

"It is the influence of Cernach fab Clydno, I suppose," said Tryffin, with a gesture of disgust. "And where are Meligraunce and Luned, in the meantime? Not a single word from the Captain since the message he sent to me from Anoeth, and the pair of them may be right in the heart of—of whatever it is that is really happening in Cuachag. I begin to fear the worst."

"Of course," said Lord Balin, stroking his beard, "you intend to meet this with force of arms."

"I can't see that there is any other choice. They are in blatant defiance of the Emperor's decree. And the sooner we get this business over with, the better." Tryffin turned toward Lord Macsen and said regretfully, "I fear this means we must delay the wedding."

But Macsen was shaking his head and beginning to glower. "All the more reason to make haste to the wedding, to seal the alliance. It will take several days to gather our forces, and in that time Tifanwy and her women can complete their own preparations. It will not be so grand and impressive an affair as we originally hoped—no doubt she will be disappointed—but concessions must be made in time of war."

"Lord Macsen," said Mahaffy, "I had not expected to marry your daughter for another month. As for myself, I want nothing so much as to claim Tifanwy for my own. But it can't have escaped your notice that ever since the day we were formally betrothed, your daughter has taken a deep aversion to me. It seems to me that it would be infinitely better to give her *more* time to adjust to the idea of our marriage, instead of *less*."

"If there is no marriage, there is no alliance. And if there is no alliance," said Macsen, growing flushed and heated, "then no men of mine will accompany you into battle. If you should fall, which God forbid, I would have Tifanwy a widow, lawfully wed, with all the status that gives her.

"I will not have it said of her, later," he added under his breath, "that Mahaffy Guillyn chose to die in battle rather than take her as he had promised."

Mahaffy and Tryffin exchanged a pained glance. Situated as they were, with so many of the men they might have called on so far distant, Macsen's army was vital to the success of any campaign.

"Lord Macsen, I implore you, for your daughter's sake," said Mahaffy. "Don't force her, so unnecessarily, into something which is plainly distasteful to her. She wears my ring on her finger. In the event of my death, all honor will be paid to her. And if I live, I will come and claim her, and do all in my power to make her a kind and loving husband. If you can't even trust me for this, if you believe that my word is not good, then I wonder that you are willing to give me Tifanwy in the first place."

"It is not your word that I doubt," said Macsen, placing a friendly hand on his shoulder. "But what others would say of her. And do not suppose that I care nothing for my daughter's peace of mind. She doesn't dislike you. She is only nervous, as young maids will be before a wedding. I have spoken with her, and she assures me that this marriage is as near her heart as it is to yours. I believe that delay will only increase her apprehension."

But what *else* could the girl say to her father? Mahaffy wondered. When Macsen had his mind set on the marriage and so much depended on it. Tifanwy had no choice but to say what her father most wanted to hear. As Mahaffy must also.

"If that is so, Lord Macsen," he answered with a sigh, "then of course I will marry your daughter within the week."

* * *

Three days later, Meligraunce and Luned arrived, a weary and bedraggled pair, who had some difficulty getting in through the gate, until Conn arrived and identified the Captain as someone Prince Tryffin most definitely wanted to see.

Hand in hand, they entered Lord Macsen's Solar, where Tryffin was sitting with Grifflet on his knee, discussing battle plans with his host.

"Tinkers, by God," said Macsen, surveying the big, dark sinister man and the little dark-haired woman, who (he had to admit) had a certain thorny wild-rose beauty about her. "You keep very strange company, Your Grace."

"Allow me to present Luned, Lord Cernach's cousin, a wise-woman of great power and impeccable lineage," Tryffin replied, only prevented by the child in his lap from rising to embrace them both, as dirty as they were. "And present to you, also, the captain of my personal bodyguard, a man of infinite resource and many disguises."

He gave Grifflet a gentle nudge. "It is your very good friend, Captain Meligraunce . . . don't you recognize him? Or is this how you greet the man you have been asking for, ever since Caer Clynnoc?"

The little boy shook his head and wrinkled his brow. "I know that it's my uncle, Captain Meligraunce . . . but who is she?"

Tryffin could only smile at the Captain's sudden entrance into the family. He bent his head and whispered in Grifflet's ear. "I believe that she is the Captain's sweetheart. So you must try to make friends with her for his sake—as she, no doubt, will endeavor to make friends with you."

Apparently reassured, the little boy slid down from his father's lap, catapulted himself across the space between, and attached himself to the Captain's knee. Meligraunce laughed a little self-consciously, gently detached the clinging child, and swept him up into his arms.

"Well," said Luned, raising a dark eyebrow, "I am glad to

see that you make such a charming 'uncle.' It bodes well for our own children, I think."

At this, the Captain blushed faintly, but the Governor rose from his seat and gave his henchman a rough embrace— which, since it included Grifflet, was slightly more gentle than it might have been otherwise—and congratulated him warmly. "This is welcome news. We will have to see what we can do to make it more palatable to others, but as for myself, I am well pleased."

Then it was time for Meligraunce and Luned to reveal what they knew of Cernach's plans and devices, of Lord Branagh's compliance, and Math's reluctance. It was a long recitation, so long that a chair was brought for Luned to sit on, and the Captain went down on one knee beside her. When they came to the end of their story, Tryffin sent for the letter of defiance and handed it over to Meligraunce for a thorough examination.

"Your Grace, I don't know Math's hand, but the phrasing reminds me more of his grandfather or Lord Cernach," said the Captain, after he read through it slowly. "I hope, if you have the opportunity, that you will spare the boy, but as for the others . . . they are both bold and bloody villains, and the sooner you gather your forces and march to put them down, the better that will be."

Tryffin nodded. "I don't suppose there is much chance, by now, that we will arrive before they can put this magical weapon of theirs, this golden cauldron, to work. It's unfortunate that you had to spend the extra days finding me here, where you did not expect me. That may cost us dearly."

He turned to Lord Macsen. "Tell me, how quickly do you think we can complete our preparations and ride to Cuachag, if we direct all of our energies to the task?"

Macsen made a swift calculation. It was already late in the day, but messengers could go out during the night. "I believe that we could be ready to leave by dawn of the day after tomorrow. Lord Balin and some of the others can go home and gather their men, and meet us along the way."

The Governor sent a servant to find Lord Balin, then motioned to Meligraunce. "I am sorry to put you to so much trouble when you are just arrived. But you will know which of our men are the swiftest and trustiest messengers. Bring them here to speak to me as quickly as you can assemble them."

The Captain nodded, bowed deeply, and hurried off to complete his task.

Meanwhile, Lord Macsen drew Mahaffy aside for a private word. "I will tell my daughter that she must be prepared to marry you tomorrow evening. It is precipitous, I know, but after all, all that is needed is the priest, the ring, and the chapel. And the bridegroom," he added, with particular emphasis.

"The bridegroom will be there," said Mahaffy. "I swear to you that I will not fail."

About the bride he was not so certain. And the truth was, he was almost beginning to hope that she would change her mind and not appear at all.

In the end, it was a hurried affair, between midnight and dawn. Mahaffy was down in the courtyard, inspecting armor and weapons by torchlight, when one of Macsen's servants appeared at his elbow and announced that the lady, her father, and the priest were waiting for him in the castle chapel.

"As this is your wedding night, don't be in any hurry to return," said Prince Tryffin, with a sympathetic glance. "We can spare you here the next few hours, so spend the time with your bride instead."

Mahaffy stopped and stared at him. "And do you think it would be possible for me to woo and win the lady in a few short hours? Should we consummate our marriage in the same hurried fashion that we are going to celebrate it? By God, I think Tifanwy would be right to loathe me if I imposed on her tonight."

Tryffin drew him aside. "I'm not suggesting that you go

to bed with her. Just take time to eat supper with her, send the servants away and pass an hour or two talking privately. If you avoid spending time alone with her, she will be utterly humiliated."

Mahaffy nodded his head. "That makes sense. I . . . perhaps I won't be back very soon, after all. But if I am needed here, don't hesitate to send for me."

After the bustle in the courtyard, the silence in the stony corridors leading to the chapel was almost eerie. Mahaffy walked slowly, almost reluctantly. Perhaps he ought to have taken the time to remove his armor, change into something more suitable for a wedding, but it was too late now. And when he arrived in the chapel, it was only to discover that Lord Macsen was also in armor, as were the handful of petty lords who were there to witness the marriage.

The bride was surrounded by a huddle of women. She wore a leaf-green gown and the silvery, shimmering veil. Her dress was elaborate, with a long train and dagged sleeves, and an intricate interlace border of thorny vines embroidered above the hem. Mahaffy thought that Tifanwy's women had probably made the gown especially for the occasion.

One of Lord Macsen's servants stepped forward and draped a cloak of the same color over Mahaffy's shoulders, whispering in his ear that it was a gift from the bride. She had woven the cloth, dyed it, and stitched the cloak with her own hands, in the time since their betrothal. *And how many bitter tears went into its making?* Mahaffy wondered.

He took Tifanwy's hand in both of his. Her skin was like ice, he noted dispassionately, and her fingers stiff. The priest nodded to him, and Mahaffy drew his bride toward the altar. After that, they both did what they were told: knelt, stood, spoke vows, Mahaffy lifted Tifanwy's veil, exchanged a cool kiss. The wedding party escorted them to a private chamber with a bed, where a late supper awaited them on a table by the fire, and then left them alone together.

Mahaffy sat down in one of the chairs, and glanced

numbly around the room. The chamber was sumptuous, with purple and gold hangings on the bed, rich tapestries on the walls. But there was nothing of Tifanwy, no sign of the interests she had described to him during that brief period when they were beginning to be friends: no herbs, no harp, no wolfhound bitch lying by the fire. "This is not, I take it, your own bedchamber?"

She removed her glittering veil, cast it on the floor with a listless gesture, glided across the room to the other chair, and sat down facing him. She was very pale, paler than she had been at the betrothal. "No. We had it prepared for . . . for tonight."

Of course, he thought. She would want to keep those other things private for herself. She was ready to dutifully yield up her body, but her dearest possessions must remain untouched, unpolluted.

They ate in silence, only occasionally punctuated by some civil remark, an equally civil (and distant) response. They both avoided looking at the bed. When they had choked down as much of the meal as they could, there was nothing left to do but stare at each other across the table.

"I wonder," he asked softly, after about a quarter of an hour of this, "if it would help at all if I said that I love you."

She shook her head. "You can't love me," she answered, just above a whisper. "You hardly know me. And I am not the sort of woman that—that men grow infatuated with."

Mahaffy frowned at her, across the miles that stretched between them. "I wonder how you can possibly know that. Are you acquainted with many men, besides your father? Have you ever allowed any of them to become acquainted with *you*? Has any man ever seen you as anything more than a shadow behind a veil?"

"I am not a cloistered nun," she replied wearily. "And I only took up the veil when I grew tired of watching men—and women, too—cringe at the sight of me."

Mahaffy began to feel bored, and even a little resentful. He supposed that there might really have been a time when her scars were as bad as she said; it was hard to say. Probably, though, she had always been more conscious of her own imperfections than anyone else was. "Were you always this vain . . . even before you were scarred?"

Tifanwy drew in her breath sharply. "Yes," she said, with a gleam of defiance. "Yes, I believe that I was. And you, Lord . . . have you always had such a wicked temper?"

"Lady," he said, "you have not yet begun to see the extent of my wicked temperament. Pray God that you never do."

He rose and moved toward one of the windows, stood gazing out across the torchlit courtyard, the castle walls, and the fields beyond. There was an ashen light on the horizon, indicating that dawn would soon arrive. Only a little longer, thank God, only a little longer and he could mount his horse and ride toward Cuachag. Whatever awaited him *there* could hardly be worse than what he was experiencing here.

It occurred to him that perhaps it was not his own clumsiness to blame after all. *Maybe she just doesn't like me. Maybe she thinks she deserves better . . . Lord Macsen's daughter, with her immense dowry. What do I have to offer in return, except a ruined castle, a few blasted acres, and a tenuous claim to the High Seat?* And that touched on his pride, which was always fatal. He felt a pulse in his temple begin to beat.

Mahaffy turned and faced her. "It is almost time for me to go. No, don't bother to leave your seat, and for God's sake, spare us both any platitudes that may come into your mind. You have been honest with me up until now; at least that is something. And comfort yourself with this: You may be lucky, Lord Branagh or Lord Cernach or young Math may oblige you, and I won't come back."

Her mouth trembled, but her chin came up defiantly. "Perhaps," she said, quite distinctly, "we may both be fortunate."

After that, there seemed to be nothing further to say, so he crossed the floor, went down on one knee, and pressed a cold kiss into Tifanwy's even colder palm. Then he rose and walked out of the room without even a word of farewell.

He berated himself all the way down to the courtyard. *Mother of God! What entered my head to make me say that? Why not say it plainly: "Be kind to me, Lady, for I am going into battle and will probably die." Of all the weak, shabby* . . . He had always regarded with contempt the men who used such tactics to gain a woman's favors. Now that he had done it himself, he realized it was just as despicable as he had always imagined.

What I should have done . . . oh God, what I should have said . . . ? Mahaffy stopped, thought for a moment, then turned right around and headed back toward the bedchamber.

He burst into the room and caught Tifanwy standing by the window, gazing down at the courtyard. The utter dejection of her pose made something catch at the back of his throat. Without a word of explanation, he swept her into his arms.

Perhaps he just took her by surprise, perhaps she was just caught up in the moment as he was, but he found that she was no longer cold or stiff. She melted immediately into his arms, her mouth warm and pliant under his. The taste of her tongue, lips, and skin was like fire in his blood. And when he was through kissing her—on her mouth, her throat, and the little scar over her eyebrow—they were both weak and trembling.

"But I will come back," he told her. "If only to do that one more time."

❧❧❧

Gwenlliant wove a spell around Maelinn, binding her with a net of words. Here in Atlendor's tower, this school of Wizardry, she was obliged to fall back on the old, familiar Witchcraft. In Dame Ceinwen's cottage, she had learned to make ropes of sand, spin silk out of straw and twigs and mayblossom; this was much the same, but she worked now with the mutable elements, making a chain of air and water out of her own breath.

When the spell was complete, Gwenlliant released her grip on Maelinn's shoulder. She knew that her enemy could not escape her now, not so long as her will remained strong, and her attention never wavered.

"Will you slay me?" Maelinn asked.

Gwenlliant shook her head. "I don't know yet. Perhaps it won't be necessary. For now, you must follow me."

Together, they left the library, climbed down a spiral staircase to the hall. Gwenlliant spoke the names that opened the triple gates, one after the other, then led the way out into the raging storm and down the long stone staircase to the sea. Great chilly waves washed over them, the wind shrieked in their ears, and when they reached the last step, the water came boiling up to meet them, as if eager to draw them in.

"We will go as seals," said Gwenlliant as the sea tugged at her skirts.

So as grey seals they swam to the mainland. Even so, it was a long, cold, dangerous journey through the wild waves. When the sea finally cast them up on a sandy beach, they lay there for a time, side by side, panting and exhausted, until Gwenlliant pulled herself up and spoke in the language of seals: "Now we will go as wolves."

By now, the storm had subsided. In the grey light of a winter's day, they went south as two rangy white wolves, skirting the city of Findias, traveling through rocky, windy country, until they reached the lightly forested region between Findias and Cuan, where Gwenlliant had first met Rhufawn and the others.

When they came to the ravine that marked the border, Maelinn asked: "Where are you taking me?"

Gwenlliant looked at her with her wolf's eyes, spoke to her with a wolf's voice. "Can't you guess? We passed through that place when I followed you here. Didn't you even recognize it? Did the place have no meaning for you at all?"

"No," said the other wolf. "I saw nothing familiar along the way . . . for my mind was intent on escaping you."

They descended the path as mountain cats; as cats they padded out of the cleft on the other side of the border. They traveled through rolling foothills until they reached the village at the foot of the mountain. Avoiding the houses, they climbed that mountain, ran down the slope on the other side. As otters they swam across the wide river. At last and again they came to the forest of thorns and dying, skeletal trees.

Gwenlliant slipped back into her own shape, and Maelinn did likewise. "Do you know where we are now?" the girl asked, as she sat down on a stump.

Maelinn's gaze shifted uneasily from a withered oak to the bones of an elm covered in thorny vines. "Why don't you tell me . . . since you are so eager that I should know?" the priestess replied, stretching her red lips into something that was more like a grimace than a smile.

Still in the boy's garb she had worn on the island, Maelinn sat down on a fallen tree, and began to untangle her dusky curls with one slender white hand. Though she affected indifference, Gwenlliant could tell that she was nervous. With Gwenlliant's spell on her, there was no possibility of deception between them.

"It is the sacred forest of Achren. It is your own wood, Maelinn, yours and the Green Lady's—after a hundred years of withering. Do you remember how beautiful it was and what a good, rich life we led here, with Regan and Pali, Ceri, Pethboc, and the rest? Do you remember the bounty of berries and nuts, sloes and brambles . . . even the ivy we brewed for the sacred ale? Do you remember how you and the other priestesses danced under the trees on moonlit nights, with the wolves and the foxes? But no one can live here now. No one serves in your place as the Lady of the

Wood and the Well, or worships your goddess in her own glades."

Maelinn tossed her head contemptuously. "I no longer worship Goleuddydd. I serve the *true* Cailleach, the Goddess Cerridwen, inasmuch as I serve anyone but myself."

For all that, she appeared to be troubled. There was a deep line between her eyes, and she angled an arm behind her, put a hand back to feel between her shoulders, as though the place where Tryffin had stabbed her with his silver dagger still pained her.

"Poor Gwenhwyach," she said, using the name that Gwenlliant had gone by in Achren. "Did you bring me all this way, hoping to impress me with a proper sense of my own iniquity? Then you have failed, because I regret nothing."

"Still," said Gwenlliant, with a sigh, "I am going to keep on trying." Because if she did not succeed, if she could not bring Maelinn around to a better way of thinking, she was going to have to do something so harsh and so cruel, she might never get over regretting it as long as she lived.

For a day and a night they sat in the thorny wood—from noon to twilight when the owls came out, twilight to misty dawn, then from sunrise to a scorching afternoon among the withering trees—while Gwenlliant tried to reason with the recalcitrant Maelinn.

"It is no use," said the priestess. "If I could lie to you, bend my knee and do some penance to gain my freedom, I would do it. But with your spell on me, I could never deceive you, and so I dare to speak the truth: What I have done, I have done, and it was all for the best, because it served *my purposes*. There is no higher morality than that. It is only because you are so small yourself that you don't understand this."

"I believe," said Gwenlliant, "that the real Maelinn would understand *me* perfectly. She was a woman who lived and breathed, and therefore, whatever her mistakes were, she was able to learn from them. I don't doubt that she later regretted her own part in the tragic events that led up to the slaughter in Penafon, the curse on the land. And the things that you have done since . . . she would never have even contemplated such wanton wickedness."

Maelinn shrugged. "After all, she was only a weak, flimsy, passing thing. She has been dust for a thousand years. While I—I who was born in the same instant she was, I continue on. And though I may seem to die in this body, I will still go on existing in some other place. I know this for certain. I have traveled through the shadows, and seen myself at a hundred different moments in my life." She lifted her head proudly. "You call me a ghost . . . but in truth, you are the ghost, the shadow. Your span of years is brief, but I am immortal. So what do you think you could possibly teach *me*—what could that other Maelinn teach me, if she was here?"

Gwenlliant sat drawing a pattern in the dusty crumbling leaves, considering how she might answer. "We could teach you compassion," she said at last. "In truth, I pity *you*. Your so-called immortality must be a wearisome, confining thing, because your world is so small, Maelinn, that it can only contain you. There is no room for anyone else, apparently."

"My world," said Maelinn, "is as vast as I am. You can't conceive the depths of my knowledge, the extent of my wisdom. You have seen what I was capable of doing when I was in your world. I was not bound by my flesh as I am here. I could be wood, stone, fire, water. What can you do that compares with that—what can you do that I cannot do as well or better?"

There seemed to be no answer to that. Gwenlliant sat staring down at the ground, thinking and thinking, but nothing occurred to her. Until the child moved in her womb, a tiny fluttering movement.

"I can create a new life," she said. "You can't make anything that didn't exist before; you can only destroy what others have made."

Maelinn sneered at her. "Perhaps you *could* make a child, but you never will. You weak, frightened, foolish little virgin. Remember that I know what you are and all that you have been—all your terrors and all the tiny errors and cruelties that make up your miniscule life."

But she doesn't, Gwenlliant realized. *She only carries the memories she stole from me in Achren. She knows nothing of what I have felt or done since.*

"I can see that it is no use reasoning with you, no use talking to you at all," she said out loud. "You are as set in your wickedness as you are in your ignorance. You don't even want to learn any better."

The priestess laughed uneasily. "And now that you have finally reached that conclusion, what do you plan to do with me . . . now that you have gained the upper hand by treachery?"

"I have no other choice," said Gwenlliant. "I am going to bind you irrevocably to this time and place. You will be a prisoner here in the wood, but within the forest you will be free to do as you wish."

Maelinn sprang to her feet. "And you call yourself compassionate? Don't you realize that you are condemning me to a slow, agonizing death? The place where the silver dagger entered my flesh already pains me, and if I remain here, this body will wither like the forest."

"I don't think that you will die," said Gwenlliant. "You are not so close to your own time as that. And I am very sorry to be condemning you to a wearisome, painful existence, but you must see that I can't let you go."

"Then kill me now, swiftly and cleanly rather than cage me," pleaded Maelinn. "Or if you haven't the stomach to kill me in cold blood, let it be a fight to the death, a duel of sorcery between us."

"No," said Gwenlliant. "I am sorry, but I can't do either of those things." To kill Maelinn by magic in cold blood would be to taint herself and her magic forever, and might even affect the child that she carried within her, transfer some part of the guilt, confer some evil destiny, simply because he was there at the time. As for the other way—"It would be wrong to risk letting you go, to work such evil, to cause such suffering as you have in the past."

Maelinn had lost all her color; there was no doubt that she was really in pain now. "My flesh burns; you cannot imagine the agony, the torment, and it will only grow worse. Gwenhwyach . . . Gwenlliant, I beg of you, do not do this thing to me. Show your compassion; kill me or release me."

Gwenlliant felt the blood drain from her heart. This was far worse than she had imagined. How could she condemn Maelinn to weeks, months, perhaps years of torment? And what if—by some chance—the bindings did not hold? Maelinn, driven deeper into her madness by the suffering she had endured at Gwenlliant's instigation, would be even crueler, even more dangerous than before.

"I am sorry . . . so sorry. But there is no other way."

"There is," said Maelinn, lowering her voice to a hoarse whisper. "Listen to me: If you are willing to give me my chance, if you will fight me fairly, I will make you a promise never to venture into your world, and never to lift a hand against anyone dear to you. Such a promise, given while your bindings are still on me, then sealed by your death, you know that it would hold me. Then you would gain something either way. If you win our contest, I will cease to exist. But if I win, you have still accomplished what you set out to do."

And all I would lose would be my own life . . . and the life of my child, thought Gwenlliant.

How could she risk that precious unborn child? How could she risk the possibility that Tryffin would never even know the child had been conceived, would never be able to hold their son in his strong, loving arms? It was too much to ask.

But when she closed her eyes, she could see those other children, the ones that Maelinn had murdered, their tiny, bloodless bodies, so incredibly fragile, laid out on the hard ground in an endless row. And she could see Tryffin with another child in his arms: a little redheaded boy, as cold as death . . .

Gwenlliant shuddered and banished that image from her mind. She knew what she had to do, for the sake of Grifflet—that other small life that she held in her heart— and for all the other children in Mochdreff. And so that Tristan, if she lived to give birth to him, would have a chance to grow up and live a good life, free of those onerous burdens of destiny that had cursed her line for so many years.

"Very well," she said, rising slowly to her feet. "It will be a duel arcane between us. But first you must swear to me that you will be bound by all those conditions you have just offered me."

"I swear," said Maelinn. "I swear by my own name, and by the death of whichever one of us falls here . . . whether it should be you or I."

"Then so be it," said Gwenlliant, as steadily as she was able. And she hoped that Maelinn would not hear the tremor in her voice, or guess how frightened she really was.

I am the sow who devours her own farrow
  The carrion crow, feasting after the carnage
I am she who waits beside the ford . . .
                                    —*From* The Song of Donwy

21.

Nightmares Walk Abroad

They left Caer Wysg an hour after sunrise: Lord Macsen and the knights and squires of his household riding in the vanguard, under his standard of the moon and thornbush; the Governor and his party; the Lord of Scoithan and his household; then the men of Glyn, Brennan, Chenoweth, Killian, and Eifion. Behind the cavalry and the mounted archers, marched the common foot soldiers and bowmen, under the banners of their various clans.

The last of them had scarcely passed beyond the castle gates when a rider was spotted, cutting across country in order to intercept them on the road, a messenger who—it became evident as he drew closer—was wearing Lord Balin's colors. On the Governor's orders, everyone halted to watch him approach, in case he should carry any vital news that might alter their plans.

He drew up beside Prince Tryffin's party in a great cloud of dust, and after some questioning was finally allowed to approach Tryffin himself. Meanwhile, Lord Macsen and some of the other petty lords broke ranks with their own troops and rode over to discover what it was all about.

The messenger was white-faced and sweating; he looked like a man in shock. And his speech was so hurried and

286

disjointed, it was some time before they could get him to utter anything intelligible.

"Men and women are dying in great numbers in Cormelyn. Nightmares come to life . . . a kind of horror goes out before them. Many go mad, or drop dead from sheer terror. Ah God, I have seen it, and the hair stood up on my head, there was a grue that ran over my flesh. Lord Balin says please come to aid him, but I have heard such tales along the way . . . they say that this unnatural army extends from Cuachag, through Llech Obrwy, Scoithan, and Barra, Duleiven, and finally into Cormelyn."

Tryffin turned to Meligraunce, who was riding beside him on a horse provided by Macsen. "You will know best where to find Luned . . . ride back to the castle and bring her back here at once. God knows, it would be impossible to make any logical decisions about how to proceed without consulting a wise-woman first."

Luned had originally volunteered to accompany them, certain that her services as a healer would be called for sooner or later, but Tryffin had asked her to stay behind. With Macsen's fortress so poorly defended, he wanted her there to protect Grifflet and Tifanwy, both of whose political importance had been greatly increased by recent events.

The Captain nodded briefly, turned the big grey stallion back toward the castle, and soon disappeared inside the gates. While they waited for him to return, Tryffin spent the time questioning the messenger more closely.

"Horses, dogs, and cattle do not see or sense them, but the pigs squeal and the goats bleat at their approach. Such creatures I never heard of before . . . they stink like carrion, they are death incarnate, and how can you kill what never had life to begin with? Yet I did see a man stop one with a long spear, when he pierced it through the heart." The messenger shook his head despairingly. "For all that, there were too many of the others, and they overwhelmed him, swept on and past him, leaving nothing but the broken body behind."

Luned arrived, riding behind Meligraunce, just in time to hear the last of this. She had dressed in a hurry, and her dark hair was tumbling around her shoulders, over the rough brown cloak that someone had lent her along the way. Sliding down from the saddle, she listened attentively to a complete recitation of all they had learned so far.

"It seems that Lords Cernach and Branagh have made use of their golden cauldron already. And under the impression that I was still in Cormelyn, have sent their army of horrors to meet me there," Tryffin concluded. "What course would you advise, Lady? Should we ride to succor Lord Balin, or is the need likely to be greater elsewhere?"

"If I understand the numbers and the symbols governing the cauldron—and God knows I should, having helped to create the thing—Brangwengwen may use it to brew up another army of phantoms once in every twelve hours," said Luned. "If someone does not ride to Caer Rigor and put a stop to her activities, there will be no end to the number of enemies the rest of you have to face." She considered for a moment longer, standing there silent and meditative among the impatient horsemen and their restless mounts. "There are not many men in the garrison at Caer Rigor, and unless Cernach has added to them from the troops at Castell Emreis, a small army would be enough to take the place."

Tryffin thought that over. To those around him, he appeared as calm as ever, broad and solid in his black armor, sitting there astride his big roan charger . . . yet there was a white shade around his mouth, and his hands were clenched tight on the reins. "If a natural army from Castell Emreis is on the move, I suppose it must be well on its way to Cormelyn by now." He glanced over at Lord Macsen. "I intend to go on to Cuachag. No doubt there will be plenty of fighting along the way as we meet with the cauldron creatures, and I will need to take the bulk of our forces with me—but if you or any of the other lords and chieftains wish to take a few dozen men and go to the aid of your friends or kinsmen, I won't dispute your right to do so."

"I must defend my own people in Duleiven," said Lord Macsen. "And I will send my sons, along with such men as you can spare, to my cousin Lord Balin's aid."

But when Mahaffy offered, half-heartedly, to accompany him, he reached out and put a gauntleted hand on the younger man's arm. "No, it is your place to ride with the Governor. I would not expect otherwise, son-in-law, though it is good of you to offer."

"Before you go," said Tryffin, "let us all listen to what the lady can tell us about these creatures. I take it there must be some defense against them, because otherwise she would already be advising surrender on any terms that we can get."

Luned nodded grimly. "I believe they can be killed in a number of ways, the most obvious being by the iron of your swords, by salt, and by holy water. But it is a matter of getting close enough to do so. As Lord Balin's messenger has said, they can kill or send men mad by their very presence. So only the very bravest will be able to face them, let alone defeat them."

She thought a little longer, though her hands were busy now, plaiting her dark hair. "If you should need to fall back and regroup at any time, head for a churchyard. I don't believe they be able to attack you on consecrated ground, nor in the vicinity of a cross, steeple, or church bells. They have little respect for Christian symbols, you understand, yet these things are invested with a certain amount of power, through tradition, belief, and use."

"But what," said Tryffin, "of the heretical churches? I am thinking not of the harmless sects, but of the Black Canons and their ilk. Surely they are allied to the power that animates this cauldron."

"Ah, you are right. It is good that you thought of that," Luned replied, her black brows drawing together. "Yet we know that while the cult of evil is very ancient, it never lasted in any one place or under one name for very long. So you will wish to approach only those churches or ruins that show signs of continuous use over a period of many centuries. And particularly those which are located near the site of a holy well or a barrow, or some other relic of the Old Religion in its more wholesome aspects . . . for these things also have a power that ought to be inimical to the creatures of the cauldron."

Tryffin nodded, and thanked her for the advice. Then he turned away as though to dismiss her, and began giving orders to his men. But Luned stopped him, reaching up to put a hand on his knee. "Shall I come with you after all? It seems to me that you may be glad of a wise-woman's help, even before you arrive in Cuachag."

"No," he said, but this time there was a note of uncertainty in the soft southern lilt, just the suggestion of a doubt in the steady brown eyes. "Or rather . . . I cannot say. But it may be more important than ever for you to remain behind. If all of us who go on to Cuachag should fall, if the prophecies of Dame Ceinwen and Dame Brangwaine should fail, and Grifflet were the only remaining heir . . . he will need you beside him, not only to keep him safe, but to fight for his rights."

She withdrew her hand and stepped back, bowing her head in acquiescence. "You see farther than I do. You are correct and I will stay. And if—if there should be no one else for him to count on, rest assured that your son will find a staunch friend in me."

"I could ask no better," said Tryffin quietly.

They rode for several hours, but it was not until noon and a village in Barra that they found the first bodies.

It was just a small village, home to a handful of herders and cottagers, and most of them lay sprawled on the ground outside the houses: men, women, and children, wide-eyed and staring, with flies buzzing over them. Many had apparently died of sheer terror; when Tryffin and his men stopped to examine them, there was not a mark or a wound to be seen. But a few had bruises on their throats, faces that were livid and contorted, as though they had died struggling for breath.

"This child was strangled," said Tryffin in a colorless voice, as he knelt on the ground beside one of the bodies. Whenever his face and voice went blank that way, Mahaffy knew he was in the grip of some powerful emotion. "Someone . . . or something . . . cut off her breath with his bare hands."

Mahaffy stood in the middle of the street, absently sheathing and unsheathing the dagger he wore in his belt. Two men in rustic sheepskin tunics lay dead at his feet. A little farther on, there was a woman and two small boys. From where he was standing, he could see at least a dozen corpses, and there were likely to be more inside some of the cottages. This was not the first time he had seen such a slaughter, but it *was* the first time since he had begun to think he could be Lord of Mochdreff. A pulse began to pound in his head, and a suffocating rage to build inside him.

"These are my people . . . *my* people. Lord Cernach and his creatures killed them, and I was not there to protect them, not there to raise a hand in their defense," he said. "What good did I do healing the land, if something like this can still happen, and I can do nothing to prevent it?"

The Governor came and stood beside him, placed a comforting hand on his shoulder. "You could not prevent it, because you didn't know that it would happen. Even when you are Lord of Mochdreff and sit on the High Seat, you will only be able to do so much. It is a hard, hard bitter lesson—one that I was a long time learning myself—but one you are going to have to learn. You must do your best, you must do all that you *can* do, and when there is something that you cannot help . . . then you must direct your efforts elsewhere."

"To do what?" said Mahaffy, clenching his fists, continuing to stare down at the crumpled bodies at his feet. "To do what . . . in the face of such horror?"

"To save any lives that you can. To die fighting for your people, if that is the best you can do, but also, if you are able, to live for their sake instead. When the battle is over, you must offer what comfort you can to the living. And finally—the last and the least important—you can avenge those who have died."

Mahaffy wanted to tear something apart with his bare hands. He looked up at Tryffin, his eyes growing wide in disbelief. "The last and the least important? You can see all this and still say that?"

Prince Tryffin shook his head. "When you have wasted as much of your life as I have paying the wages of revenge, you will know just how paltry a thing vengeance can be . . . it feeds no orphans, unwidows no wives, and God knows, I have never known it to offer anything more than a passing satisfaction."

While he was speaking, Conn and young Cei came up beside him. Both boys were pale and there was a sheen of sweat on Cei's face. He looked sick, shocked, and shaken. *Probably,* thought Mahaffy, *I look exactly the same.*

The grip on Mahaffy's shoulder tightened as the Governor gave him a slight, bracing shake. "No doubt you are thinking this is a poor time for a lesson. But listen to me now: The creatures that did this were born of spite, malice, envy, and greed. If we carry anger and malice in our hearts when we meet them, we make ourselves vulnerable, we create a breach in our own defenses, through which they can enter and destroy us."

Mahaffy nodded his head wearily. "Then tell me what I should feel, and I will try to feel it. Tell me what I should think, and I will try to think it."

Tryffin gave him another gentle shake. "That emotion you were feeling a little while since—the love of your people, a desire to protect them—that was a good emotion, a true emotion. Concentrate on that, make that your armor in the coming battle."

Was that love? Did I really feel it? Mahaffy wondered.

Was he really capable of anything so fine, so noble, so disinterested as the emotion Prince Tryffin was ascribing to him now?

But it was no time to demoralize the others by whining about his own incapacity. So Mahaffy swallowed hard, tore his gaze away from the bodies in the street, and spoke as steadily as he could.

"Then I will love my people, even if I never live to lead them. And if I may . . . I will save Mochdreff not only with my sword and such courage as I can muster, but with the strength of my love."

And the Governor smiled—that rare warm smile that was wholly open and sincere, not the one he used so often to mask what he was really feeling.

"There is no better way," he said. "Believe me, Mahaffy, there is no better way."

They mounted up, strapped on their helmets and their shields, and rode for another quarter of a mile before they finally encountered the cauldron-born. Even before they caught sight of the first ranks, a kind of horror came on ahead, a cold terror that shivered across the skin, that made the hair on the arms and the back of the neck literally rise. And then there was the smell: a sick, sweet, gut-wrenching stink, nearly debilitating in itself.

All around him, Mahaffy heard a babble of panicked voices. Some of the men turned their horses and fled, even before the creatures were more than a line of dim figures moving in the distance; others shrieked and toppled from their horses—dead or unconscious, Mahaffy could not dismount and find out which. He was too busy trying to control his own rising sense of panic, waiting for Prince Tryffin's order to charge, hoping that his courage would be sufficient. And the stench and the terror only grew worse as the army of horrors approached.

After all that, his first good look at them was almost disappointing; the long-limbed creatures, with their emaciated faces and queer, disjointed gait, were as ludicrous as they were terrible. Mahaffy wanted to laugh . . . until he saw what some of the creatures were carrying over their shoulders: loose-limbed corpses of women with their hair hanging down, small children trussed together in twos and threes like freshly caught game, one old man in priestly robes, his habit rucked up to show his skinny dangling legs . . . then Mahaffy felt like gagging instead.

The air was suddenly filled with a ghastly wailing, a banshee howling that made him want to grind his teeth and cover his ears. It was a moment before Mahaffy recognized the sound for what it was: Prince Tryffin's wild Gwyn-gellach battle cry, as the Governor and his two squires went riding past. Mahaffy drew his sword, settled his shield on his arm, and, kicking his warhorse into action, followed after them as closely as he could, galloping across the countryside with the rest of Tryffin's cavalry.

Along the dusty road, up a slight rise, then into the ranks of the enemy. It was oddly quiet when they finally met, no familiar clash of steel. The creatures had no armor and no weapons . . . except for the terror they brought with them, except for their long, sinewy limbs and their strong, clutching fingers. When Mahaffy thrust his sword through one of them, the thing just seemed to melt away in a cloud of foul-smelling smoke. But there were others he could not immediately reach with his sword, things that swarmed over him, catching at his armored arms and legs, trying to drag him down from the horse, things that were only harmed by steel with a cutting edge. One of the creatures even climbed up behind him and tried to choke him through the mail aventail around his neck. Mahaffy could barely breathe and the light was already fading around him when another rider came close enough to hack the creature away.

After that, Mahaffy swung, slashed, and cut for what felt like hours. At some moment in time, he lost his sword and had to make do with his dagger. The battle ebbed and surged all around him, and the only sounds were those of men and horses dying—their cries of pain and terror, a thud when a body hit the ground. The silence between was eerie.

There was no time to think, so Mahaffy reacted instinctively. When he saw Prince Tryffin about to disappear under a sudden fierce onslaught of the clinging monstrosities, he urged his mount in that direction and made the best use that he could of the dagger, until someone—he never saw who—thrust the hilt of a sword into his left hand. Switching the sword over to his right, Mahaffy went on hacking and slashing.

A long time later, he put his blade through the ribs of one of the phantoms, watched his opponent melt away, and gradually realized that there were no more of the creatures attacking him. In the sudden complete hush that followed, he glanced dazedly around.

The other men were removing their helmets; on every face was the same exhausted, glassy-eyed stare. But these were the faces of living men; not one of the cauldron-born remained. Mahaffy unfastened his own helmet, tucked it under his arm, and took a deep breath.

"We won," he said, scarcely believing it.

The Governor rode up beside him. "We won, but it was only a minor skirmish, and we had the advantage of numbers. Also, we have yet to count or to name the fallen." The blond hair was plastered to his forehead, and there was a streak of blood on one cheek, as though something had reached through the slots of his helmet and scratched at his face. Like Mahaffy and the rest, he was shaking with exhaustion and reaction after the fight.

Conn came up a short while later, with the unwelcome news that Cynddlig of Barra, Morgan Killian, and their old friend, Llefelys Glyn, had all died in the skirmish.

"And Cei . . . has anyone seen Cei?" asked the Governor. Elffin had been left behind as too young, but the expedition into Cuachag was to be Cei's first opportunity to prove himself in battle.

"Cei is dead," said Meligraunce tonelessly, as he arrived on foot, leading his weary grey stallion behind him.

That hit Prince Tryffin hard, harder than any of the rest. He swayed in the saddle, swore raggedly under his breath. "Mother of God . . . Mother of God . . . he was my responsibility. Too inexperienced to face these things that are not even men. Why did I not send him back when I knew the danger?"

"Because," said Mahaffy, around the lump in his throat, "you knew very well that if you had, he would have turned right around the very first chance and followed after us."

It was the only comfort that he could give, and it was not nearly enough. Conn put down his head against his horse's mane, and the Captain stood staring at the ground, as if it was too much for him to bear, facing any one of them after bringing such news. It was like a death in the family—no, it *was* a death in the family, because Cei had been a member of Prince Tryffin's household long before Mahaffy. He had been Gwenlliant's page when she first came as a child-bride to Caer Ysgithr.

"I have heard that Cei acquitted himself well and that he killed many of the phantoms—before they pulled him down from his horse and broke his neck in the fall," said Meligraunce. "It is unlikely that he felt any pain, just a sudden sharp jolt and then darkness."

"The pain will be for his parents to feel when I send them the news," said Tryffin bleakly. "And for Gwenlliant . . . by God, she'll take it to heart." Yet he seemed to grow a bit steadier as he spoke.

Then he squared his broad shoulders. "We can only spare a little time to rest ourselves and our horses, to tend to the dying and the wounded. Then we must go on and try to win our way to the source of this plague."

The others nodded grimly. It was horrible to contemplate

going on, particularly so soon, but the consequences if they did not were simply unthinkable.

In the withering forest that had once been the sacred wood of Achren, the air smelled of lightning and rain. Maelinn and Gwenlliant, locked in their magical struggle, had summoned the elements to aid them.

When the priestess called up a roaring whirlwind, sent it spinning toward her opponent, Gwenlliant countered by hastily erecting a wall of air. Safe behind that invisible but remarkably solid barrier, she watched the destructive force of the wind tear at trees and bushes and vines, stripping them of their last leaves. Eventually, the cyclone wore itself out, and Maelinn with it.

Then it was Gwenlliant's turn to attack. She conjured up a ring of fire surrounding her enemy: a circle of bright orange flames burning rapidly inward, leaping higher and higher, until the hem of Maelinn's short tunic began to smoke. But Maelinn, though grey and exhausted from her previous efforts, managed to draw water up out of the earth, from hidden springs far below the surface, and quench Gwenlliant's fire.

For a moment, a cloud of steam obscured Gwenlliant's view . . . when the mist cleared, an immense boar with silver bristles and terrible curving tusks stood in Maelinn's place, grunting and pawing up pieces of turf, making ready to charge.

She had to leap high, and a yard to one side, to avoid that deadly rush—when Gwenlliant came back down again, it was in the form of a lithe golden leopard. Before the boar could turn, the leopard sprang, landing on the pig's sloping back, claws scrambling for purchase, teeth sinking into the tough hide behind the bristled neck.

There was a squeal, a stench, and Maelinn became a badger, twisting inside her skin. She nipped and clawed at the leopard's face, until Gwenlliant was finally forced to release her hold on the badger's furry scruff.

The battle continued: Gwenlliant returned to her own shape and threw rocks and thunderbolts; the badger that was Maelinn went burrowing under the earth to escape her wrath, then came up suddenly behind her, changed into a great, lumbering bear, and crushed the girl between heavy arms covered with rough fur. But Gwenlliant countered by going smaller and sleeker as a brown otter, and managed to wriggle out of the bear's grasp.

Two wolves tore at each other with great bloody teeth . . . two mountain cats spat and fought . . . Gwenlliant wove a net of vines, but Maelinn became a golden honeybee and flew out through one of the holes. The battle went on for hours, through a hundred transformations, through a hundred different spells. Always there was the counterspell, and the two were so evenly matched that it hardly seemed possible that either one would ever gain a clear advantage.

A fox and a hound . . . two white unicorns slashing and parrying with their long spiral horns . . . a stoat and a serpent . . . a bull and a lioness . . . a dragon and a wyvern, rattling their batlike wings, stabbing with their barbed tails.

Then the ground shook, there was a mighty clap like thunder, and a great crack opened under the wyvern. Before she could stop herself, she slid into the abyss. The two sides of the crack came together with terrible force, crushing the wyvern between them. Her opponent *felt* her die, their minds tangled by the bindings of Gwenlliant's spell, felt the air forced out of her lungs, the pain of shattering bones, the brain bursting inside the skull . . . then silence, dark and infinite.

The dragon became a young woman, pale and trembling with reaction. Her knees buckled; gasping for air, she fell down on the broken ground beside the sealed fissure. Then the world went from grey to black, and she knew nothing more after that.

I am a storm in summertime
I am the White Flood
I am the sea rising
I am the Lady of the Castle of the
        Silver Wheel
                                        —*From* The Song of Donwy

22.

The Lady of the Ravens

They met the cauldron creatures again in Scoithan, and again there was a skirmish with many losses. Battered and weary, Mahaffy sat on his horse and listened as one of Tryffin's men recited the names of the fallen; Cadllyn Lochein . . . Garreg and Ciag, two loyal guardsmen who had accompanied Prince Tryffin on his fateful visit to the Otherworld . . . the list went on and on.

Too many people who we know have died, he thought numbly. *And it isn't over yet.* In a way it was too much to comprehend. For personal losses, Lord Cado's rebellion, two years ago, had been nothing beside this, and there was no telling how many had been killed in Cormelyn, how many familiar faces were gone. Perhaps Lord Balin, Lord Macsen and his sons. When Mahaffy returned . . . if he returned . . . Tifanwy might be utterly alone. And how would he then dare to intrude on her grief?

As Prince Tryffin and his men approached Cuachag, they were engaged in one battle after another in swift succession. Soon, it began to feel like there had never been and never would be anything but the endless hacking and slashing, charging, retreating, rallying and charging again, all accom-

300 • *Teresa Edgerton*

panied by the same fear, grief, and bone-grinding weariness. In the face of all that, it was hard for Mahaffy to remember what he was fighting for, to think only of duty and responsibility, and not let hatred, despair, and a thirst for vengeance govern his actions.

Prince Tryffin, however, was truly amazing. After he recovered from the losses of that first skirmish, he was a bulwark of strength. He seemed to be everywhere during a battle, wherever the fighting was the most fierce, remarkable not only for his energy and his valor, but because he was always shouting words of praise and encouragement wherever they seemed to be needed most. Mahaffy tried to be like him, to follow his example, and soon his voice was hoarse with so much shouting. And somehow, he was not sure how or why, it really seemed to help—wherever he went, Mahaffy saw men redouble their efforts, he could *feel* their flagging spirits rise. This was what it meant to be a leader of men, and it had a certain addictive charm—even while it cost him so much to see the men he was goading into such heroic deeds continue to fall before the endless onslaught of the cauldron-born.

Yet still, for all their strength and courage, their hope and comradeship, there were too many losses. And too many empty towns and villages along the way . . . empty except for the bodies of the fallen.

In the midst of a battle that had already lasted from sunrise to noon, Mahaffy saw Conn snatch up Prince Tryffin's fallen standard, and give the wailing, banshee cry that was the call to a rally. Mahaffy made his way through the press, urging his weary steed on, until he arrived under the dragon banner just as Prince Tryffin and several others came up as well.

"Meligraunce says that he remembers passing this way fleeing from Cuachag, and there is a church with a holy well not far distant," Conn shouted through the bars of his helmet. "No more than a mile to the east," he said. "Shall we head that way?"

The Governor nodded. Somewhere in the fighting, he had lost his own helmet. He was pale, hollow-eyed, and sweating, dirty and unshaven; he looked like some cruel mockery of the man he had been only a few days past. Yet he managed a smile . . . not very hopeful, but the effort meant something, and the fact that he even tried cut Mahaffy to the heart.

"We will ride to the churchyard, and regroup there," Tryffin shouted hoarsely, "where we can rest for a bit and plan what we mean to do next."

It was a wild ride to the church, with fighting along the way. Conn went down, but Mahaffy put his sword through one of the creatures as it was attempting to pull off the boy's helmet and strangle him, threw his dagger, and pierced the other. Conn staggered to his feet, but his horse was nowhere to be seen, so Mahaffy held his own mount steady until his friend mounted up behind him. With twice the burden, progress was slow, but at last the black gelding made a courageous leap over a low stone wall surrounding the churchyard . . . and collapsed among the gravestones, throwing off both his riders. They went sailing over his head and landed in the grass.

Stunned by the fall, Mahaffy spent several moments gathering his wits before he climbed to his feet and went over to inspect the gelding. The horse was dead. Mahaffy turned to find Conn standing beside him.

"Jesus, Mary, and Joseph, Conn . . . I thought we had lost you," he whispered, leaning against a granite tombstone for support. "Damn you for giving me such a fright."

They went to find Prince Tryffin and Meligraunce, over by the little stone church, and ask for further orders. "We rest," said the Governor. "There are no provisions left—that I know about anyway—but at least there is plenty of water." He indicated the well, which was ringed with white stones, and had a thatched roof over it. "And they say that the water has restorative powers. It is dedicated to St. Teilo, a good northern saint . . . and was probably associated a long time past with some beneficient aspect of the Goddess Celedon."

As Mahaffy took off his helmet, Tryffin suddenly reached out and drew him into a quick, rough, armored embrace. "I can't begin to say how proud I am of you and Conn."

But when the young knight showed signs of breaking down, the Governor gave him an affectionate shove in the direction of the tombs and monuments. "Try to get some sleep, if you can . . . if sleep is even possible, with those monsters standing outside the fence, staring in at us."

Mahaffy nodded, and went off to find a soft bed of grass on one of the graves. Once there, he stretched out, and despite his armor, fell instantly into an exhausted sleep.

He opened his eyes a short time later, when Conn shook him awake. The sun was still high above the horizon, so he knew that he could not have slept for more than an hour; he lay there blinking up at that glaring sky, while the words that Conn repeated over and over slowly sank into his mind.

"Men have come . . . strangers they appear to be, and I can't say yet whether they are friend or foe. Do you want to come with me and hear what they are saying to Prince Tryffin?"

"Yes," said Mahaffy, rising to his feet with a groan.

Over by the well, the Governor, surrounded by his surviving guardsmen, stood talking to a group of strangers armored in various combinations of leather, mail, and plate—by the look of them, common men-at-arms in the service of some petty lord. A blond boy, in a mail shirt much too large for him and a ragged dark blue cloak, appeared to be their leader.

"I knew nothing about the contents of the letter until it had already been sent," the boy was saying earnestly. "And I wasn't even there when Cernach boiled up his monsters in the cauldron . . . though probably I should have stayed and tried to stop him, instead of running like a coward." And under the dirt and the sweat and the blood, Mahaffy finally recognized his rival, Math fab Mercherion. "Your Grace, you can do whatever you choose to do with me later . . . hang me, strike off my head . . . I won't raise a hand to stop you, nor speak a word against your justice, whatever you decide. But for now, I beg of you, allow me to stand by your side and fight for you. It is more than I deserve, as I would be the last to deny, yet I may prove useful."

"I will vouch for him," said Meligraunce, coming up just then. He extended a hand to the boy, who gripped it with both his own. "Let my word be his surety, my life the forfeit if he violates your trust."

"That is unnecessary," replied the Governor. "This is no time for men of good will to be divided. And I am not going to punish you, Math, because your grandfather was a villain and you were his pawn."

When Math spotted Mahaffy, he went down on one knee in the grass and lowered his head. "I renounce my claim," he said humbly. "You can be Lord of Mochdreff. I—I never really wanted it that much to begin with, and it is clear to me now that you deserve it far more than I ever could. I'll swear any oath—"

But behind him, Prince Tryffin was silently shaking his head, and Mahaffy already knew what he had to do. "No, you must not say any of these things to me now," he interrupted the boy gently. "You might regret the impulse later. In truth, I do want your friendship, Math, and I will be honored to accept your oath of fealty when it is more appropriate for you to offer it. But in the meantime . . . well, aside from the fact that you might someday feel I had taken unfair advantage of you, it may yet turn out that you will have to take my place if something should happen to me. And I wouldn't want you to compromise your position then by hasty words now."

Prince Tryffin nodded his approval, and Math gave Mahaffy a grateful glance as he rose to his feet.

Meligraunce drew the boy aside to ask a few questions. "How did you come here with Cernach's men, and where did you come by the armor?" Mahaffy heard him ask.

"The guards at Caer Rigor all turned against Cernach as soon as he boiled up his cauldron full of monsters. That is, they felt too much loyalty to his family to raise a hand against him, but they did desert their posts to go off and fight against his creatures. I met these fellows about ten miles from Effron. They are very valiant men . . . but, of course, you know that, or we could never have gotten this far," he added, running a hand through his dirty hair. "After the first skirmish, I started scavenging armor and weapons from the fallen. I have yet to find anything that quite fits, but I do well enough."

"And Captain Iolo? I don't see him here," said Meligraunce. "Or did he alone remain behind at Caer Rigor?"

Math shook his head sadly. "He fell in our first battle. And Isaf Danan, he was with me when I left the castle. When we met the cauldron-born, he tried to cast spells against them but . . . but as you may know, he was not much of a warlock really. They ignored his chanting and the signs he was making with his hands, and one of them picked him up and shook him until—until his neck snapped."

Meligraunce passed a hand over his eyes. "Well, he was a good man and many people loved him. He will be sorely missed."

And that was as much of a eulogy as anyone received, these days; there was no time for anything more. The crowd around Prince Tryffin began to disperse as everyone went off to look to his weapons and armor. Someone gave Mahaffy a new horse, a sturdy white mare, which one of the men had found roaming the countryside without a rider, and Conn had a new mount as well.

All the rest of that day, and for a time after moonrise, the Governor and his men made sorties out of the churchyard. They killed many of the cauldron-born, but there were always more of the creatures remaining to be fought, and their own losses were too great to be ignored. Also, the horses could continue to crop the grass that grew in the graveyard, but the men obviously could not. Everyone was growing weak with hunger, and unless they found something else to eat, they would have to make up their minds to kill one of the horses that were so badly needed. By morning, Prince Tryffin decided to move on toward Cuachag.

"It is useless, no matter how many of the creatures we kill. There will always be new ones every twelve hours, unless we can reach Caer Rigor and put an end to Lord Cernach and his cauldron. I had hoped that more men would arrive, that some of our allies who were separated from us during the last battle would find their way here, to swell our ranks as we move toward Cuachag, but I see that hope was a vain one. We must take whoever will come and—"

He was interrupted by a cry from one of the men he had stationed by the wall to act as a lookout. And another of the guards came up in a hurry to warn the Governor: "There is a black cloud rising in the direction of Cuachag . . . more of Lord Cernach's sorcery, I make no doubt."

Everyone looked to the northwest, where (by now) it had become apparent that no ordinary storm cloud was moving their way; it was a great flock of birds, a vast multitude obscuring the sun with their black wings, flying rank upon rank toward the churchyard.

"Crows," said Meligraunce, in a flat, discouraged voice. " 'The blackbirds that will eat the harvest.' This bodes very ill."

But a light came into Prince Tryffin's eyes, and a sudden hope suffused his face. "Ravens . . . not crows but Rhianeddi ravens, and heavily burdened by the look of them. Don't you see what they are carrying?" he asked as a great shout went up from his men.

It was already falling from the sky, manna from Heaven, in the form of bread and fishes, which the great black birds brought from who-knew-where, carried in their beaks and their talons, and now let loose as they swooped over the churchyard.

Everyone scrambled to pick up this unexpected bounty.

The bread they devoured as quickly as they could lay hands on it. The salmon and the herrings they split open with knives and daggers and ate raw. It was chaos for a while, but it was a welcome chaos, and everyone was talking at once, shouting and laughing with amazement and delight.

"But what does it mean?" said Conn, when he had eaten his fill. "Is it . . . could it possibly be a miracle, made just for us?"

"I believe it means that the Lady of the Ravens is soon to arrive," said Tryffin. "And that Cernach's dreams led him astray, because she is going to be fighting on our side, slaying her thousands for our sake."

Even as he spoke, a grey mist began to gather in a corner of the churchyard, a luminous fog that made the air shudder and the earth tremble. At the heart of the Breathing Mist a slender, female figure started to form: first no more than a grey shadow, then something more solid, finally a pale-haired young woman in a green dress and a tartan mantle.

As his young wife stepped out of the Mist, Prince Tryffin ran to meet her, dodging around the men, the horses, and the gravestones, catching her up into his arms when they finally met. Mahaffy, like most of the others, turned his eyes elsewhere, having no wish to intrude on their reunion. But he could hear the lady Gwenlliant laughing breathlessly with relief at finding Prince Tryffin still alive, and the Governor's eager questions.

There followed a brief, quiet time, when they were probably kissing . . . only, no, Mahaffy could see that was not the case, because Prince Tryffin was already striding toward the horses and calling out to his men, and his lady had moved toward the well.

"Mount up at once and follow me," the Governor shouted. And when Mahaffy was close enough, he spoke in his ear. "Help me to lead them toward higher ground—that ridge over there to the east. There is no time for questions or answers, so just do as I say. The sooner we go, the sooner Gwenlliant can begin to do her work."

It made no sense, of course, but Mahaffy blindly obeyed, and the other men did likewise. They had to fight their way through the ranks of the cauldron-born to do it, but the manna delivered by the ravens had not only strengthened their arms but raised their spirits, and they fought with a new, relentless energy. Soon, they had left their enemies far behind and were thundering across open country toward the ridge.

"But why?" said Mahaffy as he came up abreast of Tryffin.

"The water in that well is holy . . . or perhaps it is the well itself that has some beneficient power. Gwenlliant says it is fed by underground springs and there ought to be a sufficient supply. But for God's sake, let us go swiftly, before the flood catches us and sweeps us away."

"The . . . the flood?" said Mahaffy. Reining up for an instant, he looked back over his shoulder, and saw a pale, slight figure standing on the stones surrounding the well.

Already, water was gushing up out of the earth, overflowing the sides of the well, and the graveyard had become a rapidly expanding pool of roiling water. The creatures of the cauldron tried to escape, stretching their long disjointed strides, moving faster and faster, but the flood followed after them, faster and faster still, and as soon as the water touched one of them, the thing simply melted away.

In fact, the waters were coming so swiftly, Mahaffy realized that he would be hard put to reach the ridge before the flood reached *him*. He gave the white mare a kick and the command to start moving again, and prayed as he rode that he had not delayed too long.

It was like watching the end of the world, it was like watching the Biblical deluge, sitting on the ridge and watching the flood move across the countryside, a tumbling, swirling mass of furious white water.

"If her strength holds and the springs don't run dry, she will flush out all of the phantoms between here and

Cormelyn," said Prince Tryffin, standing with one hand on the bridle of his roan gelding.

"Can you see her?" asked Conn. "My eyes are dazzled by the sun on the water, but I thought there was something—"

"Something like an otter or a seal, swimming toward Cuachag," Tryffin cut in. "It hardly seems possible that she could drown in her own flood, and the one she was named for at that.

"I think," he added with a sigh, "that she is going to Caer Rigor to deal with Cernach once and for all. God knows, I wish I could be with her when they meet."

After a time, when there really seemed to be nothing more worth watching, they all sat down in the grass and waited for the waters to subside. By noon, the flood had receded considerably, but Prince Tryffin's spirits had fallen along with them. He sat at the top of the ridge, staring down at the ground, looking uncharacteristically tired and ill.

Mahaffy climbed up to sit beside him. "I hardly think there will be much loss of life due to the flood," the young knight ventured. "It will only be the creatures of the cauldron that suffer from its touch, and—and it isn't very deep. People who are not able to swim can wade to higher ground."

Tryffin shook his head. "The very young, the old, and the weak will drown, swept under by the fury of the waters. Perhaps not many of them, but there will be some losses. And I must help Gwenlliant to bear it all, when she realizes what she has done." He looked up at Mahaffy, and his expression was bleak. "She has never had to kill anyone before—though with such powers at her command, it was perhaps inevitable—certainly not take innocent lives in order that other innocents might live. It is going to be very difficult, very painful."

He began to shudder, deep, wracking spasms, as though his body would tear itself apart. Mahaffy knew that it was just the shock, a natural reaction to all that had happened, but it was like watching a mountain fall, seeing that monumental composure crumble, like watching the sun drop out of the sky, so little had he ever expected to see Prince Tryffin break down.

"God . . . oh God, how did I ever allow it to come to this?" he was murmuring under his breath. "The High King charged me with the safety of his people. The Mochdreffi *trusted* me to keep their women and their children safe, and now this slaughter that goes on and on and on . . ."

"None of this is your fault," said Mahaffy, desperately searching for something comforting that he could say. "There was nothing that you neglected to do or to say. You have labored ceaselessly to bring peace and order, and you can't be blamed if other men are foolish and greedy and envious, and unable to realize what is best for everyone. No one could have accomplished half as much as you have. And when the day comes—and I believe now that it will come soon—that I take your place, then it will be you that I have to thank if the task is a light one, because you have already done all the difficult parts."

Tryffin shook his head. "It will *have* to be soon, because as God is my witness, I can't continue much longer. I am tired of war, I am weary of politics and government, and I am sorry to say so, but I am sick to death of your damned Mochdreff. I need to take Gwenlliant and Grifflet and go home."

But already the spasms were growing less, and his voice was becoming steadier. He went on talking, more for his own benefit than for Mahaffy's. "I need to go home to Tir Gwyngelli and raise my family in peace. Gwenlliant has never been there, you know, and she has yet to meet either of my parents, but there is no doubt at all that they will love her as much as I do . . . my father with his wisdom, and my sweet, compassionate mother." He smiled faintly, taking comfort from his own words. "She has the loveliest voice, my mother; it used to be said that she could charm the birds right out of the trees. And I promised Gwenlliant a grand and glorious wedding in my father's hall, to make up for that hurried affair in Perfudd, and that simple ceremony last year. I want to spread the wealth of Gwyngelli at her feet, the gold and the fabulous gemstones out of the mines."

He was talking his way back to courage and sanity. But you could always depend on the Gwyngellach to talk their way into or out of *anything*, Mahaffy thought wryly—that was one of the eternal verities. Even they were not immune to their own powers of persuasion.

The pain and the guilt would probably still be there, though not where anyone could see them, and perhaps the vitality and confidence would be a little dimmed, but Tryffin would again be the solid, sensible man who they all needed him to be, for as long as they needed him. That was something you could depend on, too.

"I want to introduce Gwenlliant to her grandfather, Meredydd fab Maelwas—the most brilliant liar in all Gwyngelli, and that is saying a great deal!—and I want to take Grifflet to all the places around Castell Maelduin, the places that I loved as a boy. The secret valleys and the hidden pathways, and all the rooms and passages under the hill. I have two sisters, the prettiest and the best-humored girls in the world, and a host of nieces and nephews, and I want Gwenlliant and Grifflet to know them too."

And it was a strange thing, but as Prince Tryffin spoke of the people and the places that he loved in Tir Gwyngelli, Mahaffy began to think of all those who were dear to him, right here in Mochdreff . . . all the men and women and children he had met over the last few years, those fierce, proud, indomitable Mochdreffi . . . all the stone castles and the villages of reed-thatched cottages, the meager little farms, the bogs, the stony barrens, the moors covered with heather, whin, and broom, the occasional woodland. Not very much of Mochdreff was good to look at, but it was his home, the only home that he had ever known. Soon, it was all going to belong to him, every single acre, and he realized now that *he* already belonged to it. His heart began to swell in his chest and burning tears came into his eyes.

And that was the day that Mahaffy Guillyn began to

believe in miracles. It was a greater day than the one when he worked the magic to heal the land, a wonder that even eclipsed the loaves and the fishes that had descended on the churchyard. Because right there on that grassy ridge, surrounded by so much death and despair and destruction, he learned the healing power of love . . . and learned also that the power was his, his inheritance, his birthright, part of the common human heritage, Guillyn or not. He could feel it, he could bestow it, and from this time forward he would be ready to receive it.

. . . *and the youngest son of the King took the hideous old woman into his arms and gave her a kiss on the mouth. And when he had done so, he realized that he was no longer holding a loathsome hag, but was embracing a lovely young maiden in a green gown. On her feet, shoes of gilded leather, on her head a golden crown, and around her waist a girdle set with many beautiful and precious gemstones.*

"You have broken the spell that was on me," said the Daughter of the Moon, "and by doing so have gained yourself a loving wife, as well as ransoming your father. By courage and honor have you won me, yet many dangers and tests are still ahead of you."

The Prince was too dazzled by her beauty and by the magnificence of her raiment to make any response, and so she continued without interruption. "I have lived for many long years and in many different places, and you are not the first man to seek my favors, for my other name is Sovereignty. Do not fail to treat me with respect, but love me and keep me well, and your days will be long and filled with honors.

"But the man who betrays my love or makes ill use of the power that I can bestow on him will find me an implacable enemy."

—*From* The Book of Dun Fiorenn

23.

With a Single Touch

For the last ten miles of her journey to Caer Rigor, Gwenlliant had to travel on dry land. It would have been a long, wearying trek, after already swimming so far, had she not been able to sense a sturdy little island pony running wild in the countryside, that she summoned to bear her the rest of the way.

Yet it was unfortunate that she had no means to call up the Breathing Mist, to cut her journey in half, by allowing a shortcut across the marches between the worlds. That was how she had been able to travel earlier that day, when, arriving at Dame Ceinwen's cottage after the final battle with Maelinn, she learned from the crone where to find Tryffin and under what dangerous conditions. Between them, the two women had summoned the ravens, put the necessary compulsion on the whole flock, then sent the birds on ahead, while they brewed up the Mist to send Gwenlliant after them. The girl did not like to think what would have happened had the ancient wise-woman not kept a prophetic eye on Tryffin and Mahaffy the whole time that Gwenlliant was wandering in the Shadow Lands. Without her timely arrival this morning, Tryffin might not be alive now . . . and still, it might all be useless if she did not reach Caer Rigor before Lord Cernach could brew up more trouble in his cauldron.

When she reached the castle, the gates were closed and she could see no guards up on the wall, but the girl kept on knocking until someone responded by opening the gate and raising the portcullis. Inside the gatehouse, she met two nervous women: an elderly servant who did all the talking, and a slatternly wench wearing too much face paint, who appeared to be mute.

"This is a bad place for you to come, Lady," said the older woman. "For our master is a dangerous man, and truth to tell, we fear that he has lost his mind. He won't come out of the tower where the dwarfs used to live, except when he goes to bring in water . . . and the worst of it is, we think he has turned cannibal. There was nothing at all to eat in the tower when he first went to live there, and not only have the dwarfs disappeared, but we smelled meat boiling a week ago. What glimpses we have caught of Lord Cernach since, he does not appear to be a man who is starving.

"If you go anywhere near him or even anywhere that he can spot you," she added with a shiver, "he may try to cut you up and devour you too."

But Gwenlliant shook her head, and replied with great determination. "It is Lord Cernach who ought to fear *me*. I have come here to rescue you from a bad master, so if you will kindly show me the way to find him . . ."

It was not, of course, so easy as that, because the women required a great deal of convincing. As time was short, Gwenlliant finally grew so impatient that she put a compulsion on the old serving woman, who then led the way across the inner courtyard, and pointed out the tower that Gwenlliant wanted.

She found Lord Cernach in the goldsmith's workshop, laying sticks for a fire . . . remarkably clean and fastidious for a man who had been feeding on human flesh for more than a fortnight. But his eyes were vacant, and his face oddly slack. Her gaze slid past the golden cauldron, came to rest on a pile of bones, a scrap of red hair, and some gaudy rags shoved into one corner, probably all that remained of her old friend and nemesis, Brangwengwen the dwarf.

And here, thought Gwenlliant with a grimace, *is a man who has taken more lives than Maelinn, Lord Cado, and the Princess Diaspad combined. For no better reason than ambition, pride, and an inflated idea of his own capabilities. It is an affront to every notion of decency that the man still lives.*

"And who might you be . . . and why have you come here?" he asked, looking up from his task. He appeared only mildly surprised.

"I wonder that you should have to ask," said Gwenlliant, shaking the pale hair out of her eyes, "since you have been courting me all this last year. I am your death, Lord Cernach, and it is past time that we met."

He stared at her for so long, she was beginning to think he was not going to answer, when a spark of recognition came into those empty eyes, and he finally spoke. "Ah . . . I know you now. You are the Cailleach, the Hag Who Devours Her Own Young. But what a curious thing. I was certain that you would be dark like my cousin Luned. I don't quite care for that pale childish face of yours, and, truth to tell, I was expecting someone considerably more seductive."

So the women at the gate had been right, and Cernach was utterly, irredeemably mad. But he had not been mad when he first listened to Maelinn's vile whisperings and found them good, nor when he first made his plans and put them into effect, those schemes that would lead to so much death and suffering. Then why should he escape his deserved punishment merely because he had conveniently lost his reason somewhere along the way?

Yet Gwenlliant hesitated, not willing to kill him out of hand, not willing to taint her magic, or the child that she carried. Lord Cernach had to attack first.

"I see your sword lying there on the table," she said, with a gesture in that direction. "You had better pick it up and defend yourself."

"Against you?" he said. "I would not be so foolish, so presumptuous."

Gwenlliant ground her teeth, growing impatient for this man's death. She could bind him with one of her spells, take him back to Caer Ysgithr to face the Governor's justice . . . but that would take much too long. Having wreaked so much destruction with her flood, how could she possibly spare *him*, even for a single day?

Then a darkness took hold of her mind, whether rage or despair she could not say, and with it, a sudden resolve to kill him, reckless of all consequences. Perhaps he read that resolution in her face, perhaps some spark of reason returned to him there at the last . . . however it was, as Gwenlliant moved toward him, Cernach lost his nerve and reached for the sword.

Like most madmen, he was remarkably swift in his movements. In the time that it took Gwenlliant to blink her eyes, he took two steps, wrapped his fingers around the hilt of the sword, and picked it up. But she was even faster, moving with a shapechanger's wiry strength and agility.

A small pale hand on his chest, a *word* spoken under Gwenlliant's breath, and Lord Cernach's heart simply stopped beating.

When Tryffin, Meligraunce, Mahaffy, and Conn arrived at sunset, she was still sitting in the goldsmith's workshop. Even though Cernach was lying dead on the floor by her chair, with the sword under him, even though there were no signs of a struggle, the dazed look on her face, the dejection of her pose, were frightening. Mahaffy and Conn exchanged an apprehensive glance, while the more practical Meligraunce turned over the body for a closer inspection.

But the Governor went down on one knee beside Gwenlliant's chair, put out a gentle hand to smooth back the fine light hair tumbling over her brow. "How is it with you, Cousin? Did he hurt you somehow . . . or is it only that you are weary after doing so much, saving so many lives?"

The blue-violet eyes filled suddenly with tears. "I have taken lives as well. Until now, there was no time to realize the—the enormity of the things I have done. But besides all the people that must have died in the flood, I crushed Maelinn to death under the earth, and I forced Cernach to attack me so that I could kill him, too. Do you know that I can slay a man, just by touching him? And if you do know . . . how can you bear to touch *me*?"

He took both of her hands and kissed them, one after the other. "Dear Heart, I have known what you are and what you might be capable of doing someday, ever since the first time I met you. Not a day has passed since then when I didn't love you, and I doubt there is anything you could ever do to change that. You are going to be the most powerful witch, the greatest wise-woman who was ever seen on Ynys Celydonn, and I would not have you any different than what you are."

She smiled tremulously and blinked back the tears on her

dark lashes. "It is good to hear you say so, because I have something to tell you," she whispered. "It appears that I am going to be the mother of your children, and that I am already carrying your son."

It was really amazing, thought Mahaffy, to see the change that came over Tryffin with those few simple words, the sudden illuminating smile on the Governor's face. Pale, haggard, and unkempt as he was, he nevertheless began to glow again with all the old confidence, strength, and vitality. Before the eyes of his young companions, Tryffin seemed to grow broader and more solid—and to look at him now, the last agonizing week of horror and despair, weariness, and grief had never been.

After all, the young knight told himself, *what better medicine could there possibly be for a man with a wounded spirit than the promise and the fulfillment of his dearest wish?*

⚇⚇⚇

Lord Macsen was dead. That news greeted Mahaffy as soon as he arrived at the iron gates of Caer Wysg, and by the time he had dismounted by the stables, turned the white mare over to one of the grooms, and begun the long walk to Tifanwy's apartments, he was already uneasily aware of the curious stares, the avid speculation, on every single face that he passed.

With Macsen dead, all the power he had represented in one person was now divided among his four sons and his three young wards; though his daughter still offered a considerable dowry, both in lands and goods, her value as a political asset had greatly diminished. And of course, word that Math fab Mercherion had renounced his claim, that Mahaffy had accepted the boy as his squire and exchanged the oath of fealty after the final battle, had preceded him by several days. With no one standing in his way, Mahaffy's ascension to the High Seat was virtually assured, with or without the support of Macsen's sons.

They are wondering if I mean to put her aside, now that I no longer need her to advance my cause, he thought as he opened the gate to Tifanwy's herb garden and stepped inside. It was green and damp and fragrant in the garden, smelling of earth, mulch, mint, and lavender. There were rosebushes, just starting to put out leaves, also some climbing vines, a brass sundial, and a pool of clear water in a white marble basin. He stopped to inhale the complex odors, to absorb some of the peace and beauty of the place, then passed through to the door on the other side. He walked down a long, echoing corridor, climbed a broad staircase to Tifanwy's bedchamber, and again he was aware of the sidelong glances, the questioning looks.

Making it all that much more piquant must be the fact that everyone knew the marriage had never been consummated. Even if Tifanwy had slept in the bed after he left her, Mahaffy was certain that the servants had eventually gotten around to examining the sheets for signs of blood and semen, and had gossiped afterward.

He entered her room without knocking, and surprised her sitting by the fire with her pages and handmaidens around her, reading out loud to them from an illuminated psalter. She was dressed all in black, as pale as wax and haggard with it, her great dark eyes smudged and shadowy, without the customary veil to conceal her grief. Her rich chestnut hair was unbound and unkempt, falling almost down to her knees. For all that, she was the most gloriously desirable woman he had ever seen.

At the sight of Mahaffy bursting into her room, she gave a tiny gasp and lost her grip on the prayer book. It fell into her lap, where one of the little boys instantly retrieved it and whisked it away. Not a moment too soon, because Mahaffy crossed the room in three long strides, and taking each of Tifanwy's hands in one of his, pulled her up out of the chair and into his arms, with such force that he nearly knocked the breath out of them both. He held her so for a long time, while she clung to his neck and wept out her grief, her fear, and her sudden vast relief.

Though it was hardly a joyous homecoming, it was one that he would remember for a long, long time. And Mahaffy could not help thinking—as he buried his face in her hair, as he murmured every word of comfort and endearment that came into his mind—how infinitely sweet and poignant it was to hold this warm, vital, vulnerable woman in his arms and know that they would belong to each other for the rest of their lives.

They ate supper that night in the banquet hall with the rest of her family, and it was a sad, quiet meal, with everyone in mourning—not only for Lord Macsen, but for Lord Balin and for other kinsmen as well. Sitting at the High Table on Mahaffy's left, Tifanwy did no more than pick at her food, take a few sips of wine to wet her dry lips. And when she finally pushed back her chair and rose from the table to go to her bedchamber, she stopped him from following with a silent shake of her head, indicating that he was not to follow her immediately.

Mahaffy felt a sinking sensation. Even though Tifanwy had been so glad to see him return, there was still a barrier between them, and how he was going to breach that barrier he did not know.

An hour later, he entered her bedchamber, dressed only in his shirt, breeches, and hose, and when he sat down on the edge of her bed, tried to take her hand, she pulled away and refused to even look at him. And for all his coaxing, his words of love and caresses, he could not make her meet his eyes.

"But why . . . *why?*" he finally asked. "I thought you had finally decided to like me; I was even beginning to hope that it was more than that."

"I *do* like you," she replied in a fierce whisper. "God knows that I do. But you can't possibly understand what I am feeling now . . . when you are so perfect yourself."

"Perfect?" he said, with a bitter little laugh. His pulse was racing, his head pounding, and he was more than half-aroused by the sight of Tifanwy in her thin cambric nightdress. The truth was, he was feeling too much, too many contradictory sensations and emotions, and it made him irritable when he wished to be patient and gentle. "I am very much afraid, Lady, that you have mistaken me for somebody else. I can't even claim physical perfection . . . or did you happen not to notice the scars on my hands?"

'Her lips trembled. "Your scars are honorable—won through courage and hardship—mine are not."

"Honorable?" He sprang to his feet, stood staring down at her, utterly amazed. "I came by these scars because my ancestors were so wicked, had committed so many criminal follies, that it was necessary for me to do penance for their sins and my own by slashing open the backs of my hands. And I wish you would tell me how you are less . . . honorable . . . because a fool of a drunken stableboy threw a rock through a stained glass window and the shards happened to cut your face?"

Tifanwy shook her head. "My scars are neither honorable nor dishonorable. They are just—just stupid and ugly."

That was really too much, Mahaffy decided, glancing around him, searching for a mirror. But there were none in her bedchamber, nor anything at all that might serve in place of one. "When was the last time that you looked at your own reflection? Do you have any idea what you really *do* look like?"

Tifanwy tried to hide behind her curtain of chestnut hair, to shrink down beneath the pillows and the sleeping-furs. "I don't . . . I don't remember."

"Then it is high time that you were reminded," Mahaffy replied. And in a sudden fine Guillyn rage, he dragged her out of the bed and across the room. When he threw open the door, she started to struggle, pounding on the hand that encircled her wrist with a fierce little fist, unwilling to go outside in her rather too revealing nightdress.

But Mahaffy was not to be denied, and hauled her out past the door, down the stone staircase, and along the corridor, though she cursed and fought him every step of the way. The truth was, by now he was thoroughly aroused and the struggle only excited him more. She pried at his fingers, spit in his face—she was Macsen's daughter in more than name, for all she usually pretended to be so meek.

By the time they reached the garden, however, she was tired of fighting him, and only put up a token resistance as he led her over to the pond in the marble basin. When he made her look, she stood staring blankly down at the reflection of the moon in the water and her own wavering image below it.

"Tell me what you see," he demanded. They had both worked up a sweat, and standing behind her, gazing over her shoulder, he could see that the woman down in the water was wearing a nightdress that was nearly transparent and left very little to the imagination.

"My eyes are weak," she replied, in a suffocated voice. "I can hardly see anything at this distance."

Mahaffy gave a deep sigh. When she had stopped fighting him, most of the excitement had flowed out of him, but he was still hungry for her. "Then let me tell you what *I* see. I see a lovely, desirable girl who is ruining her life over something that is practically invisible in this light. I see a woman who stirs and thrills me as no woman has ever done before."

He slid one arm around her, so that the soft weight of her breasts rested on his forearm, so that their bodies were pressed close together. "Can you really be so innocent . . . so ignorant? When we are standing like this, can't you *feel* how much I want you?"

Even by moonlight, he could see that Tifanwy was blushing. "Well," she ventured after a few moments, "perhaps I can."

Mahaffy laughed softly. "Then come up to bed with me," he said in her ear, "and let us remove any doubt."

*   *   *

Even when they went upstairs, she did not give in at once. She wanted him to put out the candles, but he insisted that he wanted to see her while they were making love. She reluctantly allowed him to take off her nightdress, and then he discovered that there were scars he had not known about: on her shoulder, her collarbone, one arm, and one breast. He kissed her scars one by one, told her that they were the most beautiful scars in the world and he would not trade them or her for anything, and once they were both lying naked on the sheets, her passion finally ignited. She gave and received with a fierce energy that more than matched her previous struggles.

And after it was over, when he still lay on top of her, breathing in her scent, feeling her heart beat strongly against his, he realized that it would *never* be easy—at least not for a long time—that it would take a great deal of effort and determination to prove how much he really loved her. Yet he was not one to turn aside from a challenge, and he knew that tonight had been a promising beginning.

. . . and in the time of Mahaffy Guillyn, Mochdreff bloomed, for that was a peaceful, prosperous age. For besides that he was a man of high principles and scrupulous attention to duty, he had the wisdom to choose wise councilors and to surround himself with brave and honorable men. The warriors who served him were great heroes, whose names are still remembered: Conn mac Matholwch, Ewen Llyr, Math fab Mercherion, Ruan Glyn, Grifflet fab Tryffin . . . and Meligraunce the Stranger.

—*From* The Great Book of St. Cybi

24.

The Greening of Mochdreff

There was still much work to be done before Mahaffy could take charge. The north was in chaos, and deputies had to be appointed, warrants signed, and troops sent to restore order in most of the towns and villages between Cuachag and Cormelyn. All of this kept Prince Tryffin busy for weeks and weeks. Mahaffy traveled with the Governor during that time, but the young knight's task was an even greater one, because it was for him to listen to the heartbreaking tales of widows and orphans, to offer what comfort he could, and to provide healing for those who had given way to despair or had been driven mad by the terror of the cauldron-born.

"But you have the means to do so, and it has been with you all along," Gwenlliant told him. "The sidhe-stone cup . . . it can no longer heal bodies, but it can be used as a medicine for sick minds once I teach you how."

Wherever there was a churchyard with a well along their

way, they stopped for a time, and the people flocked to meet him and drink healing draughts from the miraculous chalice. And it was a very strange and unexpected quality of that cup, that the more it gave, the more beautiful and powerful it became, so that by the time Mahaffy's progress through the north came to an end, a mere glimpse of the vessel was sufficient to bestow peace and serenity on even the most careworn and oppressed.

When the day finally arrived that Mahaffy, Tifanwy, the Governor, and the rest of their party began the long journey south to Caer Ysgithr, he gave the cup into Gwenlliant's keeping, and assumed once again the more humble position of Prince Tryffin's knight-equerry. For all that, great crowds still turned out to meet him, and he was met with celebrations and great acclaim wherever he went. There were pageants and parades and mumshows, in honor of his various exploits, but an even more surprising feature were the various reenactments of his wedding to Tifanwy, which seemed to have taken on some mysterious significance in the minds of the people. Meligraunce might have explained what it all meant but no one consulted him, so the Captain, typically, held his peace.

"It is because neither Morcant nor Goronwy married, and Calchas died young. It must seem to the Mochdreffi that their Lords have been barren for nearly as long as the land has been blighted," Conn ventured to guess. "And when they see you with your bride—how devoted you are to her and she to you—and when they see the wonderful changes all around them, is it really surprising that they connect the one thing with the other?"

It was true that what they had all been looking for and hoping for ever since autumn had now come to pass. Particularly in these regions which had not been invaded by the creatures of the cauldron, it was a glorious spring: The grass grew long and green on every stretch of uncultivated ground, wildflowers bloomed in abundance, the crops were flourishing, and all the children who had been born during the winter just past were remarkably beautiful, strong, and healthy.

"But it hardly seems fair that I should receive all the credit, when you and the Lady Gwenlliant have done so much. Far more than I ever did," Mahaffy protested as he rode beside Tryffin.

"It is right and natural that they should shift their affection and their allegiance from me to you, because I will be leaving soon and you are the one who will rule them for the rest of your life . . . which I hope will be a long and fruitful one," the Governor replied. "I get sufficient praise for all that I have done, though it comes more quietly.

"Besides," he added, with a wry smile, "once I am gone—and I am no longer here to remind the Mochdreffi that I was a creature of flesh and blood, an earthy man who liked to eat his three meals a day, and more when he could get them—my legend will undoubtedly grow. Before they are through with me, you will hardly recognize me, and you will more than likely grow tired of hearing yourself compared and found wanting beside my supernatural goodness and wisdom."

Mahaffy laughed, but he had to acknowledge that Tryffin was probably right. Soon enough, this love affair with the Mochdreffi would begin to pall, and he might just as well enjoy it while he still could.

At Caer Ysgithr, Captain Meligraunce easily slipped back into his customary routine. It was true that he now occupied a set of rooms apart from the other men, quarters that he shared with his lovely new wife, but other than that, his days swiftly assumed a familiar pattern. He rose early, left Luned sleeping alone in their bed, and went down to the barracks to break his fast with the other men and then put on his armor. He performed his duties with his usual meticulous precision— the only difference was, that he was now impatient for evening and the time that he spent with Luned.

Their marriage was everything he had hoped it would be, and nothing he had feared. It was true that they often quarreled—they were both strong-willed, so there was nothing surprising in that—but Luned was a woman with such a generous spirit that she harbored no grudges, and he realized now that neither their frequent clashes nor any hardships they might meet with in the future would ever wear out her steadfast devotion.

All in all, his present situation was entirely satisfactory. For years, he had only *thought* himself satisfied, being far too busy playing the perfect servant to the perfect master to examine either his motives or his true desires. But far from making him dissatisfied with the life he had been living, those few weeks of comparative freedom—when he roamed the roads as a ragged vagabond, and never had to give a thought to propriety, dignity, or even simple cleanliness—only confirmed his opinion that the position he had worked so hard to attain was exactly what he wanted for himself. Not for him the life of a romantic adventurer hiring his sword wherever he pleased; the pleasures that life offered were entirely too trivial. And as much as he honored his father, his uncles, and all the other men who lived close to the soil, the life of a farmer and herdsman was not for him, either. He was a man with extraordinary capabilities, and in order to make the best use of them, he had to attach himself to a man with extraordinary responsibilities. Up until now, that man had been Prince Tryffin, but Meligraunce was fairly certain that as soon as the Governor retired from public life, a similar position would be offered by Mahaffy Guillyn. It would be painful, of course, to watch Tryffin go and not to follow him, but Meligraunce knew that his own happiness depended on being where things were happening, where he could actually make an impression on the events of his time.

A week or so after their return, he was summoned to a private audience. When he went up to the Governor's quarters, he found Prince Tryffin seated at a table, shuffling through a pile of papers and warrants.

"Ah, Captain, it was good of you to come so promptly," said Tryffin, looking up. "I have reached a decision which I am eager to communicate to you."

Meligraunce assumed the customary pose of respectful interest and waited for the Governor to continue. He was completely boggled when Tryffin went on: "I have decided to make you a knight, my friend, and I wondered if you had any objections to receiving the accolade on Midsummer's Day."

This was so very far from anything he had ever expected to hear that he actually forgot to breathe for several seconds.

"Impossible . . . absolutely unthinkable," he stammered, when he was able to speak again. Then the Captain blushed as he realized what he had just said, and he attempted to recover by amending the statement. "That is to say . . . it is hardly for me to say what you can or cannot do, but have you considered whether this is something you are really permitted to do?"

Tryffin smiled faintly, shaking his head. "I wonder, Captain, if you remember to whom you are speaking. It is true that if one of the petty lords were to take it into his head to knight a man of your humble origins, there would be no end of fuss and courts of chivalry, and no doubt the thing would be eventually undone. But *I* am a Prince of the Blood and of Tir Gwyngelli, besides being Governor of Mochdreff—which is a position that never existed until I held it and carries such perquisites and dignities as I choose to claim for it—and if I decide to knight the wooden post at the foot of my bed, let alone you, there is no one to say me nay . . . except my father perhaps, and the High King certainly."

He indicated a chair, and Meligraunce was glad of the opportunity to sit down. "My father," Prince Tryffin continued, "is not only of the opinion that good men should always be rewarded, but he carries the unshakable conviction that the grace of a Prince of Gwyngelli is sufficient to elevate anyone he chooses as a friend. In short, by knighting you I only make public what has been true all along. As for the High King," he added with a shrug, "he writes to tell me that he is immensely pleased that I have brought the situation in Mochdreff to such a successful conclusion. Though we, who have seen so much death and grief, may account the price a high one, taking the long view—as he clearly must—the fact that several thousand people died in an obscure corner of Mochdreff must appear trivial to him beside the fact that the larger political questions have finally been resolved. I am convinced that he will be glad enough to approve your knighting when he realizes this is a matter close to my heart."

It was, of course, all true. Tryffin never said anything that was not the literal truth. Yet the Captain was still shaken by this unexpected turn of events.

"Perhaps . . . perhaps you might wish to turn your cousin King Cynwas's favor to some better account by asking something for yourself," he ventured at last.

For which he was rewarded with a glance of patent disbelief. "And ask for *what*? What could I possibly require or want that I don't already have? Wealth, rank, power if I want it—though in fact I am presently concerned to divest myself of what power and influence I now possess—and what is much more than any of these things, a wife I adore, a son that I love, and another child on the way. My only unfulfilled desire at this point is to see you and Luned comfortably established—and I ought to tell you that if I can't have this, I am going to be greatly disappointed."

Put like that, there was little that Meligraunce could say against the plan, even if he had wanted to.

"Besides," Tryffin added, "you are going to need some sort of rank when you are living at Castell Ochren. It would be ludicrous for you to be master of even such a crumbling and ruinous fortress and not be even a knight."

Meligraunce cleared his throat. "I was not aware, Your Grace, that any such plan—"

Tryffin dismissed that with a wave of his hand. "Mahaffy is determined to give it to you, and I believe you will be doing him a favor by taking it. It can hardly be considered a desirable residence for a man with so many fine castles and fortresses suddenly at his disposal, besides carrying a number of unpleasant associations. In your case, however, any property that you own increases your status, so it does you far more good than it could ever do him. I also think that Luned will enjoy being the Lady of someplace, even if it is only Castell Ochren."

"As you say," replied Meligraunce, who was gradually regaining his composure. As surprising as this all was, he had in some sense been prepared for it by Dame Brangwaine's prophesies. He rose smoothly to his feet. "But if you will excuse me, I believe that I ought to acquaint my wife with . . . with these remarkable tidings."

"I think," said the Governor, in his amiable way, "that you ought to do so at once.

"But, Captain," he added just as Meligraunce reached the door. "There are a few more things that I want you to do for me, if you can possibly spare the time. Live long and well and happily. Make Luned an excellent husband. And raise a large family of beautiful, intelligent, healthy children."

Meligraunce bowed low, there by the door. "As the Governor knows," he said, "I always endeavor to follow his orders down to the tiniest detail."